"Perrine has penned a charming, heartwarming story with endearing characters and a lovely small town. I adored Butternut Creek and its residents."

"[G]entle, funny, romantic, and honest new series . . . The veteran author and ordained minister has a sure eye for smalltown church drama, as well as the dynamics of life in a town where everyone knows your business. Perrine does a fine job blending small and large story lines, portraying details and dilemmas of regular folks, and offering spiritual messages from real life. This is a delightful first volume in what promises to be a wonderful series."

The Matchmakers of
BUTTERNUT CREEK

Also by Jane Myers Perrine

The Welcome Committee of Butternut Creek

The Matchmakers of
BUTTERNUT CREEK

A Novel

Jane Myers Perrine

**Doubleday Large Print
Home Library Edition**

New York Boston Nashville

FaithWords
Hachette Book Group
237 Park Avenue
New York, NY 10017

ISBN 978-1-62090-620-0

Printed in the United States of America

FaithWords is a division of Hachette Book Group, Inc.
The FaithWords name and logo are trademarks of
Hachette Book Group, Inc.

The publisher is not responsible for websites (or their
content) that are not owned by the publisher.

**This Large Print Book carries the
Seal of Approval of N.A.V.H.**

Acknowledgments

This book could not have been written without the love of church members who have supported and taught me since I was a child. Thank you.

Nor could it have been written without the joy my husband, George, has brought in all our years of marriage. I give you my eternal love and appreciation.

Many thanks to my writing friends, too numerous to mention, who have generously guided and critiqued and taught me everything I know and without whom I would never have published, and to Ellen Watkins, my pal.

To my agent, Pam Strickler, and editor, Christina Boys, great gratitude. You have believed in me and made my books better.

Everyone in Butternut Creek thanks you as well. To all the nice people at Hachette, your expertise and kindness have made the way so much easier.

This book is dedicated to all who love without prejudice, who serve without judgment, and who open the circle to include all God's children. It is dedicated to those who answer the question from Micah, "What does the LORD require of you but to do justice, and to love kindness, and to walk humbly with your God?" with their lives.

The Matchmakers of
BUTTERNUT CREEK

Prologue

From the desk of
Adam Joseph Jordan, MDiv.

I continue to be a sad burden for Birdie MacDowell. Since I arrived at the church in Butternut Creek seven months ago, I've attempted to lift that weight from her shoulders and to correct the many errors she expects me to atone for.

If she were to comment on the first paragraph of this letter, Miss Birdie would point out that I wrote a run-on sentence and ended it with a preposition. Despite my earnest efforts, I have failed her again, at least grammatically.

When I first arrived here in Butternut Creek, called to serve the Christian Church, she saw me as too young and too inexperienced for almost everything. She was correct. She believes she always is.

Personally, I'd hoped the passage of time would take care of both my flaws, but Miss Birdie is not one to wait around and hope for change.

Although she's never expressed this, an odd omission for a woman who prides herself on her speaking out fearlessly, she knows that a man of my age (too young) and with a sad lack of piety could never act as her spiritual guide.

She's probably correct. I am woefully incompetent to lead another person to faith when I struggle daily with my own flaws. Thank goodness for grace from the Lord if not from Miss Birdie.

But I have discovered a few things in the months I've been here. First, I fell in love with this small town in the beautiful Hill Country of Texas the moment I arrived: the friendly people, the Victorian houses, the live oaks shadowing the streets, the downtown square surrounded by coffee shops and gift stores and antiques malls with a few businesses—the barbershop and the diner where Miss Birdie works—sprinkled in.

Second, I found out I do possess some skills. I preach a good sermon, teach an interesting adult Sunday school class, have an active youth group, and make much-appreciated hospital calls and evangelistic visits regularly. I've also improved my basketball game.

But there was one area in which Miss Birdie still

found me lacking: finding a wife and producing children to populate the children's Sunday school classes.

Yes, she wanted me to find a bride. *Wanted* is an inadequate word here. Even *determined* doesn't approach the level of her resolve. Add to that adjective *single-minded* and *unwavering* and the total comes close to her desperate need to marry me off. Do not add choosy to that list because she'd marry me off to any single woman still in her childbearing years who lives within a fifty-mile radius of Butternut Creek. Her task is made nearly impossible by the dearth of single women in small Central Texas towns.

Could be she expects God to create a mate from my rib, but that hasn't happened yet. Nor do I expect to wake up, as Boaz did, to find a bride lying at my feet. Of course, if a woman should appear in my bed, whether at the foot or cozily snuggled next to me, her presence in the parsonage would create a scandal from which neither the church nor I would recover.

Because Miss Birdie has renounced these biblical approaches to finding me a wife, I shudder to imagine what she has in her fertile and scheming mind. All for my own good, of course.

For the protection and edification of all involved, I decided to document every one of the efforts she and her cohorts, the other three Widows, have made in their attempts to find me a mate. In addition, this book will cover my next year as minister in Butternut Creek, my search for experience and a wife, as well as the joy of living here with the wonderful people who inhabit this paradise.

I send it off with my love and my blessing and in the desperate hope that someday Miss Birdie will smile upon me and say, Well done, Pastor.

Chapter One

Adam Jordan stood in the upstairs hall of the huge Victorian parsonage. A wide hallway stretched to his right with three bedrooms on each side. At the end of the hallway, a stairway led up to a finished attic. He turned in the other direction and started down the curving stairs, his shoes clicking across the hardwood floors. The sound echoed through the three-story house, an enormous space for one man.

"Hey, Pops, Janey and I are leaving for school," Hector shouted.

But he no longer lived here alone. Six months ago, Hector Firestone and his younger sister, Janey, had joined him when they were left homeless.

"Bye, guys. Have a good day." Adam watched them head off before he left the parsonage, Chewy panting by his side.

For a moment he paused on the porch to look around. To the north stood the stately church he served. From here he could see only the parking lot and the back entrances, but on the front and facing the highway, tall white pillars stood out against the red brick. On the other side of the parsonage sat the house of his neighbors, Ouida and George Kowalski and their two young daughters.

As he breathed in the clean, warm air, he noticed a partially masticated backpack under the swing on the porch. He glared down at Chewy, the enormous, ugly, and affectionate creature who had arrived with Janey. Chewy smiled back at him.

"Bad boy," Adam said.

Chewy's tail went into overdrive. Adam often wondered why the dog didn't ascend and hover like a helicopter with all that spin.

"Bad dog," he repeated, which caused

Chewy to perform pirouettes on his back legs.

Adam didn't have time right now to investigate or return the item to its owner. Since the habit had started a month earlier, Chewy brought home backpacks and sweaters and hoodies and water bottles, anything he found. Adam tried to keep the dog inside, but Chewy was an escape artist who zoomed through the front door whenever someone didn't watch carefully. He'd return home hours later, exhausted and happy and smelling of whatever disgusting substance he'd found to roll in. In expiation for that behavior, the dog delivered these offerings of his deep affection.

Reminding himself to get Hector to return the backpack, Adam glanced toward the Kowalski house. He hoped to see his neighbor Ouida, a Southern name that, oddly, was pronounced *Weed-a*. Many mornings she greeted him with a daughter hanging off one hand and a plate of muffins in the other. If not, he'd walk across the lawn between the parsonage and the church he happily served.

At six this morning, when he'd had to get up and let Chewy out, Adam had glimpsed Ouida's husband, George, heading toward the garage in back. In contrast with Adam's shabby robe, George wore a dark suit, tailored and conservative. Once Adam had seen George dressed casually when Ouida had forced him to help her plant a garden. Even then he looked successful and well dressed if unenthusiastic in spotless khaki slacks, expensive athletic shoes that never got dirty, and a shirt that fit him perfectly. Occasionally, Adam saw George pushing his daughters Carol and Gretchen on the swing, still immaculately dressed, still unenthusiastic.

He and George had waved. As Adam and Chewy started back to the house, George backed his spotless black Lexus out and headed toward his accounting business in Austin.

Now, three hours later, Adam waited, but Ouida didn't appear. Disappointed and muffinless, he headed toward the church, Chewy frolicking behind him.

🍂

Running late as usual, Ouida set Gretchen on a kitchen chair and tied the little girl's shoes. George always told her if she planned better, she wouldn't always run five or ten minutes behind. She agreed in principle, but Carol and Gretchen, their young daughters, never stuck to a schedule—possibly because they couldn't tell time—all of which left Ouida attempting to catch up all day long.

This morning Carol couldn't find her favorite socks, which turned up, inexplicably, in the bathtub. George would've told Carol to choose another pair of socks. He didn't understand that forcing Carol to choose another pair would upset her and make her even slower.

Then, after Ouida and Gretchen had walked Carol to preschool, Gretchen . . .

Well, it seemed to be one thing after another. When she finished tying the shoes, Ouida picked up the plate of applecinnamon scones. "Let's see if we can find Pastor Adam."

With that, Gretchen ran to open the front door and hurry out to the porch. "There, Mama." She pointed toward Adam's back.

"Wait, Adam," Ouida called.

He turned and smiled. She hurried toward him as quickly as a short, round woman—she was all too aware of her plumpness—carrying a plate and holding the hand of a toddler could.

Living next to the parsonage had advantages, the best being that ministers and their families were nice people. However, preachers also nagged non-members about their faith and invited them, over and over, to come to church. She and George didn't want to, they were perfectly happy as they were. Adam didn't hound them, which made her like him even more. After she'd explained, he simply accepted the fact that the Kowalskis lacked the spiritual gene. "Do you like scones?"

"I like anything you bake." They chatted a few seconds before Gretchen tugged on her mother's hand in an attempt to pull her mother back toward their house.

"Thanks," he said with a wave and headed to church carrying the plate of goodies.

Ouida watched him walk away, then turned toward her home, thinking perhaps someday she and Adam could enjoy a real conversation without a child distracting her. They should have him over for dinner, should have done so months ago, but she just didn't get everything done.

Once inside, Ouida settled Gretchen in the kitchen with her toys and tackled the pile of wash in the laundry room where she could keep an eye on her daughter. After she had a load of sheets churning, she pulled the plastic bag of George's clean shirts and shorts from the freezer, opened the bag, and allowed them to warm up before she sprinkled and ironed them. George had heard that putting clean laundry in the freezer killed bugs. She allowed him to think she did but, honestly, if she put all the sheets they used in the freezer, there wouldn't be room for food. Besides, they didn't have a bug problem. But seeing that plastic bag of his things kept him happy.

By the time she'd ironed a couple of shirts, dumped the wet towels and sheets in a basket, and started another load, she'd already taken Gretchen to the bath-room several times.

"Let's go outside." Ouida helped her daughter into a sweater, picked up the basket, and followed Gretchen through the back door. The breeze would dry the sheets in no time. She loved how they smelled when she made the bed, like spring. For a moment, she leaned back, closed her eyes, and drew in the warmth of the sun. Usually, the lovely day would warm her inside and out, but not today. No, within she felt a niggling that was connected somehow to the laundry in the freezer and sticking to a schedule. Something didn't feel right, but she had no idea why she felt like that.

❦

Aah, Texas! Mid-March and Adam wore a light jacket. The lack of snow in the winter and the warmth of early spring were the trade-offs for the horrendously hot summers here.

His poor old Honda sat in the church parking lot. After nearly a year of sitting in the sun, it looked worse than it had when he'd arrived. Paint flaked off by the handfuls and huge patches of rust showed through. It looked as if an especially virulent paint-eating bacteria had attacked it. Not apparent from the outside, a spring poked through the upholstery on the passenger side, which meant that any rider who didn't have a cast-iron butt opted to sit in the backseat. Still, it usually ran, and often the radio worked.

The other car in the parking lot belonged to the part-time secretary, Maggie Bachelor. The lack of vehicles could mean no one awaited him inside, or it could mean that whoever did wait for him hadn't driven. Few places in town couldn't be reached on foot.

When he entered the church office, the look on Maggie's face warned him all was not well. She jerked her head toward the open door of his office in a manner that tipped him off. Miss Birdie and maybe another Widow or two waited in his study and, he felt sure, not patiently.

The Widows came with the church—a group of women whose husbands had died (obviously) and who did good works. Without them, there would be no community thrift store or food pantry, no Thanksgiving community dinner or outreach to the homeless.

"Mary Baker went to the hospital this morning with chest pains," Maggie said, scratching Chewy's head and sneaking him a bite of her breakfast burrito. "Jesse says his wife's feeling poorly, is going to the doctor and wants your prayers, and . . ." Maggie paused before she said in a slow, calm voice, "And Gussie Milton called about ten minutes ago." She glanced at Adam and winked. "Here's her message." She handed it to him with another wink.

Like everyone in town, Maggie showed great interest in his love life. Although it was non-existent at the moment, they all had high hopes for his eventual marriage and fatherhood. In fact, they hoped he'd be a modern Abraham, the father of a multitude. He had no expectations of such a prospect despite the Widows' shoving every woman in town at him until they finally settled on Gussie being the perfect mate. For that reason, he attempted to keep his expression neutral. Impossible. Only hearing the name *Gussie* made him want to laugh and sing and celebrate. If they heard one of those sounds, the Widows would start planning a wedding.

So he nodded and took a deep breath before heading toward his office, preparing himself for whatever was coming.

"Hear you haven't found a wife yet," Birdie said.

Miss Birdie sat in what she considered *her* chair: in front of Adam's desk but slightly turned so she could see the door as well, in case someone interesting stopped by.

Winnie Jenkins sat next to her and smiled at Adam. "Good morning, Preacher." She wore her white hair swept back and had a nice smile. An engagement ring sparkled on her left hand.

Miss Birdie wore her aggrieved look-what-I-have-to-put-up-with face, her usual expression with the young, inexperienced man who'd foolishly assumed he'd minister to her.

Short, no-nonsense hair and thick-soled shoes completed the picture of the pillar of the church. Because she barely topped five feet and had that snowy white hair, Miss Birdie resembled one of Santa's kindly and jolly but skinny elves. Ha! Amazing how quickly those lips became a straight line, her expression hardened, and disapproving words gushed from her mouth in time with her waving index finger.

But she had a good heart.

Yes, he repeated to himself, she had a good heart and was a beloved child of God.

"Sit down, sit down." With her right hand, the pillar waved graciously toward the chair behind his desk as if this were her office.

He could tell from the way she cradled her left arm that her shoulder hurt. Tough injury for a waitress.

After he placed the plate on the desk, he sat and tossed the message from Gussie next to it.

The pillar's eyes pounced on that piece of paper. He could read her thoughts, knew she was considering reaching over, picking the message up, and reading it. After an internal struggle that showed in her changing expressions, she must have decided that this would be ruder than even she dared to behave.

"It's a lovely morning, isn't it?" Winnie glanced at the plate.

With no reason to keep Ouida's goodies for himself, he took from his drawer the stack of napkins that he kept just in case something delicious showed up.

Each took a scone and savored it. He hoped it would distract the pillar from her purpose. Once in a while, he succeeded in slowing her down, but like a blue heeler, a favorite breed of dog among Texas hunters, she returned to the scent every time. "Mercedes will be here soon," Winnie said. "She had a meeting."

That explained the absence of the third member.

"I saw in the *Butternut Creek Chronicle* that Mac was initiated into the honor society," Adam said in what would be a failed effort to head the pillar off. Still, he tried. She expected it. He enjoyed it.

"Yes, she was, and Bree was named to the district third team in both volleyball and basketball. Don't try to distract me by mentioning my granddaughter, Preacher." She leaned forward to capture his eyes. "You know how proud I am of those girls, but that's not why I'm here." Once she knew he was paying attention, she settled back and smiled.

Now in charge, she was in no hurry. In every conversation, Miss Birdie considered him either the bait or the victim. Didn't much matter which. Neither came to a good end.

"What time are you leaving for the youth retreat tomorrow?" the pillar asked.

"I'm going to pick the kids up from school at three."

"Who's going?"

She knew this, but if it kept her from confronting him with whatever was on her mind, answering didn't bother him. "Your granddaughters, Hector, and his friend Bobby."

"What are you going to do there?" Winnie asked, sounding interested. "At the retreat?"

"I'm leading a small group and preaching at worship Sunday."

"What are you driving?" The pillar continued her interrogation with a glare at Winnie to leave the questions to her. "Not your car, I hope."

"Howard loaned me his van."

"About that sermon." She leaned toward him. "Don't make it long and boring. Young people like short."

"Right." His agreement always made her happy.

For a moment, the pillar studied him while Winnie grinned at the engagement ring the general, father of Adam's best friend, had placed on her finger only weeks ago.

"Will Gussie Milton be there? At the retreat?" Miss Birdie spoke casually, almost tossing off the comment.

Exactly what Adam had expected was the reason for her visit. He tensed, almost feeling the trap vibrate milliseconds before it snapped shut. *Dear Lord, please grant me patience and wisdom*, he prayed silently. *Patience and wisdom. Amen.*

"Yes," he said aloud.

"She's a nice young woman. Unmarried, as I remember."

As if she didn't know that. "Yes," he said.

Then, in a quick attempt to change the subject, Adam turned toward the other Widow and said casually, "Winnie, now that you're going to marry Sam's father . . ."

"Don't know if she will," Birdie grumbled. "They may live in sin for tax purposes."

"Birdie." Winnie put her hands on cheeks that were turning pink. "How could you say that? Mitchell and I . . ."

"But don't try to sidetrack me, Preacher. *You're* not married yet, not engaged yet. That's our biggest worry and failure," she said with a sorrowful sigh that told of the unimaginable depths of her disappointment.

"All in good time," he temporized. "All in good time."

Miss Birdie wasn't finished. "What I'm saying is that if Gussie Milton's going to the retreat, you'd better put those days to good use."

He heard the wagging of a finger in her voice and shuddered to contemplate what Miss Birdie had in mind. She probably expected him to marry Gussie on Friday evening and have her heavy with child by Sunday.

"About Winnie's wedding," he said, restating his topic.

"About Gussie Milton," Miss Birdie countered.

"We hear she left a message this morning," Winnie said.

"I haven't read it yet." He gestured toward the pink slip.

Both Widows leaned far forward in an effort to read that square of paper tantalizingly close to them in the center of the desk. He picked it up, folded the note, and stuck it into the pocket of his shirt.

Then, thankfully, because he didn't put it past Miss Birdie to pluck the message from his pocket, Mercedes Rivera stuck her head in the door. "Sorry I'm late. Long meeting." She hurried in and settled in a chair on the other side of Miss Birdie.

"Welcome, Mercedes," he said.

In contrast with the other Widows, Mercedes, the town librarian, had dark hair, liberally streaked with white and pulled back into a French braid. With a fuller body than Miss Birdie, she also displayed a sweet smile, one that Adam almost always trusted. She was polite and, most important, seldom harassed him.

Adam took the few seconds her arrival gave him to return to his topic. "When Winnie marries Sam's father—"

"If she does," Miss Birdie said.

"We are going to—" Winnie started to say.

"—the number of Widows is going to decrease again," Adam finished.

"We're not going to kick Winnie out," Mercedes said. "We'll still have three Widows."

"Miss Birdie," he said with deep concern in his voice. "With work and raising your granddaughters and all you do for the church, I fear you might become . . ." He paused to think of a word that wouldn't insult her. There were none. Miss Birdie was easily affronted.

"Weary in my efforts?" She glared at him for suggesting she might possess limits of any kind.

He couldn't mention her health problems, especially that bad shoulder. If he did, she'd—as they said on the basketball court—open a can of whoop-ass on him.

"You're a very busy woman. All your good works are far more important than getting me married off." He turned to Winnie. "And with your engagement . . ."

*

Birdie glanced toward the other Widows, then back at the preacher as he trailed off. In that instant, Birdie noted a fleeting expression of satisfaction flit across his face and realized she and Winnie and Mercedes had walked right into *his* trap.

"Well, Mercedes, you missed our entire discussion," she said in an effort to circumvent whatever the preacher was fixin' to bring up. "We're finished. Time to get a move on." Birdie struggled to stand, but when she lifted herself an inch off the chair, that blasted shoulder collapsed and dropped her back down. Doggone it! Betrayed by her own body, but she'd be darned if she'd let anyone know about it. She pretended she'd only changed position.

"Not quite," the preacher said. "We were about to discuss the Widows with Winnie's change in status."

Mercedes whispered to Birdie, "I didn't think that's what you wanted to talk about."

Always truthful, that Mercedes. How in the world had Birdie ended up with a friend like her?

"Let's talk about the Widows," Adam repeated insistently. He stood, walked around the desk, and settled in a chair closer to them. "You'll be shorthanded with Winnie getting married."

"If she does," the pillar grumbled.

Winnie frowned at her but remained silent. Winnie was well aware that arguing with her never accomplished a thing.

"Oh, no, Preacher. With Pansy and Winnie to help us . . . ," Mercedes began.

"Pansy is a wonderful help to the congregation, and a great cook. But she isn't a Widow and she's married."

Birdie leaned to the right, still attempting to find a comfortable position. "Pastor, you're the one who convinced me to break with tradition and make Winnie Jenkins a Widow when she'd never married. Not that I'm saying we should make Pansy a Widow, mind you." Fact was, Pansy had turned them down before. With her mother's poor health, she said she just didn't have time. Besides, if they started letting just anyone join, they wouldn't be the Widows would they?

"I have another suggestion," the preacher said.

Birdie didn't like suggestions, not from anyone, but he just kept right on suggesting.

"Blossom Brown," he said.

"Blossom Brown?" Birdie snorted. "Silly name for an elderly . . ." She paused for a second, realizing she and Blossom were about the same age. "Silly name for an adult."

"Besides, Preacher," Winnie said, "she's not a real widow. She's a grass widow."

"Her husband left her for some young trophy wife," Mercedes said. "Not that the whole situation isn't sad, but her husband didn't die. She's . . . she's . . ." Mercedes paused before she whispered, "divorced."

"Yes." He gave her a ministerial nod. "She went through a difficult divorce."

"Sad, so very sad." Birdie infused her words with sympathy before she snapped, "But she's not a real widow."

"Ladies, whether he died or ran out on her, Blossom is alone in that big house by the lake, and she wants to serve some-place."

Mercedes nodded. "I know this has been hard for her, but Blossom"—she raised her hand in front of her—"well, I don't want to sound judgmental or unkind, but she's not like us, not a bit." She dropped her hand and said, "She's rich and has a cook and a housekeeper."

"Why would she have the slightest inter-est in doing the work the Widows do?" Winnie asked.

"Guess you'll know that only if you give her a try." He paused. "She's alone. No children."

"Pastor." Birdie took charge of the discussion. "She's what we call 'high maintenance.' That champagne-colored hair doesn't come cheap. And those nails? I'll bet she gets them done weekly in Austin. How could she scrub a floor?"

Birdie shook her head. "Why would she want to?"

"And, well, she's not from here," Winnie said. "She doesn't know how to do things."

"Not the way we do them," Mercedes agreed.

"I believe," Adam said, "she was born in Louisiana, and she seems to be a true Southern lady."

"Well, I can't understand a word she says with that accent. Besides." Birdie leaned forward. "I can't see her as a Widow." She nodded, a motion that they all knew signaled the end of discussion. Not that the preacher ever acknowledged it.

"You couldn't see Winnie as a Widow but she worked out."

"Not completely. I've had to train her."

"What?" Winnie sat up straight and blinked. "Train me?"

"All right. Winnie worked out fine. Then she decided to get married." Birdie sniffed pointedly. Winnie's choice still rankled. "As for Blossom Brown, she's not really a member of the church. Doesn't she still belong to that la-di-da church in Austin? She and her husband seldom attended services here. Maybe once a month, if that often."

"And she wears *hats*, Preacher," Mercedes said. "No one wears hats anymore, except Blossom. Bird, do you remember that yellow one she wore last Easter? Prettiest thing I've ever seen and must have cost more than you make in tips in a couple of weeks."

"Which again makes me wonder *why* she'd want to be a Widow," Birdie said. "We're plain folks, Mercedes, Winnie, and I. We don't wear beautiful tailored clothing and fancy hats."

"Because she's lonely. She needs the church now. Whether she's come every Sunday, she's attended more often than some of our members. Ladies, she needs to be part of the church. She needs to be a Widow." He paused and seemed to search for words before he continued. "When I visited her last week, she told me she'd gotten the house in the divorce settlement and would be living out here permanently. She has nothing to do with her life now that she no longer entertains for her husband or travels with him."

"Beautiful house," Mercedes said. "Out on the lake."

"I hear she has a wonderful view," Winnie added. "I'd love to see the inside."

For almost a minute, Birdie exchanged looks with the other Widows, silently weighing the pros and cons. In the end, that beautiful lake house tipped the scales. But nothing had been decided, and Birdie didn't want the preacher to think otherwise.

"We will discuss this." She stood, pushing herself to her feet with her good arm. "I'm not promising anything."

"Pastor, don't forget the spring bazaar and chicken spaghetti dinner coming up next month," Winnie said as they gathered their possessions to leave.

"Make sure you get some signs out and get a few articles in the newspaper. And remember your responsibility at that retreat, finding a wife." Birdie turned toward the door and strode out, the other two following.

Once they stood in the parking lot, Birdie said, "I think we made ourselves very clear."

"Yes, you did," Mercedes agreed.

"But, you know, he doesn't always do what we tell him to," Winnie said.

A grievous disappointment to them all.

❦

Adam knew exactly how the Widows felt. Unfortunately, courting a woman was one area he had no idea how to approach. Tell him to preach a better sermon and he'd work on that. Give him a list of shut-ins and he'd visit. Mention that a kid needed a place to spend the night and he'd make up a bed in a spare room of the parsonage.

But find a wife in a town with no single women except for Sister Mary Timothy down at the Catholic Church and his friend Reverend Mattie Patillo? He had no idea how to manage that.

He reached in his pocket and pulled out the note Maggie had left him about Gussie's call. "She'll see you Friday at the retreat," he read. "Call her cell if you have questions."

He smiled. Not a particularly personal note. He'd prefer a protestation of undying love.

Then a terrible idea hit him. Certainly the Widows wouldn't track him down at the youth retreat in the thickly wooded campground south of Gonzalez. Surely they'd stop short of stalking him there, of appearing and coercing Gussie to accept his clumsy courting.

Of course they wouldn't do that.

But he wasn't about to place a bet on their ability to resist temptation.

Chapter Two

Gussie Milton wasn't a pink person. She preferred vibrant colors, hence her yellow car, the red accent wall in her bedroom, and the pile of orange and bright green and purple T-shirts that lay next to the duffel bag on her bed.

Her mother loved to tell about the time a three-year-old Gussie refused to go to church in a frilly pink dress, how she'd removed that ultra-feminine garment and put on jeans and a UT shirt. Gussie always wondered why a mother who named her daughter for a favorite uncle could expect that daughter to wear a pink dress.

"Gus," her father called from downstairs, interrupting her inspection of the jumble of colors on her bed. "Want to watch television with us? One of those singing shows is on."

"No thanks, Dad. I have a lot left to do."

She picked up the date book on her desk and turned to toss it into a tote. Three bags were lined up by the door: the red one for work, the orange one for the district youth, the one covered in sunflowers for church. Her entire life, organized in totes. She sighed. Someday she'd like to add a purple tote labeled MY LIFE, because she didn't have one now.

Always active in youth group and retreats and summer camp, she'd fallen into that again when she graduated from college and came back home. Her friend Clare Montoya had suggested the reason she worked with teenagers was because she didn't have children of her own. A possible explanation. However, even if she didn't work with the church kids, she still wouldn't have children of her own.

Little by little, she'd taken more responsibility, from working with the high school youth here and growing the group from three to fifteen regulars, to taking "her kids" to camp, to being in charge of the district youth. She loved it because working with young people gave her life meaning. Their joyful faith inspired her and pulled her out of herself.

After she put the book in the orange bag, her cell rang. She glanced at the caller ID. Jimmy Flock, a minister from San Antonio. Did she want to talk to him? Yes, despite having more preparation to do than she had time for, she'd answer. He always supported the district youth programs. "Hey," she said. "You're not calling to cancel for the retreat, are you?"

"Would I do that? No, just checking to see if you need me to do anything."

"Bless you. I can't think of anything."

Then he said exactly what he always did. "How's your love life?"

Didn't he realize what a pushy and intrusive question that was? No one asked a woman of thirty-one about her love life because chances were good she didn't have one. Maybe it had been witty banter fifty years ago, but now it was just plain embarrassing. As usual, she answered with a joke: "Oh, Jimmy, we don't have time for me to tell you the details."

"Still not married, huh?"

"I'll let you know when that happens."

"Okay."

"Anything else?" she asked.

After discussing a few details of the youth retreat, he said, "I looked over the information you sent in the mail. I see that new minister in Butternut Creek—what's his name? Adam something?—is preaching Sunday morning. What's he like? Have you met him yet?"

"Yes, for coffee a few times to discuss the retreat. Seems like a nice kid. He'll be fine." She looked at the piles of clothing and her full totes. "Hey, I've got a bunch of stuff to do, but I'll have time to talk more when I see you tomorrow."

Why, she pondered after she hung up, why did people believe her marital status was any of their business? Particularly people who didn't know her well.

Because she was a compulsive list maker, she settled in front of her laptop to check the one about what she needed to take with her. She had it all ready. As long as she was there, she sent a quick email to Clare, her friend since the church nursery and one of the few people who knew what had happened to Gussie thirteen years earlier. Gussie's other friends had moved away after graduation. They kept up by email and with occasional visits, but Clare—dear Clare—was always around. Though now that Clare had three children and lived an hour outside of Austin, they didn't get together nearly as often as they would have liked.

That finished, Gussie turned back toward the heap of clothing, picked up a TCU T-shirt, folded it, and lobbed it toward her duffel bag. As she reached for a pair of jeans, she grinned in anticipation of the upcoming retreat. She loved teenagers and always enjoyed working with the other adults. Maybe she'd get to know that young minister from Butternut Creek better, too. Seemed like a nice guy.

After filling the bag, she zipped it and slung it over her shoulder as she headed down the stairs toward the living room.

"About ready, dear?" Her mother picked up the remote and muted the television as Gussie dropped the bag by the front door.

"I have a few more things to pack. To-morrow morning, I'll grab everything and take off." She sat next to her mother on the sofa. "You'll be okay?"

"We old folks will make it through the weekend, especially with all the help you've rounded up and the freezer full of meals." She patted Gussie's hand. "You worry too much."

She knew she did, but this was her mother who'd loved and cared for and sup-ported her during the most terrible months of Gussie's life. Without her parents, she'd never have made it through. She owed them everything.

"How's your blood sugar?" Gussie asked. "Can I get you a cookie or a glass of milk?"

"Stop hovering, dear. I'm fine."

"Hey, Gus, looks like you're ready to abandon us." Her father came from the kitchen with a glass of tea.

"Henry, don't say that. You know how much she hates to leave us."

Maybe she shouldn't go to the retreat. If anything happened to them while she was gone . . .

"Gus, don't worry. We've been taking care of ourselves for decades."

"Find yourself a nice young man while you're there," her mother said. "You know, we'd like grandchildren while we're still young enough to play with them."

Must be a symptom of growing older, the desire to match everyone up, like Noah taking the animals onto the Ark two-by-two. Or it could be biblical, that Be-fruitful-and-multiply section of Genesis. Maybe it was a biological instinct, preservation of the species. But for her parents, maybe it was as her mother said: They'd like to see a grandchild before they died.

"Yes, Mother, of course. That's exactly why I go to these retreats with lots of high school kids and married ministers. To find a husband."

"Leave her alone, Yvonne. She'll get married when she finds the right man."

Her mother sighed. "But how will she do that, Henry? She never meets any single men."

"Leave the girl alone."

"Yes, leave the girl alone." Gussie laughed and headed toward the door. "I have to run in to work for a few hours, finish up some stuff." The daily drive to Austin to her photography studio was an accepted trade-off for her choice to care for her parents in Roundville.

Everything would be fine. She knew that, but her mind kept running, making sure. A compulsive fixer, she knew all the checking, planning, thinking, and analyzing she did was in an effort to control a life that had spun out of control. Think everything over and over, make lists, foresee every possible risk, and make absolutely sure nothing, not the tiniest thing, could ever go wrong. At times she felt as if she were juggling armadillos.

"Okay, God," she whispered. "Be my strength. You and I can handle everything together."

❧

"We have to do something about the choir." Birdie leaned closer to Mercedes. The Widows—this afternoon only the two of them because for some odd reason Mercedes had insisted they not include Winnie—had met at their usual place, the diner where Birdie waited tables. Both had a cup of coffee. Between them sat a few slices of banana bread from Butch's bakery left over from breakfast.

"What?" Mercedes groaned. "You and I can't sing. Not that we'd be any worse than Ralph and the three women who mumble the hymns."

"They're pitiful. It would be nice to have them sing something, like a prayer response, instead of having them sit up there in the choir loft and watch the congregation."

"I swear, last Sunday Ethel Peavey was doing a crossword puzzle inside her music folder." Mercedes broke off the corner of the last slice of bread and nibbled on it. "And Ralph Foxx fell asleep. Terrible to have an elder sitting behind the minister and snoring through the sermon."

"You know I occasionally disagree with the preacher." Birdie fixed Mercedes with a glare that dared her to comment on the statement. "But he does deliver a good sermon. We don't have a choir up there, only four people who don't even stand for the hymns."

"And what will we do about a fill-in organist? With Jenny on maternity leave, who's going to play?"

"I don't know who's available in town,

but we have to have someone. The choir can't lead congregational singing, and you know how terrible the preacher's voice is."

Her friend glanced down at her coffee, studying it as if she could read fortunes in the grounds, not that she'd find any in a pot Birdie brewed. She recognized her friend's slight hesitation and knew it to mean nothing good. Before she could jump in to forestall Mercedes's words, the other Widow lifted her eyes toward Birdie and asked, "What do you think about Farley Masterson?"

"What should I think about him?" Birdie shook her head. "He's a grumpy old Methodist . . ."

"He's our age, Bird. Maybe a few years older."

"Okay, he's a man our age who's a Methodist and grumpy."

"He's nice looking for a man of his age, and you two have a lot in common." Mercedes blinked twice.

Oh, she knew that expression, too. She'd first seen it when Mercedes had grabbed Birdie's Betsy-Wetsy doll back in the church nursery. It meant nothing good.

If there was one thing Birdie didn't want

to talk about, it was what she and Farley had in common. They'd both lost daughters to drugs. Oh, the two girls—women now—were still alive as far as Birdie knew, but their addictions had ruined them, made them leave their homes and families and go to some big city where getting drugs and finding a way to pay for them was easier.

But Birdie's daughter, Martha Patricia, had left behind her two daughters for their grandmother to raise. Sometimes the stress of rearing teenage girls made her feel more than her nearly seventy years of age.

A friend for most of those years, Mercedes could read Birdie's face easily. "You know you love those girls. You'd've shriveled up and died after Elmer passed if you hadn't had those girls around."

"Mercedes Olivia Suárez de Rivera, I have never, ever, in my whole life contemplated curling up and dying."

"But you do dote on those girls."

"I swan!" The woman was so persistent Birdie wondered why she'd put up with her for all these years. "Where is this conversation going?"

"I'm only saying that you and Farley Masterson have that in common."

"He's not raising his grandchildren."

"No, but . . ."

"Mercedes." Birdie raised her right eyebrow. "Why are you talking about Farley Masterson? I haven't seen the old coot"— she stopped and changed that description—"I haven't spoken to the man in years."

"You know he used to keep company with that widow over in San Saba."

Birdie scrutinized her friend's face. "Are you interested in Farley? Do you want my permission to keep company with him?"

"Oh, for heaven's sake, no." Mercedes shook her head. "You know I've been seeing Bill Jones down at the bank for years. We're comfortable together."

"So why did you mention Farley?"

Mercedes blinked again. Birdie knew her friend wasn't trying to sneak away with her favorite doll, but the expression did mean she had something devious in mind.

"You aren't suggesting that I—that *I* should keep company with Farley Masterson, are you?"

"Would that be too horrible? When you

are alone—and you will be, Bird, when the girls both go off to school—wouldn't you like to have a man in your life?"

"I'm gobsmacked," she said.

"I'm not sure that's the word you want," Mercedes said. "That's fairly new British slang."

"What does it mean?" Mercedes always thought she knew everything. Drove Birdie crazy.

"Astounded, bewildered . . ." Mercedes began counting the words off on her fingers.

"Then it is *exactly* the word I'm looking for." She paused for maximum effect. "I'm absolutely gobsmacked. In the first place, I know Farley from back when he was sheriff. He picked up my daughter about every week, brought her home. We spent quite a bit of time together. Our relationship was not particularly friendly back then and hasn't improved."

"And in the second place?" Mercedes encouraged.

"In the second place, have you forgotten that the challenge for the Widows is to find mates for other people, for our minister, not for ourselves? I'm happy with my life as it is, extremely happy." She snorted, which *should* have suggested the topic was closed.

"I . . . ," Mercedes began.

"Don't have time for anything more in my life, much less a man. Now let's talk about what the Widows can do for others."

Her friend closed her mouth, but Birdie could tell the subject wasn't finished. Mercedes was as stubborn as she was. Probably the only reason they'd remained friends all these years.

"Is this the reason you didn't want Winnie here? Because you wanted to talk about the old . . ." Birdie paused. "You wanted to talk about me and Farley"—she rolled her eyes—"in private?"

"Well, not only that. I miss you and me, the two of us being alone to chat."

Birdie didn't believe that excuse for a moment, but before she could respond, Mercedes asked, "What do you think about inviting Blossom Brown to be a Widow?"

"*If* we were to invite her, what would she do? What skills does she have?" Birdie asked, then answered herself. "She couldn't plan a sympathy dinner. She's always had a cook."

"Don't need her to plan meals. Pansy has that well in hand. She's always done that. Pansy's a good worker even though she's not a Widow."

"Blossom's always had servants. She wouldn't like to clean the thrift shop."

"We don't know that. We could give her a chance," Mercedes said in the pleasant voice that fooled so many people into thinking she was so very sweet and so completely unlike Birdie. "Make it sort of like a test. If she can't do it, we could train her, you and I. You're a great trainer."

"Pfutt."

"We could make her a provisional member, like we did with Winnie. It wouldn't hurt. With the bazaar and dinner coming up, she could help. More hands would lighten the load." Mercedes glanced at her old friend. "Not that we *need* the load lightened."

Birdie pondered Mercedes's words for nearly a minute. "All right. We should probably do this. It'll make the preacher happy."

"If he's happy, he'll be less suspicious of our efforts to get him married." Mercedes broke off another piece of banana bread. "Why don't we invite Blossom to go with us next time we visit the preacher or ask her to join us for coffee some afternoon. Get to know her a little better."

Good idea. As much as she'd like to punish Mercedes a little bit for suggesting she allow Farley Masterson to court her, not even at her most difficult—which could be pretty darned difficult—could Birdie turn down a sensible proposal. She nodded. "You ask her. She's more likely to come if you call. I scare her. Winnie probably does, too."

Chapter Three

Adam ran his finger around the collar of his shirt, attempting to loosen it. He wore one of his three dress shirts to the office every day but seldom buttoned it or wore a tie. He'd noticed last Sunday that the shirt collar seemed tight around the neck. He'd solved that by using the neck expander— a button and an elastic loop—he'd found in his desk, left, he guessed, by a previous minister with a similar problem.

Because he'd planned to preach at the retreat Sunday morning in a shirt and tie, he tried on another. Also tight, and not only around his neck but in the shoulders. The next one felt snug as well.

Could he have put on a little weight? Maybe some muscle? He couldn't weigh himself because he didn't have a scale. The total always depressed him because as much as he ate, he never gained a pound.

Maybe he had. Could be all those meals Miss Birdie forced on him, the food the congregation dropped off, and Ouida's treats had begun to work. He studied himself in the bathroom mirror. He looked less skinny. He'd either have to buy new shirts or invest in a few more neck expanders. Fortunately, the knit shirts still fit. He'd preach in one of those. He tossed a few in his duffel bag and left it open to finish packing in the morning.

❧

The next day, on the drive to the retreat, Mac sat next to Adam in the front seat of the borrowed van. Bree lay on the bench seat at the far back because Hector and Bobby had taken the comfortable swiveling seats in the middle. "Long legs," the guys had explained.

As they pulled into the campground, the

sun was heading toward the horizon. They got out of the van and stretched. Adam noticed the sound of crickets at the same time the smell of wood smoke from the lodge greeted them.

The setting didn't impress the guys.

"This is really . . ." Hector paused to think of a word.

"Rustic?" Adam suggested as he popped the back of the vehicle.

"No, primitive."

"Yeah." Bobby nodded. "Do they have running water?"

"Haven't you been to camp before?" Mac pulled two small bags from the vehicle.

"Basketball camp, but that's in dorms on a college campus. I have to check this out." Bobby swaggered toward the recreation hall. Nice kid, Adam knew, but Bobby loved to show a little 'tude.

"Not luxury," Adam said. "But . . ."

He didn't finish because Gussie exploded out of the building in typical Gussie fashion, waved, and shouted, "Welcome."

"That's Gussie," Bree said to Hector. "She directs the retreats and camps every year. She's great."

Wearing jeans and a bright green T-shirt

with WALK IN FAITH printed on it and her dark hair curling around her smiling face, she looked very different from the professional woman he'd met before. The kids with him grinned because no one could *not* smile when she did. Adam both smiled and blinked. Fortunately, his mouth hadn't flopped open. He glanced at the kids, hoping none had noticed his response.

Mac had. She wore a sly smile that looked exactly like Miss Birdie's at her most dangerous.

"It's okay," she whispered. "I won't tell Grandma you like Gussie. I know what she's like."

He had to believe she'd keep her word. No other acceptable choice.

"Come on in. Time to get your packets. Don't forget to pick up a T-shirt and sign up for chores."

"Sign up for chores?" Bobby grumbled. "Hector, what did I let you talk me into? I could've stayed home. My mother has a whole list of chores for me."

After Bree and Mac gave Gussie a quick hug, they led the grumbling Bobby and Hector into the enormous and echoing all-purpose room. Several adults and about thirty kids wandered around and greeted one another.

"Pick up your stuff, then take your bags upstairs and find a bunk," Gussie said. "Girls on the south; boys on the north. Meet us down here in a few minutes at the basketball court."

"You gonna play?" Hector asked Bree.

"Sure. I play on the team at school. Varsity." She glared, looking tough. "You know that."

"Yeah, but . . . don't want you to get hurt," Bobby said.

"Let's wait and see who gets hurt," Bree challenged.

Later in the day during a quick pickup game, Adam watched as both Bree and Hector went up for a rebound. Although Hector had five inches in height and fifty pounds on Bree, she had sharper elbows and more determination. She came down with the ball.

"Hey," he said as he rubbed his side after the game. "You don't play like a girl."

"Told you."

"We were taking it easy on you," Bobby said.

"Next time, don't." With that, Bree dribbled

toward the dining hall. She reached the edge of the court, turned, and shot. As the ball swished in, Adam cheered.

Before Bobby could grab the ball, Gussie came out with a bag. "Looks like a terrific game, guys." She smiled at everyone and motioned for them to gather around her. "Tonight the youth group from Roundville is setting the tables." She grinned at the groans from her youth. "Hey, don't complain. You get to do this because you're special." She clapped to quiet them. "Dinner in twenty minutes. We have just enough time for Slinky races on the steps down to the pool." She started flinging the toys around. "Winner doesn't do chores tonight." With that, everyone took off toward the pool.

❧

After dinner, Gussie stood and waved at the group. "Welcome!" she said and the kids all clapped and stamped their feet and shouted, "Gussie! Gussie—"

She quieted the group, made announcements, then asked, "Anyone want to sing?"

Campers shouted song suggestions.

"Okay, let's start with this one. Everyone join in. 'If you're happy . . .'"

Gussie had a wonderful voice, strong and clear. She walked around the tables as she led the group, encouraging and bringing the voices together. When they began "Silver Spade," she coaxed harmony from the group with a movement of her hand.

Was there anything Gussie couldn't do?

After several songs and a glance at her watch, she said, "Cleanup crew, get started. Adults, meet at the center tables. Vespers at seven."

As Hector stood to start his chores, he said, "Gussie's got a great voice. We need her in our choir."

"She'd sure liven up the service," Bobby added. "You know, it's pretty boring."

Bree laughed. "She'd sing a solo every Sunday and probably keep Mr. Foxx awake."

Then Mac grinned at Adam. If he'd thought she hadn't noticed how much Gussie had entranced him during the singing, he was wrong.

❧

At the counselors' meeting after dinner, the adults listened while Gussie handed out schedules and took questions. Then she introduced Adam as "the new kid on the block." She smiled at him in exactly the same way she'd smiled at Jimmy Flock, the gray-haired minister. Pleasant, happy to see both of them. Darn. The attraction obviously didn't go both ways.

"We're going to need a patrol outside from midnight to two o'clock," Gussie said. "After that, those most determined to escape should be asleep and we can get some rest. I'll take it tonight but need another volunteer and two for tomorrow night."

"I'll join you tonight," Adam said before anyone else could speak.

"Terrific. We can get to know each other," Gussie said. "Who'll sign up for tomorrow?"

The schedule of vespers, games, refreshments, and corralling campers attempting to escape the building kept him busy after the meeting. By midnight, the youth were simulating sleep while the adults had dozed off as soon as their heads hit the pillows.

The time had come to meet Gussie in the dining hall and start on their rounds.

And it was time for Adam to consider how to behave with Gussie. Oh, he wouldn't back her against a tree and kiss her passionately until she begged for more. Not that he'd turn that down if the opportunity appeared, but it didn't seem realistic. Nor would he attempt to gaze longingly into her eyes. In the dark, she wouldn't notice anyway.

As he opened the screen door to enter the dining hall, he still had no plan. He saw Gussie at one of the tables waiting for him, her face pensive. She was lovely in repose. Usually, all that joie de vivre lit up her face. The vibrancy was what everyone noticed. Now, in this moment of calm, he realized she radiated beauty as well.

"Hey," she greeted him with a smile. "Let's get going. You're the muscle and I'm the mouth. If we find anyone, you grab them and I'll lecture."

She handed him a flashlight, and they stepped outside into the glare of the halogen lights that surrounded the dining hall. Moving beyond that, they headed toward the lake.

"The lake's man-made, of course," Gussie said.

Man-made lakes. Exactly the best choice of subjects for a romantic rendezvous

between a man and a woman alone beneath the glow of a full moon and surrounded by the soft darkness and a sweetly
scented breeze.

"Of course?" he asked. Pitiful effort, but
that was the best reply he could come up
with to begin his wooing.

"Caddo's the only natural lake in Texas.
The rest are manmade."

"Interesting." He sounded like an idiot.
He wished he could come up with a daz-
zling and witty comment about manmade
lakes, but no flirtatious responses leaped
to mind. "Where's Caddo?"

"Over on the border with Louisiana.
Pretty place. You should go there someday."

"I should."

Those words pretty much stopped the
tête-à-tête. As they moved down an uneven path, he thought about reaching out
to help Gussie over a log but knew she
wasn't the kind of woman who wanted or
expected a gentleman to take care of her
and make sure she—a delicate flower—
didn't trip.

"How are things in Butternut Creek?"
she asked after they'd walked nearly the

length of a football field—Adam had adjusted to this normal measure of distance in Texas.

"Are you asking about the state of the church or how Miss Birdie and I get along?"

She laughed. "Yes, that's really what I wanted to ask. How are the two of you doing? I'd imagine a young, single minister wasn't what she had in mind."

"You know her well."

"Not really. I've met her, but my parents have known her forever. She's a legend in the churches of Central Texas."

"She's working hard to train me. If I'd only do everything she wants exactly as she wants it, she's sure I'd be much happier and more successful."

"Perceptive of you."

They arrived at a picnic table halfway around the lake with a clear view of the dorms above the dining hall. A halogen light stood twenty yards away and lent a hazy glow to the area.

"Why don't we sit here and keep an eye out?" he asked.

Silence fell between them again as the two looked across the lake. A comfortable silence. A *friendly* silence.

"Why the need for a patrol?" he asked. "Do kids often sneak out of the dorms?"

"Usually not. These are good kids. They'll stay up and talk and fool around, but most of the time, the adults keep them in line." She paused.

He read into that an unvoiced concern. "But?" he prompted.

"It doesn't hurt to have the campers know we're out here, just in case. We've had a few incidents, but only one that amounted to anything, one best forgotten." Her voice lost the usual animation. "One that really upset me."

He couldn't read her expression because the tree branches trapped and diffused the dim light, but he could read her slumping shoulders.

Before he could ask another question, Gussie jumped to her feet.

"Well, enough of that." Her voice sounded happy, and her stance looked filled with confidence.

Which was the real Gussie Milton? Oh, he knew people had good moments and bad, but the change in her had come so suddenly that it took him a few more seconds to realize what had happened. That quick flash from a melancholy Gussie to a high-spirited Gussie confused him.

"Let's get going." She headed toward the other end of the lake. "While we're sitting here, someone could be climbing out a rear window."

"Aren't there enough adults inside to make sure that doesn't happen?" He took several long steps to catch up with her. "Aren't adults sleeping by all the doors and windows?"

"Yes, but after a long drive and a couple of hours rounding up kids, the adults sleep deeply. Kids can crawl over them and right out the windows."

"But the dorms are on the second floor."

"That makes it more of a challenge." She laughed. "Besides, there's a flat roof over the kitchen with a big tree next to it."

"Sounds like you've had experience."

"Hey, kid, I wasn't always an elderly stick-to-the-rules counselor. That's why I know how to handle the campers."

"Hey, lady," he said. "You're not that much older than me."

She laughed, a sound that expressed complete lack of agreement.

❧

Saturday, the second day of the retreat, started warm. By one thirty, it had increased to just plain hot. After the morning group meetings, lunch, and the usually ignored hour of rest, Gussie settled on one of the benches surrounding the basketball court where Adam and four players from Butternut Creek battled against a team from Kingsland in a playoff game of the annual challenge. Didn't seem quite fair because Butternut Creek had three high school starters—Hector, Bobby, and Bree—but Adam seemed to be the force the other teams couldn't match up against, and Mac held her own.

As everyone watched, Adam drove and hustled and focused, pointed out the defense, distributed the ball, shouted instructions to the others, and had a great time doing it all. This was an Adam Gussie hadn't seen before, didn't realize existed. This was a man who took charge with confidence.

"Dish the rock," he shouted at Bobby, who liked to hog the ball. Then Adam said, "Good job," after Mac successfully battled for a board. A few seconds later, he set a screen for Hector for a shot from downtown.

Halfway through the game, the players were soaked with sweat.

Oh, my. Adam not only played ball well, he looked great. Gussie blinked several times but couldn't ignore him. No longer *Pastor Adam*, in her mind he'd assumed a completely different identity: *Basketball Adam.* Sweaty and hunky *Basketball Adam.* His T-shirt clung to broad shoulders she hadn't realized he had, and to a nicely muscled body. Skinny but, she hated to admit, very appealing. Since when had she found "sweaty" attractive?

The realization threw her off balance and made her feel as if a weird and wonderful force had taken over her being and filled her with lustful thoughts and desires she hadn't experienced for years. *Good heavens, Adam is a hottie.*

She felt slightly blasphemous having such thoughts about a minister.

꙳

After their second win, Adam passed bottles of water to the other players, then picked up one himself and poured most of it over him before he took a deep drink.

"Great game, guys," Adam said.

"Thanks, Pops!" Hector high-fived him,

then Hector and Bobby did a complicated handshake that included fist bumps.

"Hector, box out better on the rebounds," Adam coached. "Mac, great hustle."

When they'd cooled off, Mac said, "Let's sit down and study the competition."

"Hey, girl," Bobby answered. "We're good. We don't need to watch them."

After Hector glared at him, Bobby headed to the side of the court to study the competition.

"Sometimes he has a problem with attitude," Hector explained before he joined Bobby.

"You coming?" Mac said. "Good view of Gussie from where Hector and Bobby are," she whispered.

Adam attempted to give her the same glare Hector had used. Didn't work. She just grinned at him.

"Mac?" he threatened.

"Okay, Pops. I'll shut up." She joined the others, and he followed.

Although determined to watch the other two teams fight it out, Adam's eyes slid toward Gussie, who concentrated on the competition and cheered for both sides. He did have a good view of her.

"Great play!" Gussie's shout echoed around the court as she smiled. He really liked Gussie's smile.

Adam felt an elbow in his side, then Mac whispered, "If you're going to fool anyone, you have to stop looking dopey."

So he watched the game and forcefully kept his eyes on the players until the team from Llano won.

❦

In the break before the final game, Gussie went back into the cool of the main building to splash water from the drinking fountain on her face. Fortifying herself, she glugged down several gulps of water.

"You okay, Gussie?" From one of the tables, Jimmy Flock watched her with concern.

"Fine, just really hot out there." Water trickled down her chin as she fanned herself.

"Okay. Be careful." He dropped his eyes to his book.

Odd that the minister who always questioned her about her love life hadn't recognized the fact that lust had just broadsided her.

She forced herself back outside to watch

the final game. She had to face and accept the fact that she'd felt again, that attraction had filled her, had sizzled inside her. It still did. Yearning had escaped from the core of her being, and she could ignore neither her attraction to Adam nor the despair it caused. She preferred to think of all men as being gender-neutral but couldn't manage to believe that about Adam anymore.

For a moment, she longed to go back in time thirteen or fourteen or twenty years, to be the young Gussie Milton who'd believed in love and goodness, who trusted others. But that person had died nearly half a lifetime ago.

She watched the game, her gaze following Adam all around the court.

"Go, teams," she cheered as the team from Llano was able to get the ball over midcourt for the first time in a couple of plays.

How old was he? Twenty-five, she guessed. Twenty-six? Had that been on the application and the background check they'd had to run? Probably. Six years younger. The age difference made her feel like a dirty old lady, sitting here, ogling him.

After the game, she'd put all thoughts of his manly features back in the lockbox in her brain that she bolted securely. For now, she'd allow herself to watch and enjoy. She stood and clapped after Bobby made a spectacular jumping, twisting dunk and joined in the cheers when Adam stole the inbounds pass.

"Cut," Adam yelled, and Bree worked her way under the basket for an easy layup.

"Pops," Hector shouted after he'd stolen the ball. With a perfect bounce pass, he fed Adam, who made a long shot.

Then Bobby dribbled inside for a dunk and Mac made a pair of free throws. The game was over, and Butternut Creek had won. Gussie stood and clapped. "Great game," she shouted.

Then she very firmly locked up her feelings again.

❦

"Time for vespers, guys." Adam tossed the last of the crumpledup napkins in the recycle bin.

"You religious people sure spend a lot of time praying," Bobby said. "Not that I mind 'cause I know this is a church thing, but wouldn't one prayer a day pretty much say what you need to? Why not make it a little longer so you get everything in? Or maybe bless all the meals at the same time."

"Yeah," Hector agreed. "I mean you say them at every meal and in the morning and a couple of times at night. I bet you people pray before you take a shower."

"Or play basketball," Bobby added.

"No, never before a game of basketball." Adam turned toward the guys. "I don't pray then because I want the other team to pray while we run all over them."

"Pops, that was weak." Hector finished wiping the tables. When he tossed the dishcloth toward the dish basin with sudsy water, Adam swatted toward it and missed. "See, you can't even block my shots."

❦

Adam watched Gussie during the group skits later after vespers. What in the world had happened? Her smiles and laughter seemed forced and artificial. When his group had parodied a gospel group singing rap, she looked distracted while everyone else laughed.

After they'd finished the skits, he caught up to her as she stopped to check her message box. "Hey," Adam said. "This is a great retreat. Thanks for all the work you do."

She glanced at one of the notes in her hand before she looked up at him. "It's fun, isn't it?"

"Something like this can change lives. I hope it has for Hector."

"Me, too."

"I first considered going into the ministry at summer church camp," he said at the same time Gussie scanned another message. "Anyway, you look busy. Thanks again and good night."

She nodded. "Night."

❦

Gussie could kick herself. It wasn't Adam's fault that his presence scared and befuddled her, but she couldn't allow him or anyone else to see how much he attracted her. For heaven's sake, she was Gussie Milton, old maid, and she had a yearning for this . . . this *kid.* Not that she planned to jump his bones—where had that phrase come from?—although the idea didn't horrify her as much as she'd thought it might.

But the attraction didn't mean she should behave rudely, even if she had no idea how to act. She called after him, "Loved your group's skit."

He turned, waved, and walked away.

❦

After the closing prayer Sunday morning, Adam picked up his bag to stow it in the van. As he turned back toward the dispersing youth, he noticed that Hector had picked up Bree's duffel bag.

Well, well, well. A romance? Not that he'd kid either Hector or Bree. He figured Bobby and Mac would take care of embarrassing them.

Once everyone had settled in, he checked on the seating. Bree and Hector shared the back bench. Bobby and Mac took the chairs, and Adam drove alone. Just as well. The kids would fall asleep anyway and be useless in keeping him awake.

As he started the van he glanced at the crowd, searching for Gussie. Stupid because she had no interest in him, but he kept looking. Finally, as he drove out of the campground, he saw her in the rearview mirror watching their vehicle pull out.

❦

At eight forty-five Monday morning, Adam heard the door into the reception area from the parking lot open and knew trouble had arrived. Couldn't be Maggie. She didn't show up until later. He guessed it was at least one Widow, maybe more. Right now, he didn't feel like facing any of them. Could he sneak out a window?

Stupid response. He couldn't hide from the Widows. He'd known they'd descend on him as soon as the pillar had debriefed her granddaughters and they could gather. Oh, maybe he could dodge them for an hour or two, even a day, but they'd catch up to him eventually, hunting him down like a pack of Miss Marples.

At least he'd arrived early to prepare himself. In front of him, he had a cup of coffee and a Bible. He'd spent a few minutes in meditation, but they hadn't given him enough time. He wished he had another thirty minutes to brace himself, but he didn't. He folded his hands and awaited the inevitable.

"Pastor, are you here?" Mercedes called.

Before she'd finished the sentence, the pillar stomped into his study, folded her arms, and stared at him while she stood at the door like a rock in the middle of a creek. The three other Widows—Blossom had joined them—flowed around her and headed toward the chairs in front of the desk.

He stood and reached toward Blossom. "Welcome. Good to see you."

She smiled as she shook his hand. Then all the Widows, including the newest, sat.

Except for Miss Birdie. When she finally strode toward the desk, she stood behind the chair Blossom had snatched and glared. "We came to discuss the retreat," Winnie said.

Before he could say anything, Blossom looked over her shoulder at Miss Birdie. She must have felt the intensity of her expression. "Why aren't you sitting down?" she whispered.

"Because you are sitting in my chair," Miss Birdie whispered back. The pillar had the loudest whisper of anyone Adam had ever heard. When she whispered, people obeyed.

Including Blossom. She leaped to her feet, scuttled to another chair, and sat down. With a smile, Miss Birdie lowered herself into her place.

"You'll notice, Preacher, Blossom has

joined us *this morning*." Miss Birdie's voice underlined the temporary nature of Blossom as a Widow—it was the pillar, after all, who had the final say.

"Good to see all of you," Adam said.

"We came to discuss the retreat," Winnie repeated.

"Went very well. I believe the young people had a great time." He smiled at Miss Birdie. "What did Bree and Mac tell you?"

The pillar leaned forward. "They told me *nothing* happened between you and Gussie." She sat back and shook her head in disgust.

"Oh, dear," Blossom said. "Is that good or bad?"

Birdie ignored her and plowed ahead. "That's what my granddaughters say. Nothing happened."

"I don't know why we bother to send you off on these weekend excursions," Winnie said, "if you aren't going to take advantage of them."

Adam could explain that his finding a wife had not been the purpose of the retreat but he'd said it so often and the explanation did so little good, he didn't.

"Bree did say that you and Gussie patrolled the grounds Friday night," the pillar said.

"Alone," Mercedes added. "Only the two of you."

"Did anything happen?" Winnie asked. "Did you make a move?"

"Yes," Adam said.

Three of the women scooted forward in their chairs and watched him like a boggle of weasels eyeing a terrified rabbit. Blossom moved forward a few beats later, which made him think the newest and possibly temporary Widow didn't realize exactly what was going on.

"I . . ." But he couldn't say any more, because he'd started laughing so hard at their hopeful expressions. Three of them looked at him as if his response had exceeded the bounds of decorum. Blossom still looked confused and uncertain. Their expressions made him laugh harder.

When he could finally speak, he said, "Do you really believe that *if* anything happened between me and any woman, I'd tell you about it?"

When the comment made them look

both confused and exasperated, he added, "Not that anything has happened between me and a woman recently, but I *do* have a private life. You may deny that, but I do deserve a little space of my own."

"I guess you do," Winnie said grudgingly. She turned toward Miss Birdie and said, "He does have that right. He doesn't have to tell us everything."

The pillar narrowed her eyes and said, "We still expect you to do something about . . ."

"Yes, yes, I know." He grinned. "Thank you, ladies, for your concern. It's good to see you. Now, tell me about plans for the spring bazaar and chicken spaghetti dinner."

"We're meeting every afternoon, the ladies of the church, to start on crafts," Mercedes said. "Blossom's a real hand with colors and painting."

Miss Birdie counted on her fingers as she said, "Pansy's getting the food organized, Winnie's getting donations from the businesses, I'm working with the community center on the setup, and Mercedes is in charge of publicity."

"Sounds as if everything is well in hand." Not that Adam doubted that. He hurried to introduce another topic before they were tempted to return to their own. "I've heard Jesse's brother still needs care. Can you tell me anything about him?"

❦

Sunday evening, Ouida stood on the porch and drew in the beauty of Butternut Creek. She loved the town at this time, as the day wound down. The sun had set and the sky had paled to gray. The girls were in bed, sweet smelling from their baths, and she had a moment of quiet.

"Ouida, would you get me a newspaper?" George called. As she went back inside and crossed the living room, she picked up the newspaper and headed toward the kitchen.

When George placed his shoe-shine box on the kitchen table, she handed him a section. He placed his shoes on top of it. His best pair. Oh, he had other pairs, but this was his favorite: Italian and expensive but, he always said, very comfortable. They were gorgeous. A little flashy for George, Ouida had always thought, with the narrow silhouette and the midnight-gray trim a little lighter—only a tiny bit—than the glossy black leather.

He sat down and, using a special rag, began his favorite Sunday chore by gently cleaning any dust or dirt that dared to settle on the glossy leather surface.

For a moment, she wondered if George loved those shoes. He took such good care of them. Cleaned and shined them every week, never wore them on a rainy day, never two days in a row. The consideration made her blurt out an unexpected question.

"George, do you love me?"

He stopped wiping the shoes for a second before he said, "Of course." Then he put the rag down, opened the box, and took out the brush and polish he used only on these shoes.

"Why?" she asked.

"Why wouldn't I?" Keeping his eyes on his work, he carefully and evenly spread the polish and rubbed it in. After inspecting the right one to make sure he'd covered every millimeter of surface with polish, he set it down and picked up the left to repeat the process.

As if realizing that Ouida's minute of

silence meant he hadn't answered cor-
rectly, he said, "You're my wife."

"And?" she prompted.

"And you take good care of me?" His
statement became a question, as if they
were on some kind of marital *Jeopardy!*

She didn't answer. Darned if she'd help
him out on this. She really needed to know
how George felt, not how she hoped he
felt, but he didn't speak, either. Finally she
said, "How?"

He shrugged, still focused on the shoes.
"You always have dinner for me when I
come home and you iron my clothes."

"So you could hire a cook and a laun-
dress and I'd be *de trop*?"

After he finished precisely covering the
left shoe with polish, he put it down, looked
up at her, and blinked as if he couldn't
understand why she'd brought this up.
This conversation did not appear on his
schedule.

Poor man, he had no idea what to say,
but she had to know. Did he keep her
around to take care of this huge house because she cost less than a maid? Had she
accepted being banished to this small

town with their two little girls—a town she loved and girls whom, heavens knew, she adored—anyway, had she done this for a man who'd pretty much abandoned his family for his office in Austin?

With another blink, George shook his head. "You take care of the children, too."

"So add a nanny to the staff."

"And . . ." George's cheeks actually turned pink before he looked down at his shoes. He took a few seconds to test how dry the polish was before he mumbled, "And I like you in bed."

"Aha! So you could hire a . . ."

"Ouida, don't say that." This time he spoke sharply and looked her in the eyes. "You know what we have is special."

"How?" She took a step toward him. For once in her life, she felt powerful, intimidating. Hard for a round woman with lots of freckles to do, but she did. George watched her looking, well, intimidated.

"Because . . . it's you and me. We've always been together."

"But you're never home, George. I'd like to see you sometimes. The girls would like to get to know you."

He stood as if that change of position would place him in control of the situation. "I've just started a business."

"Years ago. But if it were new, would that make up for nearly abandoning us?"

"I haven't abandoned you. I make a good living for this family. As the owner of a business, I hire people who depend on the company to support their families. That's important."

She closed her eyes and shook her head. She hadn't reached him. She still couldn't make him understand. She sighed. "And your family isn't," she whispered.

"Of course you are. You . . ." He fumbled for words. "Ouida, my shoes are dry. I have to finish up." He sat back down and picked up a brush.

She stopped trying. She knew George's priorities. Work first, family, distant second. Now she had to figure out what was best for Carol and Gretchen and for her. The girls needed a father, she knew that, but they didn't have one now and she didn't have a husband except for those treasured moments at night. That wasn't enough any longer.

In their usual places at the diner at two o'clock Monday afternoon, the Widows awaited the appearance of Blossom Brown. Winnie Jenkins, still bursting with pride at being a real Widow for six months, stirred sweetener into her tea. Mercedes had arrived from the library mere seconds earlier and settled in a chair while Birdie placed cups of coffee in front of the other Widows, then put another on the table in front of Blossom's empty chair.

"When are you getting married?" Birdie asked Winnie.

Winnie blushed. Silly for a woman their age to blush, but she did. Birdie couldn't criticize. Well, she could, but that would sound spiteful.

"Oh, we don't know. Mitchell wanted to wait until Sam got married. He says his son's wedding should have first priority."

"That was weeks ago," Birdie said. "When are you getting married?"

Winnie smiled. "I don't mind the wait. After all, I've been waiting my whole life for the right man."

Sentimental dribble, Birdie thought, but

she wouldn't call Winnie out for those emotions. After all, Birdie had had her dear Elmer for nearly thirty years. Winnie deserved a good man, too.

Okay, Birdie accepted that, but she didn't need to hear about all that sweetness and light.

"Did you see Sam and Willow in church the other Sunday? With the boys?" As usual, Mercedes changed the subject when she saw conflict ahead.

"They looked happy. A great success for the Widows." Birdie smiled for a second, only until Blossom hurried in, her short hair perfectly coiffed and a pink jacket covering a matching pink sweater. She held a quilted basket, which she set on the table.

"You're late," Birdie said. "One of the tenets of the Widows is that we don't keep other people waiting."

"Oh." Blossom's round face flushed. "I'm sorry."

She had such a soft sweet voice. Birdie didn't like soft, sweet voices, not a bit.

"I didn't realize there were rules," Blossom explained. "I thought the Widows only went around doing good."

"Well, of course that's our main principle," Mercedes said gently. "But we have to plan our good deeds," she continued. "And we don't keep the others waiting."

"Of course. I'm sorry." Blossom settled into the fourth chair. "I'm a little late because my cook just finished making this." She opened the basket, pulled out a plastic container, and opened it to show a coffee cake. "Doesn't that look delicious? It's still warm."

Mercedes had a look on her face that said, *Don't you know you don't bring food to a restaurant?* But she'd never express that thought aloud.

"Don't you know you don't bring food to a restaurant?" Birdie said.

"They sell food here," Winnie added.

"We all take turns paying for our treat," Mercedes said.

Blossom's little pink mouth formed an O. "I . . . I didn't think. I wanted to bring you all something special, to show how much I appreciate your inviting me to be a Widow."

"You haven't been accepted as a Widow yet, not completely," Birdie said. "There are steps."

"I haven't?" Blossom blinked. "There are?"

"I had to go through a provisional period before I became a real Widow," Winnie added.

"I didn't understand." Blossom reached for the pastry. "I'll put this away."

"No, no," Birdie protested. "As long as it's here, we might as well enjoy it." She reached out to break off a piece, took a small bite and chewed. "It is really good." She cut herself a large piece and pushed the plate toward the others. "Try a little."

Winnie frowned. "Shouldn't we be getting down to business instead of eating?" She pulled out a notebook and pen.

Bossiest woman Birdie had ever met, but she also noticed that Winnie served herself nearly a quarter of the coffee cake.

"We need to discuss the preacher . . . ," Birdie said.

"I think we need to leave him alone for a while." Mercedes daintily wiped her mouth with a napkin.

With the addition of Blossom, Birdie became more aware that nearly everything her friend did was dainty and lady-like. She could only hope the two would not join forces and attempt to change Birdie, to make her softer and nicer. That dog wouldn't hunt.

"Why do you think we need to leave the preacher alone?" Birdie demanded. "One of our missions is to get the man married."

"I know, but maybe we've pushed too hard, Bird."

"Pushed too hard? We've left him alone for days."

"Yes, and we need to leave him alone for a while longer."

"Can't believe you'd say that, Mercedes. Can't believe you believe it. The man is not making the slightest effort to find himself a wife. If we don't try to find him a woman to marry . . ."

"Well, that's the problem, isn't it?" Mercedes said. "There aren't many women around. Who's left to fix him up with? Pretty soon, any unmarried woman is going to run if she sees us." She sighed. "And the preacher is beginning to ignore our efforts. Was he the least bit thankful when we mentioned Gussie Milton? No."

"Oh, tell me." Blossom clapped. "Are we trying to find a wife for Reverend Jordan?"

That woman didn't understand a thing

about being a Widow. How could she become one if she didn't comprehend who
they were and what they did?

"Didn't you figure that out when we were
in his office Monday?" Birdie asked.

"Oh." Blossom blinked. "That's what we
were doing. I thought we were discussing
the youth retreat."

"Dear," Mercedes explained patiently.
"As well as doing good, we attempt to
match people up, to get them married."

"Back when we had more young, unmarried people in town, we were extremely
successful." Mercedes sighed. "With websites and singles bars in Austin and all the
young people leaving town after they grad-
uate, matchmaking has become quite a
challenge."

"We matched Sam and Willow, and, if
you look at the faculty in the schools, you'll
see a number of our successes," Birdie
said. "The track coach and that third-grade
teacher have been married for ten years.
And the assistant principal and the school
nurse are expecting their second child.
But it is much harder now."

"The process has become more difficult

since all my children married," Mercedes added. "We found mates for two of them."

"I don't know many young people, but I'll help in any way I can." Blossom paused and thought for a few seconds. "Maybe we could invite all the singles in Butternut Creek to my house for a party."

The woman did have a lovely house.

"Problem is, that would be Pastor Adam and the minister from the Presbyterian Church," Winnie said. "We've already tried to get them together."

"I talked to a couple of divorced teachers at the middle school but they weren't at all receptive to our efforts," Birdie said. "Very rude, in fact."

"But that's a good idea, Blossom." Winnie wrote that down. "Maybe we'll try that later, after a few more divorces."

The four women considered the suggestion for nearly a minute while they each took another piece of the coffee cake.

"Well, enough of that," Winnie said. "What else do we need to discuss?"

Bossiest woman Birdie had ever met, but she did have a point. Unless more had happened between Gussie and Adam at the retreat than her granddaughters had told her, the matchmaking had hit a dead end.

"Cleanup at the thrift shop Friday, nine o'clock," Birdie said. "Bring brooms and cleaning material and hangers. With the big sale on Saturday, we have to sort everything, get it ready to set up in the parking lot."

Chapter Four

"Hello, Mrs. Boucher. I'm Adam Jordan, the minister of the Christian Church," Adam said as a smiling brunette opened her front door.

When she heard those words, her smile disappeared and she stepped back to close the door. "Thank you. Not interested."

"No, I'm not here for that. I have Aaron's backpack." He held it up.

"Oh." She shoved the screen door open and took it. "Thank you. He leaves everything he owns all over the neighborhood."

"Maybe it's not Aaron's fault." He gestured toward Chewy. "My dog has a bad habit of running off with stuff." Then he showed her a hoodie. "Is this Aaron's?"

She shook her head. "Try across the street. That may belong to April Higgins."

Mrs. Higgins was delighted to get the hoodie back. As he left, Adam said, "If you don't have a church home, we'd love for you to visit."

Had Chewy become their best tool for membership growth?

❦

When he got to the office, Adam wondered where the Widows were. Not that he missed them, but it was over a week since their last visit and they hadn't descended on him again. The lack of a second visit made him realize Mac hadn't squealed. He felt safe.

He'd worked for nearly fifteen minutes when Chewy leaped to his feet, woofed, and danced.

Ouida stood in his door, a plate in one hand and Gretchen dangling from the other, as usual.

"Exactly what I need," Adam said. "I don't know how I'd get along without you."

"You'd probably starve to death." She

shook her head. "It's my mission to fatten you up."

She scrutinized his chest and shoulders, which made Adam more than a little uncomfortable. "You've gained weight." She nodded decisively. "Makes you seem older, better looking." She nodded again. "Not that you weren't a good-lookin' guy before, for a minister." She snapped her mouth closed. "I'd better stop before I insult you any more. I came to talk to you."

In the same way she'd studied him, Adam scrutinized Ouida—but only her face—for a hint of a hidden motive. Surely she wasn't in cahoots with the Widows, was she? Was *fatten you up* code for "get you married"?

As Gretchen broke loose and ran to pet Chewy, Ouida glanced toward her daughter before she looked at Adam. "It's about George. My husband."

"Yes, I know who George is." He shouldn't have said that. If his professors in counseling had told him anything, it was *not* to stop communication with a smart answer. "I'm sorry. What about George?"

His reply had put Ouida off. She hesitated and studied him without saying a word.

"I really am sorry, Ouida. Sometimes I say the wrong thing."

"We all do." She took a deep breath. "We've been married for ten years." She seemed to consider her words. "He wasn't always like he is now, so very sober and driven and focused on work. I wouldn't have married him if he had been."

He remained silent but in a pastoral manner. His counseling professor had called it watchful empathy.

"George drives me nuts. At dinner, he eats one bite of chicken first, then one of potatoes, finishing with a forkful of green beans, then repeats that."

"But didn't you know that before you got married?" He stood and walked around the desk to sit next to his neighbor.

"Oh, yes, but back then I didn't know about the other things. His closet is perfect, colors together. He hates disorder. He hates . . . well, he hates everything that is family life and children."

"What? He has a wonderful family."

"Yes, he does." She shook her head.

"He changed right after he began his own business seven years ago, right before Carol was born. Probably not good timing with the stress of a new business and a baby."

"Tell me more about George when you first met him. Why did you fall in love with him?" There, that sounded ministerial but not overly so.

"Oh, he's always been a little staid and controlling, but I did see *moments* of spontaneity, of exploration and joy." She caught his eye as if attempting to sell him on her words. "We complemented each other, I thought. My messy life and emotions balanced his purposeful actions and solemnity. And . . . and I felt safe with him." She sighed and glanced at Gretchen, who seemed too occupied with the dog to be listening. Nevertheless, Ouida leaned toward Adam and lowered her voice. "He was raised by his grandmother. His parents died when he was seven. She was strict and unemotional, which probably has a great deal to do with his being quiet and introspective. I loved him because I knew who he was inside, how much he needed me and how hard it was for him to show it." She shook her head again. "I never should've allowed this isolation, his closing down, to happen to him, to the girls. They don't know he loves them."

"How can I help?"

"Adam, I don't know." She sighed again. "He's getting worse, much more distant. I don't know how to reach him anymore, especially since he's not around."

"Have you talked to him about that?"

"I tried. Didn't get anyplace."

"You know I'm always available to talk to. What can I do?"

"Thanks." She smiled. "Listening's probably all you can do now. I'm sorry I dropped all this on you, but it's been building." She tapped her chest. "Inside."

When she stood, Adam got to his feet.

"I'll talk to him again. Sunday, when the girls nap, I will." She reached her hand out to her daughter. "Come on. Let's go. Adam has work to do."

Gretchen gave Chewy a final pat and ran over to Adam for a hug. Then the two exited, leaving Adam to wonder what in the world he could do. There were things in ministry he was inexperienced in and unprepared for. Counseling scared him. What did he have to say that would help anyone?

He hated to use the Kowalskis' marriage as a learning experience. He should probably study up, read a little. He moved toward the bookcase and perused his books until he finally found one on marital counseling in a stack behind the desk. His sermon could wait.

❦

Adam encouraged his ancient car toward the thrift shop. Although it threatened to die on him at the only major intersection in town, he did get there. The vehicle putted and jumped as he pulled into a parking space. He'd need to call Rex.

No better mechanic in the state than Rex. Only one who had been able to keep the old car going consistently, and he charged Adam only for parts. As a good Catholic, Rex felt God expected him to help the preacher and that old car was part of his witness, his true mission. Adam kept his number on speed dial.

Turning the engine off—although it still chugged and sputtered for a few more seconds with the key out of the ignition—he got out of the car, flipped open the trunk to pick up the few boxes remaining from his move, and walked inside the shop.

The thrift shop was always closed on the Friday before the quarterly Saturday sale. He expected Miss Birdie to be there. He never knew what days she took off from the diner and probably never would. Once when he'd asked her about her schedule, she'd let him know that although she was a poor workingwoman, she didn't waitress 24/7. He never asked again, simply accepted that if there was work to be done, the pillar appeared.

"When you find a shirt that is too worn for anyone to wear, chunk it in the trash." Mercedes pointed toward a barrel as he got to work.

"*Chunk*?" Adam asked. "Do you mean *chuck*?"

"She said what she meant, Preacher." Miss Birdie glanced up from her sorting. "Chunk, you know, throw it."

Another word for his Texas vocabulary. "Okay, what do I do after I *chunk* the worn shirts?"

"Put the nice ones back on the shelf

and the in-betweens in a box for the sale," Winnie said.

After fifteen minutes of packing and chunking and chatting, they heard the sound of a car pulling up outside.

"Is that Blossom? I told her to be here at nine." The pillar glared at Adam as if the late arrival were his fault.

"Looks like her big car," Mercedes said.

"Expensive and probably eats up the gasoline," Birdie complained.

"Probably pretty fuel-efficient," Mercedes said. "The new cars are."

"Hrmph." Miss Birdie glared at her friend. "You don't always have to correct everyone."

"I told Blossom to bring cleaning supplies." Winnie leaped in to stop the disagreement. "Hope she brought a mop because the floor in that back room really needs a good scrubbing."

The front door opened and a pudgy, middle-aged woman entered toting a bucket and mop. "Where should I put these?" she asked. Not waiting for an answer, she dropped the stuff, moved back a few steps, and held the door open.

"We're always happy to have a new

volunteer." Adam hurried to welcome her. "I'm Adam Jordan, minister at the Christian Church and these are . . ."

"I know who you are and I'm not a volunteer. I'm Miss Blossom's housekeeper. She made me come. What should I do?"

The four blinked.

"She made you come? Blossom *made* you come?" Adam struggled to understand the comment.

"Where is she now?" Miss Birdie sounded oddly mystified, an emotion he rarely saw from her.

"She's in the car, getting the food out." The woman held the door open.

"The food?" Winnie echoed.

"Hello, hello!" Blossom sang as she entered the door holding a huge basket. "Coffee and pastry for all." Not even noticing the expressions on the faces of the Widows, which ranged from amazement to horror, she put the basket on the table where Winnie had been working, right on top of the nicest T-shirts.

Winnie blinked, Mercedes shook her head, and Miss Birdie—well, Miss Birdie continued to look stunned. Adam had never seen her taken aback. He'd never believed the pillar could be at a loss for words.

Both Winnie and Mercedes looked at Miss Birdie, expecting her to take over. When she didn't, Mercedes said sweetly, "Hello, Blossom. You brought your housekeeper?"

"Oh, yes." Blossom motioned in the direction of the woman. "That's Evelyn, my housekeeper."

"Why isn't she at home?" Winnie said. "Keeping *your* house?"

"You said we were cleaning. I don't clean well." She fluttered her beautifully manicured hands toward the confusion of the room.

Finally, Miss Birdie found several dozen words. "The *Widows* are cleaning the thrift shop and sorting clothing," she said in a voice so cold it could freeze the coffee Blossom had started to pour. "Not our housekeeper or our maids, but the Widows. This is a community service that *we*, the Widows, do."

This time Blossom blinked. "But I'm not at all good with this sort of thing. I'm not dressed for it." They all examined her lovely pale blue silk shirt and slacks with matching high-heeled sandals.

Because Adam feared Miss Birdie would have a stroke, he stepped forward. "Blossom, the Widows *themselves* do community service. It is their way of being servants, of helping others unselfishly."

"But I brought coffee, and my cook baked us another of those coffee cakes you all enjoyed so much." She smiled at them all.

"Not again," the pillar grumbled.

"Dear," Mercedes said. "Thank you, but as much as we enjoyed that pastry, we aren't an *eating* group. We're a doing-things-for-others group. We thought you understood that when we invited you to join."

"At the suggestion of the preacher," the pillar stated. Her tone said, *Don't blame me for this mess.*

"You don't want the coffee?" She glanced down at the three cups she'd poured.

"Evelyn, thank you for coming," Adam said. "Do you live close by? Can you walk home from here or do you need a ride?"

The housekeeper pointed east. "I'll walk." She scurried out.

"Thank you for coming," Mercedes shouted after her.

"Blossom, why don't you and I go to the

table in the back of the store and chat?" Adam picked up one of the filled cups. "Over our coffee?"

"I'm coming, too, Preacher, and I'm not feeling a bit chatty," Miss Birdie said.

"Oh, my." Blossom's ivory skin became paler, and her eyes grew enormous. "Am I in trouble?"

"No, no, only a misunderstanding," Adam assured her as he pushed her toward the back. Once there, he held out a chair for her. Skittishly, she perched on the edge of the seat.

"I don't believe you understand the mission of the Widows," he began.

"We take care of other people, ourselves," the pillar interrupted from where she stood next to the table. "We do the work. We don't have our servants do the work."

Because Blossom looked as if she was on the verge of tears, Adam took Miss Birdie's elbow and escorted her, forcefully, toward the front of the store. "I'll handle this," he said with a confidence he didn't feel. Taking a stand against the pillar had never been one of his favorite actions.

"*We* are the servants," Miss Birdie said

loudly as he headed toward the table again and she stomped back to the work area.

He took a chair across from Blossom and took a gulp of coffee. "Great coffee."

Blossom brightened a little.

"I have a favorite Bible verse, from the book of Micah. I'd like to share it with you," Adam said. "'. . . what does the LORD require of you but to do justice, and to love kindness, and to walk humbly with your God?'"

"Very pretty," she said. "But," she leaned forward and whispered, "that Birdie Mac-Dowell isn't a bit humble. Not a bit."

Because he couldn't refute her observation, he hurried on. "Those words from Micah are how the Widows feel. They serve others. When I arrived a few months ago, they got donations to furnish the parsonage. Because of that, we could open it up to an injured woman and her family. Now two homeless kids live there. The Widows furnished the bedroom, provided all the linens. The Widows take food to shut-ins and volunteer within the community."

"Maybe this was a mistake." Again she fluttered her fingers toward the Widows. "I really don't feel that way, you know, humble and kind, and how could I do anything about justice? I probably wouldn't fit in. In fact"—she folded her hands—"I don't, not a bit."

Adam allowed her words to hover between them before he asked, "What will you be doing with your time?"

"I could play bridge." She sighed. "But I'm tired of that. A lot of gossip, and I know too many rumors were going around about Jason and me to enjoy it anymore." She paused. "I could become a docent at the art gallery, but that's in Austin."

"A long drive, and you wouldn't be making new friends here in Butternut Creek."

She bit her lips, then shook her head. "I don't know." Tears appeared in her eyes. "I'm really not good at anything except taking care of Jason and being his hostess."

Adam handed her a couple of tissues.

She swallowed and dabbed at her eyes. "Pastor, I have no skills. I've had hired help all my life, even as a child. They've always done everything."

"Aren't you in charge of the help? Didn't you plan the receptions and dinners and parties for your husband? I imagine you're a good organizer."

"Well, yes, I am that, but there's no need in this group for an organizer with Birdie and Winnie around."

"Maybe you'll find another way to fit in. Please, give it another try. I truly believe you'll be a great addition."

She nodded, wiped her eyes once more, then placed the tissues in her purse.

Had the message gotten through? Adam could only hope it had. Blossom needed the Widows. He only hoped the Widows saw accepting her as an act of kindness.

❦

"Good morning, Adam."

A glorious morning was always made brighter when he saw Ouida with a plate covered by a napkin.

"I'll carry this to the church," she said as if he couldn't quite manage that.

Following her, Adam couldn't help but notice that the short overalls Ouida wore made her backside look as wide as a football lineman's—not that he made a habit of watching women's derrieres. She wore a yellow striped T-shirt, sunny and happy like Ouida, but today she seemed determined about something and her usual stroll had become almost a march. Because Chewy slept in, only Adam followed.

"Where's Gretchen?"

"She's spending this week with my sister up in Plano."

By the time they'd entered the church, waved at Maggie, and entered the minister's study, she'd slowed down a little. She placed the plate in the middle of Adam's desk and turned to look at him.

"Umm, do you do marriage counseling?"

"I can and I do," Adam said although he didn't feel nearly as confident as his answer sounded. "What do you need?"

"Oh, not for me and George." She shook her head. "But I have some friends . . . All right, it's about George and me." She dropped into a chair in front of his desk. "You know that from what I said before."

When she sat, he did, too.

He waited. She didn't speak. He templed his fingers and watched her. He'd learned long ago—actually, last year in seminary— that listening brought more information than asking questions, usually. If it didn't, he could ask questions.

"You won't try to convert me, will you? You know we aren't religious people."

"Yes, I know. You've told me that."

"That's right." Apparently convinced he wouldn't force faith on her, she said, "You probably think we're an odd couple, George and I. I told you that before, but it's the way I need to lead into what I'm going to say." She stopped. "And to get my courage up to share. I told you I loved his logic and his thoughtfulness, his ability to deliberate while I leaped into things."

Adam nodded this time.

She sighed and sat back in her chair. "But he doesn't help me with logic and I can't make him less serious because I never see him."

"Never?" Adam repeated.

"You know he's always working. He works weekends. The girls barely know who he is."

"He's runs a business, Ouida."

"Don't take his side," she warned.

Adam sat back to listen, only listen.

"Besides, he was like that before he started his company. He's away so much I sometimes wonder how the girls were conceived."

Adam didn't comment on that, only hoped she'd move to another topic.

And she did.

"*Kowalski.* Preacher, do you know the origin of that name?"

"It's Polish, isn't it?"

"Yes." Ouida picked up a muffin and broke off a piece. Once she finished that, she placed the partially eaten muffin back on the plate and said, "It's the housekeeping I have problems with. George—his middle name is Miloslaw. If you spell it in Polish, it has lines through both *l*'s."

"Interesting. I didn't realize the Polish alphabet—"

But it seemed Ouida was really wound up. Her words poured from her over his. "George is third generation of the family born here. His great-grandparents immigrated nearly a hundred years ago. Everyone in the next generation was Polish. His mother came from that background, and you should see her kitchen. Do you know how often she mops her kitchen every day?"

"Once?" he asked, although that seemed excessive to him. Before the arrival of the Firestones, he only mopped when the floor got so sticky his shoes made sucking noises when he walked across it. Since then, Hector and Janey shared that chore on a weekly basis.

"Five. Five times a day, after every meal and again if anyone has a snack."

"Really?"

"Polish people are very neat, clean people. That's fine but I'm not Polish and I'm not Susie Homemaker." She nodded decisively. "Oh, not that there's anything wrong with being Susie Homemaker if a woman wants to be that. Or a man, although he'd probably be Stanley Homemaker." She forced her lips together as if trying to keep the words from tumbling out. "What I mean," she said slowly and clearly, "is that we're all different. George's mother and grandmother may have been really tidy people, but does that mean I have to do what they did?"

"Of course not."

"Of course not," she agreed and leaned back in her chair.

This certainly wasn't a marriage counseling session. For one thing, the husband wasn't here. For another, it had taken off without him. This seemed more like the crumbling of a dam during the spring thaw with all the flotsam and jetsam of Ouida's life gushing through the gap.

"Ouida, I'm not sure . . . ," he began in an attempt to harness the flood and sift through the detritus.

"George expects me to be the same kind of housekeeper, but I'm not."

She sniffed. Adam handed her a Kleenex.

"You have two little girls."

"His mother had five children, but she kept the house spotless." She blew her nose. "My mother was neat but she wasn't irrational. We didn't mind a little dust or an unmade bed or a footprint on the kitchen floor. Do you?"

"No, I—"

"George's mother took those embroidered linen runners off the top of the dresser every week, every single week. She'd wash, starch, and iron them before she put them back on." She sat back in the chair. "Starched and ironed those dresser scarves every single week."

"What's a dresser scarf?"

"It's a piece of linen about this size." She measured length and width with her hands. "It goes on the dresser for . . . I don't know why. Maybe decoration. Could be to protect the dresser but they don't. They aren't waterproof. A spill would go right through." She shrugged. "But his mother gave me a pair that she'd embroidered at a wedding shower. I should have known they meant trouble. I should have realized I was not the kind of woman who'd take good care of those dresser scarves, not like Magda did. But it's the boxer shorts I hate most, ironing them." She sighed.

"You starch and iron George's—" Adam stopped, pretty certain he didn't want to discuss this and wondering why he'd asked for clarification.

"No starch. Just iron." She nodded. "That's how he likes them. That's what his mother did for her husband and all the wives in the family back through the centuries of Polish women who married Kowalskis. And his shirts. Those I do starch."

"Why not take the shirts to the laundry?"

"George has a chart. It shows how much better and cheaper it is for me to do his shirts, less wear and tear on the fabric so the shirts last longer. Besides, he says I use the right amount of starch and the ones done at the laundry irritate his neck."

"Have you ever heard of permanent press, wash and wear, no-iron?"

"They don't look as crisp as George likes.

He wants the front—" She placed a hand on her chest. "He wants it crisp and without wrinkles. But, you know, I think it's the boxers I mind most. Who sees them?" She stood, looking resolute. "That's where I'm going to start, with those boxers," she said with a vigorous nod. "I'm going to tell him I'm not going to iron them anymore." She held a hand in front of her, palm forward. "Don't try to talk me out of this. If he doesn't like that, he can take care of them himself." With that, she placed the remaining muffins on a napkin on Adam's desk, picked up the plate, and stomped off.

❧

Why hadn't she thought about this long ago?

Ouida nearly skipped across the parking lot and the lawn of the parsonage.

She'd been a limp rag for too long. When she'd started to date George, she'd been overwhelmed that he was interested in her, amazed this tall, handsome, intelligent man had fallen in love with plain old her. In exchange for his love, she'd done whatever he'd asked: given up her dream of being an artist, quit school to work so he could finish his MBA, and moved to Butternut

Creek because he thought that would be a great place to raise a family.

She'd give him the last point. She loved the little town and she loved her children and, truly, she loved George. But she was overwhelmed suddenly by her complete loss of who she was, her individuality—which she'd been pretty certain she'd had when she'd entered UT.

Now she wanted more—or, perhaps, less. She wanted to find out more about herself, like why had she given up painting? And why had she allowed herself to change so much?

She entered the house and looked around. Much like their lives, everything was neat as if it had been lined up with a yardstick. George had charted out the financial burden of children, and had showed on that chart—expenses of college, et cetera—that they should have another child in two years, then stop. On his chart, the last child would be a boy.

She didn't want that. Oh, not that she didn't want another child, but the scheduling of their entire lives on an actuarial table no longer sat well with her. He'd probably also plotted out the date of conception.

She used to think George's compulsiveness added structure to her life, but no longer. Now it drove her nuts.

She would take charge of their lives now, in little ways like those boxers, and move ahead bit by bit. Perhaps she'd find time to paint again.

Slowly she turned to study the room. It was spotless, and George wouldn't be home for hours. Why did she struggle to keep it perfect when George was sixty miles away? She and the girls could live here like normal people, then quickly pick up toys and sweep and make it immaculate right before George got home. No more mopping the kitchen five times a day. George might have to get used to a footprint here and a dirty fork there.

She looked out the window toward the church. Poor Adam. She'd gone to him and asked for counseling and she'd hit him with all her woes. She must have overwhelmed him, but after all, wasn't counseling mostly listening?

Thanks to him, she'd come to a big conclusion: She had no desire to leave, only to change. She wanted to set up a studio on the third floor, taking up a little of the space where the girls played, and paint the beauty of the Hill Country. All she needed was time and maybe a skylight.

Yes, George did run a business, but he could darned well wear freshly washed boxers with a few wrinkles and no one really *needed* dresser scarves.

Maybe after that, she'd stop ironing the pillowcases.

🍒

After Ouida left, Adam had looked out the office window and watched her cross the parsonage lawn toward her house, walking with a determination he seldom saw her use.

How had the session gone? Not at all like the case studies they'd discussed at the seminary or he'd read in those marriage counseling books. Ouida had taken off and left him far behind. He hadn't helped her discover her feelings. She'd pretty much done that herself.

He remembered a line John Milton wrote: "They also serve who only stand and wait." Maybe he'd served by sitting and listening. He didn't seem to have screwed anything up. Probably should let go of his worry that he'd been inadequate in the situation because, yes, he had been, but he couldn't go back and change what had happened.

How could he have acted differently? Short of putting his hand over Ouida's mouth, he couldn't have asked questions or offered much advice. She hadn't needed to be led. Could be she only needed to allow the words to flow out and know he'd listened.

Instead of worrying, he wrote a few comments in the file folder he'd labeled COUN-SELING, put it back in a drawer, and turned to his computer.

Adam checked his email, always hoping to see a note from Gussie. He hadn't heard from her since the retreat except for the evaluation she'd sent out to all adults. When he'd sent it back to her, he'd added a note, which she hadn't answered.

What did he expect? She thought of him as a kid, a minister, a camp counselor. She kept busy with her job, her parents, her church. Why had he thought they'd become email buddies, which might lead to more?

But after he'd answered a few messages and written a quick note to his sister, he checked the inbox one more time. Only spam.

❦

It was her last appointment Friday afternoon, almost five o'clock. Gussie was tired; Timmy and Tammy Scheltzbaum, the six-year-old twins who sat stiffly on the stools she'd placed in front of the blue backdrop, were also tired; and their mother sitting in the corner drooped.

"Can you smile?" She always asked that of children who didn't display an iota of personality in the hope they would sparkle and laugh without her having to resort to funny faces and dancing around.

Either they couldn't or they didn't.

She glanced toward the corner where their mother sat.

"Smile, sweeties," Mrs. Scheltzbaum said.

When the children's lips curled a little but no joy filled their eyes, Gussie sighed. She'd snapped a few good portraits of serious siblings but knew their mother expected sparkling as well. Good thing Gussie had curly, floppy hair, which usually amused children. She bobbed her head back and forth, up and down, to allow her curls to bounce. Tammy grinned a little and almost laughed, but Timmy frowned, already too grownup and macho to smile. She bet he was also too old to find the hand puppet amusing.

So she went with funny voices. Not imitations, but voices that ranged from thin and high to growling with odd accents.

"Hey, Timmy," she said with her voice sliding up and down the scale. "Gimme a smile?" As she kept up the schtick, the children relaxed and Tammy gave her an almost-smile.

Through the years, she'd discovered what worked. Impersonating a witch scared children, of course. Pretending to be a dog embarrassed even her and she was nearly impervious to humiliation. Not everyone liked clowns. She'd tried roller skates but discovered the difficulty of taking a picture as she flew by.

The final option? "The Lord said to Noah," she sang. By the time she finished the chorus, the twins were clapping and laughing and she got a great bunch of pictures.

That evening, Gussie sat at her computer while her parents watched television downstairs. She read and reread the note Adam had sent with his evaluation. "Hey," he'd written. "Had a great time at the retreat. Meet for coffee?"

Pleasant but no matter how many times she read it, she could not find a great deal of passionate interest in those eleven words. Actually, she could detect only *friendly* interest, perhaps rote politeness for the old lady from Roundville.

All for the best, of course. She had no interest in romance, certainly not. But companionship would be nice. Talking to a man who sparked excitement within her could be very pleasant.

But maybe not.

Had she felt lust for Lennie? Probably so. He'd been tall and handsome and flashy, but she couldn't remember. Didn't want to remember.

Chapter Five

Adam headed home from the Butternut Creek skilled nursing facility. He'd walked over to see the father of a church member while his car kept Rex company. He breathed in a lungful of fragrant Central Texas air. It was a great day, the kind of spring day everyone waited for. Warm and sunny and the exercise felt great.

Out on the highway west of town, reports of the arrival of bluebonnets had been coming in for nearly a week. When he got the car back, he'd take the kids for a ride to see them. Watching the bluebonnets and Indian paintbrush and what Lady

Bird had called "those damn little yellow flowers" was a Hill Country tradition he aimed to join soon.

He missed the spring flowers of Kentucky: a purple crocus poking through still-cold ground followed by lawns covered with sunny daffodils. Add to that forsythia that bloomed bright yellow and redbuds and dogwood trees. Oh, he'd seen those trees in Texas, but in Kentucky their appearance signaled a transition from winter to spring. The seasons had little separation here.

Mercedes had told him to look forward to the sweet-smelling mountain laurels and the glorious magnolia trees, which couldn't survive winters farther north. And tulips, Ouida had told him. She had a plot in her garden, but he always thought of them at Churchill Downs for the Derby. Add the fragile azaleas and hearty crepe myrtle and spring displayed itself in colorful splendor here, too.

As he walked, he thought about Hector's visit with his father in prison last Saturday, a trip he made by bus every month or two. Each time, he returned solemn and remained quiet for a few days, withdrawn and worried.

He never took his sister, and Janey never asked to go. She'd had a rough life with her mother dying when she was a toddler and her father's addiction. Hector said his father had never laid a hand on Janey because he knew Hector would hurt him if he did. Nevertheless, Janey was afraid of the man, afraid of the kind of people who'd come to the house, of the shouting and the fights and the occasional gunfire.

Adam couldn't blame her. He'd be traumatized, too. He'd attempted to get her into counseling but she'd curled up in the corner of the office and refused to talk to the psychologist he'd found who worked with kids. She found her safe place with Hector. She seemed fine in the parsonage and did okay at school. Neither Adam nor Hector could figure out why, as much time as she spent studying, she didn't make better grades. Due to trauma as well? Until he could find someone she'd talk to, they wouldn't know.

Adam strolled down the highway, then turned on Church Street. As he headed toward the church, he could see six or seven cars in the parking lot. The women getting ready for the bazaar, he guessed. On the front porch of the parsonage, he saw two people on the swing with their heads together. After a few more steps, he realized the two were Hector and Bree. Janey sat in the rattan chair and read.

Well, well.

"Hey, guys," Adam said. "What's going on?"

"Just hangin' out." Hector's glare warned Adam not to tease him about Bree's presence. "Knew you wouldn't like us inside without you around."

When Janey glanced up at Adam, a smile flickered across her face. Her smile gave him hope that, little by little, she was healing.

"Pops, we need, we really need, a goal on the parking lot." Hector pointed toward the exact place he envisioned it. "We could have been playing ball while we waited for you."

"And, Pops, we"—Bree indicated herself and Hector—"emailed Gussie Milton and invited her to speak to the youth group the Sunday after Easter."

Adam blinked. Gussie? Here?

"She didn't want to come at first," Hector said.

"Something about her parents," Bree said. "And work and the church and other stuff."

"She has a busy life." Adam sat on the wicker chair.

"But when Bree told her we needed her to talk about summer camp so we can bring more kids, she agreed," Hector said.

Bree must have learned that from her grandmother, using guilt as the ultimate motivator.

"Where'd you get this idea?" Adam asked.

"Mac suggested it," Bree said.

Aah, Mac. Matchmaker-in-training, taking after her grandmother. At least she hadn't told the pillar about his attraction to Gussie, and she'd behaved far more subtly than any of the Widows.

"We're all going to ask friends who don't go to church to come, try to get them interested in church camp this summer," Hector said. "We should have that basketball goal up by then, Pops. That'll bring the guys out."

"Not enough time. First, I have to take

that up with the property committee and the board."

Hector shook his head. "Churches. The hoops you have to go through just to get a hoop."

He and Bree laughed at that, but Adam was still trying to get his mind around the idea of Gussie's visit here in a couple of weeks.

"The Widows are going to serve refreshments," Bree said. "Food always attracts people, especially high school people."

"What time?" Adam attempted to mentally picture his calendar, but Gussie's smiling face popped up in the little squares.

"She's going to leave Roundville after church and get here about one thirty. We'll start at two," Bree said. "Grandma said after the meeting the Widows will put together a light supper for you at the parsonage so Gussie doesn't have to drive home hungry."

Oh, yeah, that driving while starving, always hazardous, but not nearly as terrifying as a matchmaking Widow.

But why worry? Spending a few hours with Gussie was great, even if she hadn't wanted to come. The idea of spending a few hours with Gussie under the eye of the Widows didn't count as a positive, but he didn't care. She'd be here.

Of course, they wouldn't be alone, so he couldn't put a move on Gussie. Actually, he'd never put a move on Gussie at any time, surrounded by people or not. The realization would have depressed him greatly if he allowed himself to dwell on the fact. Instead, he grinned in anticipation of Gussie's imminent appearance.

"Why're you smiling, Pops?" Hector asked.

"Sounds like fun," Adam answered.

"Yeah, a lot of kids will be here and Gussie's great," Bree said.

"You two should get together," Hector said. "You and Gussie. She'd make you laugh more."

"That's right. You two would be great together," Bree agreed. "Why don't you ask her out?"

Exactly what he needed. Dating advice from teenagers.

❧

Gussie stared at the screen of her computer, perusing the email she'd sent to Bree. What had she done? She'd agreed to visit the church in Butternut Creek, to talk to kids about camp and the youth program. The event didn't present a problem; she did that all the time.

The problem was, she hadn't done it before with Adam Jordan around.

Too late to back out. Not that she could. This was her ministry, what she did, how she served. She'd remember who she was—an old maid who'd substituted the young people for her children—and who he was—the minister of Butternut Creek. With those identities firmly in mind, she'd be able to be professional and not see Basketball Adam when she looked at Reverend Adam, at least not when she was close to him.

Oh, sure. Someday she'd have to stop lying to herself.

❧

Adam had finally found a donkey for Palm Sunday. With a sigh of relief, he sat back in the desk chair in his office, folded his arms behind his head, and grinned. Victory! He felt like singing loud hosannas but he knew he couldn't carry it off; he would only upset Maggie and it would serve no real purpose.

Jesse Hardin had actually found it. Thank goodness for Jesse. Last year, he'd given Sam Peterson horseback rides to build up the muscles in Sam's thigh as part of his physical therapy. And now he'd tracked down a donkey for Hector to ride on Palm Sunday. Jesse would go to the ranch early Sunday morning, load Maisie into his horse trailer, and bring her to church. The Methodists planned to use the donkey fifteen minutes later and the Catholics after that.

When he'd finished savoring that victory, Adam scrutinized the outline on his computer. As usual, when he had no ideas and the sermon had no oomph, he stared into space, searching for inspiration. None came. He stood and looked out the window. Still nothing.

The silence was broken by a bloodcurdling shriek from the reception office. He turned, ran to the door, and threw it open to see Maggie, his secretary, leaping from chair to chair, moving faster and jumping higher than he'd ever thought she could. Finally, she clambered onto the corner file cabinet, pulled her legs up beneath her, and continued to scream.

Standing by her desk were two redheaded

boys: Leo and Nick Thomas. When the paperwork was done, they'd be Leo and Nick Peterson. Their mother Willow had married Sam Peterson in February.

As Adam moved farther into the office, Maggie kept screaming. The kids looked at him, eyes wide, their faces covered with shame, surprise, and a thin overlay of machismo.

After a few more steps, Adam saw the open box on the floor with a stiff, dead animal inside.

"In there, Preacher." Maggie pointed at the container. "The dirty, filthy creature's in there."

"What is it, boys?" Adam asked.

"It's a squirrel, sir," Leo said.

"It's dead, sir," Nick added. "I don't know why it would scare her. It can't attack."

"Women are like that," Adam said. "They don't like dead things." He turned and pointed toward his office. "You two need to explain this to me."

"No," Maggie shouted. "Preacher, you are not leaving me alone with that . . . that thing." She pointed toward the box with a shaking finger.

"Guys, you know this could be dangerous," Adam said.

"But it's dead," Leo said before he added, "sir."

"Rabies, other diseases." Adam pulled a ragged jacket from the lost-and-found, wrapped the box up, and stuffed it into a plastic bag. "I'm going to take this outside, put it in the trash, and call animal control. You boys, go to the restroom and wash up carefully. Maggie, go on home and try to forget this happened."

She slid off the cabinet onto a chair, leaped from that, grabbed her purse, and ran.

By the time Adam had washed his hands in the tiny private bathroom off his study and explained the situation to animal control, the boys stood in the front office. "I'm going to call your parents," he told them.

"Oh, no, sir. Please don't." Leo cleared his throat. "We'll do anything if you won't tell them."

"Mom gets sad and *really* disappointed in us." Nick's lips trembled. "And Sam, he expects better of us."

"You know Sam's my friend. I can't keep this from him. Is he home?"

They nodded.

Adam suddenly realized it was a weekday. "Why aren't you in school?"

"Teacher in-service day," Leo said. "Sam was supposed to watch us, but he's studying. You know he's taking a lot of math classes from Tech so he can get certified as a teacher."

"He was real busy studying and didn't notice when we left," Nick said. "He thinks we're in the backyard, but Leo remembered he saw a dead animal over in that lot next to the church Sunday. He made me come with him."

"Did not," Leo said. "You wanted to come."

"Did not," Nick contradicted. "Your idea."

"Listen, shorty, you—"

"Okay, guys." Sam held his hand up. "So you both sneaked out of your backyard . . ."

"It wasn't really sneaking," Leo said.

"We've never completely fixed the fence at Sam's house." Nick smiled. "At *our* house. He says we'll get around to that someday."

"Okay, I'm going to call Sam." He picked up the phone and punched the number in.

"Please don't."

"When he gets here, you're going to explain how that creature ended up on the floor of Maggie's office and scared her to death." He frowned at them. "You know Sam expects you to respect women."

Both nodded. Their eyes spoke of coming doom, but that didn't deter Adam. Great kids, but they were also very active and imaginative.

Only a few minutes later, Adam stood at the window in the reception office and watched Sam's yellow Mustang pull into the lot. The captain got out. An amputee from Afghanistan, Sam still limped a little, but today he strode with confidence.

Once they were all seated in Adam's office, Sam said, "Okay, guys, explain."

"I saw a dead animal in the back after church last Sunday so we came back to look at it," Leo said.

"You told me you were going to stay in the backyard. I trusted you and you lied to me," Sam said in a tone that reminded Adam that the captain had commanded marines.

"We didn't," Nick began.

"Man up, son," Sam said.

Both boys nodded and said, "Yes, sir," in unison. Probably, Adam thought, the entire conversation would be more suitable if they both stood at attention while Sam interrogated them.

"We lied to you and sneaked out to get the animal," Leo said. "Sir."

"But we didn't plan to pick up the squirrel." Nick added, "Sir."

"Then why did you bring a box with you, Gyrenes?" Sam asked.

Both boys looked so crestfallen that Adam almost felt sorry for them—until he remembered Maggie's terror.

"We wanted to bring it in here and show the preacher. We thought he'd want to see it," Leo said.

"'Cause he's a guy," Nick added.

"Yes," Adam spoke solemnly. "Dead squirrels count as a particular favorite of mine."

Sam's lips quivered for only a moment before he became serious again.

"After that, we were going to come home and show you, Dad," Nick finished.

"How did that box get on the floor and

the secretary end up on top of the file cabinet?" Adam asked.

"Nick dropped it."

"Did not. You pushed me."

"Did not . . ."

Sam held his hand up. "Enough. I don't care how it happened or who pushed who. You both handled a dead animal, which could have made you very sick. You both brought it in here and scared the secretary. You both knew she'd be frightened by a dead animal. Your actions may also have contaminated the offices."

"We didn't mean to," Nick said, his eyes wide and round.

"Doesn't matter," Leo said. "Actions have consequences." He sounded exactly like Sam.

"Yes, actions have consequences," Sam said. "We'll work those out when your mother gets home tonight."

"Do you have to tell her?" Nick asked.

All Sam had to do was raise his eyebrow. Both boys nodded.

"Of course you do," Nick said.

"She's our mother and she loves us and she has to know," Leo said.

Words they must have heard from Sam several times.

"I don't keep secrets from my wife." Sam grinned when he said the word *wife.* "I don't lie to my wife and you don't lie to your mother."

"Sir, no, sir," the boys said.

"Thanks, Adam." Sam stood. "We'll handle this at home. Can you think of a service these two could perform at the church?"

"They could write an apology to Maggie."

"They will," Sam said. "What else? We don't have a lot left to do at the house."

"We could finish that fence, sir," Nick suggested as the three left the office.

Adam smiled. Yes, great kids, but he was glad he hadn't inherited them.

"Oh, hey, guys," Sam said. "Wait for me by my car. I need to talk to the preacher."

"Is it about us?" Nick asked.

Sam raised his brow again and the boys shouted, "Sir, yes, sir," and ran out.

"Don't find another dead animal or break a window or anything else while you're out there," Sam shouted at their backs, then he turned toward Adam and grinned. "They might kill me yet."

"You love them. You're happy."

"Never thought I would be again, Preacher, but I am." He paused and glanced at the wall over Adam's head before he said, "Umm . . . I hear Gussie Milton's coming to town in a couple of weeks."

Adam nodded. He didn't bother to ask how Sam knew that. He'd either heard it from Winnie Jenkins, the Widow who was engaged to his father, or he'd heard it the small-town way: Everyone knew everyone's business and everyone talked with everyone else about it, over and over, with embellishments. Actually, didn't much matter which.

"Yes," Adam said in a neutral voice. "She's going to talk to some of the kids about camp this summer. Bree invited her."

"So," Sam said in an equally neutral voice, keeping his gaze on the wall. "How do you feel about that?"

"Pretty angry that everyone in this town is determined to find me a wife."

"What's wrong with that?" Sam made eye contact with Adam. "The Widows hooked me up with Willow and that turned out great."

"I'm glad you're happy, but you would've worked things out with her by yourself."

"Maybe, but if the Widows are determined to match you up with someone, you've got about as much chance of escaping as a gnat in a hailstorm."

"Is that why you're here? The Widows told you to talk to me?"

Sam shook his head. "Willow did. I can't refuse anything she asks."

Adam laughed. "Big, tough marine."

As he finished the sentence, they heard a crash from the parking lot.

"Better go." Sam ran out of the office.

No telling what the boys were up to. Great kids, and he owed them for distracting their father.

❧

At dinner that evening, when Adam shared the news of the donkey with Hector and asked him to ride Maisie, Hector shook his head.

"Can't do that," he said.

"Why not? Afraid of donkeys?"

"Don't know, Pops. Never seen a donkey up close. But I think . . ." He paused and studied Adam seriously. "But I don't think people want a half-black, half-Mexican kid on that animal. They'll want someone more . . . well, more like Jesus. Same color."

"Don't agree with you. The church people like you. But, if they do complain, tough. I don't care."

"You don't care?"

"Besides, you're probably closer to the color of Jesus's skin than anyone else in town. He was born in the Middle East, in Bethlehem, not Dallas."

"You know what I like about you?" Hector said. "You don't go through all that junk about all being God's children, even though we are. You give it to me straight. Thanks."

"You're going to be Jesus?" Janey asked.

"Yeah." Hector smiled at his sister. "Who'd've thought I'd be Jesus in a church procession?"

❧

Birdie balanced a couple of plates on her arm. It was Friday, always a busy day at the diner. But this Friday was different. She could feel Farley's gaze on her as she delivered the order to the corner booth.

Why did the man keep watching her?

Did he hope she'd drop the dishes so he'd get a good laugh? Not out of the question because when she carried so many, her left shoulder complained, and more loudly every day. No doubt about it, if she wanted to last here until Mac got through college, she'd have to start carrying fewer plates. But that meant she'd have to make more trips, and her feet had started to ache.

When she finished placing the order on the table, she turned. The old coot—no, the a-few-years-older-than-she-was coot—still kept an eye on her. A stalker? No, not in Butternut Creek, and not Farley Masterson. He'd been the police chief for years. No history of lawlessness in his background. Besides, he was probably too old and too slow to be a stalker. Maybe he could be a shuffler or a limper, but being a stalker seemed beyond his physical capabilities at his age.

Five years older than Birdie.

For a man his age, he looked pretty good. For a man his age, he stood straight and had only a small belly that protruded over his belt buckle. Good hair, thick and white. Not bad looking. Not that she felt a speck of interest in the man.

"Okay," she demanded as she strode toward his table after she'd picked up her favorite weapon, the coffeepot. "What do you want?"

"A hot cup of joe would be nice." He pushed the mug toward her.

"I mean, why are you here?"

"Breakfast?" He sounded confused. "I mean, isn't that what everyone else is here for?" Then he smiled.

And she knew. With those words and that expression, she knew he was fooling with her and was pleased he'd upset her, gotten her attention.

"Why else would I be here, Birdie?" He winked.

She turned and stalked off.

Old coot.

Pshaah. What foolishness. She did not have to act so polite. The man was a coot. A seventy-plus coot counted as an old coot. No use trying to wrap Farley Masterson up in pretty words to hide his age.

After tossing her shoulders back in pride, she grunted in pain, then started one more round with coffee. She ignored Farley's wave but knew she'd have to fill up his coffee and bus the table. The vibration of her cell gave her an excuse not to. She wasn't supposed to check it when she was working, but she'd told her boss that if one of the girls called, she'd answer even if she had to drop a tray in the middle of the diner. There was a text message from Bree. "Coach from Hwrd Col calld. Vball."

Bree and Mac used few abbreviations in their texts because, doggone, it took so long for their grandmother to translate them. This one was easy. A coach from Howard College had called about volley-ball. It was a two-year school, but a good start not too far away and might offer a good financial package. Heaven knew, Birdie couldn't afford much. The high school counselor had told her it was a good thing Birdie's income was so low because that would help with scholarships and aid. Who knew eking out a living could be a blessing? Well, other than in the Be-atitudes.

She snapped the phone shut and attempted to ignore the realization that her granddaughters were growing up, that they'd both leave for college someday and she'd be alone, exactly as Mercedes had said.

She should rejoice, be happy to have the house back to herself, to order her life around her needs not the schedules of teenagers. But she knew the quiet of the empty house would be oppressive with only the meows of Carlos the Cat to break the silence. She'd miss the clattering of the girls' feet up and down the steps and the slamming of the front door, those things she always nagged them about.

"Coffee," shouted Farley.

She glanced at him. Not even when the girls were gone and she was lonely would she have the least interest in the man.

❦

As Adam listened to the music coming from the AME Church on the street behind the parsonage, he heard Hector come out the back door. Easy to recognize Hector's arrival because doors slammed behind him and he took huge strides that thumped across the dry yard. On the basketball court, he moved like a ballerina—not that Adam would ever tell him that—but he clumped along like a buffalo in real life.

"Hey, Pops." He sat next to Adam. "I'd . . ." Hector glanced at Adam, uncertain. "Pops, that's the church music I grew up with, when I was a kid, when our mother took us to church. I miss it." He shook his head. "I like your church, but it isn't my church, not yet."

For a moment, Adam felt incredibly guilty. "I'm sorry. I shouldn't have forced you to attend the Christian Church."

"Hey, no, Pops. I like being there. I like the people and I owe them a lot, but . . . but I'd like to go there"—he gestured to the source of the music—"now and then."

"Want to go tonight?" Adam glanced at his watch. "The service started a couple of minutes ago. We could run over there."

"You'd come, too?"

"Why not? I'll enjoy it. Get Janey."

Within five minutes, they'd hurried across the backyard of the parsonage, through the gate, and crossed the street to stand at the door of the AME Church.

"Welcome." After a start at seeing Adam, a smile creased the face of the greeter. "Find yourself a place to sit." He gestured to a nearly filled sanctuary.

After they found a pew all three of them could squeeze onto, Adam stood with the congregation and listened. Hard to believe, but the music was better inside the building.

He marveled at the skill of the pianist

who seemed to use every key, added notes and trills and beats that he'd never heard, and still pounded out the melody. Adam couldn't help but clap with the congregation and move with the rhythm.

For a few minutes, he drank it in, then turned to look at the kids. Hector swayed with the beat and Janey listened intently, her body moving side to side.

When the pianist started "Oh, Happy Day," Adam joined in. Not that he could sing well, but he knew the words and could feel the spirit moving through him. It took him a few seconds to realize the congregation split into parts, one side singing the line and the other echoing it. "Oh, happy day," his side sang. The other section sang, "Oh, happy day . . ."

He understood why Hector needed this, why he thought the service at the Christian Church was boring. Joy, this service was filled with joy.

When the pianist segued into "There Is a Balm in Gilead," Adam heard a lovely, pure voice coming from beside him. Everyone looked around but Adam looked down. Janey, her eyes closed and head lifted, allowed music to flow from her. The notes filled and swirled around the church. She sang for nearly a minute before she noticed the others had stopped. At the realization, Janey opened her eyes, closed her mouth, and dropped onto the pew, her head down. Immediately the other worshippers picked up the tune and sang on. Hector and Adam sat down, one on each side of her and each took one of her hands. He felt he'd witnessed a miracle.

As the congregation sat at the end of that hymn, the minister asked, "Do we have any visitors with us tonight?"

Adam looked around. The only white person in the sanctuary, he stuck out like a daisy in a bed of pansies. Certainly it was obvious he was a visitor, and so was the little girl with the golden voice. But the minister waited politely, his eyes moving across the congregation until falling—as if surprised—on Adam.

"Yes, brother, we're glad to have you here. Would you introduce yourself?"

Adam stood. "I'm Adam Jordan, minister of the Christian Church." He pointed in that direction. "And your neighbor. Hector and Janey," he gestured toward the kids, "heard the music and came over to join in."

"We're glad you did."

With those words, the entire congregation stood, made a line around the sanctuary, and came by the pew to shake his hand and Hector's while Janey sat with her head still down.

After a rousing sermon during which Adam had been moved to say a loud, "Amen," the minister pronounced the benediction and they all rose to leave.

"You're right. This is more fun," Adam said.

"I can't see Miss Birdie joining in," Hector said. "Or any of the rest of the congregation. But they are good folks, the people at the Christian Church."

"Janey," Adam said as they walked back to the parsonage. "I didn't know you could sing. Thank you."

She glanced at him and gave that tiny smile again. "I like to sing."

"She hasn't sung in years," Hector said. "It felt good to hear her."

Maybe it was a sign of progress.

That night, as he perused a Bible commentary, Chewy, curled up by Adam's feet, lifted his head and cocked an ear. Above them, Janey sang "Wade in the Water."

After a few measures, Chewy began to howl along with her. For a moment, only silence came from upstairs, then Adam heard Janey rushing down the stairs. She looked at the dog, put her arms around his neck, and laughed with genuine delight.

Adam had never seen Janey like this, had never known the solemn child could sing or show such happiness. He savored the moment. Inviting the Firestone children to live here had been the right thing to do. Now he was reaping the reward. He was the one truly blessed.

"I love to hear you sing," he said.

She froze when she heard his voice, then lifted her eyes toward him. All the happiness had gone, vanished.

In a second Adam was overcome by a wave of anger deeper than he realized he possessed. As a peaceful man, the emotion frightened him because, more than anything, he wanted to beat up the person who'd put that fear in her eyes. He forced the rage away and took a deep breath before he said gently, "You have a lovely voice."

"Thank you," Janey said with that tiny grin.

"Janey, you don't have to be afraid of me.

I promise, I will never do anything to hurt you."

She said nothing but looked a little more relaxed.

"I'd love to hear another song."

After a short pause, she shook her head.

He didn't want to push. "Miss Blossom left some cookies, those big lemon cookies her cook makes. Do you want one?"

She nodded.

"Let's get a few. Then we could watch something on television. What do you think?"

After they were both settled, each with a glass of milk and the plate of goodies on the coffee table between them, Adam watched Janey as she nibbled and watched the program, some reality show with singing. She had lovely dark skin. Her hair was in those intricate braids, today with yellow barrettes on the ends, a skill he knew he'd never master.

"Would you like to sing at church sometime?"

"No." She didn't look up from the television.

Okay. "Thanks for keeping me company," he said.

After a few minutes, she said, "But I'll sing for you sometime, if you'd like me to. And for Chewy."

"I really would. Thank you," he said.

And she smiled.

❦

At nine on the morning of Palm Sunday, Hector pointed from the porch of the parsonage toward the church parking lot. "Look, she's here. A real donkey."

Adam and Janey followed him toward the horse trailer as Jesse led the small animal out.

Hector stroked Maisie's soft muzzle. "I've never touched one."

Maisie lifted her head to glance at Hector as he petted her dark gray and slightly curled coat.

"She's pretty," Janey said looking up at the donkey.

"And she's a stubborn creature," Jesse said. "Hector, you're going to have to keep a tight hold of her and don't put up with any prancing around."

"Yes, sir. Bobby'll be here in a few minutes to help me with her," Hector said. "We'll keep her in line."

"Sure you will, son," Jesse said. "I'm

going to tie her to the back of the trailer and stay with her until you're ready for her."

When Adam entered the church, he saw Bree and Mac counting out palm branches on the receptionist's desk.

"We've got this under control," Bree said. "We'll go to the Sunday school class-rooms and explain it all."

By the time Adam went back outside at ten thirty, a crowd had begun to gather. The children, each carrying a palm branch, hopped out of the Sunday school wing and stood around Maisie as she snacked on the grass at the edge of the lot. Hector and Bobby wore robes and sandals and stood on either side of Maisie, both hold-ing her reins.

Leo and Nick stood a few feet from them, fascinated. A few yards behind the boys, Willow in a pale pink suit with match-ing flowered hat and high-heeled shoes leaned on Sam and grinned at her boys.

"Doesn't she look great?" Sam asked. "I have the most beautiful wife in the world."

Winnie and Sam's father stood a few feet away chatting with Blossom. Mercedes and Miss Birdie came out of the building, probably just finished putting the final touches on the cookies for the special coffee hour after the service, while Janey, Bree, and Mac finished handing out palms to the adults.

Ouida stood between her daughters as they swished their branches through the air. "They said I had to come see the donkey," she explained to Adam. "They're very excited about the whole deal."

On the edge of the lot, the bluish purple of bluebonnets shimmered. A beautiful morning, a calm, peaceful moment as the people Adam loved joined together under the light filtering through the live oaks.

Adam took pictures of the crowd, starting with one of Hector holding Maisie's reins while he grinned at his little sister. He snapped another of Bobby and Bree, laughing. A perfect day.

Then through the lens, Adam made out the head of someone with red hair climbing on Maisie's back. Before he could put the camera down and react, chaos broke out.

The donkey brayed and pulled the reins from Bobby's and Hector's hands.

"Help," Nick shouted from the back of the animal at the same moment Adam realized the red hair belonged to Sam and Willow's youngest son.

With a mighty and joyful hee-haw, the donkey took off, bucking and jumping. Maisie headed across the lawn, around the building, and toward the highway with Nick clinging to her back and Hector and Bobby chasing after them.

For a moment, everyone else watched, too startled to move. Leo stood close to where the donkey had been, his eyes wide. Then Willow started running in the direction the donkey had fled; Sam and Adam were behind her, followed by nearly everyone in the church. With a quick look behind him, Adam could see Miss Birdie sprinting toward the front of the pack with Bree and Mac only a few feet ahead of her. The general, Sam's father and Nick's grandfather, was closing in on the leading peloton. Jesse attempted to keep up but fell behind, huffing and puffing. And all of them carried their palms.

Adam glanced ahead. Nick was holding on for dear life, his arms around the donkey's neck, his bottom flopping up and down, his legs flying up beside him. How did the kid avoid being thrown off?

The pursuers hadn't gained a yard on the bucking burro. Then Adam saw Hector trip over his sandals, not the greatest shoes for running. When he stumbled, Bobby tripped over him. Both ended up lying flat on the street, watching the animal take off as they attempted to untangle their long limbs.

Willow had tossed the pretty hat to the side and kicked her shoes off. Pulling her skirt up, she leaped over Hector's legs and continued to race after her son. Although he fell behind, Sam didn't slow down.

"Go rest, son," the general shouted at Sam. "I'll get him."

The man should have known Sam wouldn't leave the chase. Although he fell back, he still followed the creature escaping with Nick on her back.

Clearly Maisie felt the thrill of independence as she ran on. When she turned her head to look back, Adam thought he saw her smile at the group before she picked up the pace. She brayed ecstatically, a sound he translated as, "Born free."

"Help!" Nick yelled again.

"We're coming," Adam shouted. He saw a sign of hope. Maisie seemed to be slowing down, winded after more exercise than she might have been used to, all while carrying a load.

Then a flash passed them: Bobby, running fast and smoothly. Maisie turned to check behind her again, saw Bobby, but couldn't find another gear. Inexorably, Bobby closed in.

Only a few steps behind him flew Hector, shoeless. "You get the kid," he shouted. "I'll stop the donkey."

That's exactly what happened. Bobby pulled up and ran in stride with Maisie, then reached for Nick—who threw his arms around the young man's neck and was dragged to safety while Hector grabbed a rein and pulled the panting animal to a stop.

Shouts and the toots of car horns came from both sides of the highway. Adam hadn't noticed the crowd until the rescue was completed. Had they stopped to watch the show or because they decided it would be better not to hit a runaway donkey with a kid on its back?

When Willow reached the four—Nick, Bobby, Hector, and Maisie—she grabbed her son and held him in a strong hug before she placed him on the street. "Wait till

I get you home," she threatened but kept squeezing Nick's hand.

Nick looked shaky, his face pale and legs trembling. He attempted to look tough, chin out and lips firm, but he did not let go of his mother's hand.

"That was so cool."

Adam looked down to see Leo standing next to him, "Preacher, wasn't that cool?" Leo asked. "But I'd hate to be in his shoes. Nick's going to be in so much trouble."

"Think we'll skip church this morning," Sam said as he reached Adam's side and put his hand on Leo's shoulder. "We need to take care of this at home. Sorry we messed up your service."

"Not your fault," Adam said. "You do what you need to do." He looked behind him to see that the congregation had gathered on the sidewalk gasping for air. They watched the Peterson family head around the church and back to the car while Hector led a now docile Maisie by the rope.

"Hector, take the donkey back to the garden," Adam said. "When you take her to the other churches, stay with her and tell everyone she doesn't like riders." He took a step toward the church and began to sing the processional hymn, his thin, wavering voice leading the way. "Hosanna, loud hosanna," he sang, and the congregation followed him back to the church waving their palms. Janey glanced up at him. Obviously feeling sorry for his pitiable efforts, she joined in. Once there, the disheveled congregation went inside and threw themselves on the pews, fanning flushed faces with the palms and breathing deeply.

That morning would long be remembered in the lore of Butternut Creek.

Chapter Six

Gussie hurried home from church after the Easter service. Her parents refused to skip that Sunday. "I haven't missed an Easter service in over sixty years," her father had said. "Not going to let a little allergy problem stop me now."

Gussie had learned years earlier not to challenge any pronouncement by her father that had a number of years in it. *I've been doing this for [fill in this blank with a number] years* always meant she'd better give in and give up.

But was that cough merely the symptom of allergies?

Oh, she worried too much.

"You've become a mother hen," her mother often said. "Silly for a daughter to turn into a mother hen." Then her mother would laugh.

However, the daughter didn't find it amusing. Her parents were in their seventies, which meant both that she had every right to cluck over them and worry *and* that she probably had no reason to believe they would change in the least because they had arrived at this age on their own and were as stubborn as . . . as . . . well, as Gussie was.

Gussie pulled into the drive at exactly the same time her father went into a paroxysm of coughs. She glanced in the rearview mirror and asked, "Are you all right?" She wanted to take him to the hospital right now, but he waved at her and nodded because he couldn't speak.

Mom turned. "Henry?"

"I'm fine," he said between coughs. "I'll get a peppermint to suck on."

Of course, once they got inside, her father didn't stop coughing but took a Benadryl, flipped on the television, and settled into the recliner to watch sports and nap.

"I breathe better sitting up," he explained. Within minutes, he was asleep and the coughing had calmed.

Looked as if he was right. It had been allergies.

🐭

Adam's first Easter in Butternut Creek. The men pulled out the huge wooden cross they'd made years ago to put in front of the sanctuary. Everyone brought flowers and put them in the holes drilled in the cross. Really pretty.

The service began with a processional to bring in the cross and candlesticks they'd removed from the altar for Maundy Thursday. Miss Birdie thought that seemed high church, but that didn't deter Adam.

He looked around the sanctuary at a good crowd gathered to celebrate. Maybe one hundred, which still left empty pews in the big sanctuary. To begin the service, Mac played an introit on her trumpet, the clear notes sounding around them and calling them to celebrate.

The joy of Easter, the thought of Christians all over the world celebrating this triumphant day, overwhelmed him. Surrounded by flowers and faith and the family of believers, they came together as God's people and rejoiced.

"Hallelujah," he proclaimed to begin the service.

❦

"George," Ouida called from her dressing table in the master bedroom.

"Yes?" George's slightly muffled voice came from his walk-in closet.

In the mirror, Ouida watched herself brushing her hair. "What would you think if I grew my hair longer?" she asked. "Do you think I'd look glamorous?"

She could hear his firm tread cross the carpet until she saw his reflection behind her, studying her. "No, I wouldn't like it long. Keep it like this. I don't want you to be glamorous."

That firmly put her in her place as dowdy hausfrau. Oh, he didn't mean it as an insult. George just didn't like change.

She could see from his reflection that he held a pair of boxers in his hand. She'd have preferred to discuss those boxers another day, any other day, or perhaps never. She'd hoped he wouldn't realize she hadn't ironed them.

"I've noticed something." He held that

blasted undergarment up. "Yesterday, I felt very uncomfortable in my . . . you know, the part of the body where I wear my boxers."

Poor George didn't like to discuss anatomy, his or anyone else's.

"Oh?" Ouida stopped rubbing cream onto her nose. Why she did that, she didn't know. The freckles would never go away. Probably magical thinking, that if she stopped, more would pop out. Maybe she could add rubbing cream on her nose to the list of things she didn't need to do. After all, George didn't want her to be glamorous. She wiped her fingers off, then turned on the bench to study her husband.

"You didn't iron my underwear." He held up the slightly wrinkled but clean undergarment, one of the dozen she'd washed, smoothed out, and folded before placing them in his drawer yesterday.

"And the dresser scarves?" He reached out to place his hand on the exposed surface of the chest of drawers. "The pretty set my mother made for you. Where are they?"

"I decided we didn't really need them. Who needs a newly washed, ironed, and starched runner nowadays?"

"I didn't say we needed them, but they are pretty and my mother made them. I'd like them back." He used the calm voice that expressed his need for her to do exactly what he wanted, as if explaining to someone with little understanding. He always seemed certain that if he expressed his wish logically and in everyday words, she'd comprehend the situation and change.

She hated it. She hadn't realized until that moment how much she hated that tone.

For a moment, she considered her options. George stood before her, tall and handsome and urbane even holding up a pair of his shorts. The man of her dreams, the man she'd loved for so long, but also the man who expected her to do exactly what he wanted.

When had she become a drudge with so little backbone? Ouida took a deep breath.

"George, with the girls and this big house, I had to cut back some. I can't do everything."

He raised an eyebrow, which made him more good-looking but twice as condescending.

She steeled herself. "I can't do everything," she repeated slowly in the same tone he used with her. "I've decided not to mop the kitchen floor every time someone enters, and not to iron your undershorts. I believe we can also get by without the dresser scarves."

He took a few steps toward her, sat next to her on the bench, and took her hand. "Ouida, I work long hours."

She nodded.

"We have a service to take care of the lawn. I work to pay all the bills. All I ask is for you to do your job inside the house. How much trouble can it be to take care of two little girls and to iron my boxers?" He handed her the garment, stood, and walked toward the bed.

She stifled a scream.

❦

Adam woke up and glanced at the clock. Five fifteen. Still dark outside.

What had awakened him? He listened but heard nothing. He shoved the sheet over Chewy, who took up most of the bed, and got up to check on the kids. After he looked in on both and assured himself they were safe and still asleep, he went back to his bedroom and sat on the edge of the bed. Within seconds, he realized what had interfered with his sleep. Actually, who.

The Widows.

Yes, the Widows had appeared in a dream. No, in a nightmare. They'd all worn black Stetsons and toted .45s. Their appearance was probably an outlet for his anxiety about the looming crisis of Gussie's coming to town and what the Widows had in mind for that afternoon.

For weeks he'd attempted to convince himself the Widows would limit themselves to serving refreshments at the youth meeting. He'd hoped they'd ignore their calling as matchmakers but he knew they wouldn't. Matchmaking was in their blood, was their prime directive.

He'd call Sam tomorrow because if he'd ever needed a marine on his side, it would be this Sunday. He hadn't seen much of Sam recently. His friend had married, become a father to two active sons, and was going to school. Not much time for more than watching a few basketball games together or meeting for pie, but *now* Sam

needed to step up to the plate. Adam refused to face the Widows alone, and Sam
owed him.

❧

Gussie kept her eyes on the road. It was
the Sunday after Easter and there weren't
huge numbers of cars roaring along. There
were also no runaway trucks coming up
behind to crash into her. No danger lurked
behind the hills and fences that, if not stu-
diously watched and carefully avoided,
might leap ahead of her and wreak destruction.

No, it wasn't the traffic or lack of it or the
possible perils on the road that forced her
to focus on her driving.

It was what awaited her in Butternut
Creek. Not really a *what* but a *who.* A perfectly nice man, a minister who cared for
his congregation. He'd built a youth program, taken in Hector and his sister, and
seemed to be getting along with Miss
Birdie. From what she'd heard, that was a
feat few other ministers had managed.

Yes, a nice, tall, skinny minister awaited
her arrival with, from what he had emailed,
the four young people she knew from the
church and ten or twelve of their friends

who didn't go to church regularly. Those kids were important. Involvement in church camp and retreats could change their lives.

Right now she didn't care about a single one of those young people. Right now she wanted to turn around, go back home, and hide in her room.

But she'd been hiding for years and it hadn't solved a single problem. Oh, yes, at first it had helped. She'd healed in solitude with her parents around to feed her and care for her, to soothe and love her. But after a few weeks, they'd forced her out of that cocoon. The right thing to do, of course, but she'd felt safer back then. Today she felt vulnerable and just plain scared.

Oh, she knew perfectly well she and Adam would be surrounded by fifteen youths, which would cut down on any frightening experiences. But the Widows would be there also. From what everyone said, they could make life incredibly embarrassing.

Thank goodness the Widows didn't know about the flash of attraction she'd felt for Adam. Gussie usually succeeded very well in hiding from her emotions since . . . since back then, over a decade ago. She had a terrible feeling that if she accepted the fact she was attracted to Adam, all those other feelings that hovered barely below the surface of her mind would flood back, engulfing and destroying her.

At one forty-five, she pulled into the church parking lot. Two or three cars were parked by the entrance to the fellowship hall. Could be there were so few because she was early. Could be some of the young people hadn't driven.

Could be she was stalling and didn't want to go inside.

Most merciful God . . . But she didn't finish. She refused to pray that Adam had a slight fever that would go away as soon as the meeting was over. He'd have to miss the gathering so he wouldn't infect the kids and she wouldn't have to face him.

No, praying for the illness of others to make her life more comfortable did not constitute an acceptable petition, certainly not one made to a merciful and loving God. In fact, the only option was a quick *Dear God, grant me wisdom and cour-*

age. With that, she opened the door, grabbed her purse and tote, and got out of the car.

"Hi!" Bree came running out of the church and waved. "We're so glad to see you. Let me help you." She grabbed Gussie's tote.

The loss of that bag pretty much cut off Gussie's plan to escape. The tote held her brain: all the information she needed about youth work in Central Texas, her calendars and schedules. Yes, her brain. It held records of all those things she did to make up for not having a real life. With no other option, she followed Bree and her brain into the fellowship hall.

A dozen kids milled around inside. No sign of Adam. She hoped he really wasn't sick. Maybe an emergency had come up. But, no, she couldn't wish a disaster, not even a small one of short duration, on others for her own well-being.

On the other side of the kitchen counter were Miss Birdie, Mercedes, and two women she hadn't met before, both with nicely coiffed hair. All four women smiled at her. She was used to a friendly Mercedes, but the curve that might pass as a smile on Miss Birdie's thin lips frightened her. Why, she couldn't explain, but it contained enough glee that Gussie wanted to run back to her car.

"Hello, Gussie!"

She turned to see Adam. He looked friendly and glad to see her but nothing more.

Was that reaction good news or bad news? If he didn't feel anything for her, she should rejoice. She didn't want a relationship. They could become messy. On the other hand, what kind of social incompetent did it make her that she was attracted to him and he liked her only as a person, as a friend, as a colleague?

Ugh. She refused to consider either of those choices, not now. She had a meeting to lead.

Unfortunately, she glanced into the kitchen and saw the intense scrutiny of the four women there. A chill invaded every cell of her body. She resolved not to show fear but she knew she wouldn't get out of here unscathed.

"Hey, Gussie," Hector said. He and Bobby walked over, each clutching the arm of a friend. "Want you to meet a couple of my friends." He nodded toward them. "This is Junior Rodriguez, and Bobby's friend is Mark Scroggins."

She shook their hands, then asked, "Do you play basketball, too?" After a few minutes of chatting about sports, the visitors looked a lot more relaxed. They probably thought because they were inside a church, she'd force them to confess their sins and repent publicly. The conversation ended when Bree called out, "Let's come together. It's nearly two o'clock."

Gussie spoke for ten minutes, then the four who'd been to the retreat gave a quick talk about their experiences. Bobby's comments were short and precise: "It was fun but we had to take out trash and wipe down tables."

At two thirty, they broke for refreshments and the fun began. Or, the mortification. The description pretty much depended on which side one favored.

"Gussie, I want you to meet our two newest Widows." Mercedes approached and introduced Winnie and Blossom.

"Aren't you the prettiest thing," Blossom said in a soft voice.

Gussie knew she wasn't all that pretty

but didn't mind the compliment. Then the platinum-blond Widow took Gussie's right hand in what seemed at first a gentle clasp but turned into an iron grip with which she led Gussie toward the sofa where—not surprisingly—Miss Birdie had shoved Adam down on the cushions and now sat next to him.

When Gussie attempted to pull away, the other Widow—Winnie? Was that her name?—took her left hand and dragged Gussie toward the preacher. She could not break away without causing a scene and possible injury. Not that they had any scruples about capturing her, but theirs had been a covert action and hers would be outright combat.

Besides they were at least twice her age. She couldn't fight them without looking like a bully.

Adam glanced up from his conversation with Miss Birdie. An I-should-have-guessed expression covered his face. He had the nerve to laugh. Did he have no idea what lay ahead?

Of course he did, but he could see the humor in the machinations of the Widows while she experienced only mind-numbing terror.

When she approached, Adam attempted to stand. With Miss Birdie holding one hand, the action was futile. He stood halfway up before she pulled him down. The landing caused the sofa to shiver and the cushion to fly up on the end as he made a resounding thud and an "Ooof."

Which of course alerted the young people who had been talking and gathered along the counter for refreshments. They all turned to watch.

Oh, terrific. Gussie didn't wonder what would happen next. She knew. With a final shove to Adam, Miss Birdie sprang to her feet.

"Why don't you sit down here." She waved to the place next to the preacher, the seat she'd just abandoned.

"I think—" Gussie could say no more before her effort to sit in a chair and her path to that chair were cut off by the two women, who were much stronger than anyone their age should be. Quickly and firmly, she'd been shoved forward, spun, and seated. The cushions were so soft, it felt as if she'd dropped into mud. She'd never get out without help. She'd been captured and imprisoned with no choice but to remain until assistance or a crane showed up.

"There you go," the blonde said in a soft Southern accent, most confusing since the woman's determination was made of iron. Before Gussie could say a word or move an inch, Blossom sat between her and the arm of the love seat so the three were packed together, shoulder-to-shoulder and hip-to-hip.

"Isn't this cozy?" Blossom cooed.

It wasn't.

"Now, you two stay there . . . ," Miss Birdie began.

As if they could move.

". . . and I'll get you some cookies." The senior Widow bustled away.

However, her departure did not signal a reprieve. Winnie and Mercedes stood in front of the love seat as if they were playing "Red Rover" and were poised to capture anyone who attempted to "come over."

Gussie whispered to Adam, "Get me out of this."

"Relax," he whispered back. "You can't

get away from the Widows. Submission is the only option. It makes the humiliation shorter and less painful."

"Great," Gussie moaned. "Thanks for the encouragement."

Miss Birdie placed a plate of cookies in her lap and handed another to Adam, then brought each a cup of punch, which she put on the end tables. Not, of course, that Gussie could pick up her punch, because Blossom sat between her and the cup. Good thing she didn't really want a drink during this odd little interlude. She attempted to shift position, but the lovely, smiling Widow held her arm securely, another reason she couldn't sip the punch.

"Now," Blossom said as Gussie bit into a lemon bar. "Why don't we chat. Gussie, why don't you tell Adam an interesting fact he doesn't know about you?"

Could this get any worse? Well, yes, Gussie figured it could.

From the refreshment counter, thirty eyes, more or less, focused on the scene, taking in every nuance, every movement, every word.

Then there were six more eyes.

"Hey." A handsome man with a slight

limp entered from the parking lot with two redheaded boys. "Sorry I'm late . . ." He stopped speaking and moving when he saw Gussie and Adam shoved together on the love seat with Blossom. "I . . . um . . ." He swallowed, perhaps attempting not to laugh. "Willow's on call this weekend and had to go to the hospital. I brought the boys with me. Guys," he said to the two, "go get yourself some refreshments and bring me a glass of punch." He sat at a table that faced the love seat. "I'm going to sit right here and enjoy the show." He grinned.

"That's my former friend, Sam Peterson." Adam glared at the man. "Thanks, Sam," he said with an edge to his voice that Gussie hadn't heard before. In an instant her brain flashed back on the image she'd stored and attempted— unsuccessfully—to ignore of Adam playing basketball with sweat gluing his shirt onto his wiry but muscular body and macho determination on his face.

With that ill-timed image firmly seared into her mind, it took every ounce of her strength to focus on the visitor and wave. "I'm Gussie Milton," she said.

"I know." Sam waved at her, then toward the treat-covered counter. "Those are my sons, Leo and Nick."

The two boys grinned at her with chocolate-covered lips.

Then everyone, every single person in the room, went back to watching the two on the love seat. Gussie ignored Blossom's request to share information about herself. Instead she chewed on a bite of cookie that had long ago lost any flavor or structural integrity but kept her mouth occupied.

"Aren't they the cutest couple in the world?" Winnie asked.

The young people looked at each other and shrugged.

"What's going on, Pops?" Hector asked.

Adam didn't answer. Probably no way to explain.

"Gussie." Miss Birdie spoke as if she and the two captives were engaged in a private little chat. "Tell Adam something about you that he doesn't know."

Other than being rude, which the Widows didn't mind doing although in such a pleasant way, Gussie couldn't think of anything else to do but answer. She refused to behave poorly in front of her kids or that man facing them from the table—Sam?—who was laughing so hard he nearly fell off his chair.

"I used to play the clarinet," Gussie said after she swallowed and before she took another bite of lemon bar.

"Were you in the band?" Adam asked, his voice filled with interest, as if that were the most scintillating bit of information he'd ever heard.

Exactly the right way to play this, Gussie realized. "Oh, yes," she said with great enthusiasm. "I was in the marching band."

"Isn't that interesting," Adam replied. "Miss Birdie's granddaughter Mac is in the marching band." He beckoned Mac over with two fingers. "Did you know Gussie played the clarinet in the marching band?"

With a grin, Mac approached them. "Isn't that interesting?" she said. "Has Adam told you about the time I led the middle school band?"

After ten more minutes, the Widows gave up. By that time, Hector and Gussie had discussed being tall; she and Bobby had discussed being an only child; and she and Bree had discussed playing volleyball. Gussie had started to relax and enjoy herself.

Miss Birdie cut into the chats. "Well, I guess that's finished." She shoved Hector and Bree toward the door, saying, "Shoo, shoo." The rest of the youths followed.

"Hey, Preacher," Bobby said before he could be pushed outside. "You need a hoop out here so we can play ball."

Miss Birdie closed the door before Adam could answer.

And they were alone, Adam and Gussie, with four Widows bent on . . . oh, she didn't know what exactly. Something evil. She heard Sam and his boys in the kitchen, probably finishing up the cookies, but she could hardly expect help from them. Sam enjoyed their predicament too much to do anything but laugh, and the boys seemed devoted to chocolate. They wouldn't notice her appeals as they stuffed down brownies.

"Preacher, why don't you take Gussie for a tour around the town?" Winnie said.

"What a lovely suggestion, but I've visited Butternut Creek often. I had an aunt who lived here."

"Oh, yes, Grace Carson, your father's sister," Mercedes said.

"Well, then, you two think of something to do for an hour or two. Together." Although devious, Miss Birdie had never been able to hide her plans well. "Then come back and we'll have a nice little supper for the two of you."

"You won't want to drive all the way to Roundville hungry," Blossom said.

"You might have one of those dreaded hunger-related accidents," Adam agreed sincerely.

"Thank you so much, ladies," Gussie said. "I didn't realize that you had this planned. I need to get home. I hate to leave my parents alone . . ."

"Such a good daughter," Mercedes said. "But sometime you're going to have to think about yourself." She paused dramatically. "And your future."

"Your parents aren't going to live forever," the pillar said, a remark greeted by shoves and "shh" from the other Widows. "Not, of course, that I'm hoping they will die soon, but we all will. Someday."

Not sure whether to laugh or scream or stare in amazement, Gussie decided to do none. Instead she said, "It's not that long a drive." She used every muscle she had to force herself up from the engulfing cushion. "If I get weak, I'll grab something on the road."

Gussie wished she had a camera to always remember the expressions on the Widows' faces. Disappointment warred with disbelief that their plan had been scuttled.

"Didn't Mac invite you?" Miss Birdie said. "For dinner?"

Gussie pulled her calendar from the tote and flipped it open. "Oh, yes, she did." She couldn't get Mac in trouble, but she had to get out of this place and away from Adam. "I . . . I'm really sorry. I forgot. Didn't check the book."

❧

Adam shoved himself up from the deep cushions and watched Gussie for a second. She looked frantic. The Widows could do that to a person. "Don't worry. Hector will eat your portion and more. If you need to get on the road, allow me to walk you to your car."

He couldn't believe he'd uttered that stupid phrase: "Allow me to walk you to your car." Sounded as if he were from Victorian England, but having Gussie here and the Widows looking on scrambled his brain. Amazing he could still utter a sentence that actually made sense, even archaic nonsense.

To make matters worse, he held out his arm, crooked at the elbow, as if he were escorting a debutante. Gussie ignored it, maybe hadn't seen it, but the Widows had and they smiled, possibly hoping he'd lure her into a compromising position over the ten yards across the parking lot to her car.

"Don't worry, Preacher," Miss Birdie said in what she considered a whisper but could be heard by everyone within twenty yards. "I won't let them out"—she used her head to point out the other Widows— "until you've finished your courting." Then she nearly shoved them from the building.

Once outside, Gussie said, "Oh, that was horrific." She started laughing so hard she leaned on his arm for support. "Horrific but absolutely hilarious." She took a deep breath and attempted to control her mirth.

He loved to hear her laugh. Sometimes it sounded like bells, going up an octave then back down. Other times it was a hoot or just a burst of happiness, but she never held back. When Gussie laughed, everyone knew she meant it and joined in.

"Adam, I'm so sorry to bail on dinner, but I've never been so mortified and so terrified and so entertained in my entire life." She pulled in a deep gulp of air and attempted to regain control. "I hardly know how to react except to laugh but I can't take any more of this. I can't stay for dinner. It's too funny and too humiliating, and way too . . . oh I don't know. Too everything." She stopped once they reached her car and beeped the doors open. "They are so very careful about every detail of their scheme and so certain they are right that I couldn't laugh in their faces, sweet ladies."

"You might believe they're sweet but they're calculating and devious and darned near impossible to ignore." He grinned to soften his words. "You don't know that because you don't have them bustling around, taking charge of your life and conniving every day to get you married."

"How do you handle it? I couldn't have kept from laughing if I'd stayed for a minute longer."

They both turned toward the church when they heard the kitchen door open.

Blossom rushed out with a large box. Gussie closed her mouth tightly, biting her bottom lip.

"Some cookies for you," Blossom said. "In case you get hungry on the way home."

The Widow stood right next to Gussie's car with a broad smile on her face while Gussie nodded and struggled not to laugh. She managed a hurried, muffled "Thank you."

Then Miss Birdie stuck her head out the door and shouted, "How did you get past me, Blossom Brown? You come inside and leave the lovebirds alone." With a start, Blossom hurried away and into the church.

Gussie whooped and tears flowed down her cheeks. "Don't they drive you crazy?"

"I've learned to laugh inside." He sighed as he handed Gussie a Kleenex from his pocket. "You met Sam. The Widows are sure it was their matchmaking that got him married. They feel flush with victory and refuse to give up on me, not while they're on a hot streak. I'm sorry they embarrassed you."

"They delighted me, too." With that, Gussie tossed the tote into the car, placed the cookies on the passenger seat, and got behind the wheel.

"Thanks, Adam. This was wonderful. I'll never forget this afternoon."

He closed the door as she started the car. With a wave, she drove away.

They'd both survived. They hadn't had their britches embarrassed off them; only, maybe, their socks. When the car disappeared down the highway, he stood there, uncertain if he should feel victorious because the Widows had failed or defeated because Gussie had fled and left him more befuddled than ever.

With so little display of interest on Gussie's part—lots of embarrassment, a great deal of laughter, but little attraction—he probably should leave things alone. He'd email her, thank her for coming. He didn't really need to stop with one email. Friends, they could be friends, and that could develop into something more. If he stopped pursuing her, even in his meandering and obviously ineffective way, nothing would happen between them. Ever.

When he'd been in seminary, his professor of church management told the story about a man watching a kid fish. Before he tossed his line into the water, the boy reached in his mouth, pulled something out, and placed it on the hook. Every time, he'd pull in a large fish and repeat the operation. The man, who'd caught nothing, approached the boy and asked how he'd been so successful. The kid spit a bunch of worms into his hand and said, "You've got to keep the worms warm."

"That's what church growth is all about," the professor explained. "Call on your visitors, invite others to come, whatever it takes to keep the worms warm."

And that pretty much described what Adam planned to do about Gussie. With every email, he could stay in touch while he worked up the courage to be more active and to figure out what to do next. He could never tell her that, of course, because he felt pretty sure she wouldn't appreciate being compared to a mouthful of worms.

❧

As hysterical as the afternoon had been, Gussie realized one important fact: The Widows would cause great havoc if they continued to play matchmakers. She had little doubt that they'd keep trying. Adam had said the Widows felt flush with victory. Perhaps that explained it. Their success with Sam and his wife primed them for more efforts toward getting their minister married. After all, they had much more invested in getting Adam married than they had in finding Sam a wife.

Although the afternoon had amused her, she felt mortified that she and Adam had been placed in this situation. If he were at all interested in her, he'd have made a move, called her, asked her out. The fact that he hadn't but Miss Birdie and her co-conspirators had forced them together embarrassed her deeply. It showed so obviously that the chemistry was one-sided.

Had anyone noticed how much Adam attracted her?

And yet, if not, why had the Widows chosen her for Adam? Had they seen her longing? No, impossible. They'd never seen her and Adam together. They were operating on hope, nothing more. Her usual good humor kicked in and she laughed so hard she nearly drove off the highway.

❧

That evening as Adam watched Janey do her homework in the kitchen, Hector threw himself onto a chair.

"I don't have enough money to take anyone to prom."

Mentally, Adam replaced the word *anyone* with *Bree.*

"A girl expects all sorts of stuff like flowers," Hector complained. "Some of the guys are going together, pooling their money for a limo. With my friends, fifty of us would have to pool our money."

Guess he'd better start giving Hector an allowance. With basketball and school on top of taking care of Janey and the work he did around the church, which didn't pay much, Hector didn't have time to get another job and keep his grades up, too.

"Wish I could help more."

"Hey Pops, I understand."

The kid needed some spending money, some—what had his friends called it?—walking-around money. For a few seconds, Adam considered the trust fund money his own father had put aside for him. He'd decided against living on it, but couldn't he share a little with Hector? No, he couldn't. It went against Adam's principles. He didn't mind tapping a parent for a worthy project here and there, but not that trust fund money. He'd never wanted to be a person who lived on someone else's wealth. If he started to accept a little here and a couple of hundred there, he might end up buying more stuff, like a new car that didn't have things falling off it and couldn't make the trip to Austin without constant prayer and Rex's laying on of hands. No, he aimed to support himself on his own money.

"Bobby thought he'd get the family car, but his father has to go in for a late shift."

Bobby's father worked as an aide at the hospital and always tried to take on extra shifts.

"We thought about walking to the civic center but that's not cool." He grinned. "Of course, driving your car to the prom isn't too cool, either, but if we park it down the street, no one will see it."

"You going to meet up with anyone there?" Adam asked casually.

"Maybe. I asked Bree to save me a couple of dances." Hector grinned. "Pops, how're you going to get to the prom. You're a chaperone again, right?"

Adam nodded. "The Episcopal priest's picking me up. Ministers are very popular chaperones. We seem to exude morality and serve as examples of honor and virtue." *And*, he added to himself, *celibacy*.

❧

Friday before prom, Adam dropped by the diner, sat at the counter, and ordered a cup of coffee. "Prom tomorrow," he said to Miss Birdie.

"None of the girls are in school today," she said as she filled a cup and placed it in front of him. "The juniors spent the morning decorating the civic center. This afternoon the girls get their hair done."

"They skip school to get ready for a dance?"

"Preacher, this is the *prom* we're talking about." She leaned forward to scrutinize him as if he were an alien being. "Tradition. Elmer took me. Our first date. It's a special evening. Missing one day of school won't hurt."

Adam nodded. Probably not something a man could understand, especially an outlander like him.

"Bree's so excited. She got a new dress and sparkly shoes. Problem is, the heels are so tall and thin that she walks like she's got a basketball between her knees. I'm afraid she's going to fall on her face. Tonight she's going to practice dancing and moving in them." She shook her head and smiled. "She tried everything on yesterday. Looked real pretty when she wasn't walking."

"She have a date?"

"No, she's going with a bunch of friends. They do that." She picked up a fresh pot of coffee and topped off his cup before she headed toward her other patrons. Going table-to-table, she freshened everyone's coffee until she arrived at one where Farley Masterson sat. Adam had met the man a few weeks ago when Farley visited the Christian Church. Adam didn't know why he'd showed up; he usually attended the Methodist Church.

Just as she had when she'd spotted Farley in church, the pillar carefully headed away, pretending not to see the man. If she hadn't been so obvious, she could have carried it off. But she had and she didn't.

Farley grinned and shouted, "I'm gettin' to you, aren't I, Bird?"

Miss Birdie mumbled something and kept her eyes away from him while she served another table.

Did the pillar have an admirer? Looked to Adam as if Farley fancied Miss Birdie.

Well, don't that beat all, he thought. He almost patted himself on the back as he noticed how much he'd improved his use of Texas phrases. He understood Texan a lot better, too. Now, if only he could use *fixin'* without thinking about it, he'd sound like a true citizen of the Hill Country.

While Adam was congratulating himself, Farley looked up at the ceiling and said, "That fan pulls right smart through here, don't it?"

Adam had no idea what the man had said. Obviously his vocabulary hadn't grown as much as he'd hoped.

❧

Along with most of the ministers in town and dozens of parents, Adam chaperoned the prom. The adults circling the walls, at the refreshments table, and guarding every door made sure that, at least until midnight arrived and the kids adjourned to post-prom activities, no one had the slightest opportunity to misbehave. If they did, punishment would follow immediately, administered by a throng of the righteous.

When he first entered, Adam glanced toward the photographer, hoping to see Gussie. Silly because she'd have let him know if she were coming, but still he hoped. No, a man set up the equipment in front of a large sketch of the Eiffel Tower under an EVENING IN PARIS banner.

The kids were having a great time. Hector and Bree danced in a distant corner, as far away from Adam as they could find. None of the kids knew how to slow-dance. They embraced and moved around the floor like Siamese twins joined at the shoulders. They performed the fast dances with jerky and repetitive movements. He shouldn't laugh because, all long arms and legs, he bet he'd looked goofier at his prom.

"Hey, you're looking good." His friend Mattie, the minister of the Presbyterian Church, stood next to him and put her arm through his.

Had he changed in any way? Yes, he had to admit he had, a little. He'd bought some new shirts at Bealls to replace the old ones that were so tight around the neck. Tonight he'd worn a daring light blue one instead of the usual white. With it, he had on one of the ties Blossom had given him when she cleaned out her husband's closet, black with light blue swirls. Far more exciting than the three ties he already possessed.

Mattie looked nice in a dressy dress that showed more leg and décolletage than he'd ever seen a minister display. Not that she looked cheap or showed too much, but she didn't look much like a lady preacher tonight.

He knew well enough not to tell her she looked *nice.* "Great dress," he said. "I like your hair." She'd piled it on top of her head with little curls dangling down. "You look different tonight." At her frown, he added, "In a good way."

She studied him for a moment, "You know, you are getting better looking. Not as scrawny as you were when I first met you. Maybe you've finally stopped growing and reached the age you can put on a little muscle."

Had she really said something nice about him, in which case he should thank her? Or had she merely moved him up the scale one step, from scrawny to just plain skinny. That didn't feel at all like a compliment.

Then she smiled and squeezed his arm. For a moment, he panicked. She'd looked at him as if he were a man instead of the eunuch who served the Christian Church.

Fortunately, one of the junior girls pulled

Mattie's arm. "I need you to help me. My dress ripped a little."

Mattie hurried off and Adam, perfectly content not to wonder about Mattie's message, watched the dancers with less of an eagle eye than the pillar expected him to use.

"Hey, Preacher," Gabe Borden said. He'd been a hotshot guard five or six years earlier at UT, where he'd been nicknamed "Flash." Adam had heard of Flash and followed his career. After a couple of years in the NBA, Gabe retired. No known injuries, simply stopped playing and went back to school for a master's degree and worked as an assistant at UT. He'd landed the job of head basketball coach at Butternut Creek High School nearly a year earlier.

"How're you doing, Coach?"

"Okay. Having fun?" Gabe looked across the crowd of students.

Adam sometimes questioned the even-handedness of whoever dispensed physical gifts. Gabe had everything. He looked like . . . well, like a former NBA player. Handsome, confident, and charismatic. From what Adam heard, the man had invested well, had piles of money, and sponsored several charities. However, Adam had two inches on him, which evened things out a bit.

Here in Butternut Creek, Gabe attempted to look like a normal guy but he wasn't. He could wear jeans from Walmart, cheap T-shirts, and knockoff athletic shoes and still look like an ad for men's cologne. But Adam couldn't help but like him. That charisma.

"How did you get dragged in?" Adam asked.

"I'm a junior class sponsor, one of the joys of teaching here. We spent most of the day setting up. Fortunately, I like being around high school kids. I'm not as fond of wrapping flowers around poles or covering the ceiling with dark blue crepe paper."

"Lovely. Looks just like Paris."

Gabe raised an eyebrow. "Have you ever been to Paris?"

"Yes, but this is still pretty good for a makeover of the community center." Then Adam tossed out the words, "Coach, do you have a church home?"

Gabe didn't respond. Instead he seemed busy ignoring a willowy blond chaperone who had her eye on him.

"English teacher, recent divorcée," Gabe explained. "She's aggressive, but not quite as pushy as a minister who asks if you have a church home when he's chaperoning the prom. No, not nearly as pushy, but close."

After a few seconds of silence during which Adam felt warned not to ask again but pleased that he had made an effort to reach out, the coach said, "I want to talk to you about Hector." Gabe's eyes searched the crowd for the young man.

"Is there a problem?" Adam hoped not. Next to Janey, basketball was Hector's life.

"Not really. I wanted to pick your brain, get your opinion. I'm thinking about changing his position from a three to a two, from small forward to shooting guard or maybe what they call a point forward, a combination."

"You know I'm not his guardian, right? That he's an emancipated minor. He lives with me, but I don't tell him what to do. Much."

"I don't expect you to, but you know something about basketball so I thought I'd talk this over with you." He paused. "You know, Hector's too thin and too short to play forward in college. He's not a wide body, which is what everyone looks for."

Adam nodded.

"He's a smart kid and a great shooter, good passer. To play guard, he has to improve his ball-handling skills. With my background, I can work with him, coach him to be a guard."

Oh, yeah, Flash would be a great teacher for Hector. "Makes sense. You think more schools would be interested in him as a guard?"

"I think he'll add more to the team and attract more attention as a guard than a forward. What is he? Six-three? Six-four? But he needs to bulk up a lot to play as a wide body."

"Do you know how much that kid eats? If I didn't have the same problem putting on weight, I'd wonder where all that food goes."

"Yeah, he works out in the weight room for hours but can't build muscle. Too young."

For a minute or so, the two men watched the young people dance and listened to the music.

"I'd like to have him dribble the ball every-

where he goes to make him more comfortable with it. Are you on board with this?"

"Sure," Adam started but before he could
say more, a student looking very sophisti-
cated in a long red dress took Gabe's arm
and pulled him into the crowd to dance.

Adam laughed at Gabe's discomfort
until another young woman grabbed him.

Chapter Seven

May whirled past. After prom, Adam attended the spring sports award ceremony,
the choir concert at the high school and
one at Janey's elementary school, track
meets, and everything else that crowded
the last days of the school year. In no time,
summer church camp loomed ahead. He'd
see Gussie for almost a week.

Here was his chance: the promise of six
days together, nearly a week to pursue . . .
no, to court . . . no, to woo . . . Oh, forget
what verb he should use. He wanted to
get to know her better and to find out if
she felt anything for him. He'd accept the

tiniest spark in the hope he could fan it into a great passion; he'd even settle for a warm ember of interest.

He and Gussie had kept up their emails for six weeks, most of them professional about the coming events and also sent to the other adults who'd attend.

But every now and then, he thought of something that happened at church or a particularly Miss Birdie moment he wanted to share with her or news about the youth group. From time to time, she'd answer. They fell into a comfortable and, sadly, friendly rhythm.

❦

Senior high camp started June 8. In addition to the five who'd gone to the retreat, three more kids from the high school were joining them. For that reason, the elders had rented them a larger but utilitarian van.

So much went on the first day and evening, Adam had no chance to put his plan to woo Gussie into action. Crowds of people surrounded Gussie at every moment, asking questions, seeking direction, or just plain talking to her because she was so much fun to talk to.

Adam waved and smiled at her, and she

returned a harried grin. He couldn't get close to her.

He glanced down at the sheaf of papers she'd shoved at him in passing. She'd prepared the list of patrols, and they were not together. He'd ended up with Mrs. Hayes, who taught high school French in Liberty Hill. Gussie had paired herself with the minister from San Antonio. Maybe he could switch with Jimmy. No, that would call too much attention to his interest.

Monday morning, he got a call that Jesse's brother had died and he needed to get back for funeral arrangements.

"I hate to leave," he told Gussie.

"I understand." She didn't look unhappy about his departure.

Had he hoped she'd cry? Throw herself at his feet and beg him to stay because she couldn't stand to spend the week without him? Or, maybe more realistically, look a tiny bit disappointed? Would've been nice.

"You'll be short a male counselor," he said.

She shrugged. "Nothing we can do about that. Your church member needs you." She placed her hand on his arm, then pulled it away quickly.

What was that about?

"I'll be back after the funeral."

But when he got back to Butternut Creek, every emergency possible hit. The mother of a member had gone into hospice and the family asked for his visits. The niece of a friend of Mercedes needed to get married. Maggie scheduled the wedding for Thursday evening as well as sessions with the bride and groom Tuesday and Wednesday.

On Wednesday, he called Gussie to tell her he wouldn't be back and that he'd pick up the youth on Friday at noon.

So much for wooing or courting or even speaking to Gussie.

❦

Adam said a quick word to Gussie when he picked up the kids but nothing more. The place was chaos, and after driving to the hospice in Lubbock twice to spend time with ailing members and their families, he'd worn himself out.

The kids squeezed into the van, stowing the luggage under their seats and in the aisle. Most fell asleep almost as soon as Adam turned on the ignition.

As he drove out, Adam saw Gussie in

the middle of a group of kids, laughing and attempting to point them toward the waiting cars.

"Sorry you had to miss camp, Pops," Hector said from the passenger seat.

Adam pulled out on the highway and sped up. He enjoyed a vehicle with acceleration.

"Yeah, wish I could have been there." Adam looked in the rearview mirror to see Bree sleeping in a seat next to her sister. "Why aren't you sitting with Bree?"

"Haven't seen you for a while. Wanted to catch up. Too bad you weren't able to see more of Gussie."

"What do you mean by that?"

Hector grinned. "Don't make me spell it out. You gotta know Mac can't keep a secret for long."

Adam groaned.

"We're gonna keep it quiet. Don't worry." He slid his hat over his eyes. "But, you know, I'm beginning to think God doesn't want you and Gussie together." Then he pretended to fall asleep.

At least, Adam believed the sleep to be feigned. He bet Hector had been warned by junior matchmaker Mac not to push.

Hector did bring up a good point. Why did he have such bad luck around Gussie? Before the week of camp, he'd had such high hopes. Seemed like he was snakebit. Nothing worked out as planned.

Maybe the kid was right. God didn't want him and Gussie together. Maybe God was doing everything a deity could do to keep them apart because He had different plans for them.

Of all the stupid ideas. Like God would kill Jesse's brother or have a teenager get pregnant and ask for a quick wedding—all just so Adam didn't have a chance to court Gussie.

Adam always thought God was busy enough with the universe that He didn't mess in people's lives or favor certain football teams despite the fact that in Texas, a majority believed He was a rabid fan of the Cowboys. Adam preferred to think God was more concerned with opening hearts so the hungry could be fed and the naked clothed and wars stopped.

The sort of thinking that made people believe God was the mighty micromanager who did petty things to mess people up or solve the small problems they could take care of themselves always astounded him. Reminded him of his aunt Hazel who believed God had nearly killed her in a car wreck and put her in a coma to get her to stop smoking. Surely, Adam had always thought, the creator of the heavens and the earth, omniscient and omnipotent, could have come up with a better plan than almost killing the woman now to save her from dying of lung cancer later.

If a Gussie-and-Adam combination truly didn't suit God's plans, then God could make this far easier by putting a lovely single young woman in Butternut Creek to distract him from Gussie. However, he truly didn't—couldn't—believe God worked that way, like a great matchmaker in the sky.

For a moment, Adam considered the idea that God had franchised that arm of the business to the Widows. If they had a divine covenant for their efforts, he might as well give in, accept the inevitable, and marry whoever they found.

❦

Gussie watched the packed van drive off and bemoaned the fact she hadn't seen much of Adam.

"He's a hottie, isn't he?"

Oh, my Lord. Had she said those words out loud?

Gussie looked to her left to see Marcy Swenson, one of the college students who had come to camp as an assistant counselor.

"Who?" Gussie glanced at the girl.

"Reverend Jordan," Marcy said.

"Adam?"

"Haven't you noticed?" Marcy whistled. "How could you not see that?"

"He's a very nice young man. The young people from his church really like him."

Marcy's mouth dropped open. "You haven't noticed?" She jabbed Gussie in the side with her elbow. "Why don't you ask him out? You're about the same age. You're both single. He's hot and you're hot, for your age."

With those depressing words, Marcy took off to help her campers load their cars.

Hot for her age? Gussie had no idea how to respond to that statement. Probably better to dismiss it and concentrate on getting camp cleared.

❦

Adam hated middle-of-the-night phone calls. He always hoped they were wrong

numbers or drunks who couldn't dial, but
most often they came from a church member in trouble. Last month it had been a
heart attack and a quick trip to Austin.

By the third ring, he was sufficiently
awake to grab the phone. "Adam Jordan,"
he said.

"Ouida fell. She wants you to come
over."

"I'll be right there," Adam said before he
realized George had already hung up.

It took only minutes to dress, comb his
hair, and push his feet into Nikes before
he ran out of the house to the Kowalskis'
front door.

Before he could knock, George opened
the door and pulled Adam inside. "She's
right there."

He pointed with a shaking finger as if
Adam couldn't see Ouida lying motionless
at the bottom of the steps, a small pool of
blood growing where her hand lay close to
a few shards of glass.

For a moment Adam could only stare.
Was she dead? "Did you call nine-one-
one? What happened?"

George nodded. "Called them right before I called you." For a moment, he struggled to speak. "She fell."

Ouida moaned. Adam strode toward her and knelt.

"Hey, Preacher," she whispered.

At least she was coherent and awake. Good. But she didn't move, her leg bent at an odd angle, and she was so pale she was the same color as her light blue nightgown now liberally spotted with red.

Shock. He tried to remember the first-aid course he'd had years ago. Treatment for shock: Cover the patient, keep her warm, and raise her head. Or maybe raise her feet. He couldn't remember which but that didn't matter because he wasn't going to touch her. EMS would do that.

"Cold," she whispered.

"Get some blankets," Adam said. "Or coats. Something to cover her."

When George didn't move, Adam stood and, in two steps, reached the front closet. He opened it and pulled the winter coats out. None felt very heavy—in Texas, no one had thick, warm coats—until he found a tan topcoat, which he lay across Ouida.

"That's my best coat," George protested.

When Adam glared at him, he added, "But, of course, that's fine."

With Ouida covered, Adam carefully picked the largest shards of glass off the floor before anyone could get cut. He stood to toss them in a decorative thingy in the entrance hall, then turned to study George. How was he doing? As he'd have guessed, George wore silk pajamas and nice leather slippers. Other than the man's pallor, George looked like his usual, well-turned-out self: great haircut with minimal bed head, immaculately clothed for the occasion, and in charge. Except, of course, George's bewildered expression showed he wasn't in charge and had no idea what to do next except to pace at a safe distance from the puddle of blood.

With a glance around the hallway and upstairs—no sign of Carol or Gretchen yet—Adam pulled out his cell and hit speed dial. After a few rings, Bree answered. Or maybe it was Mac.

"Hey, I need you at the Kowalskis'. Ouida fell. Can you two and your grandmother come over? ASAP?"

"Who is this?" the young woman mumbled.

"Adam Jordan."

"Oh, yeah, Preacher." She yawned. "This is Bree."

"Bring your grandmother, too. Okay?" When Bree didn't say anything—had she fallen back to sleep?—Adam said, "We need you now, for Carol and Gretchen."

"Of course," she said, immediately awake. "Be right there."

As sirens sounded from a few blocks away, Adam knelt next to Ouida. Still pale. Still cold.

He glanced up the stairs to see a floppy slipper on the sixth step up. Didn't take a genius to see what happened: Ouida had slipped, fallen, and landed here, probably broken her leg. Cut her hand on something. Those were the obvious injuries.

George had stopped pacing and hovered about five feet away. "Should we get her on the sofa?" George asked. "Make her comfortable?"

"No, the paramedics need to decide that."

"I fell," she whispered. "Hurts." Then she started to gag.

"George," Adam motioned toward him. "Why don't you come hold Ouida's hand."

"He doesn't like blood or vomit," she whispered.

Who did? Neither was among Adam's favorite fluids.

"Thirsty."

"I'll get water." George grabbed the reason to escape and ran toward the kitchen, leaving bloody footprints behind him.

They wouldn't give Ouida anything to drink, that was a decision for the paramedics, but the errand got George out of the way and doing something purposeful. Maybe that would either calm him down or rouse him. Adam had no idea which George needed.

Ouida attempted to move, then stopped and groaned.

Thrashing and anxiety, those meant something but darned if he could remember what. He'd take another first-aid course as soon as possible.

When the sirens stopped outside the house, Adam jumped to his feet to open the door. The paramedics ran up the walk and into the house, then took in the scene.

"I'm Shelley," the lead paramedic said. "That's Aaron." Within seconds both she and the stocky EMT knelt next to Ouida, threw the overcoat on the floor, and examined her.

"Mommy."

Adam glanced up the stairs to see Carol and Gretchen sobbing and holding hands.

"Mommy," Carol shouted over and over. And all this time, George stood to the side of the action holding the tumbler of water.

"George." Adam pointed toward the girls. "Take care of them."

George didn't move. If his color hadn't looked fairly normal, Adam might have guessed he suffered from shock.

He did. Of course he did. Finding his wife at the bottom of the steps bleeding must have frightened him deeply, but his daughters needed him now.

"How long ago did this happen?" Shelley asked.

George shook his head.

"George called me about ten minutes ago," Adam said. A stupid comment because they probably had the time of the 911 call, but George didn't seem able to give more information.

Ouida was getting great care from the paramedics, but they needed information and the girls needed to be comforted.

In the movies, the hero slapped the hysterical heroine, which always seemed to work. Adam had always wondered why that wasn't considered abusive. He couldn't imagine that slapping George would have the desired effect—and the man might slap him back. Instead he shouted sharply, "George."

The word woke him up. George chugged the water, placed the glass on the table, and said, "I don't know. I woke up about twenty minutes ago and she wasn't in bed. When I came down, she was there."

While George spoke, Adam headed toward the back stairs to avoid the huddle of health care workers in the hall. Once upstairs, he sat on the top step to the side of the girls, pulled Carol and Gretchen into his arms, and carefully turned their eyes away from the sight of their mother. "Your mother fell," he said as he rubbed their backs gently. "But she's going to be okay."

The girls looked up at him.

"These people will take care of your mommy, patch her up, then take her to the hospital."

"I want Mommy." Carol attempted to turn back and watch her mother.

Had his explanation made them think they'd be left alone? What could he do to comfort and distract them from the scene below as Shelley prepared an IV?

"You're going to be fine, I promise. You won't be alone."

The girls lifted their eyes.

"Are you going to take her to the hospital?" George asked from below.

Shelley nodded. "We'll take her to Burnet and life-flight her to Austin. We don't have the facilities in Burnet to do more than basic care."

"Mommy?" Carol sobbed.

"She'll go to the hospital so very good doctors can take care of her." Adam lifted the girls in his arms. "While your mommy is in the hospital, friends will be here with you."

Mercifully, as the crescendo of crying increased and Shelley repeated another question to George, Miss Birdie strode in followed by her granddaughters. The cavalry had arrived. *Thank you, God.*

He'd known the pillar would come and not due *only* to curiosity. As much as she attempted to hide it, Miss Birdie had a heart of gold beneath that crusty exterior.

She took charge immediately. "Upstairs," the pillar told Bree and Mac.

"You," she told George. "You come here and hold your wife's hand and give the information they need to these EMS people. Preacher." She looked up at Adam. "The girls and I'll take care of Carol and Gretchen. You come down here and support George." She infused those last words with scorn that a man, a husband, would act like George.

Fortunately, George didn't notice. George seemed nearly catatonic.

Within seconds, Bree had led the little girls away from the top of the steps and their view of their mother. When he arrived in the foyer, Adam gave George a slight shove toward his wife.

At the top of the stairs stood Miss Birdie, studying the scene below her, legs apart and arms folded in front of her. She looked like a bulldog—although a skinny one—but Adam knew the frown showed concern and the crossed arms were the way she'd learned to cope with shoulder pain, supporting one arm with the other.

George didn't know that. He glanced up at her and took a step toward his wife, then another. While George read judgment in the pillar's scrutiny, Adam saw her assess what she needed to do. He bet cleaning up the front hall after the crowd dispersed would be her first priority.

"Sir, we're going to need some information. Full name, last name first," said a young man who held a small computer.

George recited the elementary material.

"Date of birth?"

After he entered that information, the young man asked, "Do you know her Texas driver's license number?"

George rattled it off.

"Social Security number?"

George knew that, too.

"What health insurance do you have?"

"It's with Greater Good. Group number is 546C3. Identification number 1212HH1344."

The man did know numbers.

After the EMTs had stopped the bleeding and hooked up an IV, they covered Ouida with several blankets, put a collar around her neck, and carefully strapped her on a board, then a gurney. Believing everything was well under control, Adam headed toward the back stairs to check on the girls and to talk to Miss Birdie.

In one bedroom, Bree rocked Gretchen, who was sleeping soundly. In the other, Mac read to Carol. Both glanced up at Adam when he peeked in.

"You're mother's going to be fine," Adam said. "We're taking her to the hospital."

When tears started down Carol's cheeks, Adam entered the room and stooped in front of the child. "I promise I'll come back as soon as I can. Miss Birdie and her grand-daughters will stay with you."

Once downstairs, he pulled out the cell again and called Hector.

"Hey, I need you at the Kowalskis'. Ouida fell. Can you come over and talk to me? ASAP."

"Who is this?" Hector mumbled.

"Adam Jordan."

"Oh, yeah, Pops." Hector yawned. "Be right there."

After he closed the phone, Adam joined George. "I'll drive you into Austin."

When George nodded, Adam noticed a cowlick sticking up in the back of his head. He'd never seen his neighbor with a hair out of place. The fact that it was said a lot about the man's condition. That he'd accepted the ride so willingly said even more.

"Hey, Pops." Hector entered the foyer with his usual highenergy gait but stopped as soon as Ouida was whisked past him.

"Didn't expect all this." Hector waved toward the crowd: George, the paramedics disappearing with Ouida on the gurney, Miss Birdie still at the top of the steps. Before Adam could say a word, Hector said, "Hey, Miss Birdie, you don't want to be standing. Let me get you a chair." With that, he took off into the kitchen. The next time Adam saw him, he was upstairs helping the pillar sit on one of the kitchen chairs.

"Isn't that better?" Hector asked.

"Yes, thank you." Wonder of wonders, Miss Birdie actually smiled at the kid, nearly cooed.

"Be right down, Pops." He disappeared again, showing up almost immediately in the foyer.

"That was nice of you," Adam said.

"Well, she's not exactly a spring chicken, and she shouldn't be standing," Hector explained in a low voice. "But don't tell her I said that. Annoys her." As if Adam didn't know that. "What'd you want?"

Realizing he was pretty tired as well,

Adam leaned against the wall. "I'm going to drive George's car to the hospital in Austin after the ambulance leaves. I'll leave mine here. You'll have to pick me up."

"In your car?" Hector asked. "Pops, you've got to be kidding. That old blue thing won't make it. I'll be broken down by the side of the road." He grinned. "Why don't you let me drive that fine Lexus George has and you pick *me* up?"

Ignoring the words, true as they were, Adam said, "I'll call you when I'm ready. It may be this afternoon."

❦

Immediately after they arrived at the hospital, nurses hurried George off to another area of the hospital to be with Ouida. While he waited, Adam drank so much coffee he could actually feel caffeine pumping through his body. It stimulated every nerve and woke up a brain that hadn't had enough sleep, but it made his hands shake as well.

On the muted television, an anchor silently mouthed the news as pictures of earthquake damage flitted past. In the corner of the waiting room, a couple slept on short love seats. Otherwise, the area was abandoned. He could hear the pings and buzzes and an occasional voice from the nurses' station far down the hall. But here, only the snores and grunts from the sleepers interrupted the solitude.

After a while, George entered the waiting room and threw himself into a chair with sagging cushions and wobbly arms. Before they'd left Butternut Creek, George had changed from his pajamas to immaculately tailored jeans with carefully ironed creases; a soft Carolina-blue shirt with a logo Adam didn't recognize, probably because George hadn't bought it at Adam's favorite discount mall; and a pair of running shoes so expensive that Adam had once tried a pair on for fun. If George hadn't dropped his face into his hands, Adam would've assumed his neighbor felt as calm and in control as his clothing suggested.

Nevertheless Adam asked, "How's it going?" to check on his neighbor's mental condition.

George looked up. Terror and anguish alternated across his face and reinforced Adam's earlier concern: George didn't handle this type of stress well. Whenever he'd talked to George—which wasn't all that often—his neighbor seemed cool and logical. Not tonight.

"She's—" George began in a quivering voice. He stopped to clear his throat and continue, "She's in surgery, has been since a few minutes after we arrived. I had to sign some paperwork. That's all I know."

A few minutes later, a woman wearing a lab coat over scrubs approached them. "I'm Dr. Ramirez." She reached out to shake Adam's hand. "Are you Mr. Kowalski?"

"No, I'm her minister." The words fell from his lips because that's what he always said in this situation. He opened his mouth to continue, *Not really. I'm her next-door-neighbor but I'm acting sort of like her minister because she doesn't go to church but I need to be here with George this morning.*

Instead he said, "That's Mr. Kowalski," and pointed to George.

"Mr. Kowalski, I'm the doctor who cared for your wife in the emergency room." She sat in a chair across from the men. "Sorry I didn't get to see you earlier. We've had a blitz in the ER tonight. To catch you up, we got the bleeding on Mrs. Kowalski's hand stopped." With a glance at her notes, she added, "Her shoulder is dislocated and that right leg is broken. Spiral break. As you know, she's in surgery now."

"What are they doing, Doctor?" Adam asked. George looked stunned and long past the point of putting two or three intelligent words together.

"They'll put that shoulder back into the socket—that won't take long—stitch the hand up because those cuts are very deep, and set the leg. They may have to put a rod in her leg."

"The break is that bad?" Adam asked.

She nodded. "She may have to be in traction for six to eight weeks, to heal. You'll know more when the surgeon gets in there with more information."

"Six to eight weeks?" George said as if that were like the wait for the second coming, which he probably didn't believe in.

"Yes, at least. Mr. Kowalski, we're going to have someone from social services talk to you later this morning when we have more information about her condition."

"Social services?" George asked.

"Her shoulder will be immobilized for ten days or so, and that leg—" She shook her head. "Mr. Kowalski, your wife's going to need a lot of care. I suggest a skilled nursing facility. We have many good ones here in Austin."

George lay back in the chair and closed his eyes. Adam feared the man had passed out until he said, "She's going to need care for weeks? In a nursing facility?" in a desolate voice.

When no more words or questions emerged from George, Adam asked, "How 'bout one located in Butternut Creek?"

"You'll need to check with social services. As I said, one of the clerks will be up with information and some papers for you to sign, Mr. Kowalski." The doctor stood. "Please check at the nurses' station if you have any questions. She'll be in surgery for several hours, but a room should be assigned by ten. You can wait there."

When George nodded, she walked away.

"I've told her a dozen times not to carry a glass." George sat up and opened his eyes. "Especially not at night, in the dark. You don't know what you might trip on." He shook his head and looked beseechingly at Adam as if expecting agreement or at least understanding of that edict.

"Dangerous," Adam said. "That's what happened? Ouida fell holding a glass?" He pretty much figured it was. After all, he'd seen the shards of glass and the blood. But he imagined his neighbor needed to talk.

George glanced down at his hands as if seeing blood flowing from his palm. "I don't know what happened or why Ouida went downstairs. Guess Gretchen asked for water, but I didn't hear her. I don't usually hear them. Ouida takes care of that."

Adam nodded while George shook his head.

"And I don't know why she had those slippers on. I've told her not to wear those big floppy things. Too easy to step on, to trip over." His voice sharpened. "She doesn't listen to me."

Adam had no answer, so they watched the silent television and pictures of destruction someplace in Asia for two or three minutes.

"Bad tsunami," George murmured as he looked at the screen.

"Lots of people hurt." Adam agreed. *"Tsunami,* an odd word," he added, having no idea what else to talk about.

George mused a few minutes. "Japanese," he said. "Literally means 'harbor wave.' What we used to call a tidal wave. Silent *t.*"

"Interesting," Adam said.

"You don't have to stay," George said after another long pause.

"I know. I want to stay. I'm your neighbor. Besides, Miss Birdie said I had to call her as soon as we knew more about Ouida."

George nodded. "Wouldn't want to cross her." A note of respect and fear colored his voice. "Not Miss Birdie."

Twenty minutes later, George said, "You know I care about Ouida."

"I know."

"She's the one who takes care of all this." He waved around the waiting room as if she were the hospital's chief of staff. "I mean, she takes the kids to the doctor. She . . . well, she does all the home stuff. The only time I've been in a hospital was when the kids were born."

He leaned forward and fixed Adam with the stare that probably said *trust me* to his clients but only said *I'm out of my element here* to Adam.

"I'm a good accountant," George said. "But—and Ouida knows this—not exactly high on the taking-care-of-others scale. I handle the money. She handles the children and the emergencies at home."

Adam knew that from his conversations with Ouida. She'd also told him George always acted calm and in charge, but not this morning.

"What am I going to do about work?" he asked. "Someone's going to have to take care of the children." George glanced up at Adam. "You probably wonder how I can wonder about work when Ouida's undergoing surgery, but this is how I support my family and I have a dozen employees. If I don't keep the business running, they don't have jobs and we don't have money to live on." His shoulders drooped. "Six to eight weeks?"

"We'll work things out together," Adam said. "Once you know more about the prognosis, we'll work it out."

"What about that mess at home?" George sat up suddenly. "The blood all over?"

"Miss Birdie will take care of that. Don't worry about the house now." He spoke calmly and clearly. "George, the doctors know what they are doing, and their training guided their hands. You and Ouida have friends and family who love you and will be with you. We all hope Ouida will soon be home healthy and whole, in the best possible health." His words were actually those he used in prayers before surgery, but without what George would consider the spiritual stuff.

"Yeah. Okay. Thank you." George nodded and settled back again, but he didn't look as miserable as he had before that stealth prayer.

Two hours later, the surgeon approached to talk with them, pretty much repeating what the ER doctor had said. After that, George spoke with the clerk from social services, who said Ouida would be in the hospital for a few days, then taken to a skilled nursing facility. Adam requested she look into a place close to Butternut Creek.

Later, they went to the room assigned to Ouida. When the bed was wheeled in, she had her hand wound in bandages, her arm bound to her side, and her leg in a cast and hanging in traction. Looking pale and groggy, she waved weakly with her good arm. Immediately a nurse threw the men out so he could hook Ouida up to some machines.

As they waited, Adam's cell vibrated. He clicked on a text message and read it.

"Hector's here with my car," he said. "With Ouida back and probably sleeping, I'm going to take off. Will you be okay to drive your car home?"

George nodded. "I think I'll go to the office and get some work done."

"No," Adam stated. "You need to stay here with Ouida, then you have to go home. You have two little girls who need to know their mother is okay and have their father at home with them. They need that security."

George sighed. "I'm not very good with this father stuff, but, you're right. I'll stay with Ouida for a couple of hours, then go home."

"I'll come back again tomorrow." Adam shook George's hand, then headed for the elevator.

"How's she doing, Pops?" Hector waited

in the cafeteria, his calculus book open on a table in front of him.

Adam shrugged. "Okay. She'll be here for a while."

"Oh, man." Hector closed his book and stood. "You can't drive that wreck into Austin every day to see her. That's dangerous."

"Too far to walk," Adam said. "Come on. Let's go. I want to stop and get some breakfast or lunch. Where's Janey?"

"The Olivers down the block are taking care of Carol and Gretchen. She's helping."

As tired as he was, Adam let Hector drive. When they pulled up at the speaker at Sonic, Hector lowered the window. When he finished with the order he mashed the button to put the window up, but it didn't move. The sound of grinding came from inside the door. Never a good sign.

"Great. One more problem with the car. Can't close the window on this side." Hector turned to frown at Adam.

"I had this happen in another car. Grab that edge of the window, the glass you can still see, and pull it up."

"You had this happen on another car?" Hector shook his head. "Have you even had a car that had all its parts and ran well?" As the waitress skated to the car, he handed her a bill, took the change, and handed it to Adam before taking the food. "And isn't your father rich? Can't he buy you a car."

"I like to make it on my own."

"Man, you're crazy. And if you keep driving this car, you're goin' to be dead."

When they'd finished, Hector backed the car out, opened the door, got out, and tugged on the window to close it.

"Remind me not to open it again," he said when he got inside.

🍎

When Adam entered Ouida's hospital room the next evening, she was alone and snoring. On the windowsill sat a vase of tulips and baby's breath. A potted plant stood on a shelf.

He didn't want to wake her up. He reached in his pocket to pull out a card and a pen to write a note.

"Adam?" Ouida mumbled as she opened her eyes.

"Hey." He took her hand. "I came by to let you know everyone at church is . . . thinking of you."

"You can say they're praying. I don't mind." She squeezed his fingers and smiled.

"I sent George back home. He's not comfortable in a hospital."

George didn't feel comfortable anyplace away from work, Adam guessed, but he didn't say that.

"He won't feel more comfortable at home, either," she said.

"The girls will be glad to have him around." He settled in a chair. "How are you feeling?"

"I hurt. Guess that's expected. They are managing the pain. Even started physical therapy already, moving my fingers around and lifting my arm a little." She shifted in the bed. "Could you get me a glass of water? Help me drink it?"

That action reminded him how incapacitated she was. Couldn't even pour or drink water with only one arm. She faced a long rehabilitation. How would George handle that?

"What's next?" he asked after she'd taken a few sips.

But she fell back to sleep before he'd finished the question.

On the drive home, Adam had to slow down for four or five vultures to fly away from the corpse of a deer in the middle of the highway. Texas offered up a variety of roadkill. Lots of deer, armadillos, and the occasional rabbit, possum, or raccoon.

He gave a sigh of relief and a silent prayer when his old car made it back to the parsonage. He needed a car to drive into Austin without asking Rex to lay healing hands on it before every trip.

Maybe it was time to buy a new car or a less used one, but he had no money. What he had left over from his salary after utilities and food—which had increased about one hundred dollars a month since Hector arrived—went into the little extras for Janey and clothes for Hector, who seemed to grow several inches a week. Adam could see his legs getting longer if he watched for a few minutes.

He'd allowed Hector to drive Old Blue around town, but, for the kid, this was a strictly inside-the-city-limits vehicle. Yes, Adam needed to put aside a little bit, save fifty dollars per paycheck. But fifty dollars a month added up to only six hundred dollars in a year. What kind of car could he buy with that?

❦

That Sunday after the service, Adam stood in front of the church and watched the cars pass on the highway. Janey had gone back to the parsonage while Hector had sprinted out with Bobby to change and hit the basketball court.

Those kids had a lot more energy than Adam. Driving back and forth to visit an improving but frustrated Ouida, working with the Widows to make sure the girls were okay, and attempting to do the other church work and come up with the passable sermon had worn him out. He wanted nothing more than a good nap.

Well, one thing more. He also wanted to avoid Sam. Sounding more and more like a matchmaker, Sam had asked him about Gussie as he left church. When Adam saw Sam's car still in the parking lot, he started to run toward the parsonage.

"Hey, Preacher."

The voice didn't surprise him. He'd heard Sam's uneven footsteps behind him as well as the sibilant sounds of the boys shushing each other, but it did foil his escape.

"I thought if I ignored you, you'd go away," Adam said, still keeping his back to Sam. Sort of like magical thinking. Didn't work.

"Let's talk about Gussie."

Adam took a few steps away.

"Okay, now I understand why you didn't take advantage of that week of camp. You weren't there, but buddy, what are you doing now?" Sam moved to stand in front of Adam and studied him as a marine captain would scrutinize a raw recruit.

Adam should've known Sam was unignorable. As an exmarine, he homed in on his objective and kept up his attack until the target had been won.

"Tell me something, Adam. Have you ever dated a woman?"

"Of course I have. I was even engaged." He deked and took a step toward the parsonage, but Sam's voice and his smoothly executed military turn cut off that route.

"Tell me about them. How many, when?"

"Ummm." Adam thought back over the past ten years. "Not that many. A couple of girls in high school, a few in college, then I asked Laurel to marry me when we graduated."

"What happened with this Laurel?"

"She didn't want to marry a minister. Said she wasn't into teas and good works."

"And the others? Did you have to pursue them?"

"No, we were friends first, then began to date."

"So, you're telling me you don't know a thing about courting a woman?"

"No, they always just threw themselves at me."

Sam's glare told Adam both that he didn't believe those words and that humor did not fit here.

"All right," Adam confirmed. "I know nothing about this. I dated women I already knew and was attracted to and comfortable with."

"Then we're starting with the basics." Sam straightened. Not that Adam had seen his posture sag in the least, but he'd pulled himself up so he looked even taller and tougher. "Welcome to boot camp for the romantically challenged."

No escape. The parking lot had emptied out. Willow waited in the car, reading. Even Leo and Nick had headed toward the grass behind the parking lot. Looking for dead animals, maybe. Not that any of that family'd be of assistance in any way. Adam bet they didn't interfere or interrupt when Sam addressed the troops.

"Phase one: If you don't have a plan,"

Sam lectured, "you cannot execute it. Phase two: If you want Gussie, you can't be some passive grunt who lets life go past him. Take action. Man up."

"Man up," Nick shouted from the lawn. Sam glanced at his sons, pointed, and watched the kids move several yards farther away before he turned his iron gaze back at Adam.

"Yes, sir," Adam said, but he refused to stand at attention, even though that's what Sam's voice and posture demanded.

"I don't care what you do or what your plan is, but you have to get started. Take charge. Boot camp is over." With that, Sam turned, motioned toward the kids, and all three marched toward the yellow Mustang. Adam almost saluted.

After they drove off, Adam was left alone in the parking lot. He knew Sam was right. He walked back toward the parsonage contemplating the situation. What to do? How to approach this relationship problem?

Maybe he should pick up a copy of a men's magazine and read a few articles, but he thought of at least two arguments against that. To preserve anonymity, he'd have to drive all the way into Austin. Butternut Creek's only bookstore consisted of a rack at the H-E-B. At the bookstore in Marble Falls, those kind of magazines were kept behind the counter and had to be requested. If he went there, he was sure to run into someone who knew him and would spread news of his purchase all over the county. Ministers didn't and shouldn't read racy magazines was the consensus of parishioners.

Second, many—okay, all—of those magazines were way too steamy for him, past his depth. He wasn't looking for pointers on how to . . . well, those activities covered in risqué magazines were written for people with far more experience than him.

Maybe he'd look for help online.

That evening, he searched for "What do women want?" The experience both amazed him and opened his eyes to another world. He discovered women wanted many things he'd never thought they'd openly discuss.

Then he Googled "How to get the woman you want." The first topic he explored listed ways to get a woman into bed within fourteen minutes of meeting her. Not what he was looking for. Finally he found a couple of very helpful lists and made notes. He pondered the pages, re-read them, underlined a few ideas, and put stars in the margin on others. Oh, Sam might tell him to man up, and he was fixin' to, once he decided exactly how to do that.

But first he had to drive to Austin.

🍎

Wednesday morning, Adam and Blossom and her housekeeper, Evelyn, knocked at the Kowalskis' front door. When George opened it, his hair stood straight up, al-most as if he were a punk accountant—if such people even existed—who'd used too much gel.

"Good morning." He opened the door and waved them inside.

"Did you get much sleep?" Adam asked.

"Oh, a few hours. After Carol finally fell asleep about midnight, I slept until Gretchen got in my bed at, oh, maybe four thirty."

"She probably wanted some attention," Adam said. "Having her mother away from home is frightening for a child."

"No, she wanted breakfast. I convinced her to wait and she fell asleep." He paused.

"I'm not certain, but I may have promised her a puppy to get her to let me sleep. The kids have wanted a puppy forever."

"Puppies can be messy," Blossom said.

George sighed. When he did, Adam wanted to shout, *Man up.* He didn't, of course. Wouldn't be neighborly or Christian, and he couldn't carry it off like Sam, but George needed to take control of the situation.

A judgment easily made by a man with no children.

With a glance at Adam as if she'd read his mind, Blossom said in a voice as soothing as a pat on the hand, "George, let's go into the kitchen. I'll get you a nice cup of coffee."

"I don't know where it is," George mumbled. "There is no order to the way Ouida stores things. If I'd planned the kitchen, I'd put it over the coffeemaker, but . . ."

"I have some, a lovely blend from Costa Rica." She pulled a thermos from her purse and headed to the kitchen with George following like a puppy.

But the man wasn't a puppy and he needed to . . . okay, maybe for now, for a few minutes, he needed to be treated like a puppy because finding his wife in a heap had been a shock. He'd been taking care of the children and the house for only two days.

Still, he should have adapted by now. Shouldn't he? But, no, as Miss Birdie had said, they'd all coddled George. That was why Blossom had come. She excelled at coddling, and George had begged Adam never to set Miss Birdie loose on him again.

However, with Ouida being released soon from the hospital to the nursing facility a few blocks away, George would have to perform the tasks ahead of him. Even when she came home, she'd be laid up for eight weeks. Blossom couldn't pamper him forever.

"I brought some of the wonderful coffee cake my cook makes. I know you'll love that," Adam heard Blossom say from the kitchen.

He glanced at Evelyn, who'd begun to straighten up the living room. He hadn't wanted Blossom to bring her, but the other Widows scared George. How could a man be afraid of a bunch of women?

Adam grinned. The Widows had frightened him when he arrived here. Still did

every once in a while, especially Miss
Birdie, although Winnie could bark out orders nearly as well. Not that he'd ever let
them know they intimidated him.

As Evelyn cleaned, Adam picked up
toys and put them in baskets.

They couldn't keep sending in women to
do the housework. Evelyn was here really
as a favor for Ouida, a mere stopgap
measure so she wouldn't worry about her
family living in chaos. George had to step it
up, either hire someone or do more himself.

Chapter Eight

As Mercedes insisted—my, how Birdie hated it when she got all pushy like that—the Widows had left the preacher alone for over a week. Those few days felt like forever in the life of a matchmaker.

Not that they had anything to discuss, really. Bree and Mac had told her that during the one night the preacher spent at church camp, no sparks had flown between him and Gussie; they'd spent no moments alone cuddling or even chatting with each other, from what the girls had said. Drat the man. She needed to get him moving.

She hadn't pushed him or nagged about

the opportunity gone awry because he *had* been called away to take care of the congregation and he'd been busy with his neighbors since Ouida's terrible fall. Poor Ouida was suffering so much, and that husband of hers was nearly useless. Oh, Birdie knew that. She'd dropped in several times to bring food or to help with the girls. George nodded when she spoke and hurried to do whatever she asked but looked like he wanted to hide from her. Helpless and worthless.

However, Birdie had given the preacher enough time. If he believed he'd gotten away easy, ignoring his courting when the Widows had worked so hard to get him going and when they were all distracted by the plight of the Kowalski family, he had another think coming. Birdie knew she was exactly the person to set him straight.

She'd have to be cunning, Birdie reflected as she finished wiping the last table at the diner. Sneaky. Not let him know that she knew that he knew what she had in mind. She'd had a chat with the other Widows, which now included Blossom. She'd accepted the grass widow, realized that despite all her high maintenance, her expensive hair and clothing, she did have some good qualities, wasn't all fancy hats and no cattle. But, poor dear, she wasn't too bright.

Birdie had come up with a new plan of attack. She had an idea of exactly how to handle him.

Poor man. She laughed as she thought about what lay ahead.

Ten minutes later, she arrived at the church and opened the door. Maggie glanced up at her and froze.

"I'll tell Reverend Jordan you're here," she said.

Before Birdie could say she'd announce herself, Maggie shouted, "Pastor, Birdie MacDowell is here."

"Good morning, Preacher." As she entered the office, Birdie turned her friendliest smile toward him.

Adam stood. "How can I help you?" he said with a smile that didn't change the wary expression in his eyes or relax the tension in his shoulders. His face mirrored the same expression every minister who served the church wore when she arrived unexpectedly.

"Please sit down." Adam gestured toward a chair.

Birdie did. As the preacher returned to his chair, she took a moment to sit back and relax, to rotate that darned shoulder. It would bother her the rest of her life unless she finally gave up and had surgery, which she refused to do because how would her family eat if she did that? Who would . . . Well, enough of that. She cleared her throat—the sound caused the preacher to jump nervously—and said, "Didn't the young people have a wonderful time at camp?"

He nodded. "I heard they did."

"Yes, yes they did." She paused, attempting to act as if nothing were on her mind, but *subtle* was not one of her gifts. He watched her, clearly thought he knew where she was heading.

"As always, Gussie was wonderful." Birdie paused for a moment because she really did enjoy watching him become more wary. Baiting the preacher, not a benevolent act but entertaining. "However, that's not what I came to talk to you about."

His relief was audible and visible. He released his breath and his shoulders relaxed. But he still had that uneasy flicker in his eyes. In an effort to calm him, she smiled again because she did have an important item to discuss. Didn't work. He flinched.

"The other day, the Widows were talking about the Kowalskis." Not what he'd thought she'd say, she knew. That counted as a plus. He wouldn't suspect her real purpose.

He nodded, still wary.

"How's Ouida doing?"

"I stopped by for a minute yesterday at the nursing home. She said she felt better and looked forward to coming home in a week or two."

Birdie nodded. "That's good." She sighed, infusing worry and anxiety and concern and caring into that release of breath. "It's George I'm worried about." She leaned forward and allowed her most sympathetic look to cross her face.

"I can't talk about that, Miss Birdie."

"I know, I know. Privacy issues and all that, but I can." She leaned back. "It seems that the man is not pulling his weight, that he's not up to the task."

"He has a wife recovering from surgery, two little girls to care for, and a business to run."

"Exactly what I mean. George is like a one-legged man in a butt-kickin' contest." The baffled expression on the preacher's face told Birdie he had no idea what she meant. "That's Texan for he's not equipped for the job."

"He has a lot on his plate."

Birdie admired professional behavior in a minister. He'd said only what everyone in town knew, nothing more. She'd have to spell it out. "Yes, yes, we all know that, but he should do more. The girls aren't home that much with school and day care and church. He should be able to handle his business with Ouida in the nursing home and the girls taken care of all day. We take him food, we drive the girls around."

"I don't know that he's . . ."

Birdie kept speaking. "When she comes home, home health will come in to take care of Ouida. The Widows have sched-uled neighbors and church members to sit with her. But, even with all those people pitching in, he acts overwhelmed."

"It's a big change for him."

"But—" She sat forward again, a move-ment she knew always caught the atten-tion of any preacher. "But the man is so passive." She paused to make sure he picked up the adjective she used, then repeated it. "He's so doggone passive."

"It's all new to him."

"Oh, Preacher, I know that, but when I grew up, my daddy always taught me that if a man wants something, he should take action."

She fixed her eyes on him and spoke very slowly. "A man shouldn't sit around, passive, waiting for life to happen. If a man wants something, he should go after it." She settled back in the chair and continued to watch him.

It took a few seconds before his expression showed comprehension, the realization that Birdie was no longer talking about George, that Adam had become the topic of her conversation. He blinked once.

"Interesting observation." He nodded. "That's what your daddy used to say?"

He couldn't be teasing her, could he? Well, she didn't know. Sometimes the young man baffled her. He didn't behave like the ministers she'd trained in the past.

❦

It hadn't taken long for Adam to realize that Miss Birdie had left the topic of George

Kowalski's problems and faults behind several remarks earlier. His poor neighbor's dilemma had been only a bridge, a jumping-off point, perhaps even a metaphor for the pillar's favorite theme: getting her minister married in spite of his poor efforts at romance. He could—also metaphorically—all but feel her behind him, both hands on his back and shoving him toward Gussie.

Once she recognized that he understood exactly what she had *not* said but implied, she sat back, so pleased with herself that a genuine smile covered her face.

Lord, Adam loved the woman. Always consistent: scheming and underhanded and never afraid to try or say the most outrageous things, but she did everything because she cared. She knew that everyone would be much better off if they gave in and did things her way.

"You're meddling," he stated.

"I don't believe expressing concern about the Kowalskis could possibly be considered meddling."

Her smile became even broader, because there was no way he could tell her he knew good and well what she'd really been talking about. If he did, he opened himself up for advice about how to date Gussie.

His best course of action was to get her to leave. He needed a few moments of privacy to mull her words over. He stood, walked around the desk, and took her right hand, the one at the end of her good arm. "Thank you for dropping by." He helped her to her feet—surreptitiously, of course— and shepherded her through the door. She couldn't refuse to leave without crossing the line between aggressively helpful and what even she would consider downright rude.

With the pillar gone, Adam settled back in his chair and considered what she'd said, the hidden meaning in her words. As much as he hated to admit it, Miss Birdie was right. He had to become more assertive and less passive when it came to Gussie. When Sam and the pillar agreed, he should listen and act. He'd do that, as soon as he figured out what to do and how to do it. Although the Widows seemed unaware of the difficulty involved, Adam knew it too well. Gussie hadn't displayed even an iota of interest in him.

But he'd hidden his attraction to her. Perhaps she'd done the same. Could it be that deep within, she harbored a fiery passion for him, an unbridled lust she hid behind her quick smile and let's-be-friends exterior?

Oh, sure.

And even if she did, he saw obstacles he had no idea how to overcome. The most immediate: how to take action, to show interest in Gussie in case she felt anything toward him?

Should he call Sam? No, Sam had already given him the man-up lecture and expected Adam to act. His other friend was Mattie, but he'd never felt comfortable going to a woman for romantic advice.

He had to dive in and hope he could float. Better to know if Gussie felt the slightest bit of interest in him even if it meant facing rejection.

He pulled up his list of how to get the woman you want on the computer and studied it.

❧

Unable to put the deed off any longer because he feared if he didn't get a move on, Miss Birdie and Sam would visit him again with a stronger message, Adam ended up navigating the highways in South Austin the next day. A bouquet of roses lay on the passenger seat.

He'd picked up two ideas on the net: one, be spontaneous. Women adored spur-of-the-moment-ness. He'd decided to drop in, unexpectedly, to seem impulsive. Or, could be he was too cowardly to call.

Second, women loved flowers, but not red roses. Too clichéd, too obvious, too passé. Roses, yes. Red, no. So he'd headed toward the floral department at the H-E-B and chosen a mixture of yellow and melon and deep orange roses, four of each, because the bright colors reminded him of Gussie.

Because he had a tendency to get lost, he'd looked up the location of Gussie's photography studio and printed off a map. Only a couple of blocks south of Highway 71. He'd chosen to arrive a few minutes before ten in the hope that she'd be between appointments or could find time to see him later, perhaps for lunch. Finding the address, he pulled into a lot, turned off the ignition, picked up the flowers, and got out of the car, which still sputtered behind him, a problem Rex hadn't been able to diagnose and fix yet.

To his surprise, he found himself whistling. He hadn't whistled in a long time. Probably had known instinctively that whereas Miss Birdie could handle a minister who played basketball, she would not approve of a basketball-playing minister who whistled.

Why had he allowed her to run his life? Probably because his life was a great deal easier if he gave in to her on the little things.

He stopped in front of the door to Gussie's studio and gave a long whistle. Wow! She was really successful. Several pictures of Austin celebrities stared out of the front windows of a sleek, modern building: one of a guitar player with a ponytail; another of a well-muscled actor famous for taking his shirt off. He opened the door to a reception area with luxurious chairs, a thick carpet, and a gorgeous blonde at the desk.

"May I help you?" the receptionist asked with a broad smile.

"I'm here to see Gussie?" he asked although he hadn't meant it as a question.

"Was she expecting you?" Her smile became even more friendly, showing soft dimples as if she'd finally realized he was a man.

"No." He glanced around. He was alone in the waiting area. "I thought I'd drop by. Hope to catch her."

Justine—at least that was the name on her desk plate—grimaced. "Oh, dear. That's not a good idea. Miss Milton never takes walk-ins. She's too busy."

Well, that was good for her business.

"Right now, she's at a church down the highway." Justine gestured behind her with her head. "Taking pictures for their directory."

That was the problem with being spontaneous. People didn't expect you and weren't around to take note of the grand gesture.

"Do you know when she'll be back?"

"Let's see." The blonde pulled up something on her monitor and studied it. "She has appointments until four, shooting all day. She'll stay to finish the paperwork and clean up. After that, she'll go straight home."

He'd chosen to go to her office instead

of to Roundville because, with her parents around, he didn't feel a tryst could be either romantic or impetuous. Now driving into Austin in a failing car and not finding the object of his journey seemed foolish.

"Oh," he said.

"Can I take a message?" She glanced at the roses. "I could put them in water so they'll be pretty when she comes in tomorrow."

"No, thank you." What explanation could he possibly give for showing up with flowers? He obviously wasn't a delivery boy. "I . . ." He stopped when he realized there really wasn't one.

"You must really like flowers," the receptionist tilted her head a little and winked.

"Oh, sure," he agreed as if he carried them around all the time. "Yes, I do." She winked again, which, he feared, showed an interest in him. Could this get any worse?

Of course.

He'd turned to leave when he heard a door in the back of the studio open.

"Justine?" Gussie called from another room. "One of the ring lights broke and I didn't take an extra. I've got to grab a couple and take off again."

"You have . . . ," Justine began.

Trapped. He was trapped. Maybe he could escape before Gussie knew he'd dropped in. Adam shook his head at Justine in an ineffective and ultimately unsuccessful effort to quiet her. He even held a finger to his lips. It didn't work and he looked like even more of an idiot.

"You have a visitor," Justine finished. "A man."

"What?"

Could he hide? As he looked around him, Adam realized that action would look stupid and be useless. Oh, he'd never been cool around women, but he couldn't remember ever feeling this inept, not even when he and April Gonzalez had locked braces during a seventh-grade party.

"Hi," Adam said when Gussie pulled a curtain aside and glanced into the reception area.

The glow of her smile nearly blinded him. That moment made the entire mortifying experience nearly worth it. Then the brilliance faded and she looked confused.

"Adam? Was I expecting you?" She

shook her head. "Did you have an appointment? If you did . . ."

"No, no. I thought I'd drop by. I was in Austin to . . ." He couldn't think of a reason. "And I thought I'd drop by."

"With flowers?"

He nodded and straightened his arm to thrust the roses toward her.

"How nice of you." She smiled as she accepted them. "They're lovely."

They stood looking at each other for a few awkward seconds before she said, "Well, I've got to get back to work. There are people waiting for me to take their pictures."

"I didn't realize you took church pictures," he said in an effort to dazzle her with his scintillating conversation skills.

"Oh, yes, as well as weddings, yearbook photos, quinceañeras, bar and bat mitzvahs, school pictures. All of those pay the bills to keep this place profitable."

"Well, then I'll be going." He waved and nearly ran out.

What a complete idiot he was.

❧

"Cute guy." Justine grinned at Gussie.

"Put these in water." Gussie handed the

flowers to Justine. "Please. I have to get back to the church."

She headed toward the back running nearly as quickly as Adam had, hoping to get out before Justine could ask anything. Not that her quick exit would make any difference; she'd have to return to her studio tomorrow and Justine would be here, still curious, still commenting and digging and asking questions.

"I think he has a crush on you," Justine shouted.

Gussie reached the back door before she realized Adam's appearance had flustered her so much that she hadn't picked up the lights. She opened a cabinet, grabbed a couple, and took off.

Once in her car and headed back toward the church, she allowed herself to ponder her ill-at-ease reaction to Adam's appearance and his rapid departure.

Why had Adam been there?

Oh, she knew. She didn't want to face the reason, but she knew. A man didn't stop by with roses unless he had a deep interest in a woman. The realization made her want to smile and scream in frustration. She didn't want him to care about her. She didn't want to care about him.

But those last two internal comments were a load of baloney because yes, she did, and yes, she already did. She couldn't force herself to believe she had no interest in Adam. She had to stop lying to herself.

After what Lennie had done to her in college, she'd never trusted a man again. But Adam . . . Adam seemed different. What she hated was she'd treated him rudely, as if she didn't appreciate his interest or the flowers. She did but had trouble, lots of trouble, reacting to a man normally.

Once she arrived at the church, she shoved the thoughts back and attempted to concentrate on taking photos. But she couldn't get rid of images of Adam holding the flowers and looking embarrassed and how guilty it made her feel.

In fact, as soon as she left the church, started her car, and pulled out of the parking lot, they came back in full force. What should she do? First, as usual, she refused to think about the unpleasantness and her failure to act like a normal person. Instead, she picked up her cell and called her mother to tell her she'd left Austin. But then, she found herself back at her office. It was after six so Justine had left long ago. She wouldn't have to try to explain to her about Adam, not today, at least.

She unlocked the door, turned on a light, and found the vase of flowers on the reception desk. She took the flowers from the vase and wrapped them in paper towels. After that, she carried them back to the car, headed west, and allowed herself to think about Adam. A sweet man. A kind man who took homeless children in. A minister. A safe man.

Oh, crap. Certainly she didn't find him attractive because he was non-threatening, did she? If so, those years of counseling had been a waste of effort and money. Besides, the exact moment the attraction had hit her, he'd been sweaty and intense and so masculine that the awareness of the chemistry had rocked her. The unexpected reaction had felt almost threatening but good, really good. Exciting. As if she were ready, finally, to trust a guy, to care for him as a woman cared about a man.

For a moment, she took her eyes off the road that she traveled so often she could probably turn the driving over to her little yellow Focus and take a nap. She glanced at the roses in the passenger seat. Yellow and orange and—how to describe that third color? Orange sherbet? Lovely, exactly the colors she would have chosen. Turning her eyes back to the highway, she rubbed her fingers across the soft, velvety surface of the petals, then picked up the bouquet to bury her nose in the blooms. The softness against her nose tickled.

How would she explain the flowers to her parents? If she told them they came from a man, her father would worry and her mother would be filled with hope. She didn't want to raise their hopes or expectations or encourage them to dream, but she refused to hide the flowers. Let them decide how to feel. She couldn't protect her parents from hope or trauma forever.

Had she been protecting them as well as herself? The thought had never—well, she'd never considered that before. Obviously, she needed to think this through because she was contemplating a thaw in her relationship with the male half of the world, or, at least, one man in the Texas Hill Country.

She sat in her car in the driveway for a

minute after she pulled off the road. As usual, her father's truck sat in front of the house. As long as she could remember, her father had a truck. Even though getting into it posed problems with his bad hips and knee, he refused to give it up. As long as she could remember, he'd never used the back of the truck to carry anything, so why had he always bought this type of vehicle? Because in Texas, a man drove a truck, and usually in the passing lane on the interstate.

Aware that her contemplation of her father's reasoning only put off the inevitable—a skill Gussie had perfected—she picked up the roses and her purse, got out, closed the car door, beeped it locked, and headed toward the house.

"Hello, darling." Her mother greeted her from the sofa where she was watching *Jeopardy!* and knitting. As many sweaters and scarves as she'd made for her daughter, they should have lived in the Arctic. Fortunately, now she'd started knitting tiny blankets for newborns at Seeton Hospital.

Her mother had always looked fragile. Now, with blue-white hair and ivory skin covered with a net of wrinkles, she looked deceptively sweet and frail but she had a will as strong . . . well, as strong as Gussie's.

"Hi, Mom." Gussie kissed her cheek.

"Hello, Gus," her father said as he entered the room. Gussie still struggled to accept the difference between the buff and hearty father of her childhood memories and this thin, stooped man.

"What do you have there? Where'd you get the flowers?" he asked.

Gussie could tell them that a client had given them to her, but she couldn't lie.

"A man gave them to me," she said. "Aren't they lovely?" She held the bouquet up.

"Oh." Her mother's eyes opened wide and her lips trembled. "A man?"

Her father dropped in a chair, so surprised, Gussie thought, that he couldn't stand up any longer, although it was probably that his bad hips bothered him. "A man?" His voice echoed the shock of someone who'd given up on his daughter's ever receiving flowers again from a man.

"Yes, a man."

"One of those elderly men who come up with their society wives to get their portraits taken?" her mother guessed. "They do adore you."

"Mother, those men are flirts but harmless. They'd never give me flowers. They're afraid of their wives."

"Could be that man who owns the office next door. You've always been nice to him," her father suggested. "Watched his store when he went out of town."

She knew what they were doing, her dear parents. To protect her, they were in as deep a state of denial as she was, and she'd allowed it for years. Time to stop.

"The flowers came from Adam Jordan, the minister of the church in Butternut Creek."

"Oh," her mother said. "A thank-you for all your work with the young people."

Gussie hadn't thought of that. Had she allowed her attraction to Adam to color her opinion here? Had the flowers been a mere gift of appreciation? No, probably not. After all, he'd delivered them himself when he could have ordered them from a florist in Austin. Also, he'd looked nervous, and the dozen roses in her favorite colors must have cost more than a young minister could really afford. A note would have said thank you.

"No, the flowers mean more than that."

Her parents turned in unison to study each other. Although they said nothing, they didn't have to. Their ability to communicate silently had always amazed her. In fact, she put that trait high on the mental list she'd labeled *What I'm Looking for in a Husband* back when she'd expected to find one.

Knowing the futility of interrupting the transfer of information between her parents, Gussie waited.

Finally, her mother, with visions of grandchildren dancing in her eyes, said, "Tell us more."

Her father, who looked far less pleased and much more protective of his daughter, said nothing.

"Not much to tell." Gussie struggled to think of words to explain. She'd tried to come up with something on the drive home but hadn't, and inspiration didn't strike now.

After a long pause, her father said, "What do they mean?" He glared at the flowers as if they were a solicitation for something he preferred not to consider.

"What do flowers usually mean, Henry?"

"Back when I was courting you, they meant the young man had an interest in the young woman."

"That's still what it means," Gussie said.

"How interested is he?" her father asked.

Gussie shrugged because she had no idea. More than she'd realized, obviously.

"Now, dear, let them work this out. Although"—she turned back toward Gussie, her face glowing—"I would love to have grandchildren."

For a moment, Gussie was almost angry with Adam. He'd made her mother look toward the future. She wished she could reach out and caress the lines of worry from her father's face and lower the level of hope that gleamed in her mother's eyes.

But wasn't hope good?

"I'm thirty-one, probably too old to conceive a baby. I read the other day . . ."

"I had you when I was thirty-eight. What a surprise you were to everyone."

Her father had been forty-two. Now they were seventy and seventy-four, so dear but not elderly, truly. The age she considered *elderly* had been pushed back every year as they grew older.

"Are you considering having children with this man?" her father demanded.

"But first, you'll get married, won't you?" her mother asked. "Nowadays, that doesn't seem to be the norm, but I hope you'd . . ."

What had she started? How had the discussion gotten away from her so quickly and irrevocably?

"Adam brought me flowers. I accepted them." She shook them a little to make a point. Not a good idea. A few petals flew into the air. "Right now, I'm not considering commitment for life, neither of us is." Both parents watched her and she had no idea what to do or say. How could she ease their fears when hers played havoc with her usual logic?

"Let me get a vase for these." Gussie started toward the kitchen. "I'll put them on the coffee table where we can all enjoy them."

"Wait a minute, missy."

When her father used that tone, she had no choice but to stop, turn, and listen. Well, she did have a choice, but ignoring him would hurt his feelings, make him feel like an old man with no purpose in his life.

Also, she needed to figure this out—her

feelings, Adam's motive, the entire situation. Maybe if she talked about it, if she attempted to explain, she'd figure out how she felt. For years she'd hidden her emotions deep inside, tamped them down firmly and ignored them. Perhaps it was time to feel again.

She sat down, primly and meekly, to answer their questions and, maybe, a few of her own.

"Adam brought me the flowers today at the studio," she said. "He came into town and dropped them off. I'm not sure exactly what they mean." Oh, that was weak.

"Gussie, are you saying that he traveled all the way from Butternut Creek to South Austin to bring you flowers?" her mother asked.

"He probably was making hospital visits."

"Do you think he picked these up from a member of his congregation recovering from surgery?" her father asked as sarcastically as he allowed himself to be.

"No, of course not." She closed her eyes and attempted to sort out her feelings again. How to explain what confused her? Finally she opened her eyes and said, "I met Adam in Marble Falls a few months ago, to discuss the retreat."

"You often do that, with several of the youth workers." Her mother cocked her head. "You mentioned Reverend Jordan. I didn't think this Adam was anything different or special."

"I didn't, either." Oh, she should not lie but couldn't explain this now, not when she felt so uncertain.

"But?" Her father prompted. "I take it he's unmarried."

"Of course."

She glanced at her parents. They watched her, not saying a word but waiting. "Then, when we were at the retreat, I felt a hint of . . ." Oh, she really didn't want to share her chemical reaction to Adam with her parents. "I felt a slight . . . um . . . attraction."

"Aah," her mother said.

Her father leaned forward but said nothing.

"You know I went to Butternut Creek for that meeting in—what? April?"

"Were you at camp together?" her father asked. The man never let anything get by him. "Did you find him attractive then?"

"We didn't have any time together. I . . ."

"Did you avoid him?" he asked.

"No, Dad. He had to leave for a funeral. We really didn't spend time together. We did not have a chance to swear undying love." She shut her mouth quickly. Her frustration had made her mouth off.

"Missy," her father warned.

"I'm sorry."

He nodded, so she continued. "Then, today, he walked into the studio with flowers. I don't know what this means or how he feels or how I feel."

Her parents glanced at each other and smiled.

"What did he say?" her father asked. "When he brought the flowers?"

"Not much. I had appointments and couldn't talk to him."

"So," he said, "this minister shoved the flowers toward you and ran off without a word of explanation?"

"Not exactly *shoved*, but, yes, he did run off before I could think of a thing to say."

"Have you called to thank him for the flowers?" Mother asked, always the one to reinforce rules of etiquette. "At least emailed him? Although I think a personal note is so much more courteous."

Her mother would see that sin of omission as a nearly unforgivable breech on Gussie's part.

"I haven't had a chance. I just got home, but you're right. I'll write." Her last words were said with determination, to make sure her parents understood this was the end of the grilling, that she'd shared as much information as she could at this moment.

They didn't catch on. "Tell us more about this Adam," her mother said.

"I don't know much more. He's a minister, not from Texas. He took in two homeless children."

"He did?" her mother said. "What a fine young man. He likes children?"

Knowing exactly where her mother's thoughts headed, Gussie stifled a groan and stood. "I'm going to put these in a vase before I prick my finger on a thorn."

The roses had been de-thorned, but her parents didn't need to know that. She had to get away. She'd shared a great deal with them but refused to confess to the tumble of emotion inside, the sudden yearning the flowers had brought, the feeling that both delighted and terrified her.

She wanted love more than anything in the world.

And less than anything.

❧

"Pops, what's that closed building in the back of the church? Bree says it's a gym. Why can't we play ball there?" Hector asked. Now that it was mid-June, the days had gotten much hotter. Adam couldn't blame Hector for wanting an indoor court.

"I've only been inside once," Adam said. "When I first got here. You want to check it out?" At Hector's nod, he added, "Grab a flashlight. We don't have any utilities on back there."

After he searched his junk drawer for the keys and Hector found a flashlight, they headed across the lawn of the parsonage and the church parking lot. He hadn't heard from Gussie for days. The tour would fill time and take his mind off that lack of communication.

"Jesse tells me they locked the place up because it had deteriorated to the point it wasn't safe and the church couldn't afford to fix it up." He turned the key in the padlock to remove the chain, then inserted another in the lock, turned it, and tugged at the door. It opened with a loud shriek.

The air inside rushed at them, thick and dank and dustfilled.

"Stinks in here."

"Mold and age," Adam agreed.

Light filtered through windows high on the walls of the building, enough to allow them to see the rough wood of the court.

"This is bad, Pops." Hector stood at the edge of the court and looked around. "But has possibilities." He pointed. "A score-board, bleachers."

"Do you know how much a new floor would cost?"

"How much?"

"I don't know, but a lot more than we can afford." They wandered around the court and toward the dressing rooms. "Jesse told me they applied for grants but those went to organizations in big cities with more of a crime problem. They also tried to get the community involved, but the initial investment was too much."

Hector shook his head. "This could be terrific. Everyone in town could use it. We could have events and stuff and charge to keep it up. Rent it out."

"I agree." They walked into the dressing rooms. Lockers stood open, the doors sagging. Rust stains showed in the drains of the showers and basins. "It's the initial cost. Not only the floor but new wiring and plumbing. It's a huge project."

"Yeah." Hector nodded. "But it would be cool to have a hoop we could use closer than the park and in the rain."

❦

That evening, Adam checked email, then sent a message to his parents and to his sister, a medical doctor who wandered through Africa caring for refugees.

When the you-have-a-message tone sounded, he clicked and checked the name of the sender. Gussie. Quickly, he opened and read the email. "Thank you for the flowers. They are lovely." Nothing more. A curt but polite thank-you note that didn't show a bit of encouragement. Hard to convince himself—no, impossible!—that the note was written by a woman who adored him or felt even an iota of attraction and wanted to see him again.

Well, he'd tried. He'd been active and acted spontaneously but her reaction showed she thought of him as a friend who, oddly, brought her flowers. A nice, geeky guy who dropped into her studio without an appointment only to say hi. With roses.

What had he expected from her? A proposal? A declaration of eternal love? Perhaps even a Scarlett O'Hara, "Oh, fiddle-dee-dee, Reverend Jordan" flirtatiousness?

That sounded stupid even in his own brain.

She probably didn't understand why he'd brought her flowers any more than he did. It had seemed like a good idea before he arrived in Austin, but when he remembered her expression of amazement, he still cringed.

But first she'd smiled.

He probably would have sat and stared at the email for a few more minutes and thought of dozens of depressing reasons she'd never be interested in him.

Fortunately, Hector and Bobby clattered in. Their arrival effectively interrupted his moment of wallowing in the depths of unrequited love.

"How 'bout some hoops, Pops?"

As he'd always done, Adam'd figure out life after a hard game of roundball cleared his mind and exhausted his body.

Chapter Nine

Ouida lay in the hospital bed in the middle of the living room and savored the quiet. When she'd arrived a couple of days ago, she carefully supervised the position of the bed. From there, she could look straight ahead, through the clear square in the stained-glass window of the front door and out to the porch and a slice of the street. If she turned to her left, she viewed the side yard toward the parsonage.

Nearly three weeks after her fall, she'd recovered a little. The pain had lessened and her hand had healed well. She did exercises with a ball over and over to strengthen it. Her shoulder sling would come off in a few weeks. PT helped with pain and range of motion. As she gained a little use of that arm, she no longer felt quite as much like a turtle on its back, but she still couldn't put much weight on it. Fortunately, the broken leg turned out to be less restrictive than the doctors had first thought. It had healed enough that she'd be able to get rid of the cast shortly. Still, a long road to recovery lay ahead.

Today the girls had gone to day care. George had gone into Austin for a few hours. She sighed. The poor man was so uncomfortable, it was a good thing for him to get away from here and back to his beloved numbers. He'd left her with the remote, a phone, several books, and a tall glass of ice water. She hoped she didn't need to go to the bathroom until the nurse showed up in an hour.

Peace. It had been so long since she'd had peace. George wasn't wandering around the house looking confused and asking her every five minutes if she was okay and if she needed anything and did she know where his blue shirt or the ketchup was and did she need anything?

The girls weren't laughing or running up and down the staircase or making noise of any kind.

Peace.

It bored her silly.

Scattered around the living room were a few of the girls' toys. She loved to have them playing in here. Last night they'd left sticky ice cream bowls on the coffee table. Wonder of all wonders, George had picked them up, carried them to the kitchen, and placed them in the dishwasher without complaint. She'd had to point them out to him, but he did the rest on his own.

"Hey, neighbor," Adam shouted from the front door. "Decent?"

Not that she had any modesty left after her stay in the hospital and her dependency on everyone around. But, for Adam, she felt around to make sure the sheet was tucked in. "Door's open. Come on in." As if anyone locked their doors in Butternut Creek.

"Can I get you anything?" He wandered in.

Adam was the nicest person. Although she'd never been inside the Christian Church except for the Christmas pageant in which the girls had dressed as angels, he took good care of the Kowalski family. If she had even an iota of the spirituality gene, she'd join the church in no time, but she didn't and the whole thing seemed a waste of time. Oh, the girls loved Sunday school and went every week. They brought home crafts she displayed on the bookcase and pages colored in odd shades that showed Abraham as purple or Mary as yellow because, Carol said, most of the crayons were broken or missing. She'd have to donate several boxes, once she could get to the dollar store.

"I'm fine. Sit down and keep me company. Good to see you."

Adam tossed a stuffed animal off the sofa before he settled in. "How's it going?"

"I hate being laid up. I never get sick and I'm not used to people taking care of me. It's driving me crazy."

"How's George handling everything?"

"Okay." She shrugged. "It's not easy for him. He's trying so hard to help. He's doing the laundry and uses so much detergent that the sheets crackle when I turn over, but I'm not going to tell him that. I'm just glad he does the wash."

She really didn't want to tell him about the problems George was having in adjusting, so before he could ask more she said, "Carol and Gretchen love playing in your yard. Thanks for letting them use your swing set."

"I'm not using it much myself," he answered. "Janey loves playing with your girls."

"I've heard . . ." She stopped to consider her words but decided to go ahead. What could he do to a woman in traction? And she wanted to know. "I hear you have a girlfriend."

If there had been any doubt in her mind about the gossip, his reaction changed that. He straightened, blinked, and gulped before attempting to lounge back comfortably.

"Girlfriend?"

She didn't say anything.

"They may be talking about Gussie Milton. She's from Roundville. We know each other through the youth groups."

"Adam, I promise I won't tell the Widows. I know how they are. I've heard stories about their tactics. Poor Sam was hounded until he and Willow got together."

She lifted her free hand and pretended to zip her lips. "You can tell me anything. My lips are sealed."

He grinned. "Nothing to report. I tried to date her."

"Tried? You gave up?"

He shrugged.

"I was hoping for a wedding in the future," Ouida said.

"Oh, sure."

"Is she skittish or are you?" She struggled to sit up a little straighter and kept her eyes on his face.

He raised an eyebrow. "Do I have a sign on my forehead that says, MISERABLE AND ALONE. PLEASE HELP THIS POOR LOSER?"

"Guess that means none of my business? Okay, I'll change the subject because I have a favor to ask."

He looked wary.

"Don't worry. It's easy. Please take George for an evening. He's driving me crazy and I'm driving him nuts. He needs some man time. He also probably needs to talk to you about what's happening, about this change in our lives."

"I could do that. When?"

"What night might be convenient? The

sooner the better." She attempted to get comfortable but that darned cast and the traction didn't allow it. "Tonight?"

"I'll be home."

"And one more favor."

Again Adam looked worried, so she quickly explained. "Would you pull me up on the bed? I keep slipping down."

❦

That evening Adam wasn't surprised to see George when he opened the front door of the parsonage. "Come on in," he said and led his neighbor back to the television/living/dining-on-TV-trays room.

With his well-tailored khakis, George wore flip-flops and a UT T-shirt. Adam hadn't thought his neighbor possessed flipflops or a T-shirt. Even dressed in what passed as casual for George, his neighbor didn't look a bit comfortable. Warily he studied the hall and the room. Looking for religious symbols or holy relics?

"Ouida make you come?" Adam asked.

"Not exactly," George said. "She did suggest it. Strongly." He glanced at his bare toes. "She also told me to wear these shoes. She said when guys get together to watch a game, they don't wear wing tips."

She wasn't wrong. Sam and the boys came over pretty regularly to watch sports, and he'd never seen them wear wing tips. George shook his head. "I don't know *how* she knows what guys wear to get together to watch sports, but this is what she told me they wear."

Because Adam didn't know if he should laugh or not, if George was joking or only repeating Ouida's advice, he said, "Probably from a beer commercial on television." He waved toward a chair. "Grab a comfortable place to sit. Would you like something to drink? A Coke or tea?"

"No, no." George took the recliner but sat straight up in it.

Adam settled on the sofa. He should give his neighbor time to relax and to start the conversation on his own but didn't feel optimistic that would happen. The only conversations they'd shared had been the night at the hospital when Ouida fell and a few chats while George indulged in his one leisure-time activity Adam was aware of: helping Ouida garden.

"So, how're things going?" Adam asked.

George glanced at Adam. "Terrific," he said with a hint of sarcasm in his voice.

The tone made him feel his neighbor did have a sense of humor.

Then George leaned back and sighed. "I'm so out of my depth with this whole thing, I don't know what to do. Ouida's the one who makes sure everything at home runs precisely. I can't juggle things like work and family and cooking. Thank goodness the church ladies bring food."

"You do know that's going to stop in a few days."

George looked at him, panic in his eyes. "What?"

"The meals are to tide you over during the roughest of times."

"Oh." George considered that. "I can't cook."

"Can you use a microwave? They make great frozen foods nowadays."

They watched the pre-game show on television for a minute or two before George said, "You know I don't like to share, right? I'm not a touchy-feely kind of man."

Adam nodded.

"But this worries me. The doctors have said they don't know how well the leg will heal, if she'll have problems or a disability.

None of them can guarantee she'll walk without a cane or a walker."

Adam considered saying that there were no guarantees in life but bet George wouldn't be comforted by a cliché. "No, they can't, but she's getting great care, from home health and from you."

George scrutinized him with cold eyes. Obviously, Adam had failed as a man, a minister, and a neighbor.

"I don't know what I can say, George. No one knows at this moment, and it seems to me you're a man who likes certainty." He searched for words. "But all of us are here to help—your neighbors, the church, all of us. And Ouida, she's a fighter. You know that. She's strong."

George clenched his fists and swallowed quickly. Adam bet that was a deep show of emotion for his neighbor. If there was anything Adam knew at this moment, it was that he couldn't allow George to break down. Oh, it would be cathartic and George probably needed to share, but he'd be embarrassed if Adam had witnessed that, might even cut off all contact.

"Do you like baseball?" Adam said in a hearty, booming, manly voice.

"Yes." George nodded and blinked. "I graduated from UT. I'm a big Texas fan, any sport. With work, I don't have a chance to watch it much."

Adam decided his guest needed a break and a little privacy. "Let me get drinks and chips. Do you want pop?"

"You have red?"

"Sure." He tossed George the remote.

By the time Adam returned, put the chips and pop on the coffee table, the Rangers game had started. After a few minutes, George said, "I don't know how to take care of children."

Adam started to say, *What worries you about that?* before quickly pulling the words back. Sounded too much like a preacher, like a counseling session. "Why's that?"

"Ouida does that." George took a handful of chips and munched. "I'm not good with kids." He glanced at Adam. "I work with numbers. I'm uncomfortable and ineffectual around illogical people."

"Illogical pretty much defines children. Especially young ones, like Gretchen."

George nodded. "They're at day care during the day."

"They need you around."

"Sure."

A few minutes later, George said, "I'll have to work at home more."

"Probably."

"I like things neat."

Adam glanced at the precise cut of George's hair, the way even his T-shirt looked as if it had been freshly starched and ironed, and the neat crease of his slacks. "Kids aren't neat."

"I can handle that." He watched a double play end the third inning before adding, "Maybe."

A little less confidence than Adam had hoped for. He took a handful of chips and waited.

"I'm not good with injured or sick people, either," George said as the color commentator babbled on about the first baseman. "That's the hardest part." He shook his head.

"That's tough."

After the fourth inning, George stood. "Guess I'll go home. Thanks for the food."

Adam wasn't sure if what he'd said or left unsaid was right or wrong or the least bit helpful but felt communication was open. Maybe they'd even had a few moments of male bonding, but George was hard to read.

❧

When George came home the next day, the girls had settled on the bed with Ouida. "Come on in," she said. "The girls wanted me to tell them a story."

"Be careful with your mother's leg," he warned.

"Yes, Daddy," the girls said, scooting back a fraction of an inch.

"They're fine. The girls were very careful." Ouida looked down at the girls with a smile. It felt so good to be home with them cuddled around her.

"Mommy, tell us the story about your dog. You know, the deaf one," Carol said.

"Mommy, did you have a deaf dog?" Gretchen's eyes got round with wonder as if she hadn't heard the story dozens of times.

"Yes, sweetheart. Her name was Daffy. Short for Daffodil. She was a blond cocker spaniel with big floppy ears."

"Like this?" Carol put her hands up to her ears.

"Yes, big floppy ears, but she got an infection inside her ears."

"An 'fection?" Gretchen asked. "Did it hurt?"

"Very much. Daffy loved her people but she hurt so much when they petted her that she stayed away."

"Oooh," the girls said together.

She glanced at George and smiled. He leaned against the wall and continued to watch.

"Sweetheart," she said. "Why don't you sit on the chair next to the bed."

He shook his head. "I'm fine here."

She gave up and returned to the story. "Daffy's doctor had to clean out all the bad stuff in her ears as well as the parts of the ear she heard with. When the doctor took off Daffy's bandages, she couldn't hear."

"Oooh," the girls repeated.

"Poor puppy," Gretchen said.

"But Daffy didn't mind. She still danced and helped me load the dishwasher if I dropped a few leftovers for her. She came for dinner and played with the other dogs." She paused to allow her daughters to react.

"And then what?" Carol said.

She could see George smile. He'd heard this story and knew what would come next.

He knew the girls did, too, but he seemed to be enjoying this family time.

"One day, I had to go to the bathroom really bad," Ouida said.

The girls covered their mouths with their hands and giggled.

"I went in the bathroom and . . . um . . . sat down but didn't turn on the light because I was in such a hurry."

Gretchen laughed. "Then what, Mommy?"

"I heard tapping on the wood floor in the hall. Daffy was running back and forth, looking for me. She was my dog, you know. She became very worried when she couldn't find me."

"What did she do?" Carol pushed herself closer to her mother.

Using her fingers, Ouida explained. "She ran up and down the hall, frantic. I shouted, 'I'm in here,' but she couldn't hear me."

"'Cause she was deaf," Carol said.

"'Cause of the 'fection," Gretchen added.

"I yelled again, but she kept running back and forth. I could hear her searching because her nails tapped on the hardwood floor. Finally, when she passed the bathroom door, I picked up a roll of toilet paper and threw it at her. Not hard. I didn't want to hurt her, just to get her attention so she could find me. The roll missed her by a few inches but she stopped in the hall and looked all around her." Ouida acted that action out and the girls joined her. "And looked confused. I know she was thinking, *Why is someone throwing things at me?*"

"Did she find you?" Carol asked, knowing well the end of the story.

"No, I finished my business and went out to the hall. She was so happy to see me, she danced." She hugged the girls. "After that, I always turned on the bathroom light so she could find me."

George shoved away from the wall and took a few steps toward them.

"Doesn't Mommy tell wonderful stories?" Carol said.

The girls leaped from the bed and put their arms around his legs and squeezed.

"Mama tells wonderful stories," he said as he knelt to hold both girls.

❦

The flowers had finally died. When she first received them, Gussie'd carefully removed any petals that had turned dark and tugged off wilted leaves.

Now the few remaining leaves and petals were crispy. Holding on to them seemed maudlin. She should toss them. Instead she wrapped them in a towel to prevent further disintegration and put them on the shelf in the closet behind her hiking boots.

She'd behaved like a jerk. Because Adam's unexpected visit and the roses had startled her so much and she'd had to explain the flowers to her parents—well, all in all, she'd behaved rudely. As usual, she'd closed herself off. Probably acted almost catatonic when he'd handed her the bouquet, then she'd rushed out as if he had threatened her, which, of course, his very presence did. On top of that, she'd sent that abrupt email and pretended it took care of everything.

Aah, yes, her nemesis, that closing herself off, not responding, hoping that whatever intruded into her safe place would go away if she ignored it. Her normal operating procedure. In times of stress, she isolated herself, abandoned logic, and navigated on hysteria.

Well, she'd ignored Adam to shield herself from the situation for two weeks and still hadn't forgotten. She hadn't heard from Adam since her terse, "Thank you." Why would she? She'd hardly encouraged him to keep in touch.

Bet he wouldn't bring her flowers again anytime soon.

It would only be polite for her to write him a nice thank-you. He'd made an effort to visit her and how had she reacted?

Yes, she'd write him another, more cordial thank-you note. Not that she'd encourage him to answer because she wasn't looking for anything from him.

When had she become such a terrible liar—and to herself?

She turned toward her laptop and composed another short note, a pleasant one. An apology as well as a much nicer thank-you. After reading and editing it several times, she decided it would serve her purpose: Be polite, show interest, don't push. She paused before hitting send. Should she tell him she'd like to hear from him? Ask him how things were in Butternut Creek?

"Gussie." Her mother tapped on her open door. "Your father and I are going to bed now."

"Good night," Gussie replied as she hit SEND.

"Are you going to stay up much longer? You need your sleep."

"Only a few minutes," Gussie said.

Was this any life for a thirty-one-year-old woman? Being told by her mother that she should go to bed? As a kid, Gussie turned off her light when her mother told her to, then hid beneath the covers, read with a flashlight. But now . . .

She sighed. She still lived in her parents' home and habits were hard to break. Not that she regretted her decision to stay. She loved her parents and had chosen this life.

No reason not to get ready for bed. She had to get up by six, only eight hours away, and she liked to read for an hour before turning out the light. As she slipped into bed, Gussie took one more look toward the closet where she'd hidden—no, saved—the flowers. Not that she could see them from here.

It seemed like a metaphor for her life: hidden in a closet, nice and safe and isolated at the very time she yearned for romance, for another person in her life, just more, more of life.

Could she change? Live another way? Accept?

Could she allow herself to find another life, a different one?

Could she stop hiding?

❦

Independence Day was a huge celebration that would take place around the courthouse square, a true small-town commemoration. The high school band would play in the pavilion and, because the fire ban had been lifted, a brilliant ten-minute display of fireworks would follow.

Toting lawn chairs, Hector, Bree, Janey, and Adam stopped by the Kowalskis' at eight to take the girls to the show.

"They slept all afternoon so they should be fine staying up so late," George said after he hugged his daughters. "This is Gretchen's first fireworks display. She was too young to take last year."

"Just a minute," Ouida said before they could leave. "The mosquitoes and the no-see-ums will be all over tonight, so give me your arm." She sprayed an oily but fragrant substance on Adam's arms. "Now rub that on your face and spray it on your legs."

"What is that?" Adam rubbed his arms, which covered his hands in the same substance.

"Skin lotion, but also the best thing ever for keeping the bugs away."

Must be a Southern thing, Adam decided.

Once Ouida had sprayed everyone's arms and George had covered their legs, the group oozed from the house on the protective oiliness covering their visible skin.

"Sure hope this stuff works," Hector said, batting his hands at the clouds of biting flying creatures ahead of them.

It seemed to. By the time they arrived at the park and found a place for their chairs, the bugs left them alone. However, the stuff also made the kids so slippery that when Bree and Adam attempted to hold their hands to cross the street, they slid away.

As the sun dropped, the temperature fell to a comfortable ninety degrees.

The mayor welcomed the crowd, the band played patriotic songs, and everyone joined in singing. Janey played with Carol and Gretchen to keep them entertained.

Then the fireworks started. Brilliant flashes filled the sky and explosions went off. Carol looked up at the sky, enthralled, but Gretchen leaped into the air at the sounds. In only seconds she'd forced her body under Bree's chair, sobbing. "They're shooting at us," Gretchen shouted. "They're shooting at me."

They left immediately and watched the display as they walked home, backward, Hector carrying Gretchen. In the safety of Hector's arms, she settled down the farther they got from the noise.

When they'd returned the girls to their home and Bree had helped George wash them off and put them to bed, Bree and Hector sat on the porch swing while Adam sat inside to work on his very sketchy sermon.

Saturday, they went to a church picnic at Jesse's farm. Late that night, after finishing what might be, with the help of the Holy Spirit, an acceptable sermon, Adam checked his email. Because he hadn't checked for a few days, he had dozens of new messages.

He scrolled through, deleted spam, and read a short note from his sister before he saw a message from Gussie.

Why had she written?

Didn't she realize he had gotten her message: *Not interested*? Or did she believe he needed to read it again, over and over because he was so thickheaded? The subject line said, "Hello." Great. That helped a lot, told him exactly what the message contained. Did she plan to stomp on his ego again?

He didn't want to open it. Really did not. He'd thought he'd recovered from the rejection over the past few weeks and from the embarrassment of taking flowers to a woman obviously astounded by his appearance and not interested in him. Guess not. But it could be about the area youth program. He couldn't ignore that. He placed the cursor on the message.

Women really messed with a guy's brain. Did they attend classes for that or did they learn it at their mother's knee? Secrets passed down through matriarchs?

And yet, here he sat, gazing at the list of emails and not opening any more of them, especially not the one with the cheery

"Hello." Realizing the stupidity of doing nothing, he clicked on it.

"Sorry about the quick thank-you email I sent earlier. I really did like the flowers. They were on my desk for a week. You surprised me and I didn't react well. I'm sorry. Again, thank you."

What in the world did that mean? Did she want to hear from him?

Answering wouldn't hurt. He typed a short, friendly response that ended with, "I'd love to hear from you." No, that sounded desperate and needy and too emotional. He deleted the words, wrote, "Hope to hear from you soon," and sent it.

❧

Another middle-of-the-night call. Drat.

Adam fumbled for the phone but before he could say a word, a woman said, "Meet me at the diner for breakfast."

He rubbed his eyes and attempted to focus on the alarm clock but they kept closing on him. Only a sliver of light filtered through the blinds. Guess it was what Texans called "dark thirty."

"Who is this?" he mumbled.

"It's Mattie."

"Oh." He paused in an effort to wrap his

sleepy brain around the information. "What time is it?"

"Five fifteen."

"Why in the world are you calling this early?" he muttered around a yawn. For a moment he fell back to sleep, but he woke up when Mattie nearly shouted through the receiver.

"I need to talk to you."

"Now? Why?" Fully awake, he sat up in bed. "What happened? Did the church burn down?" Must have been some terrible emergency, a disaster, to warrant such an early call.

"No, I want to talk to you. Meet me at the diner at six."

"Are you dying?" he asked stupidly, but no other explanation had leaped into his groggy brain.

"Of course not. Meet me. I'll explain."

"Can't," he said. "I've got to get the kids going." Not true. Hector could handle that, had done it often before, but Adam liked to give the kids a heads-up, drink a cup of coffee while Hector fixed breakfast. Of course, in the summer, that didn't happen until nine thirty, but that excuse worked. He did not want to get up now. "How 'bout eight?"

"If you want everyone in town to listen in, fine."

"Everyone in town will be listening in or will hear it from a friend at whatever time we meet."

She sighed. "I know."

"Do you want to wear a disguise? Have a secret password?"

"You're really weird this early in the morning."

"My social skills aren't at their best before the sun rises."

She laughed. "Okay. See you at eight."

❦

Coffeepot in hand, Birdie gave the breakfast crowd a quick once-over. Looked fine. Everyone was eating or chatting or sipping coffee.

"Here you go, Charley." She poured a cup for Charley Parsons, the nice town plumber who was a hundred or more pounds overweight. When he sat at her table, she made him eat those fake eggs and didn't allow him to use butter on his pancakes. Actually, she never brought him pancakes, just whole-grain toast with margarine. That's why he always chose to sit at Dolores's table, but Birdie filled his cup anyway. She also picked up the sugar shaker and moved it to another table.

She looked around. No one held up an empty cup.

Except for Farley Masterson. Birdie wanted to completely ignore him but he was a customer and her boss would throw a conniption if she didn't serve every customer with a smile. Besides, he was at one of her tables and she needed the tips, both from Farley and from the person who took his place. If filling his cup would hurry old Farley along, she'd do it.

"Hey, good lookin'." He winked and held his cup up.

Old fool. Did he think she didn't know she looked like a—what had Mercedes called her?—a dried-up piece of beef jerky?

"How are you this morning?" Birdie asked in her brightest, most welcoming voice.

Obviously, Farley didn't recognize how pleasant she was behaving, because he said, "Sounds like you've had a tough morning."

She smiled.

"Dentures hurt?" he asked.

Old coot. He didn't have the slightest

idea how to court a woman. "I have all my own teeth, thank you."

He tilted his head, puzzled. "I was being friendly."

"If you have to explain you're trying to be friendly, you might should work on that more."

He winked.

Birdie was stunned. "Are you flirting?"

If he weren't a customer, she'd pour the entire pot of coffee over him. It wasn't hot enough to burn him, not badly.

Fortunately, he stopped talking and looked behind her. "Isn't that your minister by the door?"

She turned to see Adam standing right next to Reverend Patillo. Didn't that beat all? Had they come together? How long had they been standing there?

What was wrong with her? She hadn't noticed their entrance and they had to have been waiting in line for a few minutes. Been too wrapped up in Farley Masterson and his antics and insults.

Of course, the arrival of the two ministers wasn't all that big a thing. They were friends. Often stopped by for breakfast or coffee and a piece of pie, sometimes lunch.

As much as she and Mercedes had attempted to match the two up when Adam first arrived in Butternut Creek, it had never taken. So what was he doing here with the Presbyterian minister? Trying to destroy their latest schemes?

They'd come up with a great backup plan for the preacher and now these two showed up together? Birdie wanted to tell Reverend Patillo, *You had your chance. We have someone else in mind for him.* She didn't of course. Childish. And if Gussie didn't work out, the woman minister might go back on the short list, the very short list with only one name on it.

"Birdie?" Farley said. "Coffee."

Where was her brain? She'd never served him. She carefully poured a cup and walked away, without a smile because the man couldn't recognize good, friendly service if she slapped him in the face with it.

She couldn't take her eyes off the two preachers. Actually, the two of them showing up counted as neither a good thing nor a bad thing. The entire matchmaking venture had gotten out of hand. Twenty years ago, maybe even fifteen, she'd have had the preacher married months ago. Now, with her granddaughters and that shoulder and having to train her young minister and work, she'd given up on the endeavor almost entirely.

But if, after all they'd attempted with the preacher, she did stop matchmaking, Mercedes would get after her, would make Birdie feel like a quitter. If the preacher took up with Reverend Patillo, maybe they'd get married and have children to fill up the parsonage and the Sunday school classes.

But if they *did* get married, they might fill up the Presbyterian manse instead of the parsonage, which would destroy any gain except possibly in the preacher's happiness. Not to downplay the importance of the preacher's happiness, but those children were really important to the Christian Church. The Widows were counting on at least four or five kids. The preacher owed them children to fill the parsonage and the nursery, to expand the Sunday school classes, to take part in the Christmas pageant and, when they grew up, lead the youth group.

Of course, as a compromise, the two

ministers might split their children between churches, the girls becoming Presbyterians whereas the boys attended the Christian Church. But what if all those children became Calvinists and went to their mother's church to swell that church's nursery, classrooms, and youth group?

Maybe she and the other matchmakers hadn't completely thought out that first plan, the one with Reverend Patillo.

"Miss Birdie?" Adam said as they reached the front of the line.

Birdie smiled at him. She knew she had a nice smile. She knew it didn't look like her dentures bothered her, for heaven's sake, despite what Farley Masterson had said. The old coot was dumber than a red brick.

And yet he seemed interested in her. Mind boggling.

"Follow me," she said, as if the preacher dared not to. When they settled in the corner booth, she said, "I'm not going to give you menus. Reverend Patillo, I know what you want." She studied Adam for a second or two. "Looks like you've put on some weight but not nearly enough. I'll bring you a nice breakfast."

"Only scrambled eggs and biscuits," he said. "No grits."

As usual, she paid no attention to his words. She turned over the cups and poured them coffee before she headed toward the kitchen to place the orders.

As tables cleared, she cleaned them and watched the two ministers. Oh, Reverend Patillo was nice. Her congregation liked her, but Birdie preferred Gussie Milton. Birdie could imagine Gussie's personality filling the parsonage and the church, her enthusiasm lifting the congregation, and her voice leading the choir. Maybe she should sabotage this rendezvous. But how could she without jeopardizing her job and tips?

The longer she watched, the less necessary sabotage seemed. Not all was well with the ministers. Reverend Patillo leaned forward. As she spoke, she glowered and poked the table with her index finger, over and over. Then Adam gave Reverend Patillo the look Birdie thought he reserved only for her, the one that said, *I'm fed up with this but I'm too polite to insult you.*

With Birdie, Adam would then change the subject or look grim and refuse to be forced in the direction he didn't want to go. She respected him for that. Not that she'd ever tell him. Not that she'd allow herself to be drawn off the topic, either, but she admired his efforts.

As the preacher stood, Birdie thought the discussion was over. But no. Reverend Patillo started to cry. Before Birdie could figure out the problem, another customer called for coffee. Doggone customers. Always interrupting.

❦

As much as he enjoyed the sausages and bacon and eggs and hash browns and the omelet and biscuit and all the food he'd eat now and the rest that he'd carry home with him, Adam still had no idea why Mattie had ordered him to show up.

She'd let him know when she felt the time was right, but, for now, she focused all her attention on digging out every section of her grapefruit.

He studied the grits Miss Birdie had delivered and wondered how in the world anyone liked them. Though he'd grown up in Kentucky, where grits formed the core of breakfast, to him they tasted like ground-up Styrofoam. Even covered in butter or margarine, the way Southerners preferred, they were inedible. In Texas, people used hot sauce on everything, but it didn't change the texture. Mixing them with cheese felt like a sad waste of a good dairy product. Nothing could disguise the gritty dish, so he shoved it aside and hoped they wouldn't show up in the carry-home boxes Miss Birdie would put together for him.

When Mattie finished her grapefruit, she took a couple of gulps of coffee.

"So . . ." She paused and lifted her eyes to his face. "How are things going?"

"Fine." Inside he smiled. He knew she wanted him to ask her why they were here, wanted him to force her to explain. Why make it easy for her? She'd awakened him early this morning. He refused to give her an easy out. Besides, as nervous as she was, he guessed he wouldn't want to do whatever she had in mind.

For that reason, he picked up a slice of bacon and began to eat it, nibbling off a piece and savoring the crisp texture and the deliciousness. "This is really good," he said before taking another bite.

"I need your help." Mattie slapped his hand as he reached for a second piece.

"Oh? And you think hitting me will influence me in your favor?"

"I need a date."

He raised an eyebrow.

"For a wedding. You're it."

She sounded desperate, but he didn't want to go to a wedding and he wasn't going to agree, not before she'd explained everything and begged. Maybe not even then.

"A friend of mine's getting married, to a friend of Ron's, my ex." She tapped her fingers against the coffee cup. "I have to go. Ron's best man. He'll probably bring a date. I don't want to go alone and look pitiful."

He nodded. He understood what she was saying but refused to give in so soon. Besides, the potatoes really tasted great, too. He picked up another forkful.

"Adam, I need you to go with me."

He chewed and swallowed and considered. "I don't want to go. I don't like weddings and would never go to one if I didn't have to perform them."

"Please."

"I repeat: I don't want to go. Besides, I

have enough problems with the Widows. If you and I actually go out . . ."

"It's not a date, not really."

"You said it was. They'll think it is." With a slight nod, he attempted to gesture surreptitiously toward Miss Birdie. "They'll never leave us alone."

"I don't care. I'm frantic. I've asked every other man I know but none can go. You're it."

"I'm not your first choice? That hurts, even if I don't want to go."

"You weren't even my sixth choice because I knew how hard you'd make this."

He put his fork down. "You thought I'd make this hard?" The statement stung. "I thought I was a cooperative person, easy to get along with."

"But you *are* making this difficult."

Yes, he was. He didn't want to go. He didn't want to make the effort of putting on his only suit—coincidentally called his marrying-and-burying suit—and picking out one of his few good church ties. He bet Mattie'd expect him to get a haircut and he'd have to shine his good shoes. On top of that, he knew, and she did, too,

they'd face repercussions here in town because there was no way they could sneak
out unless they met in an isolated field
and got in Mattie's car like spies.

"My car won't drive that far. I don't
trust it."

"We'll take mine." She glared, ready to
shoot down every excuse.

"See, that's the problem. Everyone will
know. They'll recognize me in your car."

"You are such a wimp." She picked up
her toast and nibbled an edge.

"Probably not the best plan, to insult the
man you're asking a favor of. Besides, I
have no idea how to act like a devoted
boyfriend. I'm not a good actor."

"I don't care," she nearly shouted.

"Shh. Whisper."

"Why?" she whispered back. "Have you
looked around? I bet everyone in town has
squeezed into the place."

He studied the crowd. "Cell phones
must be ringing all over Butternut Creek."
What the heck, the other diners had heard
most of the argument so keeping their
voices down now, when the argument had
pretty much finished in his opinion, didn't
make a great deal of sense.

Obviously, Mattie thought it did matter. She glared and poked the table with her index finger in time with her whispered words. "I need a date for a wedding and you are it."

"Do I have a sign on my forehead that says, TAKE ADVANTAGE OF MY GOOD NATURE?" he asked. "Because you sound exactly like Miss Birdie now. I don't respond well to demands." He slid across the seat and stood.

"I'm sorry." Tears gathered in her eyes.

Oh, crap. He sat down.

"I'm really desperate. I need you to be a friend." She swallowed hard and picked up a napkin to wipe her eyes. "We can do hospital visits while we're in town. I'll buy you dinner, whatever you want, but I absolutely cannot go to the wedding alone."

"Don't go."

"Not an option. If I don't show, Ron will know I don't have a date. Besides, the bride asked me to serve at the reception."

He glanced down at the last of the hash browns, but he'd lost his appetite. All this stress. "Okay," he said. "I'll go. When is it?"

She held out her arms, for a hug, he

feared. Adam held up both hands, palms forward. "Stop. All the gossips in town are here. Imagine the talk if you and I were to touch in public."

She sat back. "But thank you. It's a week from Saturday. I appreciate this and I owe you."

He nodded. "I'll collect someday, but you have to promise not to tell anyone," he warned. "The Widows will figure out we're going into Austin together soon enough, but I refuse to give up the information too soon. Make them work for it."

Then the horrible thought hit him. Gussie photographed weddings. Certainly a loving God wouldn't allow her to be taking pictures at a wedding he attended with Mattie on what was really not a date.

❧

"You had a date with Reverend Patillo?" Miss Birdie asked him.

Adam had known this would happen. Hadn't he warned Mattie? No one could hide anything in a small town. What had surprised him was that the Widows hadn't descended on him en masse hours earlier.

The wedding the previous afternoon

had been uneventful. Mattie'd navigated the crowd well, avoiding her former boyfriend while, at the same time, somehow flaunting the fact she had an escort and had not withered away from loneliness, thank you, a talent Adam could only recognize and admire. After the ceremony she greeted the happy couple, served a few cups of punch and several slices of cake. Before Adam had a chance to pick up a plate for himself, she dragged him out of the church.

They made a couple of hospital calls, grabbed dinner at a family restaurant, then headed back to Butternut Creek.

The picking-up and letting-off part hadn't gone as well. Mercedes had been watering flowers in front of the church when Mattie picked him up and had stood to watch the entire event, from Mattie's beep on the horn to his running down the steps in what he knew Mercedes would recognize as his only suit. When he got into the car and Mattie took off, Adam had turned to watch Mercedes, who studied them.

Miss Birdie heard immediately. No question. Everyone else in town knew within the hour, but everyone else in town didn't worry him. The pillar did.

"It wasn't a date," Adam explained.

He'd retreated to his office, after church, intending to check messages and call the shut-ins about taking them communion. Frowning Widows had intercepted him. Even Blossom, a woman he hadn't realized knew how to frown, scowled at him.

"Not a date? Then what would you call it?" Winnie demanded.

"A tryst? A rendezvous?" Mercedes asked. "An assignation?"

"Oh, don't show off your vocabulary," Miss Birdie said.

"We're not talking about me, Bird." She turned her glower toward her friend. "This is about the preacher stepping out on Gussie Milton."

"We worked so hard to get the two of you together." The pillar focused on Adam again, mournfully.

No, actually, they hadn't done much more than embarrass the two of them deeply, but this was not the moment to bring that up, not when all four seemed so upset by his defection, by his treachery.

"We-e-ell?" Blossom asked, injecting a note of wounded dismay.

"Reverend Patillo asked me to escort her to a wedding of friends, a favor for a fellow member of the clergy. That's all."

He made a move toward the door to the parking lot but couldn't get closer than a few feet because Miss Birdie stood between him and freedom. For a moment he envied the donkey Maisie for her joyful escape, but he knew it was not a good idea to run over the pillar.

"A friend? Is that all?" Winnie demanded again.

"Ladies," he said. "I am not married . . ."

"Not our fault," the pillar stated.

"We've tried," Mercedes said. "Goodness knows, we've tried to find you a wife."

"It's been a challenge," Winnie chimed in. "But we have done everything we could, and you ruin it by running off to spend the afternoon with Reverend Patillo?"

"Ran off and ruined it all," Blossom said.

The tone of every voice suggested activities of vice and perversion that he could never have taken part in—and certainly not in the short time he and Mattie had been together.

"Ladies," he began again. "I am not married. I have not been keeping company with Gussie Milton although I would like to spend more time with her. You—" He glanced at each woman. "None of you are in charge of whom I see and when and how." He stopped to attempt to think of more words and added, "Or why." Then he waited for a reaction.

"He's right," Mercedes said as the other Widows contemplated his words. "I'm sorry, Preacher. You're right. It's none of our business." She took Miss Birdie's arm. "We need to leave him alone."

"She's right," Blossom added. "I'm sorry, Preacher."

Miss Birdie hrrmphed but allowed herself to be guided away.

And Adam breathed a deep sigh of relief. He had met the Widows and he had won.

Not that he considered this a final victory.

❧

They'd been emailing back and forth for three weeks, Gussie and Adam. Oh, there had been distractions, like when her father had been hospitalized for pneumonia a week earlier. She'd known that coughing had meant something, but had she been able to force him to see a doctor? No, and he'd only decided to when he could no longer breathe.

He'd spent four days in the hospital, then come home so weak he could barely stand. Her mother was beside herself with worry and not really strong enough to care for him. Her blood sugar had gone up due to the stress.

Gussie'd hired a nurse to come in during the day, but when she was home, the entire weight of care fell on Gussie. Not that it bothered her, not that she'd complain, but she did worry about her parents as well as about her ability to care for them as they aged.

She'd told Adam this in emails. He'd supported her and let her unload her worry on him, had probably saved her from more worry than she could have handled alone.

They'd missed church this morning because her father was still so weak. She couldn't leave him at home alone, and her mother still dithered about him. As she finished cleaning the lunch dishes, Gussie heard the doorbell.

"Don't move, Mom. I'll get it."

Worn out and disheveled, Gussie opened the door to see—oh, please, no!—Adam standing there.

"Well." She forced a smile on lips that hadn't seen lipstick for nearly forty-eight hours. Nevertheless, although she felt exhausted and knew she looked terrible, she was happy to see him. "How nice to see you."

It was. He looked great in jeans and a knit shirt. Nice plus good looking and throw in the sudden rush of pure joy and a spark of desire she wished she could ignore—all that equaled perfect man. If she were looking for one.

Oh, shut up, she told herself. Whether she'd been looking or not, an attractive man of exactly the kind she'd have chosen for herself stood in front of her.

"Who is it, Gussie?" her father shouted.

"Come on in." She stepped back to allow him to enter. "My parents are in the living room. Everything's a mess. Sorry. The maid didn't drop by today. Not that we have a maid. I'm it. Or her. Maybe she." Why couldn't she stop babbling?

She led him into a room with the Sunday newspaper spread over the furniture and covering bits of the floor. Her mother sat on the sofa reading with a glass of lemonade on the table beside her while her father, still wearing pajamas, reclined.

"Mom, Dad, this is Adam Jordan, the minister at the church in Butternut Creek. You've heard me talk about him."

Her mother's gaze leaped toward Adam, then moved back and forth between Gussie and Adam. Her father kept his eyes on Adam, searching for clues. Was this man good enough for his daughter? To Gussie's chagrin, his scrutiny shouted that question.

Embarrassed by her father's inspection and aware of how terrible she looked, Gussie still grinned because Adam was here.

"These are my parents, Yvonne and Henry Milton," she said, waving toward them.

Adam, much more comfortable and at ease than she, approached her parents and shook their hands. "I wanted to bring you something, but flowers aren't good for someone recovering from pneumonia and candy isn't good for a diabetic. Instead, I bring best wishes for a speedy recovery from the congregation in Butternut Creek. You still have a lot of friends there."

"Oh, that's why you're here." Her father continued his examination of the man who'd dropped in. "Bringing best wishes from the church in Butternut Creek?" he said, disbelief obvious in his voice.

"How very sweet of you," her mother said. "So thoughtful. Thank you."

For nearly a minute, they all looked at one another and smiled and nodded their heads. Little by little, Adam looked more and more uncomfortable until Gussie drew herself together and said, "Sit down. Let me bring you a glass of lemonade."

She dashed toward the kitchen, then through it, out the hall door, and to the bathroom. As she ran, she could hear her father peppering Adam with questions. She fluffed powder on her shiny nose, smeared on lip gloss, and combed her hair. The best she could do for now.

By the time she got back to the living room with the lemonade, she hoped her father hadn't asked anything embarrassing, like *What are your intentions toward my daughter?*

Surely he wouldn't. But she hadn't brought a young man to meet them in years, not since high school. Not that she'd brought Adam home, but . . .

Oh, sit down and stop overthinking.

She gave Adam his glass and settled on the chair next to him.

He smiled at her and her heart fluttered. Oh, dear. Had she regressed, again becoming a girl whose pulse beat faster when a good-looking man smiled at her?

Well, yes, she guessed she had. It felt good.

After nearly fifteen minutes of her father's questions and Gussie's efforts to silence him, Adam stood. "I don't want to wear you out and need to get to Austin for hospital visits," he said. "Good to meet you, Mr. and Mrs. Milton."

"Don't be so formal. I'm Yvonne and my husband's Henry."

Her husband didn't look happy that this upstart who showed an interest in his daughter should call him anything but *sir*, but he didn't oppose the suggestion.

"Why don't you walk Adam outside, make sure he knows how to get to Austin," Mother suggested.

As if anyone could get lost between Roundville and Austin, but Gussie did as directed. She'd have gone anyway.

"Thank you for coming," Gussie said as they headed down the front walk. "We all really appreciated it."

"Gussie," he said when they reached his car. "I'd like to see you again."

"With my father's illness, I don't know when . . ."

"I understand, but I want to see you."

"I'll email you." She grinned. "I have to apologize for my father's behavior."

"Hey, he's a father. You're his daughter. He cares."

They gazed at each other, Adam with questions in his eyes that she didn't want to hear or respond to. Finally, he said, "Okay," and got into the car, turned on the engine, which responded with a mighty growl, and drove off with a wave. She watched him and wished she didn't have to go inside. She knew a grilling lay ahead.

Fortunately her father had left the living room. Probably worn out already. Although his weakness usually worried her, right now she could only be glad she'd escaped his interrogation for the time being.

Not that her mother's questions would be any easier, only not quite so much like the Inquisition.

"He's a very nice young man, dear," her mother said. "How lovely of him to visit us."

"He was on the way to Austin to make a hospital call."

"Do you really believe that?" Her mother shook her head. "Don't fool yourself. He came to see you. Oh"—she held her hand up—"I know he said he came to see us, but you know very well he wouldn't have dropped in on two elderly folks if we weren't your parents."

Because Gussie didn't know how to respond to Adam's visit or her mother's observation, she said, "I'm going to my room," and escaped. She had some thinking to do.

That evening, she opened her saved emails and read all of them from Adam. Every one confirmed what she already knew. Adam was a nice man. That part didn't scare her. It was the being-close-to-him-and-feeling-his-masculinity part she feared. She knew if she didn't respond to his visit, he'd give up on her. She most assuredly didn't want that. Time to make up her mind and take action.

"Meet me in Marble Falls for coffee a week from tomorrow? Dad goes to the doctor Friday. Surely he'll be strong enough for me to leave him with Mom for a few extra hours by then."

Chapter Ten

Ouida glanced at herself in the mirror of the half bath to check her hair and makeup. George had called twenty minutes ago to tell her he'd passed through Marble Falls. He should arrive home any minute, and she liked to look her best for him. She must be getting better if her appearance had become important.

She'd never realized the joy of going to the bathroom alone before she'd needed help for that most private of activities. The cane and a walking cast made getting into the small half bath difficult but she could do it. If she stuck her foot far to the right, balanced on the sink—she hoped she wouldn't pull it off the wall—and the door-knob, she could fall gently onto the toilet. Her greatest joy came from not having to ask someone to pull her panties down. In the restricted space, it wasn't easy, but she had conquered that.

Independence. After weeks of casts and slings and the hospital and nursing home, she now measured independence in tasks she could do, and she treasured every one. She'd no longer complain about anything, not ironing boxers or mopping the kitchen. If she could go back to the week before her fall, if she could trade off somehow, have a do-over, she'd iron what-ever George wanted her to but, "Please, Lord," she whispered, "I don't want to fall down the steps to learn this lesson, not again. I understand."

Then she'd realized she'd prayed. Oh, not a good prayer. More like a mixture of magic and blackmail with a sprinkle of faith, but she'd addressed the words to God. The preacher had influenced her far more than she'd realized. Did that count as good or bad? And did she really want to pray to a God who'd allowed her to fall down the steps so she'd learn a lesson? She didn't think so, but she'd talk to Adam about that.

As she considered her odd moment of faith, the front door opened. George was home.

"Ouida," he called from the living room.

"I'm back here," she shouted.

He didn't hear her, of course. Her voice didn't make it through the closed door, across the kitchen, through the dining room, and around the corner into the living room. His did.

"Ouida?" His voice held a note of panic. He dragged out her name so it sounded like, "Weeeeeeeeeeee-da!"

Not that she'd ever compare George to her cocker spaniel Daffy, but she felt as ineffective and helpless now as she had back then. She could hear his footsteps going up the stairs and echoing above her as he ran through the second story. She heard his steps sounding softly on the stairs to the third floor, then nothing. Had he gone up to the attic playroom? How did he think she'd climb those steps?

She'd hobbled up to the second floor only once. She'd come back to the first floor by bumping down on her bottom most of the way.

She still slept in the living room, although no longer on a hospital bed. They'd moved the queen-size bed downstairs, and she got to sleep with George next to her. And he thought she'd climbed two flights to the attic?

George must have come down because she now heard him above her on the second floor. If she still had her crutches, she'd bang on the ceiling, but she didn't and the cane didn't reach that far. Nonetheless, she had to try something. Using the wall and the sink, she leveraged herself to her feet, then leaned to pick up the cane. As she did, she felt herself overbalance. Before she could catch herself, she toppled against the door. It popped open and deposited her on the kitchen floor.

She lay there for a moment and did a quick inventory of her body, fearing she'd hurt herself again. Despite an ache in her good shoulder, which she'd fallen on, and her hip, she felt okay but she'd never be able to get to her feet. No, not alone, and George was too busy running around upstairs searching for her to give her a hand.

"George," she shouted, but she didn't hear movement toward her.

She looked around her. If she could get to the kitchen counter, she could probably pull herself to her feet, maybe. That irritating boot cut down on her mobility and balance so much that she needed something to hold on to, but her shoulder still hadn't gained enough strength that she trusted it.

"George."

Crab-like, she moved along on her stomach, impelling her body with both hands and her left foot. When she'd almost arrived, she heard George descending the stairs.

"George!"

"Ouida?" he called.

"In here," she shouted.

She heard him run through the living room and dining room. When he arrived at the arch between the kitchen and the dining room, he stopped for a second before he said, "Ouida," and rushed to her. "What happened?"

When he knelt beside her, she turned her head and gazed up at him. His eyes were huge; his face, white.

"I'm fine. Just help me up." She reached her hand out, but he leaped to his feet.

"No, no, you stay there. Don't want to make your injuries worse. I'll call nine-one-one and get the preacher over here." He turned and took two long strides to reach the phone.

"George," she said, her hand still held out. "I really am fine. I fell, but I didn't hurt anything. Help me, please. I can't stand up on my own."

He came back to her, slowly, and scrutinized her. "Are you sure?" When she nodded, he took her hand and put his other arm around her to guide and support her until she stood.

"See, I'm fine," she said at the exact time a wave of dizziness hit her. She leaned on George's arm to steady herself.

"No, you're not." George nearly dragged her across the kitchen and lowered her onto a chair in the breakfast nook. "I'm going to call . . ."

"George, I'm really fine. I got up too fast. I'm a little lightheaded."

"Food," he suggested. "Do you need something to eat? I'll get you a glass of milk. That should . . . or maybe a piece of cheese?"

"George, please sit down." Once he did—all the time inspecting her face, searching for signs of terminal illness or fatal injury, she guessed—she took his hand. "I'm fine."

"Don't scare me like that." He took several deep breaths. "Are you sure you're fine?"

"Yes, dear."

They sat like that, gazing at each other and holding hands, until George said, "I've been thinking." He squeezed her hand and leaned toward her. "I never realized how hard it is to take care of this big house and the girls until I had to do that. I don't know how you do it."

She smiled. Nice to be validated. "I love it."

"I can't believe I nagged you about being punctual and keeping a schedule. I'm never where I planned to be doing what I think I should. It's about killed me. I decided to get you maid service, twice a week. Will that help?"

When she didn't answer because his statement had surprised her—no, stunned and amazed her—he continued. "I'm sorry. I never should've said that you have life easy. Trying to do for a few days a week what you do every day of the year wore me out. You need help."

"Oh, George." She caressed his hand and smiled at him. For a moment, she kept her eyes on him and treasured his concern. "Thank you, but I don't need maid service. I love what I do, but I would like to stop ironing so much."

She paused. "And I'd like to start painting again, when I can use my arm."

"Anything," he said. "Whatever you want."

Maybe she shouldn't refuse his generosity. She could accept a day or two of maid service a week, if he really wanted that.

🐛

Adam glanced around the sanctuary. Attendance usually fell during the summer, but today it had picked up with school starting in a couple of weeks. Probably close to sixty in attendance. The average had swelled to almost seventy, most of the additional number coming from the high school kids Hector and Bree had roped in. The Mexican and African American kids and a few of their parents added texture to the congregation. Not that sixty or seventy people filled the sanctuary, but it didn't look quite as empty as it had a year earlier.

Sam and his family sat on the side aisle, a consistent four. Actually, add the general and Winnie and that row was nearly filled every Sunday.

Behind Adam in the chancel, the choir still consisted of three women and Ralph. All sat quietly now as they did through the entire service. He wished he could get them to practice, to prepare even a choral *Amen* after the prayer, but that success had eluded him.

The guest organist played a soft prelude but everyone was so busy chatting, they couldn't hear it.

Mrs. Jurenka, the musician, had confessed before the service that she didn't hear as well as she once had. She'd showed him some signals he could use to communicate. The idea of motioning to her after the prayer seemed odd, but with their usual organist on maternity leave, they had to hire whoever they could find. Mrs. Jurenka was it this morning.

She'd played the first hymn well although had stopped before the last verse, which left the congregation sputtering to a halt when they realized that the music had come to an end. However, since almost no one sang except Janey, the young people, and a few visitors, the quick finish didn't much matter.

Later in service, Adam rose to start the prayer. As was his usual practice, he paused several times during the prayer to give the congregation time to meditate.

Not a good idea that morning.

At the first pause, Mrs. Jurenka must have thought he'd finished. Although he had not given her the agreed-upon signal, a chopping gesture, she began to play, "Hear Our Prayer, O Lord," before he could start the prayer again. He waited but she played on. He gave her the agreed-upon signal, then once more. And again. He felt as if he were splitting logs up there, but she didn't stop. In desperation, he hissed at her. Oh, he knew she couldn't hear him, but he felt the need to do something. Throwing a hymnal seemed out of the question. She continued playing. He'd never realized how long that response was, especially when she kept repeating it. Was there some sign he'd missed? Obviously the chopping and the hissing hadn't worked.

Hoping if she could hear him pray, Mrs. Jurenka would stop playing, Adam raised his voice. "And so we thank you for all the blessings of this day . . ." But she didn't stop. "For the beauty of the Hill Country," he said in an even louder and definitely less prayerful voice. Finally, he screamed, "And for the love of the people around us, for the peace and quiet of this place . . ."

By this time, the members of the congregation had lost any semblance of prayerful contemplation and were laughing so hard he feared Hector and Bobby would fall out of the pew. Although Willow attempted to remain worshipful and hush her men, Sam and the boys had long since given up an appearance of reverence. Why did Adam have a best friend who laughed at him during the most trying moments of his life?

As his gaze moved around the congregation, he spotted Gussie on the back row of the sanctuary. Why had she visited *to-day*? Today of all the Sundays in the world when he'd lost complete control of the service?

She was, of course, as amused as everyone else. Although he couldn't tell from this distance, she seemed to be laughing so hard she was crying, dabbing at her eyes with a tissue. He loved Gussie's laugh, but not now.

Adam had no idea what to do next because he couldn't shout any more loudly. Then he heard Ralph stand behind him, the chair creaking as he pulled his arthritic bulk up. Adam gave up completely on the prayer and turned to watch Ralph's slow progress from the choir chairs toward the organ.

What was the man going to do?

The eyes of the congregation followed Ralph's movements as well. For a moment, Ralph stopped behind Mrs. Jurenka, who had her eyes closed, obviously feeling spiritual as she began the response another time. After a few seconds, Ralph put a hand on each of the organist's arms, pulled her hands away from the keys, and shouted, "Stop."

The poor woman leaped off the organ bench. Ralph let go of her arms as she shrieked a piercing high note that reverberated around the sanctuary. "What are you doing?"

"The preacher's still praying," Ralph shouted and pointed.

"Oh." She glanced at Adam and nodded before turning and sitting again, her hands in her lap. Ralph tramped back toward the choir, dropped into his chair with a satisfied, "There," and folded his hands across his round stomach.

For nearly a minute, Adam waited in the hope he could somehow redeem the situation, but the laughter continued. Finally, he said "Amen" and sat down. He'd never get the congregation back.

After a few minutes, he stood to deliver a shortened sermon. The service ended in plenty of time for everyone to get to Subway long before the Methodists.

As he greeted people at the entrance, Bobby filed by. Unable to say a word because he was laughing so hard, the young man gave Adam a punch in the shoulder.

"Pops, that service wasn't boring at all," Hector said and he shook Adam's hand.

At the same time Hector left the narthex, Adam realized he was alone with Gussie. Except he knew they weren't alone, not really. Even though he couldn't see them, he knew the Widows lurked nearby. Smiling, probably, gloating, and, he knew, listening. Gussie approached him and held out her hand.

"Hello," he said with an effort to sound detached so the Widows couldn't pick up on how happy her presence made him. He failed. "How nice to see you in church today." He sounded like an idiot. He could hear himself nearly chirping with pleasure. "How nice to see you," he repeated in the deep, professional voice he used for prayers. Now he sounded like a minister welcoming a guest. All he had to do was shake her hand and invite her back. So he took her hand, shook it, and said heartily, "Good to see you this morning. Please come back to worship with us another time."

She smiled up at him and he didn't worry about how stupid he sounded. Her expression assured him that whatever reason she had for visiting the Christian Church during one of the most embarrassing moments of his life was positive. She was here. Maybe this morning's service would be counted as a good. Maybe even something they could laugh about together for years to come, he hoped.

Super-cool as always, he demanded, "What are you doing here?" Chirpy, ministerial, demanding—why couldn't he figure out how to talk to Gussie like a normal person, like a man who found her attractive?

"I wanted to see you." Her voice wasn't what he considered her usual *Gussie* voice. No, it sounded a little tentative. Gussie Milton uncertain?

Maybe that was good, too.

Then she let go of his hand and took a step back. What did that mean?

"Aren't we meeting for coffee tomorrow? I mean, not that I'm not glad to see you, but . . ."

"I wanted to see you *today*."

How much better could life get?

"Preacher."

A voice cut its way through the warm cloud of bliss surrounding him and Gussie. Adam rearranged his muddled thoughts and turned to focus on the speaker.

"How can I help you, Howard?"

"Hot enough for you?"

Adam nodded. He never knew how to answer that question.

Then the elder looked back and forth between the two and grinned. "Nothing, Preacher." He took several steps back. "I'll leave a note in your office."

He hurried away. When Howard reached the door from the front of the sanctuary to the back hallway, Adam could hear soft whispering. The Widows had captured Howard and were now grilling him. Poor man.

"Why don't we go to my office?" Adam asked. "We can talk with a little more privacy."

"Can we escape the Widows?" She used her head to point in the directions of the women.

"I have a secret route. They'll never know we've left."

Feeling like a spy in a bad movie, he led Gussie around the church, surreptitiously checking for Widows, then through the office entrance and into his study without seeing anyone. Once there, he unzipped his robe, hung it on the coatrack, and reached for his jacket.

"Hello, Gussie." Miss Birdie's voice came from the doorway.

"Miss Birdie." Gussie nodded and smiled at the pillar. "So nice to see you."

"What are you doing way up here? So far from Roundville?"

"I was in the area and thought I'd drop by. It's so good to see you."

Signs of struggle crossed Miss Birdie's face. She bit her lips and blinked several times. Adam had learned to read her expressions. This one meant goading Gussie for more information crossed a line between civility and rudeness that even Miss Birdie couldn't force herself to step over. And yet she knew no one merely "dropped by" Butternut Creek.

"How nice," the pillar finally said. Then, fists on her hips, she turned to glare at Adam. "Don't forget where you are and who you are. You are a minister and an example to our young folks. Don't close this door when you're alone with a woman." She gave an emphatic nod.

Adam felt as if he were in eighth grade when his mother found him in the closet with Susie Page. He glanced at the door just to make sure he hadn't closed it. Still wide open.

Then, with a charming smile, the pillar said, "Gussie, I know you've had a long drive and have another going back home. The Widows have prepared a nice snack for you in the garden. Don't worry about Hector and Janey, Preacher. Bree's taking them out for a hamburger." Her voice sweet still, she added, "Don't tarry." She strode out.

Once they could no longer hear her footfalls in the reception office, Gussie fell into a chair and laughed. "Don't you love Miss Birdie?" she asked.

He had to think about that. "Sometimes," he said. "Not always."

"Preacher?" Blossom called from the front office. "Lunch is ready."

The garden was a euphemism for the five-by-five grass squares on the back and sides of the church where every other inch of ground was covered with asphalt. On this side, the west, they were screened from the highway by the gym wing of the building so they could enjoy a modicum of privacy.

"Hector keeps the garden up," Adam

explained to Gussie as they neared it. "He earns a little spending money taking care of the lawn in front of the church and the parsonage." He held a chair for Gussie. Once she was seated, he settled in the chair across from her, slightly aware of the scent of mosquito repellent, ubiquitous in the summer. The Widows must have sprayed out here to make sure not even an insect intruded.

"There you are," Mercedes said with enthusiastic delight, as if they'd wandered off in the wilderness and had finally returned. From her tray, she took forks and crisp, white napkins and placed them in front of each followed by glasses of iced tea, then stood back and beamed at them.

Blossom followed with another plate, which filled up the rest of the space on the table. "Here are a few cucumber sandwiches," she said. "From an old family recipe."

"They look delicious." Gussie smiled at Blossom. "Exactly right for a warm afternoon."

Miss Birdie arrived with a bowl of fruit salad and looked around for a place to set it. Seeing none, she took the spoon from the bowl and scooped a serving onto each plate.

He should never underestimate the wonders the Widows could perform in no time at all. They possessed abilities and powers he could only marvel at.

"You young people go right ahead and eat," Mercedes said. "We'll be here in case you need something."

Three Widows watched him, looking like buzzards, keeping an eye on a particularly flavorful deer carcass.

Adam guessed Winnie was with her fiancé, which was a relief. Although he had encouraged Mercedes and the pillar to increase the number of Widows, he realized he was paying for that at this moment. Three Widows watching them closely, listening to every word, studying each movement frightened him. All four women together would have rendered him incoherent and, possibly, androgynous.

Adam remembered a story his friend had told him, that the Widows had set up a date for Sam and Willow and then sneaked away to leave them alone. And yet, here they stood, as if protecting his honor and Gussie's.

"Thank you," he said. "I think we're fine." He attempted to fill his voice with a nuance that said, *Leave us alone.*

Didn't work.

He repeated, "We're fine," and winked.

When that met with silence, he said, "I don't know if the three of you remember, but this kind of thing usually isn't done with an audience."

"Yes, Pastor, but we're not so sure you know anything about courting," the pillar said.

Could this get any more embarrassing? Of course it could.

"You know, he's right," Mercedes stated. "We should leave them alone."

Blossom nodded. "He's going to have to take over at some time. How can he make his move with us watching?"

Gussie picked up her napkin to hide her smile but Adam wanted to sink through the garden.

"Oh, all right." Miss Birdie took a few steps back and wagged her finger at Adam. "Don't leave a mess. Take the plates in the kitchen and wash them. Detergent's under the sink. Leave them to dry in the drainer."

"Thank you, ladies." He didn't mention

he'd been doing dishes himself for years and cleaned up the church kitchen after meetings. No need to pick a fight now. Besides, the sooner he agreed, the sooner they'd leave him and Gussie in peace.

Why didn't the Widows consider it wrong for the two to be alone in the kitchen? Did they believe the presence of a detergent and dish drainer would keep him on the straight and narrow, remind him of his position in the community, and stop him from seducing Gussie? It was satisfying that the Widows believed it could happen, if not for the presence of the plates to be washed and placed in the drainer.

Of course, the agony wasn't over yet. The pillar turned to Gussie. "He's a good young man but he's not much of a ladies' man."

Such positive words. Why didn't they just come right out with it, say, *The man's a hopeless idiot with women*, and leave it at that?

"You may have to help him along," Mercedes added helpfully.

Gussie straightened and placed the napkin back in her lap. "Thank you, ladies," she said seriously, although Adam thought he detected a quiver in her lips.

Exactly what he needed, for Gussie to find him and his plight amusing.

"And, Preacher—" Miss Birdie paused for emphasis but he'd heard that waving-finger tone in her voice. "—don't make a move on Miss Milton inside the church."

Aah, yes, that good-example stuff again.

For a moment, Gussie and Adam listened to the galloping clatter of the Widows as they headed around the building and toward the parking lot. A minute later, after what Adam imagined was a short powwow, he heard cars start and drive off.

He had survived, not even seriously wounded.

"Oh, my!" Gussie grinned. "Aren't they wonderful?" Checking Adam's expression, she said, "Well, maybe not. I'd guess having them around all the time and pestering you isn't as much fun as *watching* them nag you."

"Fortunately, Howard warned me about the Widows before I arrived. They do so much for the church and community, I can't stay mad or frustrated for long. Miss

Birdie is priceless, but there are times when they treat me like their youngest grandson who isn't very bright and can't figure anything out on his own. Then I don't find them amusing."

He took a sandwich and offered her another.

"No thanks," she said. "I'm really not a great fan of cucumber sandwiches. But the fruit is wonderful."

❦

Gussie watched Adam eat. She enjoyed merely being here, sitting close to him. In the warmth of the sunshine and the whisper of the breeze, she was glad she'd come. Her action had been completely out of character. She'd driven here on a whim, at odds with her usually logical behavior.

Why? Why had she set herself and Adam up for this kind of attention? She should have realized her appearance would send the Widows into a matchmaking frenzy.

She'd stewed about the meeting in Marble Falls all day Saturday, one reason for coming to Butternut Creek. This morning, she'd gotten up, dressed, told her parents good-bye, and hopped in the car.

Impulsive didn't describe her, but today it felt right.

While she studied him, he glanced up, not saying a word. Probably wondered why she was here, expected a fuller explanation than she'd given him right after the service.

"I'm sorry I've acted like an idiot every time you show up." She paused to think of words. "Both times, you startled me. I'm afraid I was rude."

"Not rude," he said. "You didn't have any warning. Besides, you already apologized." Then he smiled and leaned forward, reached his hand toward her, and touched her fingers.

She nearly leaped from the chair. Then she settled down and froze.

Oh, no. She'd hoped she'd gotten over that reaction. She'd thought the attraction to Adam, the years of therapy, and the love and support from her parents had healed her. Would she ever, ever be okay? Would she ever recover? How could she allow those terrible minutes from years ago to influence—no, to destroy—her life even now? Wasn't she better and stronger and more faithful than that?

Seemed not.

She gave a shaky laugh. "I'm sorry. You startled me."

"I could tell. Ministers are good at reading body language." He kept his eyes on her face. "When a woman leaps into the air at the touch of a hand, it's a sign of something. Usually not something good."

Obviously he didn't accept her reaction as being startled. No, he recognized it as another kind of response. She could only hope he couldn't read the truth in her eyes.

"I'm fine, just overly vigilant." She waved a hand around and attempted to change the subject. "Isn't this a lovely place?"

What was that? Adam dropped his hand back on the table and studied Gussie. Her eyes were wide, her face was nearly white, and she gasped to catch her breath. She'd jerked back, not in surprise. He'd frightened her, a response he hadn't expected. One she hadn't expected, either, he bet.

He remembered a teenager in his student church who'd been abused by her father. She'd reacted in nearly the same way when he'd lightly touched her shoulder to get past her. That poor girl had performed a long jump that could have qualified her for the Olympics. After that, she nearly fainted and he'd kept his distance.

Slowly color returned to Gussie's face, and she attempted to smile pleasantly and normally at him. He didn't buy it. He didn't believe her explanation for a second, but out here wasn't the place to discuss her problems. This didn't feel like a good time, either.

He acted as if he didn't see her struggle for control as he sat back in his chair to leave her plenty of space. "I'm not fond of cucumber sandwiches myself. Not very filling. Let's look in the fridge and see if there's anything there."

Standing, he picked up his plate and glass and other stuff. Usually, he'd have picked up hers as well, but extending an arm in her direction and invading her space didn't feel like a good idea.

Gussie gave him a smile that began with a quiver before, slowly, becoming the one he recognized as hers. "I'm sorry . . . ," she began, then seemed to realize where they were and that neighbors could be watching from the houses that backed onto the parking lot and grassy area. With a sweeping motion that looked a lot more like the Gussie he knew, she grabbed her place setting and headed toward the kitchen door.

"I'm sorry." Her voice sounded calm and strong as they entered. She placed the plate in the sink and turned on the hot water.

"Gussie, you don't need to apologize."

Adam placed his dishes next to the sink and watched her carefully wash off the plates, then scrub each with a scouring pad until he feared she'd scour off the floral pattern. She finished the few utensils and placed everything in the drainer. Then she wiped off her hands and—he guessed—couldn't think of anything more to do, so she turned to him and shook her head. "Will I ever get over that?" she whispered as she kept her gaze on the floor.

He stayed still and silent and waited. Finally, when she didn't speak, he asked, "Gussie, why did you come here?"

"To see you." She sighed and looked up at him. "I really wanted to see you. I believed I was okay, but you've noticed I'm not. I have a problem I can't seem to get past." She took a few steps and dropped onto a folding chair.

He sat in a chair a few feet from her. She looked pale and anxious and just plain terrible. She had trouble meeting his gaze, studying her hands as often as she glanced at him. No, she didn't want closeness now.

Again, he realized he needed to prompt her to respond. "Do you want to tell me about it?"

"I do, but I can't, not right now. I'm really sorry for bringing you into this." This time she did keep her eyes on his face. "I find you very attractive, really . . . um . . . desirable, but . . ."

He'd known a *but* would follow the positive feedback.

"I'd like to have a relationship with you but . . ." She closed her eyes and bit her lip. "Oh, darn. I sound like a character in a soap opera, don't I? I'm sorry I'm so incoherent."

"Gussie, don't keep apologizing. Talk to me."

"Okay." She appeared to struggle for words before she opened her eyes and spoke to him. "I have a problem. I thought . . . I hoped I'd healed because of the way I feel about you, but obviously I haven't. And I feel it's too soon to open up about everything. I'm not ready to tell you what happened and you're probably not prepared to hear it. We don't know each other very well."

He nodded, not at all sure how to react.

"But, if you're willing, I would like to explore what I feel about you. The fact that you attract me amazes me."

"All right," he said because he had absolutely no idea what else to say.

"You are attractive. I am attracted to you," she said. "You're not the problem. I am. As I said, what amazes me is that I can admit the chemistry. I haven't felt like that about a man for a long time."

"Okay." He wished he could come up with words of healing and compassion, but he didn't know her well or what the problem was, although he could guess. He stuck to the tried and true, sounding like an idiot.

"But I'm more broken than I thought. I shouldn't have come here today, but I really wanted to see you." She gave him a grin, a little forced, but encouraging. "I'd thought about our get-together in Marble

Falls and decided not to put it off. Probably a good thing because if I'd fallen apart like this at the coffee shop, how embarrassing would that be?"

"When I reached to take your hand, it scared you. I frightened you."

"Oh, yes, frightened, panicked, terrified, completely lost and *bamboozled*—all of those describe how I felt."

Great. Of all the emotions he could raise in a woman, the best he could do was panicked and bamboozled?

But this wasn't about him. "Can you explain?"

"Not really. Not without a whole bunch of stuff pouring out." She looked into his eyes, almost pleading. "I trust you, but I've got a big problem. I'm good with kids and work and church and my parents, but . . . but . . ."

He realized as she spoke those words that the barrier was right there, right after the *but.* He guessed it had to do with men or with a man. He hated to have to clean up the mess another guy had made. Right now, he couldn't force her to complete the statement. He waited.

"Would you take on a project as difficult as me?" she asked. "I really want this, I want to accept how I feel, explore that, build on it, but I'm not sure I should ask that of you." Instead of the fear he'd glimpsed earlier, an earnest plea filled her eyes. "I can't promise anything."

"Yeah." He nodded. "I'd take that on."

"Really?" She shook her head. "Why?"

"Gussie, you are one of the most loving people I know. You take care of your parents, you work with the youth in your church and in the district. You are a person of deep faith. You're beautiful in every way I can imagine."

"Really?" She scrutinized him closely, as if she couldn't believe his words.

"Really."

She scooted her chair closer to him and leaned forward to place her hand against his lips. He didn't move closer to her, only allowed her to touch him. Amazingly, after a few seconds, she put her hand on his neck and pulled him nearer, only a few inches, and placed her cheek against his.

When at last she sat back, she smiled at him. He would have leaned toward her, touched her. More than anything, he wanted to kiss her but he had to respect the physical barrier of the hand she still held in front of her.

"Thank you for not pushing," she said.

Although she insisted she was broken, he felt blessed that she'd come to him, that she'd reached out to him, that she cared about him enough to ask for his patience.

They'd figure out everything else later.

Chapter Eleven

"Preacher, good news and bad news," Maggie said. "Which do you want first?"

Adam glanced from the Bible commentary displayed on his computer screen to his secretary standing in the door. "Neither."

"Actually—" Maggie thought for a moment. "Actually, they're both bad news."

Great. "Go ahead."

"Miss Birdie's here."

He nodded. She'd want an update on what happened after the Widows had left the church.

"And she's in the kitchen."

Sounded like good news to him. The pillar wasn't *here*, grilling him. "How's that bad news?"

"That's right. You don't know about Miss Birdie and the kitchen." Maggie came into the office and sat in a chair in front of his desk. "When Miss Birdie is upset, she cleans."

Hearing that Miss Birdie was upset did count as bad news. "How's cleaning bad news?"

"Once she finishes cleaning her house and the diner, she comes here."

"By that time, she must have blown off some steam."

Maggie shook her head. "Oh, no. If she gets here, that means she hasn't calmed down at the other places and is really wound up, has built a lot of momentum. By the time she comes here, she's like a train off the tracks. You need to head her off, Preacher."

"Why? Isn't it good that she's straightening things up?" He turned off the computer to lean forward and pay complete attention to Maggie.

"When she's in this mood, she's ruthless. A few years ago, she took all the books out of the classrooms and cataloged them and put them in the library."

"What's so bad about that?"

"A lot of those books belonged to the teachers, references and coloring books and pictures they'd bought, stuff they brought in to use with the children. Back when Effie Peterson taught the third-through-fifth-grade class, she was infuriated to find her Bible stamped as property of the Christian Church with a little pocket pasted in the back." Her eyes grew large. "You've never seen such a set-to." She shook her head as she remembered.

Adam glanced over his shoulder at the bookcase where the library had been when he arrived. He'd tossed the old, torn books out and donated the rest to the public library. He wondered if any of those had belonged to people who hadn't claimed them yet. Fortunately, no one had made a big fuss.

"And last time she cleaned out the shed, she threw away a bunch of stuff, good stuff."

Knowing the kind of things churches kept—old Sunday school material that would never be used again, broken furniture no one ever got around to fixing, ancient hymnals with brown, brittle pages filled with songs no one remembered— Adam didn't think tossing all that counted as a bad thing.

"When she starts in the kitchen, she changes everything all around. You'll go in expecting the coffee can to be right above the coffeemaker, but it won't be. Miss Birdie will put it where she wants it, although some of us believe she puts it where no one can find it so we'll have to ask her. For weeks after she straightens things up, we can't find sugar bowls or the paper cups." She sighed. "It's not a good thing. It's chaos and havoc until everyone gets used to the new locations." Then, she shook her finger at Adam. "You have to stop her. She's on a toot."

He stood.

"I'll pray for you," Maggie said.

He didn't think she was joking.

As Adam headed toward the kitchen, he felt pretty sorry for himself, too, but a man's gotta do . . .

Before he could finish the cliché, he'd arrived in the fellowship hall. From there, he could see a mound of plates and packages of napkins and saltshakers and nearly everything that had been in the kitchen cupboards piled on the counter. He guessed the pillar was behind the stack someplace.

"Hello, Miss Birdie," he called.

"Preacher, is that you?"

"You sound surprised." He headed toward the kitchen. As he got closer, he could see where Miss Birdie knelt on the floor. "Surely you knew Maggie would send me back."

"Give me a hand up." She reached out her right hand. Once on her feet, she said, "I'm organizing the cabinets."

"Oh, is that what this is called?" He gestured toward the mounds. "Looks like my office when I first arrived."

"Yes, Preacher." She glared at him. "But I'm going to put it all back where it should have been in the first place and I'm going to finish that today. A lot of your stuff is still sitting on the office floor."

A mistake to bring that up. "Do you have to take everything out at once? Can't you go bit by bit?"

"Winnie Jenkins rearranged things a

few months back, and no one can find anything. I'm only putting it all back where it should be."

"Can I help?"

She studied him. "I always knew your tall skinniness would be good for something. Put those big packages of napkins up on the top shelf."

After nearly two hours of following the pillar's orders, they'd brought order to the kitchen, but Miss Birdie still hadn't said anything about why she was there. She only grumbled and grunted and emitted a few new sounds Adam couldn't translate. The only words she used were contained in commands for his tall skinniness.

"I've heard you come here and clean the kitchen when there's something bothering you," Adam said as he placed the last forks in what had been the knife drawer. Miss Birdie had relabeled it.

She spun around to look at him. "What?" She huffed. "Who told you that?"

He didn't say.

"Well, I guess that's right," she concurred.

"Do you want to tell me what you're upset about?"

"Don't you know what I'm upset about?"

Oh, he could think of several topics, but her concern about his single state hadn't driven her into the kitchen before. He also guessed he wouldn't get out of this without a stern lecture on his bachelorhood and his lack of appreciation for her efforts to find him a mate before she confessed to her real motivation. He waited.

"You know, we've tried very hard to find you a wife." She glowered at him. He listened to a diatribe about the lack of appreciation he showed her and her efforts. She finished by attempting to make him feel guilty for ignoring all her hard work.

He didn't accept the blame, but he allowed her to vent. When she finished, he said, "Miss Birdie, what's really bothering you? I know you'd like to get me married off, but your matchmaking is more like a hobby. There's something else." He leaned against the countertop.

She didn't answer, not immediately. After nearly a minute of wiping off the already clean counter, she carefully draped the dishcloth over the sink divider and turned toward him.

"It's Bree." She folded her hands in front of her.

※

When Birdie glanced back at the preacher, she knew her vacillation showed weakness, but she couldn't help that. He responded with a look of caring, of concern. She hated that.

Birdie really disliked sharing her problems with other people, but she might as well continue because there was no way she'd convince Adam she was fine, just fine. How much should she say? After all, Hector lived in the parsonage. Would the preacher think she was putting him down?

Birdie cleared her throat. The darned man didn't say a word, didn't help her get this out. Only watched her closely. Probably because he knew what a private person she was and didn't want to intrude. Wouldn't you know the one time she wanted him to ask, he didn't encourage her to open up?

People saw her as being gruff and tougher than flint. Although she enjoyed that reputation, the preacher and a few others—well, probably the entire town—knew there

was one topic she wasn't tough about. Her
granddaughters. She cleared her throat
again. The preacher still didn't say anything, only waited for her to come to the
point.

"It's Bree," she repeated. "Bree and
Hector. Mac tells me they got friendly at
the retreat. I know they danced together at
the prom, but everyone dances with everyone else. At the reception with Gussie I
saw they held hands once. And they're
always emailing or texting each other,
sometimes even talk on the phone. They
probably spent a lot of time together at
camp."

"How do you feel about that?" he asked.
"About Bree and Hector?"

How dare this inexperienced preacher—
still wet behind the ears—how dare he attempt to minister to her? Did he think she
needed counseling from someone young
enough to be her grandson?

When she didn't say anything, just
glared at him, Adam said, "Is Hector and
Bree's interest in each other a problem for
you?"

What was he suggesting? "Do you
mean the race thing? I don't care that

Hector is Mexican or African American or black or even purple. What I care about is . . ." Then she couldn't talk. Her throat had closed up and tears clouded her vision. Doggone!

Immediately the preacher straightened, picked up a handful of napkins—the good ones, the ones they used for teas and formal events—and held them toward her. She took one napkin from him, only one because they were too expensive to blow her nose in but, right now, she needed to do exactly that.

Thank goodness, the man knew her well enough not to pat her on the back or make comforting *there, there* noises. Instead he stayed a few feet from her and kept silent. She hated herself for showing this weakness and struggling for control.

"Hector is a fine young man," he said after nearly a minute. "With his mother's death and his father's drug use and jail time, he's been through more than anyone his age should have to go through."

She nodded and wiped her eyes, then blew her nose again.

"He's taken care of Janey for years and

still keeps his grades up and plays basketball. I admire him."

"I do, too." She dabbed with the napkin.
She closed her eyes for only a second before she glanced at him. "I'm not worried
about Hector. I know how much he's taken
on and I do respect that. And Bree's a
good girl, but . . ." She gulped, a hideously
loud noise that embarrassed her both for
the rudeness and because, with that terrible sound, she'd exposed feelings she
tried to hide. "You know about my daughter
Martha Patricia. I worry," she whispered. "I
worry so much."

"Of course you do. You love the girls,
but Bree is a good kid, a really good kid."

"Mercedes says I'm overprotective,
Preacher, and I am, but I love those girls
more than . . ." The words wouldn't come.
What was happening? She couldn't even
speak anymore. When had she become
such an emotional softy? Well, since the
first time Martha Patricia had handed her
baby Bree.

But she sure didn't need to blubber in
front of the preacher. She pulled herself
straight, wadded the soggy napkin, and

tossed it in the trash. "I need to get back to the diner," she stated. "Thanks for the help."

"You know, I am your minister, Miss Birdie. There's nothing wrong or weak about worrying about people you love."

"Hrmph." She turned and headed toward the parking lot. When she'd almost reached the door, she turned around. "What can you tell me about Bree and Hector?" She tilted her head.

"Not much. I saw them together at the retreat and the prom. She and Hector sit on the parsonage porch from time to time. I imagine they were together at the church summer camp, but I wasn't there."

"You didn't think to tell me?"

"Miss Birdie, if I thought there was a problem, I'd have mentioned it to you. But, you know, I also have to respect Hector and Bree's privacy."

"Of course you do." She nodded. As she did, she realized he looked different. She studied him, searching for what had caught her eye. A new shirt? "You look nice today, Preacher. Any particular reason?"

He tried to look casual but he couldn't fool her. He didn't speak for several seconds, a sure sign of duplicity. He blinked several times, which she'd learned was his tell when he considered lying. Then he smiled at her, sweetly, which tipped her off to his intent to fib.

"Are you meeting Gussie later?" she asked. Better let him know she was on to him instead of tempting him to bear false witness. Then she held her hand in front of her. "No, no. Don't tell me. You deserve privacy in your life. I'm not going to pry."

When his mouth dropped open at her words, Birdie gloated inside. Always a good thing to keep *him* guessing, wondering, a little off balance.

With that, she left the building. After a few steps, she paused. What had she heard? What was the sound coming from the kitchen? Sounded like laughter, but why? What had she said that anyone could find amusing? Probably her imagination.

❧

Adam had to tell Gussie the entire thing. Not about Miss Birdie's fears for her granddaughter but about both her cleaning the kitchen and her newfound, and probably of short duration, respect for his privacy.

He laughed again as he drove down Highway 1431 to Marble Falls. A few miles south of Fuzzy's Corner, he heard a loud clunk. Wondering if he'd run into something, he pulled onto the shoulder, put the car in park, and got out.

Behind him and in the middle of the road lay a bumper. Had he hit it or did it belong to him? He didn't want to check, because if his bumper was missing, that would be one more sign that his car was literally falling apart. Gathering his courage, he walked to the back of the car and studied the place where a bumper used to be. Then he turned to look down the road at the bumper twenty yards behind him.

Did a car really need a bumper?

Most likely the state thought it did, so he'd better think of some way to replace it. He opened the trunk, walked back, picked the thing up, and attempted to shove it in the trunk. Didn't fit. He dragged it around, opened the door to the backseat, and shoved it in there. It fit. He and Hector would try to get it back on because he feared Rex would have to charge him more for the part than he could afford.

Finished, he glanced down at his hands. Covered with dirt. Smudges dotted the pale blue knit shirt he'd bought to wear today. He kept those little moist towelettes in his glove compartment. Actually Laurel, his former fiancée, had put some there years ago. Would they still work?

First, he went back to the trunk and pulled out a blanket he'd kept there for years, in case of emergencies. Probably didn't need a blanket in Texas. He wiped his hands on it to get as much of the gunk off as possible, then tossed it in the backseat so he'd remember to take it in and wash it. The bundle looked as if he were transporting either a body or a cache of something illegal.

After he closed the trunk, he opened the door on the passenger side, reached in the glove box, and found four small square packages from KFC. He tore one open. Dry, as were the second, third, and fourth. Perhaps if he spit on them, he'd find they still had some soap, but he didn't think he had nearly enough saliva. He grabbed his bottle of water and squeezed a little on one parched square. When a few bubbles appeared, he scrubbed his hands with that and checked his face in the rearview mirror. His body looked okay, but the shirt . . . well, he'd have to stop by Cheap-Mart on the way into town and buy another.

Thirty minutes later, Adam had settled in a booth across from Gussie. His new shirt wasn't as nice as his other but it didn't have the dark, greasy smudges, either. She, of course, looked wonderful. Happy, full of life, and beautiful, enjoying the rhubarb cream pie in front of her.

"I like buttermilk pie best, but this is a close second." She took a bite and chewed. "You should try my mother's buttermilk pie. It'll spoil you for anything else."

"Okay." He put his hand near hers, so his thumb rested against hers. "I'd love to try your mother's buttermilk pie. She seems like a really nice person. A good cook?"

"She used to be, still is, but with her diabetes, she seldom bakes." She reached for a napkin, which moved her hand away subtly but effectively. "You've met my parents, but I know nothing about yours. Tell me about them."

"They live in London."

"London, Texas?"

"No, and not London, Kentucky, either. London, England." By the time he explained that, Gussie had finished her pie. Then he told her about Miss Birdie in the kitchen. After laughing through that tale, Gussie glanced at the clock. "I need to go." She wiped her mouth and took a drink of water. "I've got a drive ahead of me, but—" She placed her hand on his for a quick touch before she grabbed the check and slipped from the booth. "—but it's been wonderful to see you."

He stood, moving in front of her before she could get away. Yes, that's exactly what it looked like, as if she were attempting to escape. "Can I see you again?"

"Yes." She paused and seemed to consider if she did want to see him again. "Of course I want to see you again. I haven't dated much recently. I sometimes forget how to act."

"Dinner? I could meet you in Austin or Roundville, somewhere closer than Marble Falls."

"Let's discuss that on email, okay?"

As he watched her pay the bill and leave,

Adam wondered what *recently* meant. Gussie Milton attracted attention. He noticed that as she walked out. Men kept their eyes on her and grinned. Even the men who were with women scoped her out. No lack of masculine interest in her, so she'd chosen not to date. He could ask her about it but, when he asked her anything personal, she often acted like a doe surrounded by wolves. She'd warned him, but he'd hoped they'd made a little headway. She'd come to see him. She hadn't flinched at his touch.

For heaven's sake, if Gussie's not flinching at his touch showed progress, they had farther to go than he'd thought.

Dear Lord, give me patience, and I could really use it right now.

❦

Rex and Adam scrutinized the back of the car and the bumper that lay on the driveway. Hector had tried to reattach it with duct tape and wire. Not surprisingly, neither worked, so Adam had called the mechanic.

"Rusted out, Padre. Don't know if anything I do can keep it on for long, but putting a new bumper on that car . . ." Rex shook his head. "Seems like a waste of money.

Maybe I could find one at the junkyard." He leaned down to inspect the body of the car. "But the car's rusty, too. To get one to hold for a while, it's going to be a little off center. I've got to attach it where I can find some good metal."

"I don't mind off center. That's not going to be the first thing people notice when they see my car. How long will that last?"

"Well, it should last as long as the car does." Rex rubbed his chin. "Of course, I didn't think your car would last this long."

"Thanks for taking care of it."

"I consider it both a work of charity and an experiment. How long can I keep this pile of . . ." He stopped, glanced at Adam. His look suggested he'd realized he was speaking to a minister. "How long can I keep this pile of rust going? We'll have to see, you, me, and the Lord."

❦

Adam hated those late phone calls. Every time the phone rang, he knew it was bad news. Who called with good news at—he blinked to look at the clock—one forty-five? He fumbled for the phone next to the chair and, when he finally corralled it, mumbled, "Hello."

"Pops, can you come get me?"

"What is it, Hector?" He sat up, suddenly alert. "Where are you? Are you okay?"

He and Hector had worked out a curfew. Ten on school nights but only with a good reason. One on weekends. First week of school and he was forty-five minutes late, not a lot.

"I just need you to . . . to come get me."

Adam noted a swishing sound on the *s* in *just.* "Have you been drinking?"

"Pops, please."

Yes, definite slurring. "Where are you?"

"At Hansen's Park, on Highway 29."

"I'll be there in ten minutes." Adam jumped from the chair, pulled his shoes on, then realized he couldn't leave Janey alone in the house. He didn't want to announce Hector's call, to explain the reason.

He picked up the phone and called the Kowalskis. "I've been called out," he said to George. "Can I bring Janey over?"

After George agreed, Adam bundled Janey in her blanket, lifted her, and headed out.

"What's happening?" Janey asked as he started down the stairs.

"I'm taking you next door. I got called out."

"'Kay," she mumbled and fell back to sleep.

Thank goodness. No need to explain further.

Nor did George ask any questions. He opened the door and let them into the living room.

"Put Janey on the sofa," Ouida said from the bed. "She'll be fine there."

Once he settled the child, Adam said, "Sorry to bother you."

"No bother," George said. "Ouida couldn't sleep so I was keeping her company."

"Thanks." Adam pulled out his keys and started toward the door before he realized Hector had his car. "Umm, one more thing. Could I borrow a car?"

"Sure." George pulled a set from a bowl on the hall table. "Take my car. Leave the keys under the front seat when you get back. We'll bring Janey home in the morning."

"Thanks." With a wave at both of them, he left.

Fifteen minutes later, Adam pulled off

the highway and into the park, a well-known site for keg parties. He had to guess that was why Hector was there. He had few delusions about the actions of high school jocks. He'd been one.

Hector stood inside the gates under a halogen light, leaning heavily against an old car with his head bowed. Bobby stood behind him. Adam stopped the car and stepped out.

"What's going on, guys?" Adam asked. "Did my car break down?"

Hector shook his head but still kept it down, not looking at Adam. "Pops, I drank too much. Don't think I should drive."

Adam waited for Hector to continue, the old allowing-the-guilty-to-fill-the-silence-with-excuses-and-explanations ploy.

"I'm sorry." He paused and forced back a belch. "I don't usually drink—oh, I've had a couple of beers before but not much."

"Okay." Adam gestured toward George's car. "Get in and we'll talk about it when we get home." Then he turned to Bobby. "How are you?"

"I'm okay. I don't drink. My mom would kill me if I did. But I came with Hector and none of the other guys were sober enough for me to want to ride with. Thought about driving Hector home in your car, but I don't trust it. We could make it a few feet and it'd die again and we'd be stuck in the middle of the highway."

"I understand, but I'd appreciate if you'd drive it home. It should make it that far without falling apart," Adam said.

Bobby looked over his shoulder at the old car. "Will you follow me?"

"Sure."

Bobby caught the keys Adam tossed him but didn't look pleased.

"I appreciate that, Bobby. Don't know how we'd get my car home otherwise. I'd let you drive this one"—he pointed to George's car and Bobby's face brightened—"but I borrowed it. Go ahead. I'll follow you, just in case."

The short caravan took off toward Butternut Creek going about thirty miles an hour. Adam focused on the off-center bumper in front of them to keep himself from lecturing Hector. That would come later. There were two approaches to driving his car: drive really fast so you got to the destination before the car fell apart, or drive very slowly so that if the car *did* fall apart, you wouldn't be gravely injured. Bobby obviously belonged to the second school. All this meant it was nearly three by the time they pulled into the Kowalskis' drive.

Seeing the lights off inside the Kowalski house, Adam parked in front, shoved the keys under the front seat, and got out of the Lexus.

"Bobby, let me drive you home," Adam said.

"Hey, I'm fine. I live two blocks north and no one in this town's going to jump me." He loped off.

As Adam headed toward the parsonage, Hector shoved himself out of the car and headed after him. He walked fairly well until he stumbled over a clump of grass and struggled to keep his balance.

"Coffee?" Adam asked when they entered. Not waiting for an answer, he headed into the kitchen and flipped on the coffeepot he'd set for six A.M.

Why coffee? Because that's what everyone on television and in movies did, although he'd heard it only changed a drunk into a wider-awake drunk.

"I'm going to . . ." Before he finished the

sentence, Hector sprinted toward the half bath.

By the time one cup of coffee had chugged out into the pot, Hector had returned to the kitchen looking terrible. Only fair, Adam thought. Actions had consequences, and if throwing up all night taught the kid a lesson, good.

"I'm going to take a shower and clean up." Hector looked at Adam. "Is that all right, sir?"

Hector never called him *sir.* The kid must be worried. Good.

Adam nodded and sat at the table, drinking coffee and rereading that morning's *American-Statesman.* He heard the water go on, then off a few minutes later.

When Hector came downstairs in clean jeans and a T-shirt but barefoot, Adam handed him a cup of coffee, sat down across from him at the kitchen table, and watched the kid. After another cup of coffee and one more visit to the bathroom, Hector still looked terrible but seemed fairly sober. Probably not the best time to discuss what had happened, not with a kid who had vomited and looked sick as a dog. But he figured Hector would sleep soundly for the rest of the night whereas Adam wouldn't sleep at all. No, he'd lie awake all night rehearsing what he needed to say over and over.

Taking care of the situation and getting a few hours' rest seemed like the best choice for him and he didn't care much right now about Hector's preference.

"Talk," Adam said. "Tell me about it."

"I'm not a drinker." Hector took a sip of the third cup of coffee, then blew on it to cool it. Finally, he lifted his eyes. "I should know better. This is how my father started. Look what happened to him."

Adam said nothing.

"Okay." Hector put the coffee down, leaned back in the chair, and closed his eyes. "A bunch of us were going to meet in the park, friends from the high school, other athletes, guys I hang with. I knew there'd be a keg there and some guys would bring the hard stuff, but I didn't plan to drink much. A little beer, that's all. But I started to feel sorry for myself." Hector sat up and made eye contact with Adam. "I wanted to feel better. Right now, my life is crap, and I wanted to feel good." He shook his head. "I should've known better. Getting drunk doesn't solve anything."

"Why did you feel sorry for yourself?"

"It's not you, Pops. You've been great for Janey and me. It's . . . it's . . . what about the future? You don't want me here for the rest of my life."

"Sure I do."

Hector's eyes narrowed. "You do?"

"As long as you need it, you have a home with me. I thought you knew that."

"I didn't know, wasn't sure." He drank more coffee. "But my education? Janey? What am I going to do with my life?"

"We can't solve those tonight, but we'll talk another time, maybe in a few days, when you're doing better. We'll figure them out together, you and I."

Hector nodded but didn't speak until he finally mumbled, "And then there's another problem." He took a long gulp of coffee. "Bree."

"Why's she a problem?"

"I really like her, but I don't have anything to offer her."

"Are you planning on getting married soon?"

Hector's eyes popped open. He considered Adam's words for a second before he laughed. "No, we aren't," he said once he stopped laughing. "Not even considering going steady, but I'd like to take her out. Like to invite her to homecoming but I don't have money for the tickets or a suit and flowers, just like for the prom. I can't swing all that."

"When's homecoming?"

He shook his head. "I don't know. Sometime in September."

"Have you asked her? Does she have a date?"

"I can't, but I don't think so. She expects me to ask her so it's been a little uncomfortable talking to her and avoiding that."

"Okay, we'll talk about that tomorrow, work things out. But right now we need to talk about tonight, what you did."

Hector nodded.

"Underage drinking is illegal."

"I know."

"While you are living in the parsonage, I expect you to follow the law. That means no drinking." He paused. "No drinking at all. Non-negotiable."

"Okay."

"How does the coach feel about drinking?"

"He doesn't allow it. If he knew we were out there, Coach would suspend us for a game or two, maybe even kick us off the team."

"Second, and here's the lecture. Drinking doesn't solve problems. If you're depressed, talk to me, talk to Coach, talk to someone."

Hector glanced at Adam. "And it's my father." He shook his head. "I'm supposed to go see him tomorrow." He glanced at the clock. "I mean, today. I hate going to that prison to see him."

"Don't go."

"He's my father."

Adam nodded. No need to remind Hector his father hadn't taken that responsibility seriously. He knew that. "How 'bout this? Cancel for tomorrow. Next Saturday, I'll go with you and wait for you so you won't be on your own."

"You'd do that for me?"

"Of course I would."

"Thanks." Hector sipped the coffee before he added, "This is going to sound crazy, but it sure would help if we had a hoop out there." He jerked his thumb toward the parking lot. "Working out makes life better, cuts back on stress. I don't worry as much when I'm playing ball."

For a moment, Adam wondered if putting up a hoop would seem like a reward for bad behavior, but he quickly tossed that theory. Hector needed this. He was seventeen, jam-packed with testosterone, recovering from years with an abusive father, and even now bringing up his sister, an obligation he was far too young for. He'd never had a role model to show him how to handle problems. Physical activity probably would help him stay more level. It always helped Adam.

He'd order it set up and worry about how to pay for it later. Sounded like the kind of project his mother could get behind: Put up a hoop and save a small-town kid.

"I knew I couldn't drive home," Hector said. "That was the hardest part, having to call you, but I figured it would be worse if I had an accident and totaled your car and, maybe, hurt someone."

"Thanks for calling. That showed maturity. I'd hate for you to have hurt yourself or another person. You have to know I care about you more than I care about my car." Adam reached out and placed his hand on Hector's arm. "Even though you have a father and you're not even ten years younger than I am, I think of you as my son. I'm here for you. Always."

Tears rolled down Hector's cheeks. His eyes looked huge in his dark face. "Thanks, Pops."

Adam shoved a box of Kleenex toward Hector. "Take a couple of aspirin and drink a lot of water. Then go to bed. We'll talk more tomorrow."

As Hector filled a glass with ice and water, Adam added, "You are going to homecoming so you should ask Bree right away, before she decides to go with someone else."

"I'll call her tomorrow morning. I'm goin' up to bed."

As he watched Hector start upstairs, a wave of guilt hit him. He hadn't done enough. If he was going to do the father thing, not merely the kid-lives-in-my-home thing that he'd been perfectly content with, he needed to do more than give quick forgiveness and easy grace. No, Hector needed to understand consequences. "Not so fast," Adam said.

"What?" Hector stopped.

"Tomorrow you're going to dig a big hole for me."

Hector blinked. "A big hole?" Then he burped. "Sorry."

"Yes." Adam attempted to sound tough, but he could seldom carry that off. "A huge hole." After a pause, he added, "One more thing. You're nothing like your father."

"Thanks." Halfway up the steps, he stopped and said, "Pops, I'm sorry. I really am."

"Go on. We'll talk more in the morning." Adam watched him disappear.

Attendance at homecoming should be easy to fix. Hector didn't need a tux or a limo. He had the dark slacks from the prom. They'd find him a great shirt and tie. Could he ask Sam to loan him his treasured yellow Mustang? Probably not, but maybe Willow would let him use her car. He knew Hector wouldn't want to drive the car with a bumper that threatened to fall off, a window he couldn't put up, and the risk—actually the promise—of more disasters. Not for the homecoming dance.

The school kept the price of the tickets low so all the kids could afford to attend. As far as he could figure, the flowers would be the most expensive part. He bet the florist would work out something in exchange for a few hours of work from Hector.

Yeah, they'd talk about that tomorrow, after the kid finished digging the hole.

❦

Adam sat on the front porch, working on his sermon while the morning breeze cooled him off. Janey sat at the small table coloring.

In a spot next to the parking lot, Hector didn't look nearly as cool. Now shirtless, hung over, and with sweat pouring off him as he dug more deeply, the kid probably felt horrid. Good.

"How much farther?" Hector leaned on the shovel and panted.

"You're getting closer."

"Hey, Preacher."

Adam looked up from his notes and waved. "How're you doing, Coach?"

Gabe Borden strolled up the steps. "I hear our boys did a little drinking last night." Gabe looked across the lawn at

Hector, who waved. Gabe didn't return the greeting.

"Hector says Bobby didn't, but, yeah, Hector did. That's why he's digging that hole."

Gabe nodded. "Good punishment. Now I need to do a little of my own. I'm going to suspend him and the other guys who participated for the first game of the season and threaten a lot more. I have a list from an unnamed source."

"Fine with me."

"I'm going to put the fear of God in him." Then he stopped watching Hector and faced Adam. "Sorry about that. Guess that fear-of-God thing is your job."

"Hey, I appreciate the extra voice. Sometimes you have to get their attention, make them listen."

"Double team."

The two men nodded to each other in perfect agreement, then folded their arms and watched Hector dig.

A few minutes later, Bree walked across the lawn. After greeting the two men and Janey, she shouted at Hector, "I heard what you did last night, you idiot."

Hector, covered with sweat and probably

aching in every joint of his body as well as both eyes and his head, put down the shovel and squinted. He didn't say a word. From Bree's posture, tone, and words, he must have figured nothing he said would make a bit of difference and that Bree probably wasn't even close to finished with him.

"You got drunk and the preacher had to come get you?" She shook her head. "I can't believe you were so stupid." She took a step closer and leaned toward him, just in case he couldn't hear her shouts.

Adam bet he wished he'd taken a few more aspirin.

"Why did you do that?" Bree demanded. "Does the coach know?" She looked up at the porch. "Coach, do you know what this idiot did last night?"

Gabe nodded. "I plan to talk to him after he finishes digging that hole."

"I can talk now, Coach." Hector dropped the shovel.

"No, you keep digging. Preacher and I'll tell you when you're done."

"I shouldn't talk to you ever again," Bree said. "I thought you were smarter."

"Okay. I did something dumb. I'm sorry.

I apologized to Pops and I'm apologizing to you, and pretty soon, I'm going to apologize to Coach and he's going to get really mad at me. On top of that, I still have to dig this hole."

"Serves you right." Bree turned and strode away.

"Want to go to homecoming with me?" Hector asked.

"That kid has a terrible sense of timing," Coach mumbled.

"What?" She turned back to face him. "You go out and get drunk with the guys, you get in trouble, and I'm yelling at you and the coach is going to suspend you and the preacher has you digging a big hole. Isn't that enough for one day? How could you ask me to go to the dance with you when all this stuff is going on?"

Hector shrugged and picked up the shovel. "Okay. If you don't want to go."

"I didn't say I wouldn't go with you." Bree stalked toward him and glared. "Are you serious?" she demanded. "After what you did? I have my reputation to think of."

"I'm not proud of what I did." Hector glanced at the men on the porch then back to Bree. "I'm sorry I disappointed you. I disappointed myself, too." He cleared his throat. "Of course I'm serious about homecoming. Wouldn't ask you if I wasn't." He started to dig again. "Want to go? Pops and I are figuring things out like cars and flowers."

She considered his words. "Okay, then. Yes, I'll go with you, but no drinking."

"Okay." He pulled out a shovel load of dirt and tossed it in the growing heap. "I'll call you later."

As Bree walked off, Hector glanced at Adam with a victorious smile before he went back to shoveling.

"Don't you think that's pretty big for a base for a basketball hoop?" Gabe asked.

"Could be, but he can always fill it in. It'll be the strongest post in town. Come inside and cool down. I'll have him dig for another half hour and tell him to stop."

As he entered the room Adam used for everything except cooking and sleeping, Gabe stopped at the family pictures on the bookcase. "Who's this?" he asked casually and pointed.

"My sister."

"Guess she got the good looks in the family."

"Thanks." Adam looked at Hannah, laughing with their parents, looking carefree and very young. The backdrop was the giant Ferris wheel in London. "She doesn't look like that anymore."

"When was this taken?" Gabe turned toward Adam with a frown.

"Three years ago."

"She's changed?"

"When I saw her a year ago, she'd changed. She's a doctor. Travels around Africa caring for people in refugee camps." Adam shook his head. "She says she loves it, that she's doing God's work, but it wears on her. I worry but she doesn't listen."

As he moved toward the kitchen, Adam saw Gabe take the photo from the bookcase and study it.

❧

Hector and Adam made the trip to Cogansville Federal Prison in a car borrowed from Winnie. They didn't talk much. Even when Adam made an occasional comment to show his support, Hector answered in a short but polite sentence, then returned to his thoughts.

As they approached the town, Hector said, "Someday you're going to have to get a better car. You can't keep borrowing them."

"I know, but people don't seem to mind."

Hector nodded. "Nice bunch of people in Butternut Creek."

On the return trip, Hector said, "My father's doing okay. He wants to come back home when his sentence is up, but I don't know if that's best for him. You know, same old crowd."

"How would you feel about his being in town?"

"By the time he gets out, I'm going to be old enough he wouldn't bother me. But Janey, I worry about her." He glanced at Adam. "She'll be in high school. Tough to be in high school when your father's been in prison. The kids don't let you forget it. And he could bother her, make her remember what life was like when the three of us lived together and his druggie friends slept there."

"Hector, we'll work on this together. If your father comes back to Butternut Creek, you and I and Janey will face that together. Until then, we'll go visit him as often as you need to."

"Thanks," Hector mumbled, then turned

away and stared out the window for a few minutes. Then he asked, "Pops, did you ever drink?"

"Yeah, I had a couple of beers in high school and college, even got drunk a few times, but that's it. I stopped drinking anything when I started seminary."

"You did? I mean, you got drunk and you stopped drinking." Hector shook his head. "I've never known anyone who stopped drinking."

"I figured a minister shouldn't drink. Not because of morality but because of example." He searched his brain for the Bible verse he wanted to toss in here. "I can't remember this exactly, but Paul wrote that just because I can do something that doesn't hurt me, my example could lead another astray. There are some recovering alcoholics in the congregation."

"Really? Who?"

"Can't tell you. Confidential, you know. But suppose they see me drink a beer and that would have them start drinking again? Or a teenager saw me with a beer and started to drink. What kind of an example would I be?"

"That's a little far-fetched, Pops."

"Yeah, I guess it is, but I don't need a beer that much."

"Could put a little weight on you." A flicker of a smile appeared on Hector's face. "You're still too skinny."

"Yeah, so will chocolate. I'll stick to cake and donuts and Ouida's muffins."

Chapter Twelve

Adam looked forward to seeing Gussie. Of course he did. Her presence always brightened his day.

But at this moment, it didn't. Actually, he'd begun to wonder about him and Gussie a few days back when he'd asked her to meet him for dinner instead of coffee and she'd turned him down. And there had been a special musical program at the old theater on the square where Mac would be playing in an ensemble, but Gussie said she couldn't attend that, either.

Yesterday he'd paid particular attention

to Willow and Sam in church. They really loved each other, showed it in everything they did. Not that they made out on the pew or acted in any way inappropriate, but they held hands. Sam looked at her with such love. When they stood for the hymns, they sort of tilted toward each other, as if gravity, or another force, pulled them together. That was what he wanted.

And Gussie jumped when he touched her.

Suck it up, Adam lectured himself. He and Gussie had only been together a few weeks. There was time. He'd told her he wouldn't push. Patience.

But were they together? Really? They weren't even dating. For an hour every week, if she didn't have something else to do, they chatted over coffee and pie. The only variety came in which kind of pie they ordered. Frustrated as he felt, knowing he'd expected a little more than emailing two or three times a week or the occasional coffee in Marble Falls, he wasn't ready to give it up.

He didn't believe she was stringing him along. It was that "broken" thing. If he could get through that, find out what the problem was, maybe they could fix it. If not, at some time he might think of giving up.

But having faith and hope didn't mean he didn't notice the deeper problems that surfaced every time they met. He couldn't get through to her. She was always lovely and charming, but she'd completely closed off the part of her life that haunted her, displaying only the glorious and glossy exterior. Oh, he bet he knew more than most people about her. She'd talked, briefly, about her problem, but almost immediately she erected that barrier again.

So why did she even bother to drive to Marble Falls to meet him? And why did she continue to answer his emails in a breezy, friendly way that didn't give him any insight into who Gussie Milton was?

For this reason, once they were seated in a booth inside, each with a cup of coffee in front of them, he said, "Gussie, I want to see you more. I want to take you on a date, go out for dinner, head into Austin for a play, spend more time together."

Her smile disappeared quickly when he said those words. "But . . . but we are dating," she said.

"No, Gussie, we are not," he stated firmly.

He hated that flutter of fear in her expression but had to finish. "We meet for coffee and discuss church, that's what we do. Today we're going to discuss a tubing trip for the youth."

"I told you . . ." She stopped and swallowed hard. "I asked you to be patient."

"Gussie, I'm not pushing. Okay, I am, but I need to understand. I want to date you, I want to see you more often, to get to know you better. I'd like to know what's happening, to share whatever hurt you so much."

"I can't talk about it. Not here."

"Okay." He reached out and took her hand. She didn't pull away. "Can we talk about whatever *it* is soon?"

"I'll email you the details."

He blinked. "Email?"

"I can't talk about it."

"Can we discuss whatever this is in person, after you send the email?"

"You may not want to, once you know."

"Can we get together when I know what happened?"

Surprisingly, she put her other hand over his before she pulled both away. All the glow that was Gussie had disappeared.

She looked at him from somber eyes in a serious face. "It's not only my opinion. *You* know I'm broken, too. You recognize that. You just said you wonder why I can't give you more. Maybe we need to decide— either now or after you read my email—if we want to see each other more."

"Can I heat up your coffee?" A waitress reached between them to fill their cups. "Everything all right here?"

Everything was obviously not all right but both he and Gussie said, "Fine," and smiled at the waitress as she topped off their cups.

"This isn't the right place or time," she said after the waitress took off.

He'd lost this round.

🐦

"Someday I'm going to shoot your father," Gussie's mother said from the kitchen.

Having just walked in from the disastrous meeting with Adam, Gussie would've preferred time alone. However, with her father's life at stake, she probably should talk her mother down. She placed her purse on the sofa and went into the kitchen to stand next to her mom, who was looking out the back window at the yard.

"He has no sense, none at all."

Gussie's father pruned bushes behind the house.

"It's hot this afternoon and he's not well." Her mother turned around to glare at Gussie as if the whole thing were her fault. "He still has that cough although he tries to hide it, and he's no spring chicken. He says he's over the pneumonia."

Gussie put her hand on her mother's shoulder. "Mom, he's seventy-four years old. You've been married over fifty years. He's not going to change. We both know that."

"Of course I do. That's why I'm so frustrated. And I'm not about to change, either, you know. I'll always fuss at him." She closed the curtain as if not seeing her husband would allow her to stop worrying about him. "Oh, enough about your father. Tell me about your young man. Did you have a nice afternoon?"

"Very nice," she lied. No reason to upset her mother even more. "He's not really my young man."

Her mother considered the statement. "You said he was. Has that changed? Are you having second thoughts?" She took a deep breath before asking, "Gussie, does he know what happened to you? Have you told him?"

"Oh, that took place so long ago—"

"Gussie," she interrupted. "Does he know what happened to you?"

"Mom, don't bug me about this. It's my life."

"Yes, dear, I know, but . . ."

Because her mother didn't seem likely to let the subject go and she didn't want to upset her, Gussie forced a smile. "I'm fine, really. I'm going to go out and help Dad," she said as she turned and left the kitchen.

That evening, Gussie sat in front of her computer and studied the screen. The problem with writing about personal matters with a word processor was that she didn't have the sensual pleasure of wadding up a bad draft and throwing it on the floor.

She began to type until she had an email that covered three screens. Too much information. She clicked it into MAIL WAITING TO BE SENT and started over until she had the few words that explained what had happened. If he didn't turn away from her—and she truly believed Adam wouldn't—he could ask her more. Maybe she would answer.

She placed that one in her TO BE SENT folder because she needed to consider, to ponder, to decide her course.

❦

Monday evening, Adam and Hector had played a hard game of one-on-one at the new hoop, the inaugural game. After that, about fifteen players—male and female— chose sides and played until nearly ten o'clock.

"Gets really dark back here," Bobby said.

True. The lights had been placed in the parking lot to provide security, not luminosity.

When they could no longer see the ball and Bobby had hit Hector in the back with a fast, hard pass, the game disbanded and the players wandered off. After a shower, Adam sat in front of his computer. Would he find a message from Gussie? He had no idea what to expect, what she would say, but he hoped.

Nothing there.

Because the email didn't arrive until late Tuesday evening and he'd been too busy to check earlier, Adam didn't find it until noon on Wednesday on his office computer. He'd waited impatiently but now that he had it, he didn't want to open it.

The subject glared at him from the email queue: "Hello." Innocuous and non-threatening. He kept staring at it.

Maggie had left by then so he had complete solitude. Probably no one would interrupt unless one of the retired men showed up. They often stopped in because they had plenty of time. No one figured a minister did anything from Monday through Saturday, so they felt they should keep him company for hours. He always stopped whatever he was doing to talk because he considered those minutes to be ministry. Usually, he attempted to run them off after twenty or thirty minutes so he could get some work done.

Well aware he was allowing his thoughts to wander because he did not want to open that email, his finger hovered over the OPEN button. Would he find a way to be with Gussie after he read this? Would she permit him to see her again? He believed that as soon as he clicked that button, their lives would change. Maybe it had been better to ignore the barrier and accept what Gussie had to give.

Coward. She'd been brave enough to write him. He should have enough courage to read it.

He opened the email.

"I was raped when I was eighteen by my boyfriend."

That was all.

Oh, Lord. He closed his eyes and dropped his head. "God, please grant Gussie your healing love and bless me with understanding," he prayed.

He read the few words again. How should he answer? He had so little to go on. Finally he wrote, "I'm sorry that happened. May I come to Austin or Roundville to see you?"

That evening, he had the reply. "No, let's meet in Marble Falls for coffee Monday. As usual."

So he sent flowers, yellow and orange roses.

The next day, he sent more.

On the third day, he found an email from Gussie with the subject "STOP!" He opened it to read, "Thank you. I appreciate the flowers but save your money for something you really need."

As if he didn't really need Gussie.

❧

Adam couldn't get used to how early school started in Texas. It was the first Friday of September and the kids had been back in school for two weeks, football would start shortly, and life had settled into a steady flow.

Yes, life had become fairly peaceful, leaving him plenty of time to worry about Gussie until Jesse and Ralph came into his office, Ralph carrying a large tool satchel and Jesse a small carton.

"Hear you don't have an intercom in here," Jesse said. "You know Ralph used to work for the phone company." He nodded toward Ralph, who looked like a lineman in his white shirt, gray slacks, and heavy boots. "I'm only the gofer." Jesse wore his usual jeans, plaid shirt, and cowboy boots. "But I can do a lot of stuff. We're going to install one."

Oh, please, Lord, no. Adam had heard tales about the havoc retired men could wreak on church wiring. At a lunch meeting with the ministerial alliance, Mattie described the time she couldn't use the computer without turning on the light in the bathroom. With that, all the other ministers had chimed in with horror stories. Adam bet he'd have one to tell in a few days.

He should have more faith. "I didn't realize you worked for the phone company, Ralph," Adam said. "When was that?"

"One summer when I was in high school."

Fifty-some years ago, Adam figured.

"But things haven't changed all that much," Ralph said confidently. "And we've got instructions on the box." He held it up. "Thought we'd put a line through to the fellowship hall, too." He pointed in that direction. "Keep you from having to go down there to talk to people."

Ralph made it sound as if that area was hundreds of yards away and filled every hour with a whirl of activity and thousands of people who needed to be accessed. Adam wished it were, but at this time, AA met there twice a week, the vets' group on Wednesday, and yoga at noon on Monday.

But why object? If they wanted to set up an intercom, fine. Adam didn't want to turn anyone away, and he bet their wives would be happy for them to be out of the house and useful.

Besides, what could go wrong? Surely with wireless technology, installing an intercom was a simple matter of plugging it in.

Without waiting for his approval, the two men put their burdens down and began opening the box. Even going after the carton with scissors, a knife, and a saw, they couldn't get it open. That should have been a clue.

As Adam watched the men from the door between offices, Maggie stood beside him and whispered, "You aren't going to let them do this, are you? You do know that they'll mess up the phone system, right?"

"Have faith. How hard can this be? I probably could do this." He patted Maggie's shoulder before she huffed off. "Guys, I'm going to make some visits while you're working to get out of your way."

But they didn't hear him. They were celebrating the defeat of the cardboard box too loudly to notice.

After dropping by the nursing home, stopping to chat with Ouida, and grabbing a sandwich at home, Adam headed back to the office to check in with Jesse and Ralph. When he walked into the reception office and flicked the light switch, nothing happened.

From the silence, he realized the men had left. In the light from the door and the windows, he could see wires—telephone or electrical or both, he couldn't tell—dangling from the ceiling. He picked up the phone. No dial tone.

The light switch in his office didn't work, either. Taking care not to fall over or bump into anything, Adam navigated to the window, opened the blinds, and looked around. On the corner of his desk sat a little box with two buttons on it. One of the buttons bore the label MAGGIE; the other, FELLOWSHIP HALL. To test the system, he pressed the one for the front office. Nothing. Didn't seem to be hooked up yet. Even if it was, they'd turned the electricity off. He glanced at the dark, dead screen of his monitor. After checking that the machine was turned on, he flipped the control of the power strip off then back on.

He glanced overhead at the dangling wires. They didn't look live. No electrical charges zapped out the ends, but he wasn't going to touch them to find out. He felt pretty sure Ralph and Jesse had cut off the electricity here before they began their work. With that thought, Adam picked up the flashlight he kept in his desk, went into the hall, and opened the fuse box to shine the light inside. Yes, two circuits had been shut off.

Nothing would work.

On top of that, the heat smothered him, felt hotter than mid-July when the air conditioner struggled to cool the offices. He reached up and couldn't feel any air circulating from the vent over his desk. The ceiling fan didn't move.

Adam glanced down at his computer for the time. Of course, it didn't appear on the dark screen or on the electric clock plugged into the wall. He looked at his wrist: one thirty. The men had probably knocked off for lunch. He'd work at home, get out of their way until they finished.

❦

When Adam arrived the next morning, the electricity was still off. The wires still dangled from the ceiling. Of course, with the electricity off, the offices had no phone, no computers, and no air-conditioning.

"Might want to move your things to the fellowship hall," Maggie said. "That's what the ministers usually do after Ralph has messed with the wiring." Even in the dim light, Adam could make out her expression. It said, *I told you so.*

He flipped out his cell and dialed Ralph.

"Oh, Preacher," his wife Annabella said. "He's up in Waco. You know, he was in the army. Has his physical today at the VA."

"Do you know when he'll be home?"

"Oh, not until eight or nine at the earliest. He likes to shop, get a nice meal before heading back."

"What about tomorrow? He left some wires hanging and the electricity's off."

"Oh, dear. We're headed out in the morning to visit our kids up in Corsicana. He said they ran into some problems with that installation in the church and he needs to pick up a few parts. He'll probably finish up next week."

"Would you mention I called and ask if he would stop by as soon as possible? We do have church Sunday."

"Oh, I'm sure he left the electricity on in the sanctuary."

"Great." Realizing the sarcasm that

came from his frustration probably wasn't the right tone, he added, "I'd really appreciate his calling me ASAP."

"Of course."

After Annabella hung up, Adam called Jesse. "Hey, Jesse," he said before he realized the answering machine had picked up. "Please give me a call on my cell as soon as possible."

About all he could do. He headed to the fellowship hall.

Unfortunately, wires hung from the ceiling and the lights didn't go on there, either.

Maggie stood in the door, barely hiding her smile. "How hard could installing an intercom system be?"

"I should call an electrician."

"Not a good idea. You'd hurt their feelings."

"But look at this mess. We won't be able to use the fellowship hall, either." He paced and mulled his options. Few came to mind.

"Shove everyone outside after church to keep them away from the wires," Maggie suggested. "Have the ladies come up with refreshments. Make it like an outside reception, a special occasion."

He headed down to the diner to talk to

Miss Birdie. After he explained the situation, she said, "Sure, Preacher. We can take care of that."

Then she laughed, a sound Adam had heard only a handful of times. It always startled him with the pure delight it expressed.

"I know you can't stop them from making repairs to the church, but the past minister limited Jesse and Ralph to maintenance that didn't require the opening of walls or ceilings. He made another rule. They had to make all repairs on Monday so normalcy could be restored by Sunday." She cackled. "Guess you've learned your lesson."

❦

"How was your weekend?" Gussie smiled at him, completely comfortable as if she'd never written him that email, as if he didn't know about the rape.

Denial? Or did she feel as if telling him closed the discussion? Had she dealt with this problem from her past and it no longer haunted her? No, if she had she never would have leaped away from his touch nor told him she was broken. His best guess was not only denial but *I don't want to talk about this* as well.

He hadn't expected that response but should have. Gussie was always happy and smiling, always up except for the few minutes she'd allowed him past her facade. No, not a facade. Gussie truly was upbeat, most of the time, but he'd caught a glimpse of that other part of her. Now she'd made it off limits again. Okay, he'd accept that. For now.

❧

Gussie rubbed the handle of the coffee cup before she glanced up at Adam, who also rubbed the handle of his coffee cup. For the first time ever, conversation between the two lapsed once they'd discussed Ralph's and Jesse's repairs and her parents' health.

"I'm going to order a piece of pie," she said.

Scintillating, that's what she and her conversational gambits were.

"What kind?" Adam asked.

Poor man. He couldn't think of what to say, and she felt sure he wouldn't bring up the topic of her email. She certainly didn't want to. Even writing it had been painful. Sending the short message had taken every bit of courage she possessed.

"I like the rhubarb but I'm going to be adventurous and try lemon meringue."

"Aah," he said. "Risky. I'll try apple."

They placed their orders and, once the waitress walked off, stared at each other.

"How's Hector?"

They discussed the Firestones for a few minutes.

What else could they talk about? She'd thought she and Adam could discuss nearly everything but that one topic, the unspeakable, hung between them like a scrim in a theater. They could both see it but both refused to acknowledge it, pretended it didn't exist even as it separated them.

She'd been very clear about her privacy. She knew if they wanted to move on, to speak about what she always called "the event," she'd have to bring it up. The waitress set their pieces of pie in front of them. She took another gulp of coffee and fed herself several forkfuls she couldn't even taste.

Adam took a few bites then stopped and watched the ice cream melt down the slice and puddle on his plate. "I'm not very hungry," he said.

Okay. If Adam not eating his pie didn't signal his mood, nothing would.

"What did you think . . ." She stopped because the words stuck in her throat. After a quick drink of water and an internal repetition of the Serenity Prayer, Gussie said, "What did you think about my email?"

"I appreciate that you shared that with me." He smiled gently, then picked up his fork and took another bite of the now soggy pie.

Was that it? Had he returned to his dessert because she'd relieved him of the necessity of bringing up the subject of her email or because he didn't want to discuss it anymore?

When would she stop trying to figure people out? A bite of pie could simply be a bite of pie.

Sometimes her brain kept going and working as she attempted to figure life out. Even with that, she couldn't make sense of the situation between Adam and her, couldn't seem to figure out what to do next. Like him, she kept cutting off little parts of the pie, chewing and swallowing. She concentrated very hard on the fork as if she feared jabbing herself in the eye instead of putting it in her mouth.

"Gussie, if you want to discuss what happened or need anything from me, tell me," he said. "I'm willing. I care about you."

With several bites of that delicious pie left, she put down her fork, pulled together every particle of her courage, and said, "I'd been dating Lennie for about a month. We met in freshman composition and I trusted him."

She glanced at Adam. "I'd never been drunk before. And I've never been drunk since."

He put down his fork and listened.

"I thought, *What kind of college student has never even had a drink of anything? Isn't that the college experience? Drinking and carousing and experimenting?*"

"Gussie, you don't have to tell me this, not now, not here, if you're uncomfortable."

"If I don't tell you now, I may not have the nerve another time." She took in a deep breath. "Lennie said he'd take care of me, make sure I didn't drink too much or get in trouble. I believed him. We went to a fraternity party and I drank a couple of glasses of something fruity they were serving. Illegal because I was eighteen, but no one cared. It was good. I couldn't even taste the alcohol but it packed a punch." She reached out and grabbed his hand, holding on so tightly her fingers hurt.

She didn't like talking about this, not a bit. But as she turned to scan the other patrons of the restaurant, she realized this could be a good place to talk about the event. Here, as emotion burbled inside her, she couldn't allow herself to lose control surrounded by all these people.

"The alcohol hit me hard. I don't know why. Could be because I'm not a drinker or I drank it too fast or that fruit juice tasted so sweet—anyway, I got woozy and sick. I could barely stand up and had to lean against something—a wall or a chair—to walk." She blinked tears back. "I'm so ashamed."

He squeezed her hand. "You can stop now. You don't have to say more."

"Yes, I do." The words poured. "Lennie took me back to his apartment. He said I could sleep it off there. I didn't want to go back to the dorm in that condition. When I woke up—I don't know how much later—he was on top of me." She pulled her hand back, picked up her glass and drained it. "I never reported him. At first, I wanted to forget everything, then, as time went on . . . well, too much time had passed. The police would wonder why I hadn't reported it and Lennie had witnesses I'd had too much to drink. I couldn't handle that. I wanted to forget, pretend it never happened." She glanced at him with wide eyes. "I still do."

She stood quickly, nearly knocking the table over. "I have to go now," she said and tossed a bill on the table.

Before she fled, she noticed Adam's pale face and his eyes filled with an emotion she couldn't interpret at the moment. Feeling like the stupidest of idiots for opening up *here*, she forced herself not to flee from the restaurant but stopped at the door. A mistake because Adam caught up with her before she could leave.

Okay, what now, Miss I'll-tell-the-story-my-way? Hadn't she learned this wasn't about someone else at another time? "The event" was that *she*, Gussie Milton, had been raped by a man she'd trusted, a man she'd thought she could fall in love with.

She heard Adam tell the waitress the

money was on the table, then he held the door for her.

Once outside, he took her hand. "Gussie." He stopped speaking as if he didn't have any more idea what to do next than she did. They could not stand in the middle of Marble Falls only a few yards from the heavy traffic on Highway 281 with cars and trucks whizzing past them. "I'm sorry."

"Not your fault." Gussie fumbled through her purse looking for her keys. "Don't worry. I'm fine."

"Oh, sure, I'm going to let you drive home now."

When had she given him permission to tell her what she could and couldn't do? Well, back when she'd told him about "the event." And probably when she'd run out of the restaurant and now, when she was standing in the parking lot quivering.

"I know I can't." She closed her purse and looked at him for a few seconds before she leaned against him. How odd that she'd do that, but how great that he stood there, warm and trustworthy. "I know, but I've always run home for comfort." *And to hide*, she added to herself. She didn't say the words aloud because she'd already given up more of herself to Adam than she had to anyone other than her parents.

"We need to find a place that's more private," he said.

From the movement of his body, she could tell he was looking around for inspiration, but she didn't want to lift her head or step away from him.

"I won't leave you to face this alone." He handed her a Kleenex. He'd learned to carry a pocketful, one of his ministerial tools and necessities.

"Thanks," she said. "I'm not crying." But she was, she realized when she felt her cheeks, and she was having trouble breathing. Odd when she felt like a huge burden had been lifted from her by sharing. "It may not look like it but I feel better than I have for years." She stepped back. "Let's take a walk."

❦

Gussie had leaned against him for comfort and support. In the restaurant, she'd put her hand on his while she told him what had happened to her. A much-abridged story, he guessed, but nonetheless a step forward.

They didn't speak as they walked down

to a park overlooking the lake. "Gussie, I'm sorry that happened to you."

"Thank you, Adam. For listening and not turning away."

He wanted to question her, find out more. But not now. They found a bench looking over the lake and sat down. She even touched his hand again. Yes, he'd like more but, for now, having Gussie next to him felt like more than enough.

Someday they'd have to talk about what happened next, after the rape, but not now. He didn't believe she could take it. Instead of speaking, they watched the water. Together.

Chapter Thirteen

Adam had a spring in his step. A stupid phrase he'd never thought he'd use, a saying that went back generations. He also had a song in his heart and smile on his face. He walked like the conqueror of the world and wished he could tell Miss Birdie that he thought the Widows' matchmaking efforts could stop, be called completed and successful.

He didn't, of course. In the first place, Miss Birdie would act obnoxious in her victory. Secondly, he didn't want to talk about him and Gussie possibly becoming an "us" because what had seemed like a bridge crossed now felt like only a minor change. He'd hoped the confession signaled that she was falling or had fallen or perhaps anticipated falling in love with him. Now it seemed more like a tiny step, that maybe the idea of falling in love no longer nauseated her.

And, third, there were those other old expressions his grandmother had repeated: "Many a slip 'twixt the tongue and the lip" and "Don't count your chickens." Et cetera.

Two or three times a day, he and Gussie emailed or texted. They set up a date for Friday, the format to be decided later. Once she'd called to say she was headed toward San Saba and would he meet her for lunch in Butternut Creek? The sight of them together had made Miss Birdie glow as she bustled around them, filling nearly full glasses of tea and forcing dessert on them. After that, they'd wandered around the courthouse, sat for a while on a bench in the square, and chatted. One of his best afternoons ever.

Life hadn't changed much in Butternut Creek. Ouida continued to improve. He'd officiated at the wedding of Winnie and the general, Sam's father. They'd gone off somewhere for a honeymoon.

Wires no longer dangled from ceilings all over the church. Some of the men—not Jesse and Ralph, who'd admitted defeat— had coiled them up and capped them off, then turned the power back on. He and Maggie still had to shout at each other, but they had phones and lights as well as large holes in the ceilings of the offices and the fellowship hall.

Through the window, Adam could see the new basketball hoop in the parking lot. Great idea. Used at night and weekends, and no doubt would be a busy place this coming summer. As the coach had decreed, Hector dribbled everywhere except the church. He'd decided that wouldn't be respectful—but he dribbled the ball right up to the front door. After several accidents, Adam had banished it from the parsonage as well.

He'd emailed stories about Butternut Creek to his sister as he did every Friday. In one he told another story about Chewy and a backpack, finishing it with, "He's become one of the church's best evangelistic tools."

She seldom answered, but she needed his support. He hoped the funny stories cheered her up. He couldn't imagine anything more different from his life here and hers over there. How did she do it?

His parents wrote they'd visited Paris. The Chunnel had become a shortcut to Europe for them. They loved Europe and planned to send him a ticket so he could visit soon.

Life was good. Today he was going to wallow in being happy.

He began by looking at a computer file of church members he needed to call and chose one he hadn't seen in church.

"Hello, Mrs. Gibson," he said. "This is Adam Jordan, minister at the Christian Church."

Silence.

"How are you doing this morning?"

"Fine." Her voice sounded begrudging, as if she hated to give out even this small bit of information.

"I'm sorry I haven't gotten in touch with you sooner. The chair of the elders tells me you're a member of the church but haven't been able to attend for a while."

"That's right." Another pause followed. "What's your name again?"

"Adam. Adam Jordan, I don't believe I've met you."

"Reverend Jordan, nice of you to call." Her quiet voice quivered. "The problem is that it's hard for me to make it on Sunday morning. I have a lot of trouble with my joints—arthritis, you know—and I don't get moving until about noon. Then a migraine hits and puts me in bed, in the dark."

"Sounds as if you have a lot of physical problems. I'm sorry to hear that."

"Thank you. On top of that . . . well, you don't want to hear an old lady complaining about her aches and pains."

How to answer that? "If you want to talk about them, please tell me."

For another few minutes, she gave what his uncle Bob, a physician, had called "an organ recital," describing the appalling condition of her heart and her liver and various other ailments he didn't catch. He stopped taking notes after several repetitions of the phrase, "None of the doctors thought I'd live."

"You know, our elders take communion to people who can't make it to church.

Could they drop by this Sunday? Would that be convenient?"

Again silence. Had they been disconnected? No, there was no dial tone. He glanced at the phone to see that the *in use* button glowed red. "Mrs. Gibson?" he asked.

"I am not," she said testily, obviously insulted, "I am *not* a shut-in. I shop for myself. I play Bunco with my friends. I drive. I go to the beauty parlor. I am not a shut-in and don't need the elders to bring me anything or for you to visit."

With that, she disconnected. He knew for sure when the dial tone beeped from the speaker. Adam turned the phone off and laughed.

Although too weak to go to church, it seemed Mrs. Gibson could do anything else she wanted.

An imp inside him wanted to turn her name over to the elders, but that would only cause those leaders trouble. Instead he wrote, "Call next year. Don't treat as shut-in," on Mrs. Gibson's card and filed it.

❦

Birdie listened to the sounds of Carlos the Cat coming from the bathroom: *Whap! Whap! Whap!*

Mac had put Ping-Pong balls in the tub and the silly animal loved to bat them around. Mac said they'd given him new life. Instead of sleeping twenty-three hours a day, now Carlos slept twenty-two hours and fifty minutes and played in the bathtub for a few minutes several times a day.

She hated it when the cat wanted to continue chasing those balls and Birdie wanted to settle down for a nice soak. Whose joints were more important? The breadwinner's or those of a skinny, elderly cat? Didn't Birdie work to put food in his bowl? Nevertheless, she never bothered him.

Oh, my, had she gotten soft. Allowing a cat to inconvenience her because the girls adored him and he scratched people who tried to move him.

She stood up from Bree's bed where she'd been contemplating a far more difficult problem.

Fashion or style or just plain pornography?

School had been in session for almost a month. Still hot here in Texas, would be through part of October. Wasn't the heat that bothered Birdie. It was the clothing, those doggone tiny tops the girls liked to wear. Said it was too hot to wear regular T-shirts. So why was the district spending taxpayer money for air-conditioning if the girls had to wear those bits of nothing to stay cool?

Not that Birdie accepted that excuse. She'd been young once.

Bree told her grandmother that everyone—well, all the girls—wore tops with straps so narrow their bra straps showed. Just plain slutty, Birdie told her granddaughters that, but she couldn't make any headway. School dress code allowed it. The other girls wore it. Some even tried to get by with sheer tops, but the principal gave those girls a hoodie to wear or sent them home.

Didn't Bree understand what happened when a girl wore clothes like that? Elmer had allowed Martha Patricia to get away with anything. He spoiled her terribly and look what had happened. After Elmer died, Martha Patricia had left town with that no-good father of both her girls and it had all started when Elmer allowed her to wear tight shorts.

Mercedes had passed on a story about

a woman who dressed like the daughter to show her how terrible she looked. Said the woman had put on a tank top without a bra and that had gotten the message over to her daughter.

Might as well try it, but she refused to leave off underwear.

After opening Bree's drawer and taking out a shirt with what she'd called spaghetti straps during her youth centuries ago, she shook it out. Then she took her blouse off and slipped the shirt on over her head. It settled across her shoulders and hung down to her hips, huge on her. The straps of her old-lady bra showed white under the coral top. She studied her image for nearly a minute, aghast at what and who stared back at her. She couldn't carry this off. She'd feel mortified to show anyone else, even her own granddaughters, her desiccated torso, ropy arms, and saggy neck, much less the thick straps of her bra. She looked like the scrawny old woman she was.

When had she gotten so old? She still felt like that girl who planned to start college to be an English teacher. Then she and Elmer had fallen in love at the prom, and her life had changed because Elmer had to stay in town to take over his father's carpentry business. Years later, she ended up here, looking at her elderly self in the mirror.

Not that she'd change anything, except what happened with Martha Patricia, but she would have slowed down those years. They'd flown by much too fast.

Yes, here she stood, looking like a skinny old lady and wishing she had a few of those pretty curves Blossom had. She couldn't allow anyone to see her like this. She'd have to think of some other way to teach the lesson.

Bree was a good girl. Everyone said that, but everyone wasn't thinking about the effects of hormones on a teenager's ability to reason or resist temptation. Could be one soft, lovely evening with the moon hitting the right angle, romantic music on the radio, and a sweetly scented breeze calling out thoughts of love and lust, two young people could get carried away. Goodness knows, it had happened to enough people.

Birdie guessed she'd have to trust Bree. She sure as anything wouldn't leave the bedroom in this outfit.

❦

Adam had bought a new tie, dark blue with a gold pattern. Didn't go with his suit, but he'd borrowed Hector's prom-and-homecoming slacks. A little short but they fit well otherwise. With dark socks, no one would notice.

At last, he and Gussie were going out with Willow and Sam. Adam had issued a stern "no-joking" order to Sam and could only hope the former marine would behave. If not, Willow would put the kibosh on her husband. She handled him effortlessly. Sam was so much in love with his wife, he'd do whatever she said.

They'd take Willow's car into Roundville, because none of them trusted Adam's car enough to make it both ways, despite the fact that Adam made the trip weekly. Willow and Sam would drop him off at the Miltons', and Adam and Gussie would go to Austin and back in her car.

After greeting Mr. and Mrs. Milton—Yvonne and Henry—he escorted Gussie to the car and reached for her keys.

"Oh," she said. "Are you driving?"

He nodded, hand still out.

"Don't you trust my driving?"

"It's not that." He didn't understand this odd streak of machismo he hadn't realized he had. But he couldn't seem to tamp it down. He needed to drive. The thought of not doing so, sitting in the passenger seat while Gussie drove, made him anxious.

"Are you afraid I'll get lost? Or have an accident?"

"I can't explain it. I'm sorry." He took the keys from her hand. "I have to drive."

"Men," she groaned.

"Besides, if you drove, I wouldn't be able to open your car door." He performed that. "And help you in."

"Delicate flower that I am." She laughed as she allowed him to assist her.

Sam had made reservations at a nice place on Red River for a celebration. Sam would finish his class work and student teaching in December and had a teaching job at the middle school starting in January.

"At least I no longer have to live off my rich wife," Sam said after they'd settled at the table. "But, you know, I like being a kept man." He glanced at his wife and grinned before he turned back to Adam. "Let me give you some advice. Marry a woman who makes more money than you and can keep you in style."

Across from Adam, Willow laughed. "Oh, yes, we live in such style."

Next to him, Adam could feel Gussie tense.

"Sam and I live in the house Sam's aunt left him," Willow explained. "It's a little small but it's free."

"And we're together," Sam said.

To change the subject because the waves of adoration between Sam and Willow had become stifling, Adam asked Gussie, "What looks good to you?" as she perused the menu.

Maybe this double date hadn't been the best idea in the world. He could almost see little hearts floating between Sam and Willow and cherubs strumming harps over their heads.

And yet, he thought as he glanced at Gussie, as nauseating as it was to see such affection at close quarters, wouldn't it be nice to take part in it? To care for someone that much and show it? Through a touch? A kiss? Or a besotted glance?

Because the Petersons did nothing un-acceptable. They were deeply in love and showed it.

Yes, as obnoxious as he found the display between Willow and Sam, he probably felt that way because he envied them.

"Congratulations on the job," Gussie said to Sam after they'd ordered.

"We have more news," Sam said. "We're pregnant." He smiled so broadly, the corners of his lips nearly reached midcheek.

"How wonderful," Gussie said.

"When?" Adam reached across to take Willow's hand.

"March. You're the first people we've told, except for family."

"Boy or girl?" Gussie asked.

"We don't care. The general is hoping for a granddaughter." Sam put his arm around the back of Willow's chair. "Winnie's just excited to have another grandchild. She never expected to have any."

"Don't let him fool you. He really wants a girl." Willow gestured toward her husband. "He has big plans to spoil his little princess."

"We're going to have to find a bigger house, because there's no way we can fit another person in."

After dinner, they strolled toward one of Gussie's favorite music venues, Sam and Willow in front. Sam held Willow's hand and, again, Adam noticed how they listed toward each other, drawn together.

He wanted that.

❧

"Girls, get over here and pick up your shoes," George shouted out the back door.

Carol and Gretchen dashed in from the yard. Each grabbed her own sandals and said, in union, "Sorry, Daddy."

They hugged his legs before heading upstairs without a whimper or a complaint or a put-upon sigh, no sign of rolling eyes.

A miracle. Ouida'd witnessed a true miracle.

She wouldn't have believed this months ago. Nor would she have believed what the house looked like. The living room was neat and fairly clean but under the coffee table were some books. A few toys lurked in a corner. Crayons spread across the small table he'd brought downstairs for the girls. A little clutter, enough so that the old George would have been overwhelmed. Now he didn't even blanch when he spotted a dust bunny, which he'd always considered to be a seed of destruction and plague.

"Do you need anything?" he asked. Her husband had dressed for work in his usual well-tailored suit, silk tie, and gleaming shoes.

He looked the same—well, maybe a little harried—and sounded the same—except his voice held a note of exasperation occasionally, perfectly natural for the father of two—but he acted differently. No longer the passive man who barely lived with the rest of the family, he'd taken hold, seemed in charge.

"Help me to my feet," she said. Feeling like a Weeble—she both wobbled and occasionally fell over—she grasped his hand and struggled to stand. After a few months, she now spent most of the day out of bed, often in George's seldom-used recliner with her bootless leg elevated. She took care of herself, fixed lunch, started dinner, went to the bathroom, all that as long as she kept the cane close to lean on when she had to stand. This week, they planned to move the bed back upstairs, and she could take a bath again.

"Got to get on the road." George glanced

at his wrist. Unfortunately his expensive watch had been a casualty of a conflict over chocolate versus white milk a week earlier. He looked at the wall clock, which was a little askew. After the first fifty attempts to straighten it, he'd given up and now merely tilted his head to read it. "I'll be back by six with dinner."

That evening at six o'clock exactly—of course—George pulled into the driveway.

Dinner. Ouida pushed herself to her feet, then clutched her stomach. It had been bouncing around all day. She couldn't be pregnant, could she? No, she'd had morning sickness with the others and this wasn't morning. She'd thought making love on a bed in the middle of the living room when the girls might wake up seemed risky. George found that element of danger exciting—he was not always staid.

Carol and Gretchen ran downstairs and dashed to the window to wait for their father.

"I've got dinner," he shouted as he came in.

"What did you get?" Carol jumped up and down in excitement.

"Fried artichoke hearts with furry gravy," he said.

When the girls broke into laughter, George beamed.

But the mere thought of fried artichokes with furry gravy added to the odor of what he'd really brought home and hit her hard. Her insides clenched and burned. Must be the flu that Bree had mentioned, the one that had hit all her friends. Ouida struggled to keep her insides truly inside her.

"Hi, sweetheart," George said after he put the bag on the kitchen table and came back to stand in front of Ouida. "How are you doing? You look a little pale."

At exactly that moment and before she could even turn her head or put her hand in front of her mouth or shove him away, she lost the battle.

She vomited.

Even worse, she'd thrown up on George. When she finished heaving and spewing, she opened her eyes. Still standing in front of her, he looked down. She followed his gaze.

The eruption had hit only the bottom few inches of his beautifully tailored slacks, but his shoes—oh, dear, his beloved shoes, his adored oxfords with the lovingly cared-for, formerly brilliantly shining leather—were covered with her afternoon snack. How devastating for him.

"I'm sorry," she whispered. When he didn't answer, she lifted her eyes to his face.

Stunned, that's how he looked. He'd changed a great deal, he'd become the George she'd fallen in love with and married, but even that much freer George wasn't the kind of man who appreciated being thrown up on.

Was there anyone who did? Mothers got used to it but didn't look forward to such an occurrence. She didn't know what to say, how to soothe him, so she watched him, stricken with guilt and humiliation.

At first George drew himself up very straight. His stiff neck seemed to elongate as he stared down at the wreckage of his shoes.

"I'm so sorry. I know how much you love those shoes."

Behind him, she could see the girls clutching each other's hands and, eyes wide, watching their parents, studying the mess covering their father's feet.

He lifted his eyes to her face, his expression and body relaxed. "Gretchen, get your mother a pan from the kitchen, then bring a couple of towels. Carol, get her a wet cloth and a glass of water."

Then he looked at her gently. "I'm sorry you're sick." After inspecting her hand, he took it in his. "It must be terrible to have gone through so much and, now that you're getting better, to have this happen." He took a towel from Gretchen and tossed it over the stuff on the floor. He took the rag Carol handed him and wiped Ouida's face gently. "Rinse your mouth out." He handed her the water. "Then let's get you cleaned up and in bed."

At that moment, Ouida fell in love with George even more deeply because she knew, really knew, how much he loved her. He loved her more than his dignity, his sense of smell, and those formerly gorgeous Ferragamo shoes.

❧

"How are you doing?" George greeted Adam at the front door Wednesday evening as the preacher entered the living room to see Ouida on the sofa, with a cup of coffee on the end table at her side. She wore a bright aqua top, her shiny curls bristled around her head, and she glowed.

"You're looking well." Adam settled on a chair across from her, then glanced from Ouida to her husband. They both glowed.

"Yes, well, yes," Ouida stammered. "Adam, we've worked matters out between us, and we have some news for you."

"Oh?"

"First, I'm going to hire a manager for the firm." George sat and took his wife's hand. "A manager who'll take care of the day-to-day details and give me more time to spend with the family."

"It will mean less income but we're fine," Ouida said.

"Or maybe not. Could be more help will lead to expansion," George explained. "But I don't care, as long as I can spend more time with the girls and . . . and the new one."

"The new one?"

"Yes, Preacher, that's the second bit of news. We're expecting. I'm due in seven months."

"Isn't that wonderful," Adam said sincerely.

"Not on George's schedule at all. Earlier than he'd planned."

"But I'm really happy about it." George gazed at her with deep adoration.

This looked like a George whom Adam hadn't known existed, a completely different and much more approachable George, a George in love with his wife and not ashamed to show it.

Ouida was pregnant, Adam thought as he walked back to the parsonage. It seemed almost like calving season around here. A terrible, stupid, misanthropic thought, Adam realized as soon as it hit him, but envy had overwhelmed his good humor and usual love for others.

After all his years of being a bachelor, he suddenly discovered he wanted a family just like everyone else, his friends, his neighbors. But he'd fallen in love with a woman who didn't act as if their relationship would end up in a family. She seldom allowed him to touch her, and only when she initiated it. In fact, they were more like buddies, he and Gussie. Buddies who went to movies together or met for coffee.

He wanted more, much more.

If he broke up with Gussie, he didn't have many choices of other women to bear his children.

Whoa, had he really considered breaking up with Gussie?

Yes, they'd been "together" for nearly two months, and she still refused any physical intimacy other than holding hands now and then and an occasional kiss. Last week, he'd put his arm around her shoulders and she'd allowed it for a few seconds before she subtly twisted away. He'd gotten the message.

What was wrong with him? Why had he allowed such a platonic relationship? Why had he settled?

Oh, not that he wanted to jump into bed with her. No, that was a lie. He did, but he knew it would be too soon for her and against his belief in commitment and marriage. Plus as a minister, he'd accepted that people held him to a higher moral standard. But could they start with a little cuddling and three or four kisses at a time?

They were going to meet for coffee again Monday. Of course: coffee. He'd allowed them to get into this rut where Gussie felt comfortable and he felt frustrated: coffee in Marble Falls and once in a while a movie or a date where they drove separate cars. She seemed perfectly content with this. He wasn't.

He wanted more.

Was he expecting too much too soon from a woman who'd been raped? They should discuss that, talk about the physical relationship. Would there ever be a physical relationship?

Not that he wanted to push her. He just needed to know.

He'd bring it all up Monday. Could be she wanted more, too, and was too shy to take action. He doubted that. *Gussie* and *shy* were antonyms. If her body language when they'd spent the evening with Willow and Sam had told him anything, it was that she felt comfortable with the present arrangement but the idea of anything else—well, she alternated between fear and lack of interest.

For the first time, Adam didn't look forward to seeing Gussie.

❧

That afternoon, Adam and Gussie met at the coffee shop but decided to walk around the east side of the lake in the autumn sunshine. They chatted about their day, about the health of Gussie's parents, about church and life.

But when Adam reached to take Gussie's hand, she jumped.

Not the reaction he was hoping for. Before he could think about them, the words he'd thought all day rushed from his mouth. "I want more."

Gussie took a step back before she turned to face him. "You want more?"

"From you."

"I'm very happy with how things are," she said tersely. "Why change it? This works. And you promised not to push me."

"Gussie," he said. He paused, hoping her expression and body language would change from wary to calm and happy. When it didn't, Adam reached out to take her hand again, but she pulled it away. "That's what's wrong. Wanting to hold your hand isn't pushing. Wanting our relationship to grow isn't pushy."

"Feels that way."

"No, it's natural. It's natural for a man to want to kiss a woman he's seeing. It's also usual for her to kiss him with a modicum of enthusiasm."

"We've kissed."

He nodded. "A dozen times, when you've allowed it. I wasn't really allowed to participate as . . . umm, vigorously as I'd liked, and I felt you weren't into it."

"Whose lips were they? I was there."

He stopped himself from answering. Arguing wouldn't work, wouldn't build their relationship, but he had no idea how to explain this to her. She looked like a frightened creature, trapped. Not at all what he'd considered when he'd thought this scene through, but he should have. How could he get through to her without upsetting her?

Dear Lord, he prayed. *Please give me wisdom and courage and the right words.*

"Gussie, I don't want to argue. I'm stating a fact. Our relationship has stalled. I want more. I want to see you more often. I want to treat you like the woman I'm dating, not like my dear friend or my sister."

"Oh, so you kiss your sister on the mouth?"

He wanted to tell her that there wasn't much difference between how he and Gussie kissed and how he kissed his sister except for the part of their faces where the kisses landed. He didn't. She couldn't handle that now, and that depressed him greatly.

"What do you expect? What do you want from me?" she asked in a grim voice, as if he'd pushed her toward the guillotine.

"I want . . . I want what a man wants from a woman, when two people are in a . . ."

"I know what a man wants." She shook as she spat the words out. "I know exactly what a man wants."

"Gussie," he said patiently and clearly, "I'm not Lennie."

She took another step back.

"And I'm not attacking you."

"Feels like it."

How could he reach her? Not by doing anything that seemed threatening.

"I want a future with you, to see you more. I want to be with you more often. I care about you, and not the way a man feels toward his sister. I want to show you that. I want more."

For a moment he felt like Oliver Twist holding out his empty bowl.

"I don't have any more." She folded her

arms in front of her and pulled her shoulders forward, nearly huddling.

He studied her and felt guilty. For a moment, he considered stopping, accepting what she could give. But that wasn't good, not for either of them.

To build her trust, he worded his next comment carefully. Calming words, not confrontation. "I don't agree. You have so much love and caring and faith inside you. I only ask that you share them with me, with a man who cares for you deeply."

❦

Trapped. Gussie felt trapped. She'd never thought Adam, a man who said he cared about her, would give her an ultimatum. Not that he'd threatened anything, but she knew what he meant, what would come next. This was exactly how her previous attempts to date had ended up, only far more quickly.

This time felt worse because she'd hoped things would turn out differently. She'd prayed that Adam would be content with how she wanted to continue. Adam was a better man than the other guys. Those failures should have warned her that she hadn't healed yet, but denial ran deep.

She'd hoped Adam would stick with her while she worked her life out. But, if she hadn't done that in thirteen years, how could she ever have believed it would happen now?

"You said you wouldn't push," she repeated. Oh, stupid to say that because Adam wasn't a demanding man. Adam had been more patient than she had any right to expect. She didn't want to lose him. She'd miss the joy of picking up an email from him or meeting him for coffee, looking forward to that.

She didn't want to give up the hope that Adam could fix her.

But that evening with Willow and Sam? She never wanted to do something like that again, couldn't repeat that experience, because those hours had underlined the difference between how each couple defined *relationship*. Caring for each other deeply, displaying that affection . . . well, she couldn't do that. Not ever.

"I'm happy with how things are," she stated. "I believe our relationship has deepened and will continue to grow." She sounded like an announcer on an infomercial for a dating service. No, even worse, she sounded like a complete idiot, a frightened fool.

As her eyes caressed Adam's face, she realized that his strong, square chin didn't just make him better looking. Now it jutted out stubbornly. This was not a happy man. He was serious.

He wanted more.

"Maybe," he said slowly. "I know I'm pushing it here, but I need to know. Maybe sometime we could talk about . . . oh, I don't know, sex?"

She blinked. "How crude."

"I'm not asking for anything now. But I need to know where this is going. I've thought about marriage, but, if we do get married, I'd want a marriage in every way. Does that possibility exist in the future?"

She didn't meet his eyes.

"It's natural." He gestured at Gussie, then toward himself. "How do you think we got here? Our parents did have sex at least once or twice. I'd like to know if the idea of having a physical relationship when we get married is at all realistic."

"I don't want to even think about that."

"I know you don't, but I do. It's not a bad thing. I care for you and want more between us."

"I told you I had problems. I warned you," she stated defensively. Her normal way of reacting when pushed: Blame the other person. Really immature. She needed to learn better coping skills. She needed to listen to Adam and respond like a normal person. She was thirty-one, the rape had happened thirteen years earlier. A normal person shouldn't still be so broken she couldn't respond to a man she believed she could love, so broken she couldn't communicate with him naturally, so broken she shrank from intimacy of any kind.

"Gussie," he said, his voice soft with concern and caring. "I want to fall in love with you, but you keep me at arm's length." When she began to speak, he held up his hand. "You told me about the date rape and your distrust of men. Thank you for sharing that. But I'm not the guy who hurt you. I'm a man with normal expectations and hopes. I want to make a life with you, share a bed with you. You can trust me. After the months we've been together, you know you can trust me."

Yes, she knew that. Adam was the best man she'd ever met.

"My parents," she said. "They're getting old, not in the best health. My father hasn't been out of the hospital for so long. They supported me when I fell apart. I owe them."

"Do you owe yourself anything? Do you plan to start having a life of your own at any time? I'd like to be part of it, but I won't always be around, Gussie."

The thought of not having her parents around and Adam's having moved on tore at her, but the words that spilled from her lips weren't the ones she should say. "You're not expecting me to choose between you and my parents, are you? Because I can tell you . . ."

"Gussie." He took her hand. This time she let him. She didn't know why. But after a few seconds, his touch made her feel such tremendous longing she had to pull her hand away. He let it go.

The hope that he'd keep her hand in his and persuade her to marry him someday warred inside her brain with the idea that she couldn't do that. She just could not. Not that she could explain it, but the idea of turning her life and happiness and body over to a man, even to Adam, scared her. She might could work this out if Adam stood next to her and held her hand and forced her to face her life.

But he didn't. No, he treated her as an adult, like a thirty-one-year-old woman who should be able to make decisions herself.

Instead of doing what she wanted, even knowing Adam would never hurt her, she couldn't speak. As always, she'd chosen to passively allow her life to flow past and not to leap into it.

"Have you even thought about marriage? With me?" he asked.

"You're really going for the jugular here," she said with an awkward laugh that even she knew didn't express mirth.

"Have you?" He kept his eyes on her face.

"Umm." What a stupid thing to say. Not even a word, just a sound, but her brain seemed unable to come up with anything else. "Umm," she repeated.

He watched her for a few more seconds. "That tells me what I need to know. Let me know when you're ready for more, if you ever are." He watched her for a few more seconds. "I'm going back to get my car. Do you want to come with me?"

"Adam, please. Be patient," she whispered.

On those words, he turned away.

She swallowed hard and watched Adam walk back along the path to the sidewalk and up the street. When she lost sight of him, she knew he'd get into his ugly old car and drive off.

This didn't count as a good-bye. Impossible that their involvement with the youth of the area wouldn't throw them together. They'd see each other again, at the tubing party and other events. Maybe she should give up working with the churches and the kids to avoid ever seeing him.

No, she couldn't. Not that.

So she sat on a bench and didn't move, didn't think for five or ten more minutes.

After that, she stood and headed toward her car. Once inside, she turned the ignition, listened to the soft purr of her engine. For a moment she thought of Adam driving back to Butternut Creek in his old clunker and broke out in tears.

❧

If he could have, Adam would have wept, but he knew that wasn't macho nor particularly appropriate. He'd broken up with

Gussie. It had been his decision and that gave him no right to hurt.

Not that they'd had anything to break up. Meeting for coffee, a couple of movies, and one dinner didn't exactly signify a deep, enduring passion on her part. Besides, he'd set all of them up. Gussie hadn't taken an active part or showed much interest in their being together.

But she had shared something with him she hadn't, he felt sure, shared with many others. He could understand where she was, could appreciate the knowledge she'd trusted him that much, but he couldn't fall in love alone.

To hell with deep enduring passion. They could have their love—Sam and Willow and the Kowalskis and their new babies and happy families, he thought bitterly as he pulled into the drive.

Why had he turned on his friends? He'd become a curmudgeon, a grumpy nearly twenty-seven-year-old grouch who envied people who loved each other because he didn't have that. As a minister, as a person, as a Christian, he shouldn't feel like this. No matter how frustrated and alone he felt, he couldn't stop caring about others.

"Most loving God," he whispered. "Please help me to stop feeling sorry for myself and to appreciate the lives and joys of others. Amen." He spent several minutes in meditation and hoped that would handle his negative feelings.

The question that haunted him, the one he feared even in quiet contemplation, was how he should handle the Widows. They had high expectations. They'd grilled him about meeting with Gussie. If they didn't see him making progress on the marriage front, they'd be after him, and right now he couldn't handle that covey of matchmakers. He most especially could not handle the head matchmaker.

Which meant he wouldn't say a word. Let them figure it out. He got out of the car and headed toward the porch.

"Excuse me," said an attractive blond woman who stood by the porch of the parsonage. "My son lost his backpack and someone said you might have it."

Darn Chewy.

"I'm Adam Jordan, minister at the Christian Church."

"Diane Fuller." She shook his hand.

"I'm afraid my dog gets out sometimes and brings things home." He waved toward the porch. "We try to find who they belong to, but those two had no identification."

"The red one." She ascended the steps to the porch, knelt, and unzipped it. "Yes." She nodded as she took out a notebook. "This is Paul's." Then she smiled.

A nice smile.

"It's hard being a single mother," she said. "I'm divorced," she added with a toss of her hair. "Keeping up on Paul's possessions isn't easy."

The woman was interested in him, flirting. Amazing. She wore nice slacks, a white shirt, and black heels. All in all, Diane Fuller looked like a nice person, a pretty woman, but he felt nothing for her. Had the weeks of frustration with Gussie leached all the interest and optimism from him?

No, he didn't think so. Maybe he was just a little tired now.

He could only hope Miss Birdie didn't find out about this woman, ever.

"I'm sure it is." He paused before he asked, "Do you and your son have a church home?"

❧

By the time she reached Roundville, Gussie had stopped crying. After pulling into the driveway, she flipped open a compact and glanced at herself in the mirror. Her eyes weren't too red, but she'd better fluff a little powder on her nose.

There. No one would guess how she felt.

As soon as Gussie entered the living room, her mother asked, "What's wrong, dear?"

How did she always know? Well, today Gussie must look wrung out and red-eyed.

"Nothing, Mom. I'm a little tired."

If Gussie had thought she could go around the living room and into the hallway without saying more, she was wrong. After all these years, she should know her mother wouldn't allow that.

"Come, sit down and talk to me."

Her mother's soft, sweet tone covered a determination Gussie could admire and fear but never ignore. If she did, her mother would follow her all over the house. Into the yard. Once she'd even stood behind Gussie's car when her daughter had attempted to leave without answering all of her questions.

She sighed and entered the living room for a debriefing. Might as well get it over with. She sat in the chair across from her mother. "Where's Dad?"

"He's taking a nap again. Can't seem to get his strength back." She knitted a few more stitches before she asked, "How's Adam?"

"He's fine." Gussie counted to five— quickly—before she stood and attempted to escape. "I'm going to look in on Dad."

"No, no." Her mother waved Gussie back into the chair. "I did that just before you got here. He was sleeping." She waited until Gussie sat. "Is everything okay between you two?"

Gussie closed her eyes and attempted to come up with an answer that would satisfy her mother, not that any existed.

"Oh, dear, he's not your young man any longer. I had such hopes for the two of you."

"No, Mother, he's not my young man."

"What happened?"

"Nothing." Gussie kept an eye on her mother, attempting to read her expression. "We weren't moving forward so we decided not to see each other again."

"Aah. Very civilized and mature."

Gussie nodded.

Her mother nodded. "Well, why don't you go look in on your father. Dinner's in the oven. I'll dish it out when he wakes up."

Gussie knew better than to think she'd fooled her mother about anything. Fortunately, she was too sweet to pry.

❧

Gussie hadn't looked forward to the tubing on the Guadalupe River. It was late September and the water held a little chill, but they got a cut rate that fit the budget. Even worse than the cold water, she'd see Adam.

Mature and civilized, she repeated to herself. Mentally, that worked, at least until the first time she spotted him. She repeated the mantra, but the words did not calm her, not a bit.

He should not be allowed to wear a sleeveless T-shirt and swim trunks. Oh, the trunks were the long, floppy kind and

the shirt certainly didn't display a gratu-
itous amount of his body, but he still looked
good. She had to make an effort not to
hyperventilate. But what hurt most was
what was inside the man. He was a good
person who cared about her.

She had only herself to blame for being
too much of a coward to accept what Adam
had offered. She should talk to him, greet
him, tell him how good it was to see him.
Instead, she shouted, "Hey, Adam," waved,
and kicked away in the other direction.

Gutless, spineless coward.

❦

The sun beat down on the tubers, hundreds of them from all over Central Texas
mingling with their group of three dozen. A
great day to be on the river, and possibly
the last Saturday warm enough. Adam
glanced at Janey, who floated along a few
feet from him, drinking a root beer and
humming.

Farther away, he heard Gussie's laugh
float across the water. Six or seven of the
youths twirled her tube around in circles.

He really loved her laugh.

"Hey, guys, you're making me dizzy.
Stop!" she shouted.

With a grin which quickly changed to a frown when he realized this was as close as he'd get to her again, he watched for another minute. She waved. He waved back.

"Hey, Janey." Mac floated up next to them. "Having fun?" At Janey's nod, Mac continued, "Gussie's great, isn't she, Adam?"

He hoped she couldn't read his expression through his dark glasses, the zinc oxide on his nose, and the shadow of his University of Louisville cap.

"Yeah. Great," he agreed. He turned his head to search for Hector and found him kicking his tube beside Bree. That romance seemed to be chugging right along. As usual, Bobby flirted with several girls.

Adam hoped Mac would float away during the time he scrutinized the crowd, identifying and mentally counting the number of young people he'd brought from Butternut Creek.

"You can't ignore me," Mac said from a few feet away.

"Yes, I can." Adam grabbed Janey's tube and kicked hard. "We're going to float around and see how everyone's doing." Could he escape from Mac? Probably not.

After he'd maneuvered the two tubes across half the river, he could hear Mac behind him.

"Don't forget. I'm a runner. Strong legs," she shouted. "Slow down. I need to ask you something and you don't want me to shout it across the water."

With that threat, he paddled back toward the pillar's granddaughter, pulling Janey along with him. Genes ran true. She'd never give up.

"Why aren't you and Gussie floating down the river together?" she asked once they were within two feet of each other. "Making goo-goo eyes?"

"In answer to the second question, I've never made goo-goo eyes at anyone in my entire life." He ignored the first point. Make Mac ask again.

"Why aren't you and Gussie together?"

The kid never gave up. A true Mac-Dowell.

"We adults have to watch all of you from different places, to keep you safe." To show how seriously he accepted that responsibility, he paddled his tube around to scan the group. "I'd hate to get home and have to explain to your grandmother why only Bree made it back to Butternut Creek."

He could feel Mac's eyes on the back of his head but didn't want to actually face her. He bet she could have read his expression even if he covered it with an iron mask.

"The water's pretty low. Hope no one gets stuck under the bridge," he stated.

"You're not going to answer," she stated right back.

He kept his hold on Janey's tube and kicked away with legs that had played basketball for years. She'd never catch up.

"I'm going to tell Grandma," she threatened as he retreated.

"Go ahead," he said. Might as well get it over with. Miss Birdie and the Widows should know they'd failed and would have to start all over again. He could only hope that humiliation would make them stop looking for a wife for him.

Oh, sure. As if the Widows didn't enjoy humiliation, especially that of their minister.

❧

A few hours later, the flotilla had nearly arrived at the dock where they'd get out of the river, give up their tubes, and get in a bus to shuttle back to the departure point.

Gussie gave a deep sigh of relief. She'd survived. They'd get back to the cars and vans and head out and she wouldn't have to see Adam for months. Surely by that time, she wouldn't lust after him.

Except, of course, everyone—except Gussie and, she imagined, Adam— wanted to gather at the barbecue place on the frontage road for a last meal together, as if they hadn't spent nearly four hours in a river together. She couldn't get out of it without making a fuss, because tradition demanded that meal.

Fortunately, Adam and a bunch of kids had found a booth on the far side of the restaurant and Gussie had shoved her bunch toward the other side, where she sat with her back to him.

Once they'd settled, Gussie discovered that Mac had joined their group. No surprise. The kids pretty much intermingled.

Between ordering and the arrival of their meals, Mac leaned toward Gussie. "Have you heard," the junior matchmaker said, "about the new single woman in town who Grandma wants to fix up with Pastor Adam?"

"How interesting," Gussie said.

"Blond, professional woman. Smart, pretty."

"None of my business."

It wasn't, Gussie reiterated once she arrived back in Roundville and dropped the kids off at their homes. It had been a week since Adam had demanded more from her than she could give. Now he'd moved on.

No, Mac had said the Widows had found a new match for him. Not his fault. The Widows never gave up. Indefatigable in their efforts, unrelenting in their actions, unflagging in devotion to their cause, and inexorable. The Widows would find Adam a mate if they had to import her from Maine. It wouldn't be Gussie.

She felt implausibly sad. Why should she feel sad when she'd turned down what he'd offered? Of course, she still had her parents and the church and her business. They'd made her happy for years. Why wasn't that enough?

Maybe because she hadn't been happy all those years? Merely content or comfortable or only okay but not really happy?

Click went her brain as that idea slipped into place. She'd been treading water all these years. Yes, she'd accomplished stuff. A university diploma and a successful business. But she hadn't moved on. Stuck in the same place for thirteen years and fooling herself into believing she'd achieved her goals and dreams.

Chapter Fourteen

"Mac tells me you and Gussie Milton are no longer . . ." Miss Birdie paused to search for the word. "An item," she finished.

Adam wondered why it had taken so long for the Widows to descend on him. He figured they'd have ambushed him after church last week or the previous day. He guessed Mac hadn't squealed on him until the end of the week. Yesterday the pillar had glared at him when she filed out of the sanctuary but hadn't said a word. Probably had needed a powwow.

He could only be thankful he'd had all this time to prepare.

"Come in, ladies." He stood and waved toward the four chairs in front of his desk. He'd warned Maggie when she got in that they'd show up. He'd known they wouldn't arrive until after ten with the work schedules of Mercedes and Miss Birdie, but he knew they'd come.

Once they'd settled in their usual places, Adam sat down and asked, "How are you doing today? Busy at the diner, Miss Birdie?"

"Pfutt," she said, a sound he hadn't discovered the exact meaning for. "Don't change the subject."

"I didn't realize we'd chosen a subject of the conversation yet," he said with a pleasant smile.

"You and Gussie Milton."

"Now, now, Bird." Mercedes patted her friend's arm. "We can certainly take time for pleasantries."

"Good morning, Pastor," Blossom said, then sat forward in the chair and leaned toward him with a sweet sympathetic expression. "How are you doing?"

Darn, he could stand Miss Birdie's pushiness but Blossom's sympathy about killed him.

"Fine, thank you." He turned toward Winnie. "How are you and the general?"

"Don't try to change the subject," Miss Birdie said. "You know when you mention the general, she'll talk about him forever. Crazy about the man. Hardly thinks about anything else. Maudlin."

"I don't know if that's the word you want," Mercedes said. She stopped speaking when Miss Birdie glared at her and substituted, "Yes, Pastor, Mac mentioned that you and Gussie were no longer seeing each other."

"We have never seen a great deal of each other," he said. "She and I met for coffee or for a movie but there was no great romance."

"You two went to Austin with Sam and Willow," Winnie said.

"Yes, a very nice evening spent with friends."

After that statement, he folded his hands and watched them calmly. Miss Birdie blanched. Winnie narrowed her eyes and scrutinized him. Mercedes tilted her head as if wondering what to do next. Blossom, as usual, didn't seem quite sure what had happened.

"With friends?" Blossom asked him, then turned toward the pillar. "Weren't they supposed to be more than friends? Didn't we hope they'd get married?"

"Yes, we did," Miss Birdie snapped. "I for one am very disappointed."

"I am, too," Blossom agreed.

The remaining Widows didn't seem to have anything to add but nodded in enthusiastic agreement.

Still Adam sat at the desk, hands folded and mouth closed, until the cluster of disappointed Widows stood, nodded, and left.

For a moment he felt flush with victory. The Widows had come but they hadn't conquered him. He'd learned to handle them and felt strong and certain. For a moment.

Then he felt a sense of loss. Conquering the Widows didn't give him nearly the elation he'd always thought it would. In fact, victory felt a little flat. Playing with them was more fun. Having them attempt to find his wife, well, when the choice had been Gussie, he'd really rooted for them.

Besides, he had no idea what they might

do next, and he didn't feel nearly as confident about facing the unknown.

🍂

"What do we do next?" Mercedes asked as they stood in the parking lot.

"A disappointing development," Winnie said.

"Very disappointing," Blossom agreed.

"We're going to have to start all over." Birdie sighed. "And I don't know how." She shook her head. "I thought they were perfect for each other."

"Perfect." Blossom shook her head in time with Birdie.

"Maybe Gussie doesn't want to get married," Mercedes added. "She's over thirty and still single. Could be she wasn't as perfect as we'd hoped. Could have baggage."

"Could be her parents," Blossom said. "I cared for my in-laws for years."

The four considered that.

"Did anyone see that blond woman with her son in church Sunday?" Winnie broke in on the contemplation. "Let's check on her. I can get her name from Maggie if the woman signed the friendship register. I'll visit her and see what I can find out, welcome her to the community and ask her to come back to church."

Bossiest woman Birdie had ever met, but a good plan nonetheless. They all agreed and put Winnie in charge of that investigation before they left.

❦

"Reverend Jordan, this is Mariah Wilson calling from the elementary school. I'm the counselor here."

What had happened? "Is Janey all right?" he asked.

"Oh, yes, although we do have a concern."

He waited.

"Her teacher has noted that Janey struggles with her work although she seems like a bright little girl."

"I've noticed that."

"I wanted to make sure everything was okay at home."

"Yes, Janey seems to be settling in well, but it is an adjustment. I'll talk to her," he said.

The kids' schedule made life and discussions difficult. Janey always arrived home by four and started homework at the kitchen table. They ate late, after Hector got home from practice, then she took everything up to her room to work at her desk. She had no time to watch even thirty minutes of a television show. When the season started, they'd go to all Hector's games together, but for the most part Janey studied.

After dinner, as they cleaned up the dishes, Adam said, "I need to talk to you guys."

"Pops, I've got a big American history test tomorrow and I'm on KP tonight."

"I know." He'd listed all their tests on a calendar in the kitchen. "But this is important. Sit down. I'll take care of the dishes when we're through."

Once they'd cleared and wiped the table, they sat down.

"Janey, I received a call from Mrs. Wilson at your school today." He paused to consider how to phrase this without upsetting her. "How are your studies going?"

"Okay." She dropped her eyes.

"Are you having any difficulties?"

When she didn't answer, Hector took over. "Janey, you've always had to work really hard in school. I've noticed you study all the time but your grades still aren't good."

Tears rolled down Janey's cheeks. "I try."

Adam handed her a Kleenex. "You aren't in trouble. We know you're smart. We know how hard you work."

"B-b-but, no matter how hard I try." She stopped and wiped her eyes. "No matter how I try, I can't do as well as my friends. I don't know why. I feel stupid."

"Janey." Adam took her hand. "You aren't stupid. Your brother and I know that."

"But Amy and Cassandra always get perfect spelling papers and their tests are put on the bulletin board. Mine never are."

Adam had seen her spelling tests, the letters uneven and red marks all over.

She looked at both men. "I don't want to be different. I don't want to have special classes in a special room."

Hector said, "Janey, you're smart. I know that." He pointed back at Adam. "Pops knows that. But you spend so much time studying, hours longer than I do. Do you like to spend every minute studying?"

"No-o-o." Her voice quivered. "I'm tired of studying all the time."

Adam watched the Firestones and felt guilty. He should have noticed this. He should have gone to the school about Janey's grades and her efforts.

"Hey." Adam knelt next to her, balancing on one knee, to look into her eyes. "It's going to be okay, really. We'll talk to your teacher and the counselor and see how we can help you. Hector and I and all the people at church will make sure you're fine." He put his hand on her shoulder. "We love you and want the best for you. Do you understand that?"

Janey nodded, then slid out of the chair and onto Adam's knee. She put her arms around his neck and leaned against him. She felt warm and trusting. A wave of emotion and gratitude nearly overwhelmed him.

"I'm sorry I didn't notice earlier. I don't know much about little girls."

Janey hugged him more tightly, and Hector put his hand on Adam's shoulder.

"Most loving God," Adam prayed. "Thank you for the Firestone children. They have blessed my life so richly."

"Hey, Pops, stop or you're going to make me cry, and players don't cry."

❧

As she walked home from the diner, Birdie glanced at the sky. Getting cloudy. Forecast said rain, not good weather for homecoming. She got to the front of her house and stared at it. She'd have to paint it soon but where would the money come from? Maybe she could hire Hector. And the Adirondack chairs, the ones Elmer had made so they could sit on the porch and wave to their neighbors, needed a coat of stain.

After Elmer passed when the girls were young, Birdie'd spent a lot of time out here, praying for strength to get through the next day. With the girls' activities, she didn't have time now.

Two chairs. No one to sit in Elmer's and she never sat in the other. Maybe she should give one away. Could be she should find someone to sit in the other.

Should she encourage Farley a little?

Ptsh. She was too old for romance.

But a little companionship, that would be nice.

❧

In Kentucky, the rain usually pattered down. Sometimes it pelted but usually it pattered gently for hours or days or, in February, weeks.

Texas rain also pattered and pelted, but

many times it came down in one huge mass. At times, it seemed as if the clouds gave up on sending the drops down one by one and, as if worn out, they dropped the whole cloudful of water at once. It looked and felt as if a pail had been turned over on the Hill Country, over land too hard and dry to absorb it all.

Not that this fit any scientific explanation of rain, but it worked for Adam.

"Surely they aren't going to play in this weather, are they?" Adam asked Miss Birdie. The high school football game—the homecoming game followed by the dance—was scheduled for that night. He'd ducked into the diner when the storm started and decided to stay for lunch.

"Not if there's lightning in the area, but this doesn't look like a thunderstorm." She placed his order in front of him: a chicken salad sandwich and Coke. Then she surrounded that with a basket of more fries than he could consume in a week, a huge dish of fried apples, and a piece of cherry pie with two dips of ice cream.

"Now that you're putting on some weight, we can't let you get skinny again," she explained. Then she stood back. "A little rain never hurt anyone. The players wear special cleats and such."

"But the band doesn't march in this weather, does it?" He took a bite of the sandwich.

She stared back at him as if he were speaking classical Greek. "Why wouldn't they?" she asked, her tone scathing.

He finished chewing. "Because the field will be muddy?"

"So?" She put her fists on her hips. "We aren't some namby-pamby Kentuckians. We're Texans. What would have happened at the Alamo if Jim Bowie had decided the weather was too cold or rough or rainy to defend liberty?"

Adam thought he remembered that the siege of the Alamo hadn't been about defending liberty but stealing land, but he didn't respond. Nor did he mention that Jim Bowie had a lot of Mexicans shooting at him and had little choice whereas the students didn't really *have* to march down a slippery field. The pillar probably thought they, as Texans, did have to.

"And the area band contest is next week. Our kids placed in the top group in the region and will move on to state if they do well. They need the practice." She turned and strode away, still angry, Adam thought, that he'd questioned the fortitude of Texas youth.

If anyone was more fanatic than a football coach, it was the band director and the grandmother of one of the band members.

"And," she proclaimed from halfway across the restaurant. "If you want fields of bluebonnets in the spring, you'd better welcome rain in the fall and winter."

With that, the other diners turned to glare at him, which made Adam feel as if the whole town would blame him for a drought and the death of wildflowers should the rain stop.

That evening, he watched the players sliding and falling on the field. Adam settled in to watch a game of mud ball, glad he'd worn a sweatshirt and jacket under the waterproof poncho. "Are you all right?" he asked Janey. She had demanded to come because Bobby played on defense.

She nodded.

"Tell me if you get cold." Before they'd left, Hector had bundled his sister in several layers, then turned to Adam and said,

"Pops, I'll be home from the dance late. Don't wait up for me. Makes me feel like a kid to have to check in."

"I don't wait up because I don't trust you," Adam said. "I wait up because I want to make sure you're home. Can't sleep if I don't know that."

"Aah, that's nice." With a grin, Hector had loped off to watch Bree play volleyball.

At halftime, the band slipped all over the field, tripping on the ruts dug out during the first half, but they kept playing the program. That impressed Adam. He had no idea how one controlled a trombone or tuba while falling down, but the musicians did with only a few missed notes.

The members of the dance team, wearing their cowgirl outfits, finished the performance covered with splattered mud but with huge smiles.

Despite the slips and falls and pitchy notes, the crowd cheered every second of the performance. These kids belonged to Butternut Creek. As the students marched off the field, everyone on the home side of the stadium stood and pulled their arms from their plastic coverings to clap and cheer proudly.

That night, to keep Hector from feeling like a kid, Adam pretended to be asleep when he came home.

Didn't fool Hector. He came into the bedroom and sat on the side of the bed to scratch Chewy's ears. "Had a good time. Pop, you can go to sleep now. I'm home."

❧

As the fall grew closer to winter, leaves changed, at least the little bit they changed in Texas. Most of the green leaves stayed the same. Some of them turned a bright red, but the rest looked as if they'd rusted.

With basketball practice starting, Hector and Adam didn't get much time to play ball together, but a lot of kids in the neighborhood used the hoop in the parking lot. Adam joined occasionally and considered those contests good for the relationship of the church with its neighbors.

He and Janey rode the family-of-the-team buses to Hector's out-of-town games in Bandera and even as far as Dripping Springs. Hector's play had improved so much, Adam knew he could no longer challenge him. Not that he'd confess that to the kid. Bobby, a feisty and intelligent point guard, attracted scouts as well. The team looked great, well coached and intense.

"We're going to have a great year," Adam emailed his sister, attaching a picture of Hector going up for a rebound that had been in the newspaper.

The next day, Hannah wrote back, "What's the matter?"

He sent an email about another win, the coach, and Hector's improvement playing point forward.

"I don't care about the coach."

Adam reread those words. Hannah had never been a fan of athletes, but she sounded angry and mean. Probably under a lot of stress. He wished he could help her.

He read on. "I don't really care about basketball unless you're playing. I do care about Hector and hope to meet him and Janey someday, but what's wrong with you?"

He wrote back, "Leave me alone."

She answered, "Okay, now I'm really worried. What's wrong?"

He solved her persistence by not answering. Nothing she could do from Kenya.

Wrong. Hannah wrote their mother, who

emailed, "Your sister tells me there's some-thing wrong. What?"

He couldn't ignore his mother. Well, he could, but it was useless. She could chal-lenge the Widows for the title of most re-lentless. However, she also knew when to shut up, a skill the Widows and his sister should learn.

"I don't want to talk about it," he wrote back and copied it to his sister. "Leave me alone."

Both did.

❧

"I don't think that new blond woman is go-ing to work," Winnie said. "She's not minis-ter's wife material. Entirely too worldly and here for only six months while her bank opens a branch down on Highway 29."

"Only six months?" Birdie asked. "The preacher can't work that fast."

"Where does that leave us?" Blossom asked. "Where can we find another single woman?"

"We should send out a message to the churches in the area, see if they have any single women who might be interested in a minister," Winnie suggested. "Send it to the president of their women's group and ask for suggestions."

"Winnie, will you be in charge of that?" Birdie asked, to regain control. Then she looked at each woman. "What ideas do you have to help us find a wife for the preacher?"

"We tried Reverend Patillo, but that didn't work out."

"Oh? The Presbyterian minister?" Blossom asked. "What happened?"

"Nothing." Birdie snorted. "Absolutely nothing."

"That was the problem," Mercedes added.

"Then Bird recognized that if Pastor Adam and Reverend Patillo got married, the children might all attend the Presbyterian Church with their mother. Might could live in the manse instead of the parsonage."

"Oh, dear, no." Blossom gasped. "That would ruin everything. We need their children at the Christian Church."

"Exactly," Birdie said. "So we have to come up with something to keep those children in our church."

Each took another sip of coffee. "I could

check with my neighbors about their daughters or nieces," Blossom volunteered.

"Most important, we have to find him a wife everyone will like and will make the preacher happy," Winnie said.

"My sister in Abilene has a daughter." Immediately after Blossom said the words, she shut her mouth firmly and puckered her lips as if maybe, if she just sat silently, everyone would forget what she'd said.

"Well?" Birdie asked.

"I forgot, she's a nun. But they would share a common interest in theology and churches."

"Don't need a celibate woman for the preacher," Birdie said. Good thing Blossom had other good attributes like having a very good cook and knowing just how to entertain, because nothing she said ever contributed to the discussion.

"I'm concerned." Mercedes looked around the group. "I don't see anyone better for Pastor Adam than Gussie Milton. I really don't."

The others murmured agreement.

"I think Gussie's the one. We should do everything we can to bring them back together," Mercedes said. "That has to be our goal."

After a moment of silence, Blossom suggested, "We could invite them for dinner at my house."

"Might not be a bad idea," Birdie said as she nodded at Mercedes.

❦

As soon as Adam hung up, he leaned back in his chair and stared out the window.

What do the Widows have in mind?

When Blossom called to invite him to a little get-together at her home, suspicion filled him. It had the fingerprints of the matchmakers all over it.

And yet it could be nothing more than a thoughtful invitation from Blossom, a dinner party for him and a few others. She hadn't specified who else would join them, and he was too polite to ask. The words *Are the other Widows going to be there?* had trembled on his lips, but he'd swallowed them.

He had to warn Gussie. He didn't want her to be embarrassed and he couldn't face her again, not with the Widows clucking around and matchmaking. Of course, if they hadn't invited Gussie, the email would seem strange. But if they had, she'd appreciate the warning.

Maybe they'd invited another woman, in which case he'd have to go and act polite. Maybe they'd dug up a woman who fit him. Maybe they hadn't. Regardless, he couldn't turn down an invitation from a church member no matter how suspicious it sounded. He looked forward to getting to know Blossom and eating the wonderful dinner he knew her cook would prepare.

Just in case the invitation came from the Widows' usual motive, he wrote a quick email to Gussie and sent it. Later that evening, he received a message from her.

"Thanks for the heads-up. The invitation was on my computer when I got home. I declined. They never give up, do they?"

No, they didn't, but now he could look forward to a great meal and chagrined Widows.

Chapter Fifteen

Gussie couldn't sleep. Every night, she tossed and turned and found herself staring at the ceiling at three o'clock, knowing she'd have to get up in a few hours. In an effort to gain a little rest, she breathed in and out, deeply, and recited the Lord's Prayer. After thirty minutes, she felt closer to the Lord but even farther from sleep.

After a few days during which she dozed during slow periods at work, Gussie set a pattern to soothe her to sleep. It started with a long, hot bath, after which her skin was so wrinkled she felt like a shar-pei puppy. After that, she listened to relaxation

CDs. She followed all the instructions, but no matter how long she stayed in the tub or how far she descended on the fantasy elevator or how warm and relaxed she felt lying in the imaginary sunshine of the flower-covered meadow, she could not make the final descent into deep, restful slumber.

On the advice of friends, she drank warm milk, chamomile tea—not on the same evening—put a lavender sachet under her pillow, and ate a graham cracker. None worked. She refused to try feng shui because she could not believe having the bottoms of her feet face the door would help in the least.

Finally, she dug through the drawer where she tossed stuff and pulled out a little machine that played various soothing sounds. She'd never found sounds of the forest relaxing because the birds tweeted so loudly. Her father had ruined sounds of the sea, telling her he could hear calls for help from far away. The sound of rain made her have to get up and go to the bathroom, hardly conducive to deep sleep, and thunderstorms woke her up. She chose the soothing babbling stream. After replacing the batteries, she placed it on her bedside table, turned it on, relaxed in bed, closing her eyes and, again, breathing deeply and rhythmically.

Five minutes later, she'd fallen into a deep slumber.

When she woke up in the morning two hours later, she realized she spent far too much time preparing herself for a few hours of sleep. She needed to do something different. She needed help, and she really needed sleep.

❧

If there was anyone Gussie did not want to see that afternoon, it was Clare.

Actually, she had a list of people she would prefer not to see. It included many citizens of Butternut Creek, but Clare's name appeared at the top.

And yet Clare's huge black SUV sat in the parking lot of her studio. She was just too tired to have this conversation and yearned to drive off without stopping at the studio, but she couldn't. She had a disk filled with photos she had to download and print. Besides, she hadn't seen her best friend in such a long time.

Several times Gussie had emailed Clare that, although she and Adam had split, she was fine. Clare knew her too well to believe it. Then, in her most recent email, Gussie had foolishly mentioned the invitation from the Widows for their matchmaking dinner and Adam's warning. When she confessed she'd turned down the invitation, Clare had called her immediately. Gussie'd allowed the machine to pick up. But Clare would never give up, even if she had to show up in person towing all three children with her. When she heard honking behind her and realized she held up a line of traffic, Gussie turned into the lot and parked. Once inside, she saw Clare holding her youngest, Ashley. She knew she couldn't hold her friend at arm's length. She could not resist mother and baby. Clare had pulled out every weapon she had. How unfair.

Gussie hardened her heart—one last effort to escape Clare's loving insistence. Then Ashley gurgled.

Darn it!

"Okay," Gussie said, giving in. "Let me have the baby. Come into my office and we can talk. I don't have any more appointments today." She waved to Justine behind the reception desk. "Go on home. I'll close up."

Once they'd each grabbed a bottle of water from the fridge, Gussie and Clare settled in the two comfortable chairs and Gussie cuddled Ashley. Clare didn't bother with how long it had been and how good it was to see her, or with giving an update on her other two kids. No, she got straight to the point, as usual.

"Gus, do you love Adam?"

Gussie looked down at Ashley, who was waving her little fists in her honorary aunt's face and making baby noises.

"Gus." Clare's voice sharpened. "You know I am genetically incapable of staying out of the lives of people I love. You know I won't go away."

The two sat in silence for nearly a minute before Clare said, "But I will leave you alone. Because I love you so much, I will fight my instinct to pry into your personal life. All you have to do is tell me to leave."

"Yes, I think I love Adam," Gussie mumbled.

"Does he love you?"

"I don't know." Gussie shrugged. "He said he wanted to. I think that meant maybe he does."

"He's a minister," Clare said. "Don't you think he usually tells the truth?"

"Probably."

"Okay, let's try this again." Clare slid her chair over the laminate flooring closer to her friend. "Do you think Adam loves you?"

Gussie swallowed hard. "Yes."

"Why aren't you together?"

"You make it sound so simple. Sometimes love isn't enough."

"Gus, don't intellectualize. Talk to me."

She looked at Clare's expression of love and concern. "I don't know. I'd really thought I was okay, that I'd gotten over the rape and gotten back my life, until I met Adam. I was functioning, at least." She would've held a hand up to keep Clare from interrupting but both were full of baby. Instead she glared. "Yes, you mentioned, often, that you saw signs, like the guys I'd date for a month and break up with, but I didn't realize that.

"I don't think things will work out with Adam. I can't be with him right now the way he wants, and it's not fair for me to ask him to wait when I don't know if . . ."

Clare watched sympathetically.

"But still, I know I need to do something. I just don't know what yet. When I've worked things out—or even if I haven't—I'll get in touch with you. I promise."

Clare stood and moved toward Gussie to lean down and hug her. "I love you. And you know, no matter what happens with Adam, you need to do this for you."

"I know. I'm lucky to have you as a friend. Most of the time."

"And don't you forget that."

❦

"Nothing has worked." Birdie felt like crying. Never had she faced such a failure. She glanced around at the Widows gathered at the diner to discuss the crisis.

"It was a setback, but we haven't tried that much." Winnie spoke up—as usual. "We had that dinner without Gussie, but what else could we have done?"

"I don't know what to do next," Mercedes said. "We can't give up. If we do, we'll lose one of our core tenets."

"We could wait until another single

woman moves into the area," Blossom suggested.

"Not likely." Winnie shook her head disconsolately. "The economy and the attractions of Austin draw young people to the big city."

"But wasn't the dinner party nice?" Blossom asked. "Even if only the preacher and the three of you showed up. I had a nice time."

No use explaining to the woman that the purpose hadn't been to chat with the preacher.

"Mac and Bree tell me that Gussie is set on taking care of her parents," Birdie explained. "Seems she's very devoted to them."

"Do you think maybe she won't or can't commit to the preacher because of them?" Winnie asked.

"My, my," Blossom said. "That does make sense."

"What do we do about it?" Mercedes asked. "Other than taking dinner down to Roundville and dragging the preacher along, I don't see a solution."

"Tea," Blossom said.

The other three turned to stare at her.

"We could take tea to them." She batted her eyes. "To Gussie's parents and talk to them about the situation. A polite chat over tea."

Who'd've believed it? Blossom had come up with another good idea.

"You're right," Mercedes said. "Surely they'd be interested in what's going on."

Winnie pulled her ever-present note-book and pen from her bag. "All right, let's brainstorm."

Within ten minutes, the Widows had a plan and a purpose and renewed dedica-tion. Gussie Milton and the preacher would get married if the Widows had to follow them down the aisle with pitchforks.

❦

"Pops, you know the Widows aren't going to give up on you," Hector said as he cleared the table. "Bree told me that."

Great.

"Not going to give up on you and Gussie," he clarified, though Adam knew what he'd meant. "Bree says they thought about that blond lady but didn't think she was right for you."

Good news.

"As far as we can tell, whatever they have planned will take place sometime soon, maybe this week."

"They have *plans*?" Oh, please, no. Their ideas always meant inexorable determination on their part and deep humiliation on his. "What do they have in mind?"

"Don't know. Miss Birdie didn't tell her. Bree could tell *something* was going on because the Widows have been so secretive and she heard your name mentioned when her grandmother took a phone call." Hector rinsed a place off. "Your name and Gussie's."

Adam felt as frustrated as if he were on the deck of the *Titanic*, watching the ship approach the icebergs while he shouted, "Danger ahead!" Nothing he could do would stop or delay the impending and inevitable catastrophe.

The situation required constant vigilance. He could almost feel the ice floe forming around him, but he had no idea where the flood of destruction would come from.

He waited for the tide to submerge him.

Lots of water images and none of them worked together. He didn't care. He was a scared man, not a poet.

Despite his certainty the Widows would act soon, he heard nothing. Two days, then a week. Nothing happened. The Widows didn't converge on him. He heard nothing from Gussie. Good news that she didn't have anything to report on the Widows. Bad news that he didn't hear anything from Gussie about herself.

Still, he waited fearfully.

And hopefully.

❦

On Friday, the Widows met at the church to go to Roundville. They'd use Blossom's big, luxurious car that made them feel like they were riding in a softly upholstered co-coon.

"But you're not driving," Birdie told Blossom when they all arrived in the parking lot. "When you carried me home from the diner the other day, I thought you were going to kill me." She reached for the keys as she explained to Mercedes and Winnie. "I swan, she drives so fast and talks the entire way and fiddles with the radio and the air-conditioning, weaving all over the road. Thought we were going to run over every dog and cat on the way. Old Jacob Russell was pushing his walker across the street and nearly had a stroke. Poor man was shuffling as fast as he could."

Without a murmur of protest, Blossom handed the keys over and they all piled in, Mercedes in the passenger seat with Winnie.

Winnie got her notebook out and flipped it open. "Let's make sure we've checked everything off." For the next hour, the Widows chatted about the plan.

When the car arrived in Roundville, Mercedes said, "Slow down, Bird. I know how to get there."

"Don't show off. I do, too. We used to come here all the time when Gussie's mother was in charge of women's programs for the district."

The two argued about which road to take and which direction to turn until, somehow, they arrived at the Miltons' home. All four got out. Blossom took the keys to her car, popped the trunk, took out several huge tote bags, and they all marched up the walk.

Before they could ring the bell, the door flew open.

"My, my, my." Yvonne smiled at the women in front of her. "Birdie MacDowell and Mercedes Rivera, how wonderful to see you. It's been years."

"Hello, Yvonne," Mercedes said. "These are our friends from Butternut Creek, Winnie Jenkins and Blossom Brown, also members of the Christian Church."

"I'm Yvonne Milton. Please, come in." She stepped aside and motioned the four inside. "What's the occasion?"

"Oh, we were just in the neighborhood and thought we'd drop by," Birdie explained.

Yvonne studied their expressions closely. Roundville, ten miles from the main highway on a winding two-lane road, wasn't a place one visited on a whim. Too polite to point that out, Yvonne led them into the living room, where Henry read the newspaper in his recliner.

"Don't get up," Birdie commanded.

Because Henry knew her well and understood equally as well the futility of disobeying her, he relaxed back in the chair.

"Sit down, please." Yvonne motioned toward the love seats and took a chair. The six sat quietly and nodded toward one another for nearly a minute because—how could the Widows not have considered this?—after all their meticulous planning, they'd forgotten one thing. They hadn't decided who would open the conversation and what the chosen Widow would say.

Birdie glanced around. Not one of the Widows looked as if she would say anything. It was up to Birdie. Mercedes and Blossom were too gracious to push ahead and Winnie—well, that woman might say the wrong thing. In a tough situation, the leader had to take over.

"Your daughter won't marry our preacher because she has to stay here and take care of you." There. The problem was out in the open.

"What?" Yvonne sat up straight and glared at Birdie.

Henry lowered the footrest on his chair, stood, and strode toward Birdie. Standing only inches away, he demanded, "What gives you the right to say that? Yvonne and I would never come between our daughter and happiness."

"Birdie MacDowell," Yvonne said. The words coming from her mouth sounded as if they had brilliant vocal flames surrounding them. "You've gone too far this time."

Birdie blinked. She'd never seen either Milton angry.

"What Birdie means to say," Winnie began.

The Miltons turned toward Winnie as one and glared.

"Who are you?" Yvonne asked in a tone that successfully shut the bossy woman up.

"I'm sorry," Winnie whispered.

Henry simply glowered at the assembled Widows.

"You need to allow your daughter to make her choice, to get married if she wants to. Our minister . . ." Birdie stopped speaking and actually cowered. Never before had she cowered, but the look on Henry's face frightened her. For a moment she considered that, perhaps, she hadn't used the most judicious words. No, she'd spoken the truth. The Miltons had overreacted.

"You don't think we love our daughter?" Henry thundered.

"Now, now, now." Blossom spoke in a gentle, calm voice and held up her hand. She stood and approached Henry with more courage than Birdie could have mustered. "I think we have a slight misunderstanding."

"Misunderstanding?" Henry exploded. "That woman—" He pointed at Birdie, his hand shaking. "That woman told us we have kept our daughter from happiness."

"I don't believe she meant it exactly like that."

Yes, Birdie had, but she hadn't expected Henry's reaction. Not that she shouldn't have. If anyone had said that to her about Bree or Mac, she'd deck 'em. Birdie sat back, vanquished and annoyed because she had to allow Blossom Brown to rescue her, their mission, and the happiness of the preacher.

"Why don't we go into the kitchen, just the three of us?" Blossom pointed to herself then the Miltons and spoke in a sugary sweet voice that made Birdie want to stomp her feet.

Instead she mumbled "Hrmph" to herself.

Blossom continued, "My cook makes the most delicious coffee cake. I brought one to share with you." She turned toward Yvonne. "Cook uses real butter and fresh eggs and has little, tiny chips of walnuts and apples with a streusel topping." She took Yvonne's arm. "I know you'll like it."

Slowly and amiably, Blossom urged the two out of the living room and into the kitchen.

"And tea," Birdie heard the newest Widow say. "Cook makes the most wonderful tea. I brought a carafe of that. Or, if you prefer, she packed mocha cappuccino in a thermos. Now, I'm sure you have lovely china, but I brought my mother's favorite along."

Birdie let out the breath she'd been holding and whispered a prayer of gratitude for help coming from unexpected sources. Neither Winnie nor Mercedes said a word. Both looked a little shell-shocked.

The three Widows sat quietly in the living room. They could make out rustling sounds in the kitchen, the clink of china, and bits of conversations, a word here and another there, but nothing more. At least they didn't hear Henry shouting. Absence of loud voices probably signaled a suspension of hostilities.

"You should have known better than to

let me talk first," Birdie whispered after about ten minutes.

"We didn't know you'd make such a terrible mess of it," Mercedes said.

"We should've," Winnie added.

"Yes." Birdie sighed. "You should have. I'm sorry."

The three Widows didn't move for nearly half an hour, sitting in silence with their backs straight and hands folded in their laps. During the entire time, all Birdie could think about was that she had destroyed their mission. Their most important effort at matchmaking had failed because of her. A bitter defeat due to her incompetence.

The sound of movement and laughter came from the kitchen. Blossom returned to the living room with a happy Yvonne and a smiling Henry.

"So good to meet you." Blossom grinned at both Miltons.

"Please drop by anytime." Henry took her hand and shook it. "I'll carry your bags out."

"And make sure you send me that recipe," Yvonne said. She hugged Blossom.

Within minutes, the Widows were back

in the car. Actually, Birdie realized, three Widows and one Matchmaker.

"What happened in the kitchen?" Birdie asked, humbled and greatly chagrined for her part in what could have been a failed maneuver.

"We had tea and coffee cake and chatted."

"And?" Winnie prompted.

"And we worked things out. Yvonne is going to talk to Gussie, try to see how much of what we guessed is true. She'll handle it. We can relax. She did swear us all to an oath of secrecy. We are not to mention this to anyone. They want to deal with this themselves."

"Besides, we don't want the preacher to know we meddled," Mercedes said.

All four nodded.

"Thank you, Blossom," Birdie said, so filled with relief she could have hugged the woman if they weren't in the car. Not that she actually would, even when they got back to town. Although she had to push the words out, Birdie again said, "Thank you."

Anyone who thought having to acknowledge the success of another person in carrying out her mission didn't mortify her didn't know Birdie MacDowell very well. Her failure and the need to thank Blossom Brown humiliated her.

❦

"Dear," her mother greeted Gussie as she arrived home from work. "Your father and I need to have a little chat with you."

Uh-oh. The words *need to have a little chat* constituted the highest level of the early warning signal. *Want to talk to you* meant a serious problem but at a lower level—say, roaches in the kitchen or weevils in the flour. *Need to have a little chat* meant a severe hazard, a red-level threat, a national emergency, perhaps enemy attack or a constitutional crisis.

Or an egregious transgression on Gussie's part.

"Let's sit here in the living room," Mom said. "To be comfortable."

Oh, sure, Gussie would be comfortable for this "little chat."

Her mother wore a lacy white shirt with her cameo, another sure sign of an impending emergency and the possible arrival of

Armageddon. For a merely important talk, she wore her pink T-shirt with the rabbit on the front.

Gussie glanced at her father who attempted to look uninvolved, sinking back in his recliner with his newspaper in front of him. This was the equivalent of a high-pitched warning signal screaming, *Leave me alone. I'm not part of this.*

"Let me go upstairs . . . ," Gussie said before her mother shoved her toward a chair.

Her mother recognized the words Gussie used when she attempted to escape a crisis.

When she didn't sit, her mother took Gussie's elbow and escorted her to the chair.

Thoroughly warned that she would *not* like the coming "chat" but acknowledging she couldn't get out of it, Gussie sat.

Loving God, save me, Gussie prayed silently.

For the first time Gussie could remember, her mother had a difficult time beginning what she called "the chat" and Gussie called "the grilling." Mom sat, crossed her legs, and swung her right foot left and right. She played with the cameo, rubbing a thumb over the silhouette of a rose and fiddling with the clasp.

"Gussie," she said at last, her voice serious. "We had visitors today. From Butternut Creek."

"Not Adam." *Oh, please, let it be Adam. Please, do* not *let it be Adam.* When she realized how hopeless and hopeful her voice must have sounded—hard to accomplish that with only two words—Gussie cleared her throat and asked in a neutral voice, "Adam?"

"No, Birdie MacDowell, Mercedes Rivera, and two other women. I believe you know them?"

"The Widows?" Darn. This was serious. Again, hope and despair filled her.

"I'd forgotten that's what they call themselves." Mom nodded. "Yes, the Widows."

Gussie attempted to wait out her mother, force her to bring up the subject. She should know better. After all these years, she could never beat her mother at the waiting game.

After a long silence, Gussie asked, "Why shouldn't they stop by? Aren't you and Miss Birdie and Mercedes old friends?"

"Why do you think they stopped by?"

Gussie shrugged. As useless a reaction as attempting to stop Shaquille O'Neal when he drove for the basket.

"To talk about Adam?" Gussie asked, then paused, hating to add the rest. "And me? Not, of course, that there is an 'Adam and me.'"

Her mother leaned toward Gussie and shot her the glare of death. "They tell me," she said, "the reason you and their nice minister broke up is because of us, your father and me, because you feel as if you must take care of us for the rest of our lives and have put your happiness on hold." She leaned back and crossed her arms. "Is that true?"

"Oh, no." Gussie shook her head. "No." Again, her mother said nothing. "Well, only a little bit. You know how much I love you. If you hadn't supported me after . . ." She couldn't finish the sentence.

"After what?" her father said, breaking into the conversation.

He'd been so quiet, she'd nearly forgotten he sat only five feet from her. She swiveled to look at him, "You know," she said.

"But you can't say it." He tilted his head and studied her face. "Maybe if you could, you'd do better, maybe start healing."

"I've healed," she squeaked, which pretty much gave her feelings away. She'd *thought* she'd healed until she met Adam. If healed meant she wanted to live normally and fall in love, well, she'd missed the mark by miles.

"You were saying that if we hadn't supported you after Lennie hurt you so badly, you would have fallen apart?" Mom leaned forward, this time her eyes filled with compassion.

"Yes."

"And, because of that, you have to take care of us forever?"

"When Dad went in the hospital, I realized how . . . how . . ."

"Old and frail and sickly we've gotten?" Dad asked. "I resent that."

"No, I . . ."

"What I really resent—" He tossed the paper on the floor, a sure sign of agitation. "What I do resent is that you didn't talk to us about this, you shut us out. We didn't realize a problem existed until these . . . these Widows dropped in and told us."

"We should have spotted that, Henry. Gussie hasn't been herself recently."

"She seemed happy," her father said. "She looked great until a few weeks back. We know she does that, covers up her feelings." He paused. "You're right. We should've realized she acted happy on the surface so we wouldn't worry."

"Yes, underneath she wasn't happy," Mom said.

"Hello," Gussie said. "I'm right here. You shouldn't talk about me while I'm sitting right here."

"Dear, I'm sorry. Would you prefer to leave the room so we can talk about you more comfortably?"

"No. Talk *to* me."

"All right. We should have noticed you haven't been happy since you and your young man broke up."

Did her mother not realize that, if they'd broken up, Adam no longer could be considered "her young man"?

"We want to know if that's our fault and what we should do." Dad lowered the recliner footrest, stood, and moved to sit in a chair next to Gussie. He took her hand. "I can even quote the Bible here: 'A man leaves his father and his mother and cleaves to his wife.'" He held his other hand up when Gussie began to protest. "Think we can read that as a woman leaves her parents as well. That's what people do, they start a new family. They become one flesh, Gussie, exactly as your mother and I did."

"If you want that for yourself, we do, too," her mother said.

"If you don't, we still don't want you to give up your life to stay with your aging, decaying parents. Maybe you'd like to move to Austin, be closer to work. Most important, we don't want to be used as an excuse for you not to find the life you want. We don't want you to hide behind us because you're afraid."

Was she afraid? Well, yes, of course, for many reasons. Her parents were aging. Their health concerned her greatly.

And Adam. She thought about him, wondered about her feelings, about trusting, but the-cleaving-and-becoming-one-flesh part scared the living daylights out of her.

"What would you do if I didn't live here?"

"We lived a long time on our own, dear. We survived before you were born, while you were a child, and after you went off to college."

"I hear the Baptist retirement center may have openings," her father said. "We could buy one of those little houses. We have lots of friends there, and they all say it's a good life."

Oh, so they did have choices. Shame spread through her that she'd considered herself their only future. Humbled, she asked, "Would you like that?"

"A house takes a lot of upkeep," her father said.

"Since the dog died last year, we haven't needed a yard," Mom added.

"What we're saying, dear, is that you don't have to—in fact, you shouldn't—give up your life for us. We have other options. We want you to find happiness."

Gussie smiled. What a mess she'd made of things. "I'm sorry. I should have talked to you. I shouldn't have assumed I'm indispensable."

"Of course you're indispensable, but not in the way you think. You're our daughter. We love you, but you aren't our nurse or caregiver or keeper. You're our beloved daughter." Dad squeezed her hand. "What do we need to do? What do you need to do? Do you love this Adam?"

She looked from her mother to her father while she considered the question. "Yes, Dad, I think I do, but I'm frightened." Her voice broke on the last word.

Her mother stood and took Gussie's other hand. "As much as I hate to admit this, we should thank those Widows for dropping by. Now we can start to work on your future." Her mother paused. "Oh, and we asked them not to mention this visit to Adam or anyone in Butternut Creek."

"They agreed?" Didn't sound at all like the Widows.

"Yes, we came to a meeting of the minds on many subjects," Mom said.

"Thanks, Mom and Dad." Gussie stood, pulled both parents to their feet for a group hug. "I'm going upstairs. I need to think." This time, her mother allowed her to leave. Once in her bedroom, she settled at the computer and opened her mail. The usual: spam and a couple of notes from friends, including two from Clare. Adam hadn't written her for weeks. Not that she blamed him.

What now? Should she write him and

explain? Maybe pray for guidance? Ask him to pray for her?

No, not yet. She knew what she had to do—what she and God needed to do together. She needed to get straight, come to peace with her past in a way that didn't mean celibacy or require her to toss up roadblocks between her and what she wanted, really wanted: to be with Adam. She wouldn't get in touch with him until she knew she could give all of herself. She could only hope he still wanted her.

Chapter Sixteen

"Hello, Gussie." With a nod. Fran Finster, Gussie's counselor, welcomed her into her study. It was a calm room with light blue walls, windows looking out over Zilker Park, curtains of soft blue flowers on a white background, and enough clutter strewn around to look cozy but not sloppy. If this weren't Texas, she'd probably have a fire crackling in the fireplace. "Sit down."

Fran didn't fit the friendly setting. She wore her dark hair in an angular cut that reached her shoulders in the front. With a green shirt, she wore black slacks and what Gussie guessed were comfortable if incredibly ugly shoes.

"How are you doing?" Fran asked, her voice clipped but also filled with concern.

Nice touch, Gussie thought, that note of concern in her voice. Gussie knew the real Fran had the heart of a shark. She dug deep and never forgot a single word Gussie had uttered.

"Not so great if I'm back here." Gussie settled in a cushioned chair that faced Fran's desk and leaned back. "I need the tough lady who'll put me back together."

"I can help, but you have to do your part this time: to promise to work hard, stay with me, face what you have to, and not run away." Fran settled in a chair across from Gussie. "You left too early last time."

"I really believed I was okay, functioning well. The studio has become successful."

"And your parents?"

"Getting older but still fairly healthy for people in their seventies."

"If everything is going so well, why are you here?"

Gussie struggled for words, then took a deep breath and made herself speak before she could hide behind her usual dodge of logic. "I ran into something I hadn't expected. A man."

"You ran into a man? In your car?"

Aah, she'd forgotten Fran's play-dumb act. Not that she actually was dumb. Though her tactics differed, she was just as determined as Gussie's mother. Fran truly was *she who could not be ignored.* But this time Gussie wanted to explain, as hard as it was.

"I met a man I'm very attracted to." Gussie shrugged. "I didn't expect that. I should have realized that *not* expecting to find a man attractive meant I wasn't cured, but I didn't. As long as life remained on an even keel, I fooled myself into believing I was handling things very well."

"And this man has made you to look at yourself?"

Gussie nodded.

"Good for him! What's his name?"

"Adam Jordan." Okay, that was the easy part. She knew Fran's questions would become intrusive little by little, but that was good, really. Intrusive meant the counselor would search for the core of the problem. "We met at—"

"Before we go into that," Fran said, "I want you to tell me about your rape."

She stiffened. "I don't want to talk about the rape. I want to talk about Adam and our relationship."

"Oh, I see. You want to discuss your relationship with Adam," Fran stated. "Then explain why you are here. You could discuss that with Adam or a girlfriend or your mother."

Fran watched her expectantly.

Gussie had nothing. If she talked to her parents, they'd look sad and sympathetic, and she couldn't handle that. Clare would listen but not in silence, and Adam . . . she couldn't discuss anything with Adam until she knew how she felt. Fran was right. Gussie leaned forward, head down and eyes closed, and began the story of the rape, the one Fran had forced her to repeat over and over.

When she finished, tears rolled down her cheeks and pain ate her up inside. Until the rape, she'd hadn't realized mental pain could also become physical anguish.

"There," Gussie said. "Are you satisfied?"

"Tell me again."

"Fran, we've done this before, over and over."

"Have you told that story to anyone since our last appointment?"

"Yes. To Adam."

"How did he react?"

"Fine. He was very sympathetic."

"And you? How did you do?"

Gussie didn't want to answer that. She closed her eyes and shut herself up inside.

"You still cry and you still hurt, Gussie. I haven't seen you for three years," Fran said. "We have to start from the beginning and build from there again. This time, you have to thoroughly confront that experience, your pain and trauma, but here, in a safe place."

"I don't want to."

"You know what I always say, Gussie. The wound is where the healing starts. Doesn't do a bit of good to approach the trauma any other way, to tiptoe around what hurts. As you relive the pain, the healing will begin."

Gussie opened her eyes and forced herself to speak. "I was eighteen and in my second semester of college . . ."

After she finished the second telling, Fran said, "I'll need to work with you intensively for at least eight to ten weeks. I also want you to come to the rape survivors group every Tuesday evening."

"But most of them have been really raped. In dark alleys or in their homes by men they didn't know. Compared with them, I wasn't really raped."

"Gussie, if you did not give your consent, you were raped. You have to deal with it that way, not as something you asked for because you were drunk or because you were in a vulnerable situation. You were violated. That is the definition of rape."

"But I knew Lennie wouldn't kill me. I wasn't that frightened of fighting him off, not like women who are assaulted in an alley."

"No, but a man you trusted and cared about sexually assaulted you. Until you accept that, you won't mend. Until you get angry—furious, overwhelmed by rage—about that violation and Lennie's part in it, you won't get better. You're too detached from what really happened. You have to feel."

Gussie sighed, then took her calendar out and wrote in dates.

"I have another question. Why, Gussie? Why now? You know this thing with Adam still might not work out as you hope."

"I know, but I have to try. I have to face up to how lonely and broken I am. I want to be a normal person. I want to fall in love. I want to love a man even if it's too late for me and Adam." She nodded. "Yes, I'm ready, and I'll do it your way."

❧

Even though December had arrived, Adam didn't consider it winter. Here winter consisted of a few weeks at the end of January when the weather got cold enough for people to stop wearing flip-flops.

Life went on. The church had sponsored a Halloween party in the fellowship hall. Janey had sung a solo in the community celebration of Veterans Day.

He and Janey continued to go to every one of Hector's games. With each, Hector improved. The team hadn't yet lost a game. Letters from colleges arrived daily and had piled up as schools showed interest in Hector.

During all these weeks, Adam had heard

nothing from Gussie. He'd decided not to make contact himself, not to push her. He'd recover. A year ago, he hadn't even realized a Gussie Milton existed. Surely he could move on.

The Widows remained oddly quiet— not that he complained, but it confused him. Could be they'd run out of options. He'd heard the blond woman had started to keep company with a man in San Saba.

A minister in Austin had invited him to join a group of friends for a picnic in Zilker Park and introduced Adam to a ministerial student. They'd had fun at the outing and Adam knew she wanted him to call her, but the idea of having a long drive to see her—well, he'd done that and didn't want to again.

"Okay, it's time for you to come out of that funk," Mattie said at breakfast. They sat at what Miss Birdie referred to as "their table," where she always placed them so she could keep an eye—and an ear—on them.

"What funk?"

"Everyone knows Gussie Milton dumped you for her parents."

"She didn't . . ." He cleared his throat. No way he'd talk to anyone about what happened with Gussie, even to protect his masculine image and ego. "I'm not in a funk. It was mutual."

"Oh, yeah? Mac showed me a picture of Gussie Milton. She's way hotter than you are, out of your class."

One of the problems with a small town— that everyone-knows-everyone's-business thing.

"Thanks," he said. "Have I ever told you how much I appreciate your friendship and support?"

"No, but you can."

Uh-oh. This tone of voice sounded exactly like the one she'd used when she made him go to the wedding with her. He dug into his pancakes.

"Some friends in Austin are having a Christmas party. I need a date."

That's exactly what he'd guessed. He took another bite.

"I need a date," she repeated. "And you're it."

He chewed and took another bite because he didn't want to respond. After he finished chewing, Mattie still hadn't spoken. He wiped his mouth, took a drink of juice, and said, "I don't want to go. Didn't I make it clear the wedding was a onetime deal?"

"If I go alone, I'll feel like such a loser."

"You aren't. You've just hit a dry spell. It isn't as if single men are running all over Butternut Creek."

"I know."

"You have to come to grips with the situation. You and your fiancé aren't going to get together again."

"Don't want to."

"I'm not going with you. You have to accept the fact that you're not dating and don't let it bother you. Let go."

"Yeah, and how's that letting-go working for you?" When he didn't answer, she said, "I know. I tell myself that, but it's hard to move on."

Didn't he know that.

"Do you know how many men would even ask a woman minister out? With the handful of men in a fifty-mile radius, you are about it."

When he didn't answer, she went on. "Men are afraid of women ministers, afraid we'll have no interest in kissing, like we're nuns."

"Mattie, I don't need to hear this."

"And none of them would even consider marrying a minister. That's not the life a man wants. They're afraid they'd have to act pious and give up beer and bring a casserole to a church dinner. Adam, I want to get married. I want children."

He blinked because he wanted to ask *With me?* but felt fairly certain he'd never get those words out.

"But don't worry." She buttered her toast before she said, "You'd probably be more trouble than it's worth."

❧

When Hector pulled into a parking space in front of the dentist's office and turned off the ignition, the vehicle gave its usual five or six gasps and several huffs before the engine stopped.

This time, Hector didn't sigh. He merely shook his head and got out of the heaving vehicle. Throwing the keys to Adam, Hector said, "You can drive it back. I'm embarrassed to be seen in it."

"You're going to walk back?"

"No, I'll go with you, but I might hide in the backseat with a blanket over me."

❦

"I'm trying a new recipe." Ouida placed a covered plate on Adam's desk. "Chocolate chip muffins."

Chocolate chip muffins, a combination of two of his favorite things. Why hadn't he heard of these before? He lifted the napkin and studied the beautifully rounded morsels.

"These look wonderful." He picked one up and asked, "What's the occasion?" before he pulled the paper off and took a bite.

"George said chocolate is not for breakfast." She dropped into a chair. "He says it's a special treat, like a dessert or a snack, but not breakfast." She smiled. "George has some pretty strict beliefs, but he's trying to relax, trying to be more accepting." She waved toward the plate. "These should help. I'm serving them for breakfast tomorrow." She frowned. "Or maybe they are too rich. George may be right. What do you think?"

Busy with savoring the deliciousness of

the muffin, he couldn't respond immediately. At last he swallowed the thick richness, ignored the question because he didn't want to be involved in a discussion about the nutritional value of chocolate chip muffins, and said, "Things between you and George going well?"

"Oh, yes, Preacher. Thank you. Without your advice, I'd never had the courage to change. Without you, I'd still be ironing George's shorts and starching those dresser scarves and feeling dissatisfied."

Because he'd taken another bite— stupid knowing he'd need to respond to Ouida, but he couldn't resist the lure of chocolate chip muffins—he attempted to mumble, *I didn't do anything*, but couldn't with his mouth so full. Instead he shrugged and attempted to look both wise and caring, difficult while chewing.

"You didn't tell me *what* to do, I know that, but you encouraged me, listened to me while I worked things out for myself. Thank you."

He nodded as wisely as a man with a mouthful of muffin can. "We've started work on my studio in the attic, decided to install a skylight up there. George figures it will increase the value of the house, and I'm happy to have more light."

He nodded again. What he really needed was a cup of coffee or a glass of water because, as tasty as the muffin was, the density nearly defeated him.

"I have to warn you." She smiled at him.

He thought about smiling back at her but felt chocolate probably covered his teeth. Instead, he raised his eyebrow as if asking a question.

"We're coming to the Christmas Eve service, the whole family." She laughed. "I didn't want you to keel over in shock. Carol is excited about the candles and Gretchen loves being in church." She shook her head, the action a nice counterpoint to his nods. "They want to come so George and I have to. They like church and I have to admit attending hasn't hurt them." She stood, waved, and turned toward the door.

By the time Adam finally swallowed, she'd disappeared.

He was glad the girls liked church, glad it hadn't hurt them, and delighted George and Ouida would attend Christmas Eve.

Everyone he loved would be gathered in the sanctuary that night.

Well, almost everyone.

"Hello, Preacher."

Adam looked up to see a professorial-looking man who squinted at him through thick glasses.

"I'm Martin Hanford, the organist for Sunday."

"Hello, Mr. Hanford. Good to meet you." Adam stood. "What can I do for you?"

"Yes, well, I'd like to practice on your organ. I've played here a few times, before you arrived. Your organ has a recorder in it. I'd like to record the music for Sunday. At the right time in the service, I just mash the PLAY button." The organist showed how he'd do that. "Boom, the music starts and plays with no mistakes."

Makes you wonder why we need an organist, Adam thought but didn't say. He did say, "Sounds fine. Let me show you . . ."

"No, no. I've been in the sanctuary before and your secretary gave me a bulletin so I know what to play. But I would like to know if there's anything special you'd like for Sunday because it *is* the first Sunday in Advent."

"Can't think of anything."

With that, Mr. Hanford strode off and Adam returned to work on his sermon.

❦

Not nearly as easy as it had sounded, Adam reflected. At the beginning of the service that Sunday, Mr. Hanford played—at least the organ did—a lovely prelude. With that nearly completed, the organist glanced at Adam, who waited in the narthex. Before Adam could give the signal for him to play the opening hymn, it began.

Startled at the rapid change, the congregation leaped to their feet and Adam hurried down the aisle after Nick, who served as acolyte. Because the acolyte's candle hadn't been lit yet, Nick arrived in the chancel area with no way to light the other candles.

Still, the opening hymn boomed out from the organ. Nick look at Adam, confusion in his eyes. "What do I do," he whispered.

Willow ran forward from the narthex with a book of matches. She struck one, lit Nick's candle, and hurried away. As soon as the candles were finally lit, the second hymn emerged from the organ while Adam was still making his way to the pulpit.

The organist cursed as he madly pressed buttons and attempted to turn the recording off. He looked up, aghast that his words had echoed through the sanctuary. "I'm sorry. I'll rewind."

As Adam made announcements, he could hear a few notes coming from the organ as Mr. Hanford attempted to find the correct place. When they stopped, Adam believed the problem to be solved.

Not so fast.

When he asked the congregation to rise for the second hymn, instead of the notes of "Come, Thou Long Expected Jesus," the prelude began. The congregation stood motionless, then smiled, then titters began when the organist again muttered, "Damn." This time, he didn't apologize, just glared at the organ as if it were possessed.

He mashed a few buttons on the recorder again, harder. By the time the correct hymn began, Adam felt sure no one could sing because only he and the pillar could keep a straight face. However, Miss Birdie, with Hector and Bree doubled up next to her and nearly hysterical by this time, didn't look as if she could keep it up much longer. For that reason, Adam began the hymn in his shaky tenor. Fortunately, Janey recovered when she heard his pitiful voice and began to sing. Her clear voice filled the sanctuary and returned the congregation to a worshipful air.

At least, until what sounded like small explosions sounded from the inside of the organ.

All eyes turned again to Mr. Hanford, tie loosened, suit coat off, and sweat pouring down his face as he glared at the organ. He pressed the buttons again but nothing happened.

"Shh—" Mr. Hanford started.

"Shucks," Adam shouted over him. Now what? "Shucks, folks, let's not sing the next hymn. Let's go straight to the scripture."

While the worship leader began the Gospel text, Adam walked to the organ and asked sympathetically, "Problems?"

Sadly, Mr. Hanford didn't recognize the concern in Adam's voice. He said, "Okay, if you're so smart, play it yourself," then grabbed his jacket and stalked off.

Another organist down. Another sermon shortened. Another congregation that arrived early at the Subway.

As folks filed out, Hector said, "Pops, don't ever get a regular organist. The subs really make the service fun."

Lord, how Adam wished he could share this with Gussie.

🎵

The ladies of the church and the few men they could force to help them had decorated the parsonage for Christmas weeks earlier. As usual—well, at least like last year—the house smelled and looked wonderful and felt even more like home. Electric candles stood at each window, ready for Adam to turn on at sunset. Pine boughs wound around the staircase and decorated the fireplace. Mistletoe hung over the doors, and red ribbons and plaid bows filled any empty spaces.

Adam leaned back in the sofa, took the beauty in, and sighed with contentment. He'd just read a card from the Smiths, who'd stayed in the parsonage a year earlier. Deanne and Missy were fine. They sent love and gratitude and a huge box of homemade goodies.

"Pops, we need to buy a tree from the Letterman's Club," Hector said, interrupting his moment of peace and joy to snatch a cookie. "It's our big fund-raiser of the year and we all have to bring people to the lot."

"We have a tree." Adam pointed at the beautiful fir, huge and full, its branches laden with ornaments and other baubles the ladies had donated. It nestled in the corner of the living room with splendor.

"I was thinkin' we could move it into the front hall, by the curve in the staircase."

"It would look good there," Adam agreed.

"Then we'll put the new tree in the corner." Hector pointed. "I've got the rope in the car to tie the tree up there to bring home, and Miss Birdie gave me some ornaments."

Adam knew he wouldn't get out of this. Hector—and, therefore, Adam—had to support athletics. With a sigh because he'd hoped to spend the evening on the couch watching a college football game, Adam stood.

❦

"Pops, what time is it?" Hector asked once they were in the car. "They close at five."

"It's three twenty."

"How do you know that? The dashboard clock says four twelve."

"Subtract an hour and add eight minutes," Adam explained.

Hector sighed deeply. Adam knew he wanted to say, *Why don't you get a new car? One on which most of the stuff works.* But Hector also knew that ministers of small-town churches didn't make a big salary.

❦

The selection of trees wasn't great.

"They've been picked over a little, Pops."

Because of the disappointment in Hector's voice, Adam boomed, "Nonsense. I'm sure we'll find a great tree," with much more confidence than he felt.

The best one turned out to be four feet tall, spindly and crooked, and uglier than any tree Adam had ever seen, but the expense supported a good cause. He pulled out his wallet and handed one of the parents who ran the lot a twenty. The man kept his hand out.

"Ten more," he said.

Adam wanted to tell the man, *You've got to be kidding*, but he didn't. That statement would embarrass Hector. Instead he asked, "Throw in a stand?"

After he paid, Adam picked up the stand

and tree, which weighed less than a middle-size cat, and carried them toward the car. As he did, needles showered off.

"I'll help you carry that." Hector took a few steps toward Adam and his burden.

"I can handle it." Instead of tying it to the top of the car, Adam squished the fragile tree into the trunk because, after all, very little could make it look worse. He tossed the stand inside, tied the trunk shut with the tree hanging a bit out the side, and walked around the car.

Once home, as they moved the thing inside the parsonage, it shed needles down the hall and into the corner of the television room.

"Janey," Adam shouted up the staircase. "Want to help us trim the tree?"

He could hear her hop down the stairs and skip into the room. The fact that she now hopped and skipped and sang delighted him.

Then she stopped short and looked at the tree, her eyes moving slowly from the top, down to the trunk. It didn't take long.

"What's that?"

"It's our Christmas tree," Hector said with obviously artificial enthusiasm.

"I like the one in the hall better," she said.

"Wait until we get this set up and decorated and have all the presents underneath," Adam said. "You won't recognize it."

First problem: The stand was too big. Hector held the tree and Adam twisted the screws but when Hector let go, the tree tipped out of the stand and fell onto the floor, leaving half of its remaining needles there in a pile.

"I'll clean it up." Janey ran into the kitchen, came back with a broom and dustpan, and started sweeping at the front door.

"Duct tape," Adam said. "Get some from the tool chest."

When Hector came back with the silver roll, they put the tree back up and Adam attached it to the stand. It took nearly four feet of tape, but, at last, the stand grasped the trunk firmly.

"It's crooked," Janey said from her observation post on the sofa.

Unfortunately, when Hector let go of the tree, it fell over again, taking the tightly attached stand with it.

"It's never going to balance, Pops." Hector lifted the tree. "Center of gravity's on the front and right."

Adam walked from one side of the tree to the other as Hector held it. "I'll be right back." He ran to the kitchen, grabbed the tool chest, pulled a roll of string out, and came back. "We'll have to attach the tree to the wall to keep it from falling."

"What?" Hector shook his head.

"Hold the tree. I'll fix it." With that, Adam twisted several eyebolt screws into the frames of the window behind the tree, then cut the string in four-foot lengths, threaded each piece through the eye in the screw head, and tied it to the tree, attempting to center it.

Hard to center a tree with two thirty-degree curves.

"Hector, let go now." Adam stood back. The tree didn't fall over, but the string showed white against the dark wood of the window frame.

"That should do it," he said.

"I like the one in the hall better," Janey said.

Although he had to agree, Adam said, "Let's get the ornaments on and that Christmas tree skirt around the bottom. That should hide the duct tape. You won't recognize it when we're finished."

They got busy decorating, but, sadly, when they finished they could still recognize the tree. Only ten ornaments found a secure home on the fragile, twisted, and nearly naked branches. No amount of tinsel or shiny balls could hide the fact that this was the same skinny tree they carried in, tied up, and taped in place.

"It's really pretty," Janey said, probably in an effort to make the two men feel better.

Adam and Hector took a few steps back and studied it before all three started to laugh.

"Pops, we can never let anyone else see this tree."

Maybe they could find a big bag to cover it, but Adam didn't think one would fit—not with all those strings holding the thing up.

"It's going to be bald by Christmas." Hector choked the words out and they all started to laugh again.

Chewy wandered in to investigate all the noise. He glanced at Janey, then at Hector and Adam, then discovered the tree. He moved into attack position. His usual attack position consisted of lying on the floor with his tummy up for any thief to scratch.

But not this time. When he caught sight of the thing in the corner, he turned into a ferocious guard dog, primed to protect his home and loved ones. The hair on his back bristled, he leaned forward ready for action, his big bottom up in the air, then began to bark at the scrawny, nearly bare intruder. Although they finally got him quieted this time, every time he walked through this room, the barking and the challenge began anew.

❦

Running late as usual, Gussie pulled into the parking lot of the grocery store about four fifteen. She'd promised Kathy Grant at the Ministerial Alliance of Austin that she'd help for their holiday food drive. She parked, leaped from the car, and ran inside to the manager's office.

"Here are your flyers," he said. "There are boxes at each exit for shoppers to place their donations. You're here to remind them to do that."

Gussie took the stack of paper and found a place to stand next to the shopping carts. Not many people here yet, sort of a lull. The few shoppers who came through accepted the papers and glanced at them as they moved farther into the store.

At nearly five, the crowd hit. Hordes of women dashed through the door and inside. They converged on the line of buggies, each grabbed one, and advanced into the grocery area as if a race had started and the first to pick up dinner won.

Every time Gussie held out an information sheet, the woman either glared at her or ignored her. Not one took the piece of paper. Gussie could nearly feel a breeze from their quick rejection as they rushed past.

Perhaps she should be a little more assertive. Gussie stood in the middle of the aisle the women scooted through and blocked them from the carts.

A particularly large and determined group entered the store and nearly stampeded over her. She tried to stand her ground, but ultimately had to jump aside before she was knocked off balance as they jerked the carts free and whipped them around.

Standing in their way was not the way to go.

Recognizing failure, she tried another

tactic. Looking and attempting to sound angelic, she reached out a hand and said, "Help a person in need have a happy holiday."

The shopper didn't look, didn't listen, didn't even seem to realize she existed.

After this happened several more times, the checker closest to her said, "That's how they are on Friday afternoons. After work, these women have to pick up dinner, get home, put it on the table, then drive or send the kids off to their activities. This is the rudest time of the week. They're unpleasant to us, too."

Slight solace.

She glanced at the nearly empty collection box. Maybe she should just grab a cart and fill it herself. But first, she'd try once more.

As a harried woman moved past her, Gussie attempted to hand her a flyer. The woman ignored her and kept pushing her cart.

That was when Gussie lost it. "What's the matter," she shouted. "Don't you care about hungry kids?"

Didn't faze the woman. She probably

didn't hear her words, but Gussie was horrified by her own behavior.

"I can't believe I said that." Glancing at her hands, she realized they shook. She was supposed to be a Christian. She had shouted at a perfectly innocent stranger. Worse, she was going to do it again, verbally attack the next person who ran past her. She was suddenly, inexplicably furious. She'd never lost control like this and had no idea how to leash it. She had to get out, away from everyone.

She dropped the flyers in a checkout lane and nearly ran out of the store with the anger still burning through her and no idea what to do with it. Gussie Milton didn't lose her temper this way, never. She forgave trespasses. She handled life evenly. Yet this fury filled her, so thick and caustic she could almost taste it. She ran to her car. The rage grew stronger and hotter until it finally overwhelmed her. In the middle of the packed parking lot, she dropped her purse and began to pound on the hood of her car.

"Damn you, Lennie Brewer. Damn you!" She kept pounding, bruising her fists but not caring. "Damn you."

Oh, yes, it hurt but it also felt wonderful, invigorating, even liberating. Emotion flowed out and she felt powerful and in control even though it seemed obvious she was not. "I hate you for what you did to me," she screamed.

She had no idea how long she yelled and pounded and felt that power. Fortunately, because the motto of the city was "Keep Austin Weird," no one paid much attention to her. If she'd been bleeding or on fire or unconscious, they would have helped, but no one would interfere with a good hissy fit.

Then, as the anger slowly dissipated, every bit of strength flowed out with it. She became so weak she nearly fell down. Leaning on the side of the car, she grabbed the door handle and, with great effort, pulled it open and slid inside

"I'm fine." She waved a good Samaritan away. "Thank you."

As soon as she closed the door and found herself in near privacy from the shoppers who raced around the lot, she burst into deep, gulping sobs that felt as if they were torn from inside her. Pain and agony—as physical as it was mental—filled her. She clutched her stomach and rested her fore-head on the steering wheel.

She bawled and blubbered and wept and howled. Lifting her head, she allowed herself to beat on the steering wheel, each blow accompanied by a mental picture of what Lennie had done to her. With each wail and every punch, she felt better.

When she finally allowed herself to slump, she realized there was no way she could drive herself home. She felt completely wrung out. Her parents didn't drive in Austin anymore, and she couldn't let them see her like this. They'd be devastated.

She fumbled in her purse for her cell and hit a number on speed dial. When he answered, she said, "Adam, I need you. Can you come pick me up in the parking lot of the grocery store near my studio?"

Chapter Seventeen

Gussie sounded terrible. Her voice quivered and she hadn't said anything more after that one question, only clicked the phone off. Was she sick? Had she had an accident? What had happened?

Fortunately, he'd been in Austin to make hospital calls and to get a few supplies for the Christmas Eve service. Even through the terrible Austin traffic he drove like an idiot and arrived in fifteen minutes. He parked next to Gussie's car.

But he didn't see her. No one sat in the car waiting for him. Where was she? He jumped out of his car and ran to hers to look in the window on the passenger side. She lay across the backseat, quiet, her eyes closed.

Was she unconscious? Had she fainted?

"Gussie," he shouted and pounded on the window. He tried the door and found it open. As he scooted in, he lifted her head to his lap.

She snored.

Not unconscious. Asleep. When he shook her gently, she blinked, then stretched.

"Adam?" She smiled, a true Gussie smile. "I'm so glad to see you." She struggled to sit up.

"What happened? Why did you call? Are you all right?"

"I needed you," she said simply.

Before he could react to those words, she burst into tears and threw herself against him. He had no choice but to put his arms around her and hold her while she cried, exactly what he wanted to do.

Oh, he knew this didn't fix everything, but it was a beginning. He worried about her hysterical sobs and rubbed her back and whispered soothing promises, words of comfort. He'd do that for however long it took for her to pull herself together.

Within a few minutes, she stopped crying, wiped her tears with a couple of napkins from Wendy's, and became quiet, her head still against his shoulder. Had she fallen asleep again?

No, she sat up and leaned away from him. "Guess you'd like an explanation."

He nodded. "Considering the fact that last time I saw you, you waved merrily at me while tubing down the river, and today you called me sobbing, yes, I would."

"Okay." With one more swipe at her cheeks and nose, Gussie closed her eyes to gather herself. "First, do you know that the Widows visited my parents in October while I was at work?"

"What?" Oh, Lord. "When? What happened? How did the Widows keep this secret? They never can."

"My parents negotiated a non-disclosure pact. They didn't want anyone to know about this until I decided what to do."

After that, Gussie filled him in on that afternoon, ending with, "I don't know what they said because Blossom had a private chat with them. Somehow she got them to believe I'm using them as a shield to hide from life." She paused and nibbled her lip before she forced out the words. "And love."

He watched her, still confused. "Then what?"

"When I got home, my parents called me in for a little chat, to explain that I was not to hide behind them. Not a comfortable moment but necessary and very helpful. I realized I needed help, that I can't heal myself. I went back into counseling. I'm ready to change." She took his hand. "I have a reason to change."

"What's that reason?" He wasn't about to act on the profound hope she meant him.

"You're going to make me spell this out, aren't you?"

He nodded. "I have to know. I don't want to misread anything."

"You are the reason." She paused before adding, "And I am the reason. I want to explore what's between us." She paused and seemed to struggle to express her thoughts. "I want more. I want what you want. I want to be with you and I want to be healthy."

He should say something but couldn't think of the right words. As a minister, he should be able to come up with something.

With that hesitation, she looked down at her hands. "I care about you deeply," she murmured. "I probably am in love with you, but you know how pathetically wishy-washy I can be."

"That's one of the things I like about you." He laced his fingers through hers.

Then she lifted her eyes to gaze into his. "I want to think about marriage." She swallowed hard. "And I have thought about sharing your bed."

He pulled her close to him and held her. She didn't tug away, she didn't push him, she didn't scream. Not screaming always felt like a good first step.

"I love you, too," he murmured into her beautiful hair. Then he lowered his lips and kissed her on the lips. A lovely sweet kiss, which became a promise.

After a pleasant interlude, he realized they were, after all, in the grocery store parking lot and fully visible to the growing throng of shoppers. He stopped kissing her, content to have his arm around her, her head against his shoulder.

Then she burst into laughter, that wonderful, joyful sound. He pulled back to look at her.

"I'm sorry. I know I'm irreverent. When I used to think about finding the man I wanted to spend the rest of my life with, I pictured myself singing and dancing and laughing and incredibly happy." She shook her head. "But look at me. I'm a mess. I've been crying. My eyes are red and swollen."

"Not part of your dream?"

"No, but you are." She snuggled against his chest again. "And I'm happy."

"Why today?" he asked after nearly a minute. "What made you decide to call me today?"

She told him about the scene in the store, which made him laugh. She joined in when she realized how funny it was.

"And then the anger flowed out, really for the first time since Lennie raped me." She spoke calmly and with quiet confidence, not glossing over the attack or blaming herself.

"Healing," he said.

"I know I'm not completely okay."

"None of us are."

"I'll still need counseling for a while and will always have an underlying resentment, but I have to accept it as part of my life. That event shaped and influenced who I am. Now I feel ready to move past it. Finally."

"Have you forgiven Lennie?"

"I don't know." She paused. "No, that's not right. I may someday but I haven't yet. Facing what he did to me is a small step." She struggled to explain. "I think there may be some acts that cannot be forgiven and that rape is one of them. I won't hold a grudge or let the memory of him control my life anymore. I'd never seek revenge. But forgive him? I don't think he deserves that."

He could quote scripture and even Shakespeare about forgiveness, but this wasn't the time. She was too raw. Maybe in the future she'd forgive him. Was she right that there were some sins the victim shouldn't be forced to forgive?

She picked up his wrist and glanced at his watch. "It's nearly seven! My parents will worry."

"Call them. Tell them you and I are having dinner and you'll be home later."

❦

"Guess who called me this morning?" It was three days before Christmas, and

Blossom wore a grin of such deep satisfaction and secrecy, it made Birdie want to slap her silly. Not that she would, but her palm did itch. She looked at the other Widows around their usual table in the diner to gauge their reactions.

"Don't play games with us," Winnie warned.

Blossom, so pleased with herself, only smiled, an expression that said, *I know something you don't know.*

"Come on, tell us," Mercedes said, falling right into Blossom's trap.

"Yvonne Milton called me."

"Yvonne Milton called *you*?" Birdie couldn't believe it.

Blossom nodded. "Yes, we've kept in touch often since our visit to Roundville."

"Really?" Mercedes asked. "What did she say?"

Blossom preened for a few seconds before glancing at Birdie's frown. "She said that the preacher and Gussie had dinner together Friday, *and* yesterday he came to Roundville for supper."

"Oh," the others breathed in unison.

"And the Miltons—all three of them—are coming to the Christmas Eve service."

"Sounds like this is getting serious," Mercedes said.

Suddenly peace filled Birdie and she didn't care who took the honors for making the match. This would count as the highest achievement of the Widows' career. She would shower gratitude on Blossom.

"Well done." Birdie laughed.

"Yes, well done," Mercedes echoed.

"In no time, they'll be engaged, then married, then producing little Jordans." Birdie drew herself up in pride. "And now, ladies," she said with a confident nod, "we have a wedding to plan."

❦

Unfortunately, attempting to shield the small spindly tree from the friends who trooped through the parsonage became impossible. People streamed in with Christmas goodies and with small gifts for the kids they wanted to place under the tree. As they arrived, Janey led everyone back to the pitiful specimen of flora to leave the offerings.

By Christmas Eve, gifts were piled high around the little tree with the listing star on the top. Before they left for the eight o'clock church service, the two children stood in front of it, holding hands.

Hector shook his head. "Pops, I don't know what we did to deserve this."

"Don't worry about that. Accept love with a generous heart."

Janey took Adam's hand, held on to it tightly, and began to sing, "'Silent night, holy night . . .'"

A perfect moment. Adam could feel himself becoming a warm blob inside as joy and gratitude flooded him. Add to this the anticipation of celebrating Christmas Eve with Gussie and her parents, of all of them sharing cookies and opening presents together, and he felt incredibly blessed.

"'. . . Sleep in heavenly peace,'" Janey finished.

For a moment, the three stood in front of the tree and drank in the moment of being a family.

Then the church bells began to ring. Almost eight. "Let's go." Adam let go of Janey's hand and dashed out toward church. Without time to grab his robe, he entered the chancel as the last bell rang and stood before the worshippers gathered there to read the words from Luke that always filled him with awe: "To you is born this day in the city of David a Savior, who is Christ the Lord."

In the darkness of the sanctuary, the only sources of light came from the Christ candle on the communion table and a reading light on the lectern. Janey had volunteered to lead the congregation in the first stanzas of favorite carols interspersed with readings of the familiar Christmas stories from Luke and Matthew.

At the end of the service, Adam read from John: "Jesus spoke to them, saying, 'I am the light of the world; he who follows me will not walk in darkness, but will have the light of life.'" Then the congregation stood and began to file forward to take a candle from Adam and light it. Adam watched each pass: Bree and Mac with Hector and Bobby, followed by Miss Birdie, Mercedes, and Blossom; Sam and Willow, their boys each unusually solemn, the general and Winnie; Jesse and Howard and all the elders. Close to the end were Ouida and Carol with George holding a sleeping Gretchen.

All these people gathered here had become not only his congregation but his family; Butternut Creek, his home.

As he glanced to welcome the last few approaching the table, he smiled at the Miltons. Yvonne and Henry picked up their candles and said, "Blessings, Adam."

Gussie reached forward and took a candle from him. She whispered, "Merry Christmas," lit the candle, and moved past him to join the chain stretching around the sanctuary.

Then Adam lit his candle and joined the circle, watching each of the beloved faces glowing more brightly than the flames in front of them.

"'Joy to the world,'" Janey began, and the congregation joined.

Next to him, Gussie's strong voice took up the tune. When he looked down, she took his hand.

He leaned toward her, filled with the promise of her touch and her presence and her love.

When the congregation completed that verse, Adam repeated. "'Rejoice! For to us this day is born a Savior, Christ the Lord.'"

The organist began to play "Gloria in Excelsis Deo" as the worshippers extinguished the candles and moved out of the sanctuary, into the beauty that was Butternut Creek. The sound of their murmured greetings mingled with the scent of pine as everyone headed home.

Ahead of them, Hector chatted with the Miltons and Janey skipped toward the parsonage.

And, as Adam followed, Gussie walked beside him.

Reading Group Guide

DISCUSSION QUESTIONS

1. Adam loves Butternut Creek. He feels at home here and has created a family. Is there a place you feel particularly at home and at peace? Where is it? Why do you feel that way? If not, what are you searching for?

2. Adam never states that he feels called by God to this one place, but he has found many ways to minister. Do you believe Adam was called by God to serve only at Butternut Creek, or do you believe he could find a way to serve anyplace he went? Have you felt called to a particular place or ministry service? How did that happen? How did you feel?

3. Gussie is dedicated to serve God and others. She also has a secret, a tragedy in her past. How has she handled that secret in the past? What has helped her in this novel? Do you believe she has healed? Why or why not?

4. What do you think about Adam's reaction to Gussie's revelation? Was he wrong to tell her later that he wanted a deeper relationship? Did that change the "rules"? What did Gussie's response tell you about her level of healing at this time?

5. Gussie says she hasn't forgiven Lennie and believes there may be sins that are unforgivable. Do you agree with her? If so, what would those sins be? Could her lack of forgiveness be because she is still wrestling with the issue?

6. Have you ever had difficulty forgiving? Did you finally? What helped you? If you didn't, why not? Has that lack of forgiveness hurt you?

7. There are people who blame God for their troubles and turn away, but Gussie didn't. How did Gussie live her faith and remain faithful to God after the life-changing tragedy? Where did she find

the strength to finally face her past? Where have you found strength during times of sorrow and crisis?

8. How have people you know reacted to difficulties and tragedies? Do you know people who have turned away from God? Do you have a friend who has gone through a time when his or her faith was tested? Did you find a way to support this friend? How?

9. Gussie has to face the fact that her parents are aging and will not be around forever. How does she handle this? She believes she has to take care of them because they have supported her. Do you agree with her sense of duty and her choice?

10. Often people find themselves being faced with either their own aging or the care of aging parents. What are some decisions that have to be made? What resources can families use? Why is it so hard to accept the changes aging brings?

11. Determined to be strong, Gussie shoulders everyone's problems. She calls herself a rescuer. Have you ever felt this way? Did it help you or hurt

you? Did the people you rescued show gratitude? Why or why not?

12. Gussie's counselor says, "The wound is where the healing starts." What does this sentence mean to you? Would you find this thought to be helpful during times of trouble in your life? The thirteenth-century Persian poet Rumi wrote, *The wound is the place where the Light enters you*, which inspired the counselor's words. Do Rumi's words speak to you?

13. If we see brokenness in a friend's life—broken personal relationships, addictions—how can we speak a word of healing?

14. Teenage binge drinking is a huge and dangerous problem. How did Adam handle this? What would you have done?

15. Adam is less than ten years older than Hector and suddenly has two children. How has Adam handled it? Has he grown in his acceptance of this role and his ability to respond to the needs of the Firestones?